Jake's Ladder

Mary E. Benecke

Boone County is a fictional town in Nebraska.

All characters are fictional, as well as the events.

The author holds highest respect and appreciation for those who gamble on weather from year to year to grow our food. They are America's grass-roots. They are America's stories.

Printed in USA by
Barnhart Press, Inc.
2600 Farnam Street, Omaha, NE 68131
ISBN 0-9671698-0-1

Chapters

The Birth . . . . Page   1

The Friendship . . . . Page   3

The Courtship . . . . Page   75

The Last Concern . . . . Page 281

The Birth

Her heart pounded in fear and haste as she ran fast as she was able. She was in her eighth month, and she held on to her pregnancy with both hands to protect the unborn child; her teenage son, Alvin, ran ahead into the storm cellar while her farmer husband looked frantically outside the house for their four-year-old daughter Alice.

The tornado came closer, its heaviness a threat to everyone and everything in sight. But she concentrated on herself and her own heaviness. Her husband would find their little girl.

Out of breath, she inhaled deeply and sat down on a small stool in the hunched-over cellar; she waited for her husband and Alice. Just in time they came. With shouts from her father to hurry, Alice excitedly ran down the steps, tripped, and hit her head hard on the dirt floor.

She died instantly. And the mother, holding on tight to her swollen belly, screamed in disbelief as she caressed the stillness of her little girl.

The next day, in the pitch of emotional grief and physical pain, another child was born to her. It was a boy. They named him Jacob, the supplanter — the replacement. Jacob Robert Blackburn.

Jake Blackburn.

The Friendship

Bad things happen. But nature has a way of diminishing its tragedies by afterwards presenting something good. And good was the way of the weather the next day on the Blackburn farm in Boone County, Nebraska when Jake was born. The sun came out with extra brightness overlooking air purified by the rainstorm that had followed the tornado; and the birds returned to their songs.

The house was not hit by the whirlwind, nor were any of the crops, the barn, or tractor. Even a spade used by Mrs. Blackburn to hoe weeds in the family garden patch was still leaning up against the back porch. The two dogs and several cats were running and walking around as though nothing bad had happened.

And even though the Blackburns third child was born in the comfort of the main upstairs bedroom, the grieving couple would have much preferred the loss of that bedroom to their Alice's round and wondering blue eyes; they would have preferred the loss of their large, warm kitchen to Alice's running feet as she scampered from one childlike activity to another; even if the chimney had fallen off, its structure couldn't match the strength of Alice's hugs she routinely gave her parents at bedtime.

Alice was gone, and Jake was here, and never again did Mrs. Blackburn take motherhood for granted. She reached out to the small, slippery bundle the midwife handed her and touched the tip of his nose with one trembling finger. The baby was short, but he was alive, and his screams indicated he was also strong and healthy. She gasped again in grief, as she would for a long time to come, and then hugged her new child whose eyes had yet to focus on his new world.

The baby was aware only of the closeness of the person whose finger touched his nose and whose arms supported his helpless body. The baby did not know that the day before his father and mother had gone into town with their lifeless daughter in their arms as his older brother Alvin drove the Ford. He did not know that as his parents handed their little girl over to the doctor and funeral home attendant, his mother felt a labor pain, a premature pain that could have been due to the shock of her loss. He did not know he was born in grief which turned to joy for a little while when his parents realized he would live.

There were a lot of things Jake didn't know, and one of them was that he was born short. Even though he was born almost one month early, the doctor said another month probably wouldn't have made him any longer. Jake also didn't know that his shortness was important to other people, that the neighboring mothers exclaimed about it and suggested he might be a midget. "I don't think so," Mrs. Fallen said to Mrs. Gladson. "He's alive, that's all that matters for now, don't you think?"

The Blackburns thought so. They didn't discuss the baby's size, except for one time after Alvin grumbled a remark about his peewee brother. They explained Jake would probably grow taller as he grew older.

He didn't, and for that he was criticized. But Jake had a few years to enjoy his country life before he met the faultfinding eyes of his peers. It was these beginning years that created his love for the land and a respect until he gradually thought of the land as a person. A person to love.

***

Some sections of the country are better looking than other sections. When a born and bred city person drives out to the country to get from one place to another, and you're unlikely to find them there for any other reason unless it's to kill a deer, duck or pheasant, they can't help but notice the isolation of it, especially in the winter when there is not the intense activity of planting and harvesting.

4

The farmer's winter also brings a lack of color; barring the blue of the sky and the white starchiness of the clouds, the ground color is a washed yellow, the residual straw appearance of depleted summer crops, and this makes an outside observer wonder how anyone could stand to live like this.

It is so quiet and so far away that a person who is used to honking horns, wall-to-wall houses, and shoulder-to-shoulder city activity might think country people could easily lose their minds.

But they don't. The farmers use the uncolored winter silence as a time to repair machines and tools and to plan for the promise of what is to come in the next planting season; they are not merely holding their breath for the green growing spring. And just like window shades pulled down on a hot sunny day, the farmers relax in this sabbatical from the intensity of plowing, planting, cultivating, and harvesting while awaiting the uncertainty of the next season.

This was the setting that Jake grew up in. The black tornado sky that caused his sister's accident and death that afternoon in Boone County eventually dispersed and returned to its usual display of quiet blue and silent clouds. More than once Jake heard his father say that if God would just turn the world upside down, children would have acres of playground. Whenever there were billowy clouds in the sky, Mr. Blackburn would turn his young son's head up to the puffiness and ask the small boy if he would like to bounce up and down on them; one time Jake himself pointed at a sky full of clumpy buttermilk clouds in puzzlement, and his father laughed and said wouldn't that be great fun to skip all around those lumps? And sometimes Jake imagined himself skating, like on ice, along the flat stratus formations that streak like a painter's long stroke across the horizon.

In this atmosphere of country earth and country sky, Jake grew up. When he was almost nine months old, Mrs. Blackburn dressed him in rompers, put a protective cap on his head, and handed him to his father who carried him out into a newly sprouted field of corn; he placed his son gently down in a furrowed row of earth to amuse while he investigated the area for good crop growth and unwanted weeds. Jake, with his baby fat cheeks, looked down at the soil and the one inch sprouts of future harvest and, with chubby fingers not yet synchronized, rummaged through the soil and greenery. His father brought Jake here for more than the youngster's entertainment—he wanted him to grow up to realize that this was his life, that the land and what comes out of it is something to behold, to use, to appreciate.

***

A place in the rear of the house where chickens were once cooped eventually became Mrs. Blackburn's flower garden and vegetable patch. The ground was rich with the droppings over the years of the laying hens who were sold shortly after Alice's birth.

After Jake learned to walk, his mother took his small hand and led him to newly budded tiny flowers growing in a row next to the cucumbers, lettuce, and dainty green onions. Then she would take him to the front of the house where thick meadow grass grew and insist he play where it was clean. Sometimes he crawled up on the front porch steps and scratched on the screen for Mom to come and let him in. He ultimately learned that if he wanted to come inside the house, he would have to manipulate his one-year-old feet over large chunks of gravel and go to the side door and maneuver his way through the back porch which housed wash tubs, rubber boots always caked with dried mud, overcoats, heavy sweaters, and discarded knickknacks waiting to be trashed.

But all this effort was worth it because, once he was through the back porch which his folks and everyone else's folks referred to as the shed, he would find his mother in the large kitchen, a kitchen that had a ceiling taller than he would ever be and a table with room enough for the Pilgrim's first Thanksgiving feast. Sometimes a news-hungry neighbor sat at the table with his mother while they talked without stopping and ate leftover coffeecake swallowed by leftover coffee.

At suppertime, with Jake propped up on a chair next to

his brother Alvin, Mr. Blackburn almost always made a comment about his day in the field, sometimes with a smile and other times with a frown. Although Jake was too young to understand, his father would point at him and at Alvin and explain that if crops were planted in a proper manner, the ground would always be there. "It won't go south, boys, if you practice soil saving." Jake would look at his father in a very serious way and then throw a biscuit on the floor. "I think he got my point," the father continued as his wife reached down for the discard and threw it out the door for the dogs.

By the time Jake was three, his father had talked about the land enough times for him to realize, really know, that the ground was brown dirt and the crops were green stems of some kind. He saw how his father always tended to the fields and ignored the thick-bladed meadow grass in the front of the house. He noticed how he graded the fields with his tractor while a cow or goat manicured the front lawn. It eventually became clear to the youngster which of the two areas was more important.

To Mrs. Blackburn, however, the most important thing when Jake turned five—was school.

"Now, don't be afraid, son, there will be lots of other children your age there," Mrs. Blackburn said to Jake as she adjusted his shirt buttons and pulled up a fallen sock cuff. She didn't mention that the same age didn't necessarily mean the same height. Her son was about to meet his peers who would certainly tower over him and maybe make fun.

The mothers came with their children. One mother, Mrs. Hallgren, had to drag her son Harold out from the family's small truck and up to the light brown stucco schoolhouse. Harold Hallgren hollered all the way.

Following close behind was Jake Blackburn similarly removed from his parents' new Ford with his favorite sucking finger in his mouth, hand tucked inside his mother's, and eyes staring scared up at the massive strange structure.

Mrs. Blackburn smiled faintly at Mrs. Hallgren as the four arrived at the door at the same time, and each offered that the other go first. The mothers put the two boys side by side, emphasizing to each they were to behave while they registered them with the town's only teacher.

The boys looked at each other; Jake replaced his quietly sucked finger with a noisily sucked thumb; Harold's sobs turned into what sounded like boo-hoos. Other children, who were no braver but at least quieter, skirted themselves around and away from the pair who stood transfixed to each other out of obedient habit to their mother's command rather than out of a curiosity of a possible friendship.

Suddenly Harold stopped crying, and Jake removed his thumb; the two stood there, stiff, like a motion picture that had suddenly turned into a still life. They could do it, sure, they could be brave, the silence of their looking at each other seemed to say. Harold was taller of course, and he didn't want to be a cry baby in front of such a short fellow even if that fellow was such a baby that he still sucked his fingers and thumbs.

But it didn't last. Harold started to whine, high pitched with some tones only a dog could hear, and Jake's finger went immediately back into his mouth.

"Maybe our boys can be friends," Mrs. Hallgren suggested to Mrs. Blackburn who was trying to remove her son's finger from his mouth.

Mrs. Blackburn's anxious frown relaxed at that suggestion; maybe her meek little boy needed a boisterous pal. "They seem stuck together already. I think they picked each other out as friends. Mine only has an older brother, how about yours?"

Harold's mother nodded. "Perfect. That loud kid is the only one I've got. I feel better already about leaving him here now that he has a pal."

So, assuming the boys were locked in a friendship of their own choice, the mothers coaxed them even closer together, and there they stood—one short, one tall, side by side for the first roll call. They continued this placement until each child was registered with the background noises of Harold's sniveling and Jake's finger sucking. Neither of them said a word to each other, they didn't know how to reach out to a stranger for comfort, but they didn't separate either. Even after the teacher told them they 'needn't be so shoved in close together,' they remained in that stance until they were seated. They had become emotionally attached and only two desks were able to disjoin them.

This attachment would last for more than that first morning. Although their mothers had thrown their sons out into that famous cold, cruel world of school, they had provided them with someone else to be with ... a friend, a pal, a buddy.

The two seedlings became one.

***

They kept their hands in their pockets a lot, Jake and Harold, as they walked around the Hallgrens' barnyard in their bib overalls, duckbill caps, and thick soled high top shoes. They were two miniature old men surveying their property while deciding what to play with next. They would usually find a stick of some size with which they poked at the ground and discussed things like farming.

"My father has more land than your father," Harold would declare, although each father had one section.

"My father grows corn better than your father," Jake would answer, although that was unlikely because both fathers shared good growing expertise.

Then there was silence for awhile because neither boy knew what he was talking about and consequently were unable to follow through. If they had thought about these conversations when they became older, they would have realized that any statements they made about their fathers had nothing to do with facts.

At four o'clock, regardless of how intense the outdoor conversation had become, Mrs. Hallgren called them inside for their favorite radio show of action and fighting and shouting between villains and good guys. She beamed at Harold who finally had someone besides himself to fight the bad guys. With feet pounding on floor, threats screaming through air, and fists thrusting forward, the boys crushed the evil men who were out to kill their heroes.

The first time that Jake had come to play with Harold after school he told Mrs. Hallgren that he would walk home. "My father told me I can walk home in good weather. He wants my legs to grow strong for when I grow up to be a farmer just like him."

Mrs. Hallgren doubted this statement. Two miles was a little far for someone whose stature was swallowed up by the immensity of the fields; he would be a mere speck walking with two short legs along the road. Besides, she wondered, his legs might get even shorter if he walked too long on the hard dirt roads.

Mrs. Blackburn laughed when Mrs. Hallgren told her about Jake walking home. "Of course not, keep him there even if you have to tie him to the side of the barn until I come." She sighed. "I would prefer you lock him up inside your house instead."

None of that was necessary because Jake was an obedient child, a characteristic lacking a bit in his best buddy Harold. If they were told to not climb that tempting tree by the culvert, Harold would climb it, Jake would not. Whenever the teacher told her pupils to be quiet, Jake would hush up, Harold would not. Mrs. Hallgren soon learned the ways of the two boys and hoped some of Jake would rub off on Harold.

***

They told each other everything.

"My Mom was sick," Harold told Jake one afternoon when they were poking through a blueberry patch to find something sweet to munch on. "She was sick in bed a long time ago, I don't remember when, and she cried and she told my Daddy they won't have anymore babies."

"What do you mean?" Jake answered.

"I don't know."

Jake pouted out his lower lip which customary for him to do when he was puzzled. "I have a big brother Alvin and a sister Alice, but she's dead. Want to see her picture?"

"Sure, where is it?" Harold didn't know what dead meant when it came to human beings. Maybe the picture would tell him.

Because the Hallgrens lived closer to the school than the Blackburns, their mothers decided to let Harold's mother drive both boys to her house after school and later Mr. Blackburn would get Jake. The only time, consequently, the boys went to the Blackburns to play was so Harold could look at Jake's dead sister's picture. Their mothers decided this was a good a way as any for the boys to find out something about life's hardships.

"She doesn't look different," Harold said to Jake as they looked at Alice's memory. "What does dead mean?"

Jake looked up at Alice's picture on the dining room sideboard. His mother rarely talked about that young girl, but he did know she wasn't around to play with. "My Mom told me a long time ago her name is Alice and she died falling down stairs before I was born. She's pretty, isn't she? And I bet she's nicer than that stuck-up Colleen of yours."

Harold didn't answer Jake's tease about the redhead that he loved with all his heart but who cared nothing about him. He kept looking at the picture to see if it would tell him about what dead was.

Mrs. Blackburn came to the doorway. Jake went over to her, looked straight up into her eyes and asked, "Where's Alice? What's dead mean? Harold wants to know."

She leaned over, took each boy's hand, and sat them on the sofa next to her. "Have you ever seen a bird lying on the ground and not moving or flying, but just still and on its side?"

The boys nodded, of course they had.

"Well, that means the bird is no longer breathing. It is dead. People die too. Alice died—she no longer breathes and so she is buried in the cemetery. Jake, your Dad needs to take you there someday and then you can see Alice's grave and your uncle's grave and lots of peoples' graves."

The boys remained silent. What were they suppose to say

to that? Jake got off the sofa and leaned onto his mother's lap. "Jesus died. But he came back. Why doesn't Alice?"

Mrs. Blackburn's eyes filled with tears, but she forced a smile. "You are so very young and innocent, you two. Someday you will understand."

"I wished I had a sister," Harold shouted as though the loudness would make it come true. "Someday I'm getting married and then I'll get my own sister, even if she's dead."

Jake looked over at his buddy and then up at his somber mother. "I don't think that's the way it goes, is it Mom?"

Mrs. Blackburn swallowed hard and then laughed. "No, Jake. No, Harold. That's not the way it goes.

***

Jake didn't always play with Harold. Sometimes he came straight home from school and ran to the field to watch his father finish up the day. This usually happened after a morning bout with Alvin when the older boy would taunt him.

"Jacob, Jacob, where's your ladder?" Alvin teased. "Are you in Heaven yet?" Then he would laugh.

Jake didn't understand anything about Jacob's ladder, not even when he heard the story in Sunday School. He knew his real name was Jacob; his mother once told him his name means replacement and that he was the replacement for his sister. Mr. Blackburn had told his wife that the Biblical Jacob had replaced his brother by devious means, but Mrs. Blackburn told him that a replacement was a replacement, and she knew her new tiny baby would never be devious. "Besides," she added, "maybe our baby needs a strong enough personality to be devious. Alice wasn't strong enough to be devious, maybe that's why she died. Weak people die."

***

No one knows when a young boy's mind clicks into a particular attitude of himself; perhaps it is not one click, but a series of events that add up to that child's impression of good and bad. With Jake it was both.

Alvin either teased or ignored his young brother. So Jake

went to his mother for comfort and also to his dead sister's picture. "I love you, Alice," he would whisper while he stared at its blankness. He knew his parents still thought of her now and then, and so they must still love her. And if they loved someone dead, then they must really love him. He eventually learned to ignore Alvin, he didn't need him to feel good. Besides, Harold would always play with and talk to him. Who needs anybody more? A mother, a father, a playmate, and a dead picture. He was filled with love.

This, however, did not last. Something happened between the first and third grade at school that caused that click in Jake's mind and influenced his thinking from thereafter.

It was a blue-eyed blond girl who got all of Jake's attention and who returned it. She smiled at him, she was Alice, alive. By this time Alvin had left home to marry and farm his father-in-law's land in South Dakota. He took his caustic Jacob's ladder remark with him and for a few years Jake had no one to taunt him about his shortcomings, most of which concerned his height.

The little girl was short too, and he and she would exchange sly, shy looks. At recess after they tired of the games, they always found the same spot to rest on and to exchange more glances. They talked of unimportant things except for one—the checkered design of her dress. Jake loved checked patterns—they looked like his father's description of planted farm land—and whenever the blond love of his life would wear that dress, Jake felt especially close to her.

For this two year period between the first and third grade, Jake lived in paradise: with Alvin gone, he had all of his parents' love and attention, especially his mother's who appreciated another chance at motherhood; he had Harold, and he had that pretty blond girl. There was no one anymore to make remarks about his height except the neighbors, and he never heard them.

In the third grade, unfortunately, the atmosphere

changed. Jake's short stature never caught up with the other children. He didn't grow like the others, and especially not like his blond girlfriend. Then one day at recess when Jake reached for her hand, she pulled back, looked down and straight into his eyes, and said softly, "You're too short for me anymore, what girl would ever want to be with you, probably never, and I don't want to even speak to you again." The checkered dress and all the other dresses walked away.

Maybe if she had talked to him in a cutting tone and flounced her skirt and strutted away, Jake wouldn't have reacted the way he did. Alvin had acted that way, arrogantly, and Jake had survived him. But the girlfriend spoke quietly as with authority and finality. Jake's eyes bulged beneath his curly hair; he did not cry because of the shock of the remark, but instead held his breath and her judgment inside him. He didn't tell his mother or father or Harold what that girl said; he never told anyone; he never would.

But he did tell his mother nobody liked him, a complaint more than one mother has heard more than one time. Mrs. Blackburn was concerned when her little boy looked up at her with small eyes a little too close together and pouting with thin lips that seemed to reach from ear to ear. She told him that all he had to do to make people like him was to make them laugh. She thought this would bring her skinny son out of his sadness and give him the courage to socialize.

So Jake made his classmates laugh by saying smart things. They liked him for it, and he continued to be bright-mouthed until this way of his grew into a friendliness—a friendliness on the outside only because whenever a classmate ignored his wave across the room, Jake retreated into his nobody-likes-me attitude again. Nobody, he decided, except his parents and Harold and possibly the teacher. But then, even the lepers in the Bible probably had a few friends.

***

The years went by as usual for everyone else, but for Jake nothing would ever go by as usual. There was a festering inside him that perhaps started before he was born when his mother's grief permeated into the womb and onto the cord, traveling into Jake and planting a sense of how heartbreaking and unfair life can be. So when his girlfriend of two years rebuffed him for being short, that dejected feeling surfaced and its strength slammed a door on him, like a door inches thick of strong wood that even Paul Bunyan could not crash through.

All the love from his parents and all the attention from Harold could not make up for Jake's peer rejection. After all, parents don't choose their offspring, but classmates choose their friends. Jake took his parents' and Harold's acceptance for granted; he knew, however, that his world was more than his home and one playmate—it was having lots of friends, and having them talk to you and laugh without being coaxed with jokes and quick remarks.

By the eighth grade all of the boys had inched themselves up to a decent height, with Harold the tallest of them all after one summer of sprouting like a blue ribbon cornfield. Jake neither inched nor sprouted.

The girls continued to ignore him, and Jake wanted to believe his mother's explanation that 'those girls don't know a good man when they see one, and someday, someone will come along who will fall all over you and love you to bits.'

None of the girls really did this. They couldn't accept him for being short, he needed to be punished.

***

It was time to learn to dance, it was the seventh grade. The town had a gymnasium for this activity as well as for sports; it had been built by a wealthy farmer 20 years before for his twelve children, all of whom were boys. He had wanted his offspring to have the benefit of big city athletics. Over the years the teenage boys in the high school kept it clean by sweeping out the courts and painting the walls.

This was where the young boys and girls came once a week every spring to pair off and dance the waltzes, foxtrots, and occasional cha-chas. It wasn't easy for most of the boys to learn because not only did they have to figure out how to untangle their legs to a rhythm, they also had to face a girl close and hold her hand.

Jake was wallflowered by every girl every time. It didn't matter to them that Jake said smart things to make them laugh—nothing could make up for his shortness. While Harold and his tallness waltzed from one end of the gym to the other, Jake leaned against the wall and pretended to not notice by turning his head one way and then the other, never really looking at the dancers.

"You must learn how to dance," the teacher said at first.

"No I mustn't," Jake replied. There was a tightness in his chest as it heaved in and out to accommodate his rapidly beating heart. If he had been alone, he would have cried.

The parties afterward gave no relief. Anyway, by this time, Jake's entire insides felt like someone had reached in and removed them; he felt like a skeleton, no feeling left or appetite for treats. Harold suggested more than once, as they waited for their ride home, that Jake should push and force himself onto a girl. "They're only girls, giggly girls, buddy, no big deal." But Jake thought they were big deals; and with Harold's remark he felt even more unworthy to be rejected by 'no big deals.'

The dancing lessons finally convinced Jake that girls were a waste of his time to hurt over anymore. His father's land took over. He learned to till the soil, plant, harvest, worry, sweat, and love his impending inheritance.

Just as Jake was at the mercy of the girls, the land was at the mercy of the weather. There was this shared challenge between them, but unlike the girls, the land would never reject him. He was taller than it, and it was always there waiting for his attention. In the winter it was Jake who deserted the land while snow and cold took over, but in the spring it was there for him to put on a jacket, pull a duck-billed cap down over his forehead, stand before it with hands on hips, and exclaim to his father, "Okay, Dad, where do you want me to start?" The girls, for now, were a hundred million miles away.

***

The ringlet curly brown hair that was arranged in whatever direction his sleep went the night before sat atop a face of small, close-together brown eyes and thin lips piercing almost from earlobe to earlobe. Jake stood in front of the agriculture college building, again with hands on hips, and exclaimed in his adult scratchy voice to his buddy, Harold, "Looks like a cement prison to me—how about you?"

The handsome young man with straight blond hair flopping onto his forehead looked down with large blue eyes and dimpled cheeks at his friend Jake. Harold had grown to six feet two, and his camaraderie with Jake had grown with him. It was as though Harold thought he had to make up for Jake's jockey-height stature, and consequently, the last summer of high school he grew four inches.

"Doesn't matter if it's cement or if it's a prison. Just so there's girls inside." Harold's interest in girls, those silly, giggly girls, had intensified over his years of growing up and there were times Jake wondered if Harold would ever be able to choose just one of them for a future life together. As for himself, Jake knew he wouldn't have any trouble choosing: it would be the first pretty, nice, smart, short girl that would say yes to him.

But Jake needn't have wondered about a future wife. The only dates he had at the University were accepted by girls in the Malt Shop before he stood up from the soda fountain and showed his stature. His broad shoulders that overhung a small waist and narrow hips didn't make up for it. Girls simply did not accept a second date, some reneged on the first. Without the girls' interest, Jake eventually gave up wearing the carefully ironed slacks his mother sent with him and went back to blue jeans. As long as his height turned off the girls, there was no longer any reason to disguise his toothpick skinny legs inside of loose fitting slacks. Besides, jeans were more comfortable; he pushed them down low on his hips and secured them with a brown leather belt that had a carved outline of Nebraska on a silver buckle. Approximately in the middle of the state's outline was an engraved gold star that indicated the location of Boone County. His father had it made especially for him as a high school graduation gift, but Jake was too embarrassed to wear it then.

In college, however, the belt no longer embarrassed him because there was no one to be embarrassed with. On Friday and Saturday nights while Harold was out with one girl after another, Jake filled his loneliness by studying subjects not related to farming. He went to the library and brought back to his dorm room one book, then another and another until the trip to and from became like the path he and his father had taken to and from the barn years before. His mind became as strong as his hands, and Jake hoped that someday he would find a girl who would fall in love with brains instead of height.

***

Sometimes it seems that only good things happen to one person while only bad things happen to another. This is the way it was for Jake and Harold after their sophomore year.

Harold got married. Dolly Benson was the conclusion of his years of dancing from one end of the gym to the other and of his endless search for an endless number of girlfriends. His wedding and his father's land was all that interested Harold anymore, so he quit college, moved his bride into a farmhouse rental near his parents, and climbed onto a tractor.

While Harold was still in the honeymoon spirit, Jake's father died. It happened while Mr. Blackburn walked between rows of new growth checking for weeds and infestations. No one saw him grab his chest, stagger, and fall. But when he was late for supper, Mrs. Blackburn called Harold's father to please help her—she knew, she just knew, the situation was not good. They found him on his side between rows of young corn pushing their way out into the world. They buried him next to Alice and his father's older brother, and afterward Jake went to the place where one of his two mighty strong oaks had fallen, and he cried until he was parched. Then he clamped his hand over his mouth and screamed. So far this is what life is all about, he mourned, one rotten thing after another. There were no smart remarks left for him, no more jokes for classmates.

His father was dead. A piece of the world fell off.

Mr. Hallgren offered to oversee the hired hand so Mrs. Blackburn could insist Jake continue in college. Harold told Dolly that the reason Jake went back to college was not because of his Dad's offer to oversee or because his mother insisted, but because he didn't want to leave the library alone. Jake smiled when he heard this, even though he was still in the dumps with grief, because he thought that maybe someday his bride would come through those library doors.

She didn't. By the time Jake was a graduating senior, he knew every library employee inside and outside the building. He learned a lot about life from the various books he read, and he learned a lot about farming, because after all, that was his beloved major study.

All of the Hallgrens drove Mrs. Blackburn to Jake's graduation. They surrounded the new graduate with his oversized gown, bobbing tassel, and diploma. "I'm looking forward to getting more acquainted with you now that you'll be farming close by," Dolly said to him. "Harold has been talking about how you and he can be buddies again and help each other out at the busy times."

Jake looked up at Dolly. He wanted to cry, he felt like sitting down on the sidewalk next to what was probably the oldest, largest tree in Nebraska and boo-hooing all over the cement. What a lovely woman Harold married. She didn't care he was short. And she wanted Harold and him together again as friends. Maybe things would get better, maybe Dolly had a short, unmarried girlfriend. Maybe everything would be perfect for him also.

***

Perfect things don't happen. While Dolly unexpectedly gave birth to Harold's daughter in the doctor's office in town, Mrs. Blackburn died in her husband's favorite easy chair. She saw a vision of Jake, who was on his way to buy seeds from a dealer whose farm was on the other side of town, and then she plain and simply died.

She would never hear that Harold was so excited about his baby he ran up and down the town's main street waving his arms this way and that, shouting the news until Jake drove by and saw that something was the matter. Jake's first thought was to tell his mother—this baby could be a substitute grandchild until he gave her one of his own. He could buy his seeds later.

"Get back to your wife," Jake called out to Harold. "I'll go home and spread the news to Mom. She can call your folks, I can see you're in no condition to do anything but wave your arms about."

He found her resting comfortably in that large blue chair of his father's, positioned directly in front of the television. His heart pounded clear up to his throat because his mother never sat in that chair, and especially never sat anywhere until the mid afternoon. He felt a slow, crawly something come into his body. He stood behind the chair, arms dangling by his sides, and he whimpered, "Please, Mom ... no ... please, no."

She didn't answer. Nothing answered. And not even the birds singing outside the window could bring sound into that room where Jake's precious mother had left her life behind. He stood and stared at her, and the cuckoo clock couldn't call loud enough for the son to hear. Everything had suddenly become nothing.

For a few months Jake wanted to be utterly alone. Harold and Dolly insisted he come over and share their suppers with them, but Jake refused. He didn't want to leave his father's house, his mother's remembered warmth, and his sister's picture. "I have to face reality. I read in one of those library books that grief goes away slowly, so as to not notice. It'll be okay again." He sighed. "As okay as it ever was, anyway."

So he ate the suppers that Harold's mother prepared and brought to him. He ate them alone after she left, swallowing the food along with the tears. And he thought about the land and remembered how his mother had willed it all to him so

Alvin couldn't suddenly show up after years of silence and claim a portion.

By exclusively willing Jake the land, Mrs. Blackburn had exclusively willed her son love, because land and love were the same to him. Sometimes he stooped down and ran his hand over the surface of a newly plowed field just like when he was in rompers by his father's feet. The land, the earth, the dirt, was real. And although at times it may be muddy or dry or weedy, it was always there. It would never die of a heart attack or breathe a last breath while sitting in an easy chair. It would never go away like everything else did; Jake gradually learned to live again with the strength of the land. The land was his father and his mother and his wife, and it sort of made up for the fact that he was alone and unmarried and short.

**

The years went by. If Jake and Harold had had the time from their busy activity of farming, they would have looked at the horizon for more reason than to determine possible storms, sunshine, or overcast, and they would have noticed how naked the country appeared even though showing an occasional house, barn, clump of trees, and vehicles raising dust on the gravel roads or rocking back and forth over ruts on the hard dirt byways that Ralph the road commissioner had not yet smoothed over.

They did look down, however, because down was where the ground was, and the ground was where crops grew, and on which Harold and Dolly raised their daughter, and into which Jake's parents were interred.

Jake frequently visited the cemetery where his whole world was buried, everyone except Harold and Dolly that is. And the uncolored silence of winter was especially hard on Jake; he went to the Hallgrens a lot during that time. Even before his retirement, when he had the spring and summer crop plantings and the fall barbecue to anticipate, the winter years of being alone crept up on him like molasses moving along a stick and which eventually took the shape of a cold steel spear that penetrated his thinking and made him realize that all those meals he had with Harold and Dolly and their growing daughter was not a case of sharing their lives, but more a matter of him being on the outside and looking in.

As the years passed, the more he was on the inside of the Hallgrens house, the more he felt the outside. "Jake, old buddy," Harold would say occasionally, "do you remember when we were kids and our moms forced us together? Look at us now. I guess mothers know best, don't they?" Then he would wink at Dolly whose smiling face was her nod of approval.

But the realization that he had no family of his own was not erased by the Hallgrens' camaraderie. This reality repeated itself over the years until it became a cycle of loneliness—a loneliness that grew like a fetus conceived by that rejection in the third grade and nurtured by all the consequent rejections in high school and college.

Jake's personality on the outside did not reflect what his thoughts of himself were on the inside; Jake didn't know this. He thought his inward and outward idea of himself matched. This mismatching showed, nevertheless, whenever a potential girlfriend was around: his outside went up to her, but his inside could never convince her that he was worth her time.

He had willingly stayed in college as his mother wished, not only to learn more farming, but to find a wife. He figured if he couldn't find one in a girl-populated place like college, he certainly wouldn't find one in the country where everyone was scattered and only occasionally social.

That unmatched personality of his proved to be true, and Jake entered his livelihood of farming without a bride, and this situation remained up to and into his retirement.

Thank goodness for the Hallgrens. Thank goodness for Barney's Beer Palace. And thank goodness for Saturday afternoons because Jake, in his loneliness, sometimes thought he had retired too hastily. It happened the afternoon in Barney's when he and Harold's neighboring farmer, Big Leutzinger, verbally presented his four sons as men of the land, as born and carefully bred farmers who were looking for sections to rent.

"I only have one section, boys, as you know, but by adding your two sections, my strapping sons can farm away to their hearts' content. Would you consider selling? Then they'd have houses too."

Well, that 'selling' request certainly turned Jake off, especially because there was no way Big had the money to buy all that land and houses too. Harold didn't approve either, but he was looking for a way to quit farming; Harold offered a compromise.

"Come on now, Leutzinger," he answered. "You said your boys were looking for rent land. Now you want to buy our precious sections and the very houses we live in."

Jake turned his back. He was insulted. He gave a silent pause that said a lot, and Big realized he had pressed for too much.

He answered Harold immediately because he was determined to not give up. "I'm sorry, I overstepped. My boys will be happy to rent with option to buy after they get enough money to borrow a loan on your houses. They are good, those sons of a gun. They would do honor to your soil."

Option to buy? Jake considered that as bad as outright buying. Whose option? Jake's or the sons?

When Harold and Jake didn't respond to the second offer, Big tried desperately at one more. "How about my boys renting only the land? No houses, no options, just rental land?"

Harold raised his eyebrows. Now he was tempted. He looked at Jake whose eyebrows were not raised, but who at least had turned around. He knew Harold was interested in the last offer, so he spoke up. "Leutzinger, I would like to talk to your sons, alone. I want them to come to my place tonight."

The four young farmers sat in Jake's kitchen and didn't say anything—by suggestion of their father.

That was the first thing they did right because it created an atmosphere of desperation they might say something

23

wrong and lose the precious land.

"Well, boys," Jake started, "why do you want my land? Why not go to the city and become accountants or something like that?"

"None of us would consider that, Mr. Blackburn, we love the land too much," the oldest one said.

That answer was the second thing they did right.

Jake continued. "A lot of people love land, but they don't all work it. Some people own land for investment or just for the sake of it."

"We farm our Dad's now, as you know, but it's not enough. We're stumbling into each other. And when you have a need to plant seeds and cultivate and harvest and sell, you have to have space."

That remark was the third thing they did right.

Then the youngest, almost eighteen, spoke the final straw that broke into Jake's concern and flattened it like a mouse on the bottom of a full silo. "We hear, Jake Blackburn, that you love the land. We do too. And we would like to take your love and our love, and with all that love, show your soil that it's not taken for granted."

"I'll call Harold," Jake said. He did, Harold agreed, and that was the beginning of Jake's new life. He felt his land was appreciated by the answers the Leutzinger brothers gave. If he had a son, he would have retired even sooner. As long as he could live on it and walk on it, he decided it was all right to no longer dig on it. Now he would have more time to visit with Harold and Dolly and come to Barney's and go to the library in a town bigger than the Boone County one. He might even find a bride in the library, a woman who needed someone desperately enough to not care about shortness. A lot of jockey-height men marry taller women. He could too.

If the world's greatest philosophers had convened to analyze Jake's reason for retiring, they would have quickly and unanimously come up with the same answer: Jake wanted a wife, and he needed time to look for one and time to convince her and himself that his short stature was no longer an issue. For the first time since the senior Mr. Blackburn placed his infant son between the rows of corn sprouts in the field, Jake began to recognize there was something else in life besides the land—not instead of, mercy no to that thought—but in addition to. And when one important thing in life interferes with pursuing another important thing, then it's best to walk away from the one until the other is realized. After all, Jake was not selling. He was merely renting. His love would remain intact.

**

Barney's Beer Palace. The proprietor, Barney, had opened the only beer joint in town years ago when he was two days past his twenty-second birthday; he was younger than Jake and Harold and also the child of a farmer—a product, as some in the community jokingly referred. His father had sired ten sons by his wife and one by a mysterious lady who left town shortly after Barney's birth. She gave permanent waves to women in the beauty parlor until her protrusion became as embarrassing as the reason she was that way. The owner of the beauty parlor kept her in an upstairs apartment until she gave birth, after which the young mother shoved her unwanted baby into the father's arms and drove off.

Barney never knew who his mother was because he never heard from her, and his father wouldn't talk about the matter. Barney's stepmother, however, didn't mince hay about telling him the truth when he was old enough to understand.

The Beer Palace had only one entry, a narrow door on what appeared to be the side of the rectangular, narrow-boarded building. One of the stories, that made its way around town one year, told of a time when an especially heavy man from the next county, on his way to Omaha, stopped for a beer and had to enter and leave sideways because his stomach could be squeezed to fit through the narrowness better than his shoulders. The door opened onto a parking lot twice the size of the building but lacked sufficient gravel to notice if the stones were really there. Consequently the lot was not desirable for parking during a heavy rain when mud showed through and tires sank.

Most of Barney's patrons, which was everyone in the county interested in beer, pool, pinball machines, and conversation, preferred to park in the lot instead of the street, probably because of the shorter distance to walk.

The sheriff had once commented to Barney that he should have another door to his establishment, an exit door at least, in case of fire; the sheriff was concerned not only for the customers of which he was one, but for Barney himself who had a small apartment in the back rooms.

But Barney had shook his head no, with the excuse that the Beer Palace was his life and when it went, so would he. The sheriff never pressed the matter, mistakenly thinking there was always enough beer to douse a fire, and the windows were large enough and frail enough to crash through using any of the tables and chairs.

The interior of Barney's reflected the countryside: it was large, its contents appeared swallowed up in it, and it was quiet. The bar counter went almost the width of the room with a twelve foot mirror behind the rack of glasses and mugs which Barney continuously soaped, rinsed, and towel polished as his customers lingered over their beers and bowls of pretzels. The bar stools, whose cushions had been pressed down by the weight of the customers over the years, looked like mushrooms all lined up ready to be picked and thrown into a stew.

The table and chair area of the room, used usually only by the hunting season customers who found the bar section too crowded with locals, held an array of varied colored hard plastic tables and chairs that looked like strong toothpicks glued together. The arrangement of these toothpicks was not color consistent, however, with green chairs and yellow tables pushed together as well as the blues and reds mixing.

Barney at one time tried to keep them matched, but over the years when some tables and chairs were too worn out or damaged, he replaced them with not quite the same colors. He compensated for this lack of correct color motif with his utmost cleaning routine of scrubbing the walls—walls on which hung large photos of John Wayne, Humphrey Bogart, a Gone With The Wind poster, and occasional samplings of a calendar girl surrounding a wide-mouth picture of Marilyn Monroe—and of scrubbing the floor with a mop that he kept wet in a bucket at all times. Cleanliness was the major theme. And when the numerous large and clean windows let in the brightness of the day, one might say the room sparkled.

One year Barney moved in a stuffed moose head and hung it over the mirror. He got it from a retired farmer from the edge of Boone County who claimed his grandfather had bagged it during one of those gold rushes in Alaska. Barney didn't care if the story was true or not, he did know it was the head of a moose, probably female, and he welcomed it. He secretly named it Lover Doll, a name he wouldn't even had told his wife about, if he had had a wife.

Another year Barney padded his pickup truck with old thick bedding pieces and drove to the furniture mart in Omaha. He returned with a pool table. The farmers didn't use it much during planting and harvesting seasons, but when the winter months came and their arms and hands were not as busy, nor their time as filled, they sometimes held contests with the prize being a free afternoon of beer for the winner paid by the losers. Barney used the pool table all the time— before customers came, after they left, and when business was slow. He loved to wipe chalk on the pool tip, strike it sharply on the designated ball, and watch the balls roll away, one after another, until they were all pocketed.

Jake and Harold never touched the pool table. Jake was too short to get enough leverage, and Harold, of course, wouldn't play without his buddy.

The pinball machines were another matter. The out-of-towners were heavy users, the ones who had just bagged some pheasant or duck and liked to continue their tirade out on the metal lever. A chug of beer with one hand, a pull on the handle with the other, and wow, what wonderful merriment that was. Barney was glad the heavy use of the pinballs was seasonal, he liked the usual quiet of his establishment—unless, of course, it was he making the noise. At Christmas Barney moved in a tree and decorated it quite heavily. At Easter he tacked up an extremely large cardboard rabbit onto one of the windows. And Halloween was always cluttered with goblin stuff of rattling skeletons, bats dangling from the ceiling, and a witch mask with a nose wart on it carefully placed over Lover Doll's snout.

The Beer Palace was Barney's home as well as his business; he blended the two and, along with his shy manner, created a homelike atmosphere in the midst of the building's plainness. This was maybe why his was the only saloon necessary for miles around, certainly the only one needed in this town.

Everyone liked Barney. Although his stepmother had raised him to be a social outcast, he became less of an outsider after he turned a forlorn looking empty, very empty building into a place for farmers and townspeople to gather and exchange tales of woe and bouts of bragging. They complained together, laughed, slapped backs occasionally, and drank lots of beer usually preceded by a mouthful of pretzels.

Like Jake, Barney never married, but not so much because of rejection by women, but because of shyness. As bold as his parents were to produce him, his disposition grew up to be just the opposite. So he spent almost all his waking hours cleaning, polishing, and listening. He especially liked to listen.

***

Jake and Harold sat on their usual bar stools at Barney's, drinking their usual beers and chewing on their usual big bites of pretzels. They began doing this every Saturday afternoon from the first year they started farming over forty years ago until, and through, their recent retirements.

There had been exceptions, like when Harold's daughter was sick with chicken pox or when Dolly was in bed with flu. But today they were together and slightly bored. It was

September, the beginning of the autumn beauty and the threat of winter hibernation.

"Isn't it something how a person can get into a rut?" Jake said to Harold after swallowing an extra big gulp of beer. Jake was smarting a little from his decision to retire.

Harold directed his head up from staring into his mug of beer and looked at Jake through the bar mirror, a more comfortable way to talk to his friend than to turn to his side and look at him straight on. "How's that?" he answered in a flat tone that seemed to mean he really didn't care what rut Jake was thinking of.

"Well, take us for example. We went to grade school, high school, and college together. Then you got married and I didn't, and we both settled down on our land and never left again."

Harold shook his head at his friend's finality. "So what's rutty about that? Everybody does that with their life. There aren't too many new things out there, buddy."

"I know, I'm not dumb, I'm not referring to the usual routine stuff." Jake looked up from the pretzel crumbs he was chasing with his middle finger on the slick countertop. "I'm referring to the fact that we don't have any friends besides ourselves, we never have had, and I sure don't see any dangling from the ceiling right now."

"Another beer, Barney, thanks," Harold called out as though Barney was somewhere back in his apartment with the door closed.

Jake mimicked, "Another beer, Barn, more pretzels please."

Harold responded to the pert remark by bypassing his mirror technique and shifting his body entirely toward Jake. "You need a wife. Right now, here, this very minute. Buddy of mine, let's get you a wife."

Jake's reply came with a snort. "Hey, leave me alone on that subject, and is it necessary to shout it to everybody in the world?"

Barney swiped on the pretzel crumbs with a wet cloth

rung dry as tight as a wet cloth can be rung dry. He would be closer to the conversation now in case anything more was said on the subject of wives or of anything else.

"Everyone in the whole world knows without my shouting it." Harold smiled. "Come on, buddy, let's find us a private table and get serious about this."

Jake took a deep breath and let it out with a slow moaning whistle. He knew he was in for it now because Harold wouldn't let go until either he gave in to him or it was time to go home.

Harold settled onto a green chair, put his beer on the blue table, leaned back, and focused on Jake's eyes which were going back and forth, up and down, in an attempt to avoid the topic. He blew his nose on Dolly's carefully ironed handkerchief. "I grabbed this one by mistake—if you ever get married, be careful about taking your wife's fine lace hankies."

Jake cleared his throat. "I shouldn't have given up on the library. I should have tracked down everyone of them in every county and town in the state until I found myself a nice little librarian." He relieved a notch on his belt buckle to accommodate the beer and pretzels.

"Sit down, for pity sakes." Harold leaned back further on his chair and attempted to put his heel on the table. "You're right about the library, you should have spent all your weekends looking into them. But as far as women go, somebody will find you someday. But why not start looking now? This very instance. Right here in Boone County."

Jake went over to the window and looked out as though he would get going right away, at four o'clock, this Saturday. "It doesn't look good out there. I think we're in for some big rain. Pretty soon."

Harold pounded his fist on the table. "You've avoided it all these years, and you're still avoiding it. Hang the storm. Promise me you'll go library hunting starting this Monday."

Jake smirked, not from Harold's remark, but because he had lost the courage to act on the reason he retired. His habit of years without a woman was so strong, he couldn't bring himself to a front line assault. "The library is out. For crying-out-loud, you dummy, it's enough that women around here make fun of my shortness. What do you think they'd say if they thought I was a bookworm? A short bookworm."

Harold nodded indignantly. "Well, I'll have Dolly pounce on them if they make fun."

Jake sat down across from Harold's heel that had finally made it to the edge of the table. "It's going to pour buckets any minute now, and it's not the gossip I worry about—it's the thinking. It's starting to rain. Have you ever been looked at by Mrs. Meddlesome, our most prominent town gossip? I've never actually heard her say anything, but I've heard her think. She looks at a person and thinks, her eyes stare right at you, and she presses her lips together until there is just a slit, and then she thinks."

Harold guffawed a reply. "I've never had the stomach to look at her, and I think you have her name wrong. It's Mrs. Flappylips."

A slice of lightening lit up the windows, and the rumbling of thunder became louder as though to orchestrate disgust at all the town gossips in all the towns as well as Boone County.

Barney drew two beers and brought them over to the two buddies. "It's on the house."

Jake and Harold nodded thank you's. They knew how Barney had suffered with gossip about his real mother and decided this was his way of saying thank you for two descriptive names concerning them.

Harold raised his mug. "Here's to you, Barney, and to you, Jake, and to you Mrs. Meddlesome Flappylips."

The rain came heavy, and Harold gave up his salutations and rapped his knuckles on the table. "C'mon Jake, old friend of mine, let's shake our legs and get out before Noah sails by. Dolly is fixing a special supper for us. I can milk Brie before instead of after—she's not so fussy anymore—and then you and me and Dolly can talk longer after we've eaten. Okay?"

"Okay." Jake unconsciously leaned over to swipe a dried clot of dirt from the side of his boot. He always automatically responded to some kind of attempt to look presentable whenever a nice woman's name was mentioned, even if it was a married woman unavailable to him. "What are we going to talk about longer after we've eaten?"

Harold's reply of 'anything you want' relieved Jake's concern that both Harold and Dolly would gang up on him about the wife issue. He felt the warmth of Barney's fourth beer in him and slapped the table as the two got up and walked to the door. "Dolly is sure nice to have supper for an old bachelor as often as she does. Do you force her?"

"Me force Dolly? The mother, my mother? Grand Mom? Are you kidding? She's the one who forces me to ask you."

Jake laughed. "I see. You can't live without me, can you?"

By this time they had each reached their pickup trucks and had started to squeeze on the handles when suddenly the already heavy rain came down from an especially black cloud with such a force as though to dump a year's load in one minute.

"Wet," Jake yelled and rushed to the back of his pickup where his dog Prince of nine years and his cat Mitzie of five were whining and meowing with all the noises they could possible make. He lifted Prince with one arm and Mitzie with the other and slid them onto the inside seats, wet soggy fur and all. He sat there drenched himself. "Wet. Dang."

But he was about to get even wetter because Harold yanked open one door and Barney the other after which Jake realized he and his pets were being hauled inside the Beer Palace.

"How many years have you been a farmer?" Harold shouted at him. "Even city men know better than to sit inside a drowning vehicle."

They plopped themselves down at a yellow table this time and watched the rain run down their heads and eventually onto the floorboards which conveniently had cracks between them to accommodate the run-off.

"I smell wet dog."

"No kidding."

"Wet cat, too."

"Double no kidding."

"I wonder if they can smell us?"

"What'd suppose wet pretzels smell like when they get soaked?"

"Why don't we drop the subject?"

Prince settled by the door and panted loud enough until he was told to shut up. Mitzie slunk to hide under a table as any respectful cat who thought it had lost its fur coat would do.

They drank more beer and waited. There wasn't anything else to do but drink and wait and pant and slink.

Ordinarily Jake would never have stranded himself inside a vehicle during a possible flood. Nor would he have left his pets in an open pickup during a lightening storm. But Jake was not thinking ordinarily right now. He had been distracted with thoughts of a wife again, a phase he went in and out of over the years; today he began another aspect of it.

Prince settled down to only occasional panting, and Harold was relaxed far back in his chair with another beer and with nothing more to say. It was the calm during the storm, and the vacuum atmosphere inside the saloon allowed Jake to concentrate on his unusual behavior during the cloudburst. Unlike Harold who had nestled himself down to quiet nothingness except for what it took to bend his elbow and open his mouth for gulps of beer, Jake's mind became very active. He thought about the wife thing again, and he thought about the yearly barbecue a few weeks before.

His mind saw her repeatedly as she was that day, standing by the pot roast table of marinated, barbecued, and plain slabs of beef. The lady had a soft stateliness to her smile, a kind of real friendly Mona Lisa; her green and brown checkered dress moved as slowly as she did in the uneventful breeze.

This new woman in Boone County, Jake remembered again as he bit slowly into another pretzel, was tall and maybe unmarried and willowy with a face lined ten years younger than her fifty-five. Of course Jake didn't know her real age or her marital status, but he concluded these two facts from a thread of gossip coming out of Mrs. Meddlesome's flappy lips in the grocery store the day after the barbecue. He wishfully decided that the new woman at the pot roast table was the same one. Anyone else, along with Jake who noticed her that day, would call her a lady instead of some ordinary middle-aged woman. One might say she was someone to look at twice. Especially by the men.

With the exception of the pot roast table, the local yearly barbecue was essentially an oversized pot luck event, and it had been Jake's turn this year to host, which meant he offered his land, his one bathroom, and his kitchen's aged oven for last minute heatings.

Jake looked over at Harold, who was in a very uncomfortable sleep at the moment, and remembered how perfectly warm and cool it had been that day. Whenever it got too warm, then a cool breeze came, and when the breeze became too cool, then it warmed up again. Back and forth with a condition that Harold always referred to as nothing weather because no one could judge whether it was too warm or too cool, too breezy or too still. The result was a rare time when no one talked about the weather which was usually the most important topic.

Most farmers were used to the fickleness of the rain and sunshine and frost and drought, and they were full of many 'oh well's' and 'that's the way things go.' One year rich, the next year poor. 'We sure had a good year, didn't we?' or 'We sure had a bad year, how are you holding up?' They lived one season at a time instead of one day at a time, and in this atmosphere of similar remarks, the farming gamblers gathered every early autumn to say hello, goodbye, and how's the weather been treating you?—although everyone knew the weather treated everyone in the Boone County area about the same.

Barney brought Jake another beer because more clouds were bursting, and any hope of them quitting their outpour became less and less. Harold suddenly awoke from his discomfort and pushed his chair against the wall for more support and then nodded off again. Jake removed his friend's grasp on the mug in case Harold's body would jerk in sleep and take the mug with it. The room started to look like Rip Van Winkle.

Jake was glad Harold chose to sleep instead of talk because he was in the middle of a reverie himself, and he couldn't seem to stop. Was it the new lady who had brought out this nostalgia on such a pitiful afternoon? He thought about all those years he concentrated on weather conditions, fertilizers, insecticides, and seeds. Now he concentrated on the woman. He visualized her as a female who cared as much for the land as he did. Otherwise, why would someone so lovely still be on a farm? She should be in a town or a city, married to some big shot who could show her off, instead of staying on in the country spread out by acres and acres of uninhabited land.

He smiled when he thought of his land, for Jake considered his acres as more than mere measurement of what he owned. He considered it as the substance of farming—it was soil, or as all children and most mothers would say: dirt.

Sometimes, Jake remembered, when he was little and alone and while his mother busied herself with the family wash and food preparation, and while his father plowed through the fields on his tractor with Alvin far behind, he would stoop down to the ground and pat the earth. He then would wonder if the place he was standing on at the moment had ever held an Indian tall with arms folded over chest, or if this particular piece of land had once provided a trail for tired horses weary from pioneering across Nebraska to California as those movies in town on Saturday afternoons showed.

Barney heaved a box of bottled soda pop from the storage closet and thudded it behind the counter. The noise not only jolted Jake but reminded him of how he would occasionally pound on the hard ground as a child and think of the God he learned about in Sunday School. Was God in that ground? And why was it brown—why such a dull color for something as important as the ground? And although Jake outgrew wondering if God was in the ground, he never outgrew his wonderment of it.

This wonderment remained, like an oak remains after years of overly hot summers and ice cold winters. It was as though Jake was born, not out of his mother and father, but out of the earth which held him mesmerized and respectful. And like a baby who looks up at its mother in wide-eyed puzzled security, Jake looked down at the ground with the same intensity. The ground was always there, the mother not.

Barney looked over at Harold snoozing and at Jake gazing into space; he put the coffee pot on high. Barney had no notion that his only awake customer, Jake, was really awake. Open eyes did not necessarily mean consciousness, although Jake certainly thought he was conscious as he again recalled the woman in the brown and green checkered dress standing by the pot roasts, and how he had zealously looked at her as though this effort would keep her there forever while he mused over how she looked: she seemed to have come out of the earth, the ground, its dirt, and silhouetted against the sky like a blade of corn. Those young shoots of growth his hands had dabbled at when he was nine months old had finally matured and was standing only a short distance from him in a dress that danced on a checkerboard of brown earth and green growing crops.

She was too tall for him and probably married; he had kept his distance but continued to look at her through the meats, vegetables, apples, casseroles, and chocolate cakes; and he wondered about her just as he had wondered about the earth. He eventually and reluctantly looked away.

The barbecue grew dark, and the farmers gradually packed their cars and pickups and drove home. But the new woman's presence never grew dark in Jake's mind; he remembered her the next day and the next week and the next month, just as he was doing now at Barney's in the middle of a rainstorm; he remembered her with the same clarity and futility that he remembered his little blond girlfriend in the first grade. This lady, however, standing by the pot roasts in her earthly patterned dress was like a beautiful array of what Jake loved the most, and the memory of the little blond girl suddenly furrowed into the ground along with last year's spent crops.

Harold woke up and raised his mug. "Here's to you, good friend, may your journey home be a good one." He was still a little bit under the influence of the beers and the nap, so his toast to Jake bordered a little bit from a scene out of the knights of old when they saluted each other at the end of the day, and it showed that his mind was far, far away from Jake's right now.

Jake wiped his mouth with his sleeve—he had no wife to reprimand him for this sloppy action—and put his mug slowly, deliberately down on the table. "You evidently are not aware that neither of us may go home. We may be spending the night here with Barney, right here where we are right now at this table."

"Now, why would we want to do that?" Harold asked.

"Because there's a lot of water out there, and we're kind of drunk. Do you want us to drown and make Dolly a widow?"

"No, of course not. I couldn't live without Mama."

"You've got it turned around," Jake continued as he reached for the pretzels. "She would have to live without you. And with me dead also, she wouldn't have someone to come over and milk Brie and wash the upstairs windows and make a nuisance for her."

Harold frowned. "She could move to town and console herself with the other widows. And there are a few widowers she could acquaint herself with."

Jake shook his head as he always did whenever Harold rambled on about something that went against his real feelings. He went to the bar and leaned over. "Barney, where's your coffee?"

Barney wiped his last wet mug clean with a backward and forward thrust and held it up to the light. "No widow can whistle-clean glass like I do," he said, "and besides, you guys ain't going anywhere until you have at least two pots of coffee in you. You two may not be making a ruckus, but I can tell you're both drunker than all the beer joints in this state."

"Tell that to big shot over there," Jake said with a slight hiccup. "I don't think that crazy fool is living in the real world right now. All I did was mention the slightest possibility that maybe we would drown on the way home, and he has Dolly fixed up with every man in town." Jake resented his friend's casual dismissal of Dolly even though he knew Harold was just mouthing off.

"Hey," Barney said almost loudly. "Hey, Harold Big Shot, no more beer and no more talk about leaving. Your little lady can get along for a night without you."

"She can't milk Brie," Harold retorted.

"Sure she can. She's a farmer's wife, ain't she?"

"Yeah, but I've spoiled her. I told her right after we were married, it was on our honeymoon, that the milking is my job and the mending is hers."

Barney poured two cups of his extra strong coffee. "Sure, sure, I bet that's what you told her on your honeymoon. Probably the very first thing you said. I'll put you under that citizen's arrest thing if you leave here now." He wiped the bar top until its reflection showed the wood chandelier light from above. "Drink this coffee and then call home and tell your wife you won't be coming for awhile."

Harold swallowed a hot gulp and went to the phone. "All right, you win, you win, you win, but not because of that silly arrest threat of yours. I just decided I don't want Dolly up for grabs by some lonely widower or a wandering transient."

Barney stepped out from behind the bar. "Sorry, the phone is dead, I just remembered. Your wife will just have to worry for awhile longer. Probably won't be her first time to worry about you." He signaled for Jake to drink his share of the coffee as he poured another cup for Harold who was picking up the phone anyway. "Now, now, dialing on a dead phone won't bring it to life. And don't have any thoughts of leaving—if a phone line can't survive that stuff out there, what do you think your chances are?"

Harold suddenly came to attention like a young soldier whose sergeant had just walked by. Chances? Phone lines down? What about the electrical lines? What about Dolly tracking through the mud to milk Brie and stepping on a hot wire? He looked straight at Jake as though he himself had stepped on a hot wire; he froze for a moment. "She'll go to Brie—I know her—she can do anything if she really wants to, and she will really want to milk Brie and relieve her misery."

And before Harold unfroze his body, Barney grabbed his shoulder, and Jake slammed himself up against the door.

"No, buddy, no," Jake yelled. "She'll know better, she'll put on your rubber boots. She will—won't she?"

Harold leaned on Jake and started to breathe deep and heavy. "No she wouldn't." Then he grabbed at Jake's shirt to pull him away from the door, but before his hand could grasp the plaid, Jake gave him a bear hug around the waist, and Barney came from behind to hug around the shoulders.

The three stood there struggling in a most offensive grunting way until Harold finally wailed, "Okay, okay, I'll stay." They let go, but remained awhile by the door just in case the panicked one changed his mind.

Jake rubbed his chin which he usually did when he felt powerless. He then took his friend's helpless elbow and escorted him to a bar stool. They sat side by side but said nothing until Barney broke the silence when he picked up an already polished mug and polished it again until it squeaked.

"Hey there, buddy," Jake finally said, "I know for a fact that God won't take Dolly yet. He wouldn't do that to Himself."

Harold looked up at Jake through the bar mirror. "How's that? How do you figure that?"

"Because if He took Dolly away, He'd have to take care of us. He wouldn't wish that on Himself."

Harold shook his head and asked Barney for more coffee. He took a swallow that lasted until his breath gave way, and then he turned to Jake in a very slow, deliberate motion.

"Aside from the fact that you are partially crazy, will you do me a favor and pray?"

Jake thought for a moment. He started to rub his chin again. "I always pray when it concerns you, you ingrate, how else do you think you make it through every day? It's my prayers that does it."

"Thanks, I hope you mean it because I am in the middle of the ocean right now, and I don't have any oars."

Jake nudged Harold with his elbow. "It's okay. Everything will be okay again." Then he wondered to himself if this was the first time Harold had been without oars. He wondered if Harold knew that his longtime friend, who was trying to console him now, had himself gone through his entire life without oars—that it didn't take a rainy deluge to be left in the middle of something with no means to navigate. Jake sighed because he knew what helplessness felt like.

The blackness of night came, and the downpour stopped. "I guess the rain got lost in the dark," Barney mused, but Jake and Harold didn't respond to any form of humor.

"Let's go," Harold shouted, and Barney grabbed his lantern flashlight so the two drinking buddies, who by now were completely sober, could inspect the depth their tires had mired in the mud.

"Why don't you put gravel on your parking lot?" Harold grumbled to Barney.

Barney swung the lantern back and forth between the two vehicles and answered, "Why don't you park in the street?" without missing a beat on the swings.

"Why do you have a parking lot if you think we should park in the street?" Harold snipped back.

"It came with the joint," Barney said as he put the lantern down and turned away. "If my help isn't appreciated ..." and Barney was gone, back to his beloved saloon with a slammed door as a goodbye offering.

Harold shook his head back and forth. "We won't get out 'til spring. Brie will be just a memory by then—she will have exploded—and Dolly will have remarried. And all because

Barney won't pave this ridiculous parking lot."

Jake stooped down and scooped at the mud around his rear tires with the shovel he kept in the back of his pickup. "It's not that deep, Harold, for pity sakes, let's get out of here. Are you going to apologize to Barney?"

"Oh," Harold smiled a little in the pitch black, "Barney knows I didn't mean it."

"Apologize, Harold. Now."

Harold looked at Jake and gestured for the use of his shovel. "Why are you so on your high horse? Barney knows I'm upset about my wife and cow. I'll get to him next week."

Jake cleared his throat and offered the shovel. "You don't know what it's like to be alone with hurt feelings. When you go home after a bad to-do, you have Dolly to cushion you. It's different when there's no one there. You dwell more on an insult. It eats away like salt in a wound."

Harold handed back the shovel. "Is that so?"

Jake nodded. "Yeah, that's so. And even more so with Barney. He doesn't have anyone at all. At least I have you and Dolly."

"Will you please quit making me feel like a jerk?"

"You're not a jerk. I just feel sorry for Barney, that's all. I always have. I know what it's like to be an outsider. But at least I was born legitimate."

Harold got into his truck and started the engine. It gasped a few times, then took hold. He rocked the vehicle determinedly back and forth until it came out of the mud and onto the cement curbing. He stopped the motion, put the engine into neutral, and got out. Without a word to Jake, he picked up the lantern and stomped back to the saloon door.

Jake's heart started to pound. Why didn't he mind his own business? Harold hurt Barney, so Jake hurt Harold. He got into his pickup and slowly drove to where his dear, sassy friend would soon reappear. He wondered what Harold was saying to Barney, and then he wondered what he would say to Harold. Maybe he should pretend that bad words hadn't passed between them. This was usually how they handled their arguments. But this time was different because Harold was distracted with concern over his wife and Jake bawled him out anyway.

He started to feel his rain-soaked jeans on his legs and backside, and his whole body wanted to do nothing else but to go home and go to bed. It was so dark and still and alone with no one but himself in the parking lot, such as it was. Why was he so hard on Harold? Did his buddy hit a touchy subject when he brought up the wife stuff? Does his best friend think a man can go out and pick out a wife like you pick out books in a library or trucks on a car lot? Why did his only friend make him feel bad about being unmarried? Harold was so smug about his Dolly and their marriage. Smug. Is that what was wrong with this argument? Was he jealous of Harold's smugness?

Of course he was. But maybe envy was a better word, it was more grown-up to be envious. And it was this envy that made him pounce on Harold at a time when his friend needed sympathy over his worry about the electrical lines. Just for that he would go library hunting first thing next week. Maybe he would even make inquiries about that new woman at the barbecue. Uh-huh, Harold was right—he needed a wife, a woman to soften him up, someone to peel off his husks and expose the fine, silky strands within. That is, if there were any.

Harold finally came out. He had been inside long enough to deliver a congressional filibuster on apologies. He looked over at Jake sitting snug in his pickup.

Jake gave him a broad wave with his hand. There, that should take care of bad feelings. He nonchalantly started to drive into the street. "Do you still want me to come over?"

"Of course I do, you bazooka. You'll have to help if something happened to Dolly. By the way, Prince and Mitzie are waiting for you inside. Are you interested?"

There, that was it. Harold might just as well have shot him right between the eyes by suggesting that maybe Jake didn't care about anything anymore except proprieties and hurt feelings. So what if Dolly's mired in the mud, and so what if his pets spend the night in a beer joint. All he was concerned with was that one insult flung out into a night of worry and frustration. Yes, Harold got back at him all right, that broad wave of his hand hadn't fixed everything after all.

Jake was embarrassed. "Of course I'm interested." He had forgotten again about the only two living things that depended on him for everything. He had let his distraction about the barbecue lady interfere with the possibility Dolly may be in danger. A bird in the hand—Dolly and his pets were birds in the hand—and not that lady from the barbecue. Next time there was a crisis in Harold's life, he would apologize himself to anyone Harold offended while under stress, and not expect him to be a perfect gentleman when he bellyaches about his tires buried in mud and his wife crumbled over electrical wires.

***

Dolly had all the lights in the house and barn turned on. In the blackness of the rain and the night she figured Harold and Jake, if he came, would need a few obvious targets to aim at. Jake heard a long and very low moo come from inside the barn, and he heard Harold at the back door pounding his fist as though Dolly had locked him out.

"You okay?" Harold shouted to his wife. "Unlock this door, let me in. Dolly? Dolly. Now."

She came to the door. "Go to Brie, old man, she's long overdue. Why didn't you call that you'd be late? Is it asking too much to relieve my worry?" Dolly wiped flour from her hands and waved for Jake to hurry on in.

"The phone at Barney's was dead, woman. Why didn't you call me, then you'd know?"

"Harold, calm down. How can you ask why I didn't call you when you knew Barney's line was down? I did call you. You could have gone somewhere else in town and called me. I was worried sick. Hello, Jake."

Harold started to shout again. "You were worried? You were worried? I thought you were out here dead, and you

43

were worried? Worried sick, you say? I was worried sicker."
He let out a big sigh and put his arms around his wife.

Dolly hugged back. "I thought you might be dead too. So
what do you think of that, Mr. Hallgren?"

Although they hadn't asked him, Jake thought they were
asking too many questions. He nudged the reunited couple
aside so Prince and Mitzie could come into the shed. "Do you
two want me to milk Brie, or would you rather she
explode? Then you can worry about something that is really
dead."

Harold left Dolly's side, patted Prince, Mitzie, and then his
own dog, Proudflesh, on their respective heads and went to
his duty in the barn. He hoped his pet would follow even
though wet weather was not the animal's favorite thing.
Proudflesh was Harold's dog of his old age, a mixture of many
breeds, rickety and full of scars that he had received in
puppyhood when he had gotten into every fighting scrap he
could find. Harold named him Proudflesh because, for the
first year of the dog's life, there was always some unhealed
wound somewhere on his body. Proudflesh slowly,
reluctantly followed his master.

Dolly turned to Jake. "That man is the worry-est worrier
I've ever known. He's always afraid something will happen to
me. Would you mind cleaning up the mess he left from his
shoes? I'll get supper on the table."

Jake complied. He didn't mind Dolly's orders. What a
woman she was. Too bad there was only one of her in the
entire county. "Oh boy, what a smell," Jake grinned as he
rubbed his weather-roughed hands together at the aroma
from the oven. "Please don't take that smell away."

Dolly laughed. She was as relieved as the men were, now
that they were all together and safe. "I kept cooking and
baking all through the storm. First the plump roast, then the
baked potatoes, then the cinnamon rolls. Everything's a little
wrinkled by now though."

Harold came in with a bucket of Brie's milk and clumsily
banged the container against the shed door, something he

always managed to do with Brie's milk. Dolly had complained once that she could have recorded the number of times he milked Brie over the years by the number of bangs she had heard. Harold lifted the bucket and poured into a smaller one. "Here's your share, old buddy. Okay?"

"Sure, sure, thanks," Jake replied although he really didn't want the milk; he always took a gallon now and then when offered because Harold thought he needed it. Brie certainly didn't need it anymore.

Dolly pulled pans and platters from the oven of warmed up supper. She quickly put them on the table and motioned for the men to sit, eat. She purposefully looked at Jake. "You need a wife, young man, she would more than welcome that milk."

Harold pulled out Dolly's chair, something he rarely did, but he was so grateful she had brought up the marriage thing again. "Yeah," he added as a further gesture, "yeah, Jake, you should look for a wife."

"You two are ganging up on me."

The three dug their forks into the potatoes and beef. Proudflesh took a deep yawn, turned on his blanket three times, and lay down. Prince and Mitzie milled around in the shed until Dolly got up and let them in with orders to settle down. She patted Jake's shoulder on the way back to her chair.

"Not really, Jake," Dolly said. "But you're retired now, and you have more time to look."

Harold scooped a big bite of potato into his mouth. "Hey, Dolly, don't those new farmers to the west have a sister? Their name's Swensen. Three big guys, two widowed. Just came from Iowa a little bit ago."

Jake looked up from his food. "You're right. Their name is Swensen. Saw them from a distance at the barbecue—the sheriff pointed them out—big suckers, aren't they?" He looked down at his food again, not knowing that his casual remark about the Swensens would be the last casual remark he would ever make about them.

Dolly picked up the hot pan of cinnamon rolls, loosed the edges, and inverted them right onto the table's oilcloth. "They have a sister, and she joined my bridge club just the other day. I guess she heard at the barbecue that every woman who breathes around here is a member of the club."

Jake bit slowly into the hot cinnamon. A sister? He had heard only of the brothers. She was probably the size of an elephant if the brothers were so huge. Probably that was why she wasn't with them at the barbecue—couldn't fit into their pickup, not even in the back. "Is she like you, Dolly? I mean, does she cook and stuff like that? Is she a big one like her brothers?"

"Do you want her?" Dolly asked bluntly. "She asked about you, she wondered about our barbecue host. Didn't you notice her? She was the one in the green and brown checkered dress. A very lovely woman."

Jake swallowed hard. The green and brown checkered lady. Dolly knew her. He might stand a chance now. And she must be unmarried or Dolly wouldn't tease about an introduction. His heart pounded clear up to his ears. "Oh well, now Dolly, for pity sakes, I was just making conversation. I don't even know her name."

"Nell," Dolly smiled in reply. "You two should meet, you are both nice people. And single."

"No, no, I'm too old and set in my ways." By now Jake's heart was inside his ears, his own words became an echo; and Harold's laughter at his remark sounded like chamber music in the horror films they went to in town on Saturday afternoons when they were kids.

Harold's chamber music became louder as he continued. "So was Dolly, set in her ways, when we met. But I married her anyhow. I liked the way she was set. Still do."

Jake could hardly hear. He had to get hold of himself, for pity sakes, what was he so excited about? The lady surely wouldn't look at him twice, let alone get serious with him. He took a deep breath and let it out. The pounding gradually went with it, and he began to hear almost normal again.

"Don't pay any attention to him," Dolly said of Harold's last comment. "Don't pay any attention to me either. It is just that I know two very nice people, and if they want an introduction, I'll introduce." She had noticed Jake's veins protruding in his neck and his face motionless looking down only at his plate. She knew she had hit a very sensitive subject with the Jake and Nell business, and she didn't want Jake to run so far and fast that he would be irretrievable.

Jake reached for another cinnamon roll. His heart had returned to his chest, but his veins continued to pulse prominently in his wrists. "I'm still too set in my ways. Besides, I wouldn't know what to do with a woman anymore."

Harold snorted. "Anymore? Are you worried about that? I have never known what to do with a woman. Dolly taught me everything I know."

"Don't pay any attention to him," Dolly repeated. "And don't put so much importance on sex. It's what the two people involved want, not what everyone thinks they should want."

Jake didn't say anymore. Things were getting a little touchy. He reached for a third cinnamon roll and took big swallows of lukewarm coffee.

"Mama, I think we had better change the subject," Harold decided. "Why don't you give us an update on the latest gossip?"

Dolly's face lit up, and the conversation shifted as easily as gears in a new automobile. "Aggie Jensen called me today. She said our quilting circle might have to increase its members. We might need more money for the orphanage."

"I thought the county paid those two old sisters for the care of the children," Jake said. "Surely that huge house of theirs that they turned into an orphanage is all paid for."

Dolly shook her head yes. "It's the extras. Our quilts buy extras for the children so they can come as close as possible to having a real home."

Harold tapped his pipe on the edge of his plate. He knew

there was more to Dolly's gossip than a need for more money. He knew that when his wife had some really big news, she would back into it, toy with her listener, especially if the listener was him. "All right, all right, woman, what's the real story? Let it out, give it to us straight."

"The Charmleys. They beat each other up the other night. First one and then the other called the sheriff and yelled that the other one had started it."

Thank goodness, Jake thought, something real gossipy to distract from the Swensens' sister. He had better keep this conversation alive. "Beat each other up? What about the kids? Did they beat them up too?"

Dolly frowned as she shook her head vigorously back and forth. "No. They apparently don't beat kids. Just spouses."

Jake and Harold put down their coffee and cinnamon rolls and waited for Dolly to continue.

"The sheriff is going to watch them closely. He got real nasty to them. He threatened to take away their kids. He doesn't think that's a good atmosphere for them to be in."

"Did that scare them?" Harold asked.

Dolly said no. "They said he couldn't do that. They said they have beaten on each other in Denver where they're from, and they have never touched the kids. The sheriff asked the older child if that was true, and he said it was, that the parents wait until he and his sister are in bed."

"How nice of them," Harold said. "How old are the kids?"

Dolly shook her head sadly. "The boy is ten and the girl six. The spinster sisters at the orphanage figure they will get them someday, and that's why we need to step up production on the quilts. Besides, that shop in Omaha can't seem to get enough of our handiwork, they have asked for more than we can make."

Jake inserted a toothpick into his mouth, rubbed it rapidly back and forth between two teeth, and wondered if that Nell Swensen was a quilter. Doggone, there she was again, he was back into his thoughts about her at a time when he should concentrate on this very important, juicy gossip. He rolled his eyes and drummed his fingertips on the table to distract himself from the distraction.

"You okay, buddy?" Harold asked in response to his friend's finger drumroll. "I'd like to hear some more of Dolly's story if you don't mind."

Jake became still. What must they think? What would Nell Swensen think? Sure enough, there she was again. All roads do not lead to Rome—some of them detour to the new lady in town, or county, or wherever she lives.

"I just can't believe it," Jake finally managed to say. "The boy, Billy, bicycles over to my place once in awhile after school. He tells me everything he learned that day." Jake wondered if Nell was his teacher, and if she was, she surely must live in town. Hello Nell, do you think of me as often as I think of you? How's your husband? Please have a husband so I can quit being interrupted by you.

Jake grabbed a stack of dishes and carried them to the sink. "He brings his sister too. The prettiest and littlest thing. He stashes her on the seat behind him. She's crazy about Mitzie and isn't afraid to smile at me even though her two front teeth are missing."

"I think I have seen the two wandering around town," Dolly said. "They have a kind of blankness to them, don't they? You said the boy is Billy. What's the sister's name?"

"Nell." Jake really didn't want to say that, especially because the sister's name was not Nell. It was Angela.

"Oh?" Dolly sounded surprised. "Same name as the new woman, Nell Swensen, which I think fits her better than it does a forlorn little girl, don't you?"

Jake brought more dishes to the sink. How was he going to get out of this one? "Harold, why don't you get Dolly's hearing checked? I said 'well,' and was about to add 'her name is Angela,' but before I could finish, Dolly comes out with 'Nell' and a whole conversation about whose name fits who."

Harold leaned back in his chair and was quiet for a short while. Then he stood up. "Dolly's hearing is perfect, old chum, I think the problem is your tongue. Too many potatoes and cinnamon rolls stuffed in your mouth."

Jake took a deep breath, Harold had saved him. "I guess you're right, I shouldn't talk with my mouth so full of food." Good old Harold, he and Dolly will probably discuss his slip of the tongue after he left, but for now he had a reprieve.

"Her name is real pretty, don't you think? Angela. It's like someone from Heaven." Jake turned on the sink water and started to swish the plates with his fingertips. Then he realized he had never done this with Dolly's dishes before, and he had better quit this right now or she would ask him why his sudden interest in tidying up. Then he would have to tell her it was to get his mind off Nell Swensen. Dolly of course would then arrange an introduction, after which Miss Swensen would mutter something about his shortness and tell Dolly to forget it. Jake imagined that the new woman would even be revolted by more than his lack of height. She would probably liken him to a worm, a short worm, with skinny legs and a skinny mouth and endless nerve to think he had a chance with her.

Harold lit his pipe again. "Oh well, maybe the orphanage is a better place for those two. They'll probably get more love and attention there."

Another reprieve. "Love and attention, yes, but it's not the same," Jake eagerly added to get as far away as possible from that other dangerously embarrassing subject. "All kids want their own parents' love, even if it's not offered."

"Is that Dr. Spock?" Harold teased.

"No, it's Jake Blackburn. Things I have read about abused kids claim that a child always looks for a parent's approval even if that parent is rotten and in jail forever and ever. It has to do with identity. Kids identify their importance and worth with their parents."

"Jake's right," Dolly interjected. "But the orphanage can be a darn good substitute. Unfortunately, we can't do anything about that until the sheriff does something about it, and maybe he won't."

Jake looked at his watch. "I'd better go. Thanks for the supper. You're a good woman, Dolly." He hesitated and looked over at his friend. "So are you, Harold." Then he quickly signaled to Prince and Mitzie to follow. With his two pets beside him, he slowly, reluctantly, drove away from the Hallgrens' driveway and onto the muddy road. He turned the radio on low, the vehicle lights on high, and rolled down the window to let in the prematurely cool September air. Prince panted, took a deep breath to relieve the burden of the world, and stared straight ahead as a lookout for his master. Mitzie edged her way between Jake's legs, licked her paw a few times, and settled to sleep. Mitzie never cared where she was—when it was time to sleep, she slept.

Jake mused about the evening with the Hallgrens. While the cool air filled his lungs with energy, his thoughts filled his head with nostalgia. What a warm comfort Harold and Dolly were; how lucky they were to have each other and how lucky he was to have them. He thought about his parents and how they had loved and cared for him. But this evening with the Hallgrens and the life with his parents were gone now. They were events and people he could only think about. They were not him.

He hit a bump in the road causing Prince to bark and Mitzie to scamper to a less precarious place. He thought about the Swensen brothers. He thought about Nell.

***

The Swensen brothers and their sister had moved from Iowa to Nebraska a few months previous to the spring planting. They moved because they inherited rich Nebraska land from an obscure uncle who died debt free with a well kept-up house and well established farmland, both of which were closer to a town than their Iowa circumstance.

George Swensen, the youngest, had never married and at forty-five his chances that he ever would became less and less. He didn't lack women in his life, but he had no desire to have children. He had been slow in school and thought he might pass this on to offspring. He farmed his parents' land

and continued this after their deaths. Nell Swensen, the oldest of them all, stayed at home with her younger brother and became the housekeeper and cook. Her reason for single-hood was not due to a lack of available men in the remote northern area of Iowa, but rather the idea of waiting for the perfect man. Perhaps if George and Nell had not had each other, they would have put out an effort to find mates. Both of them would have been good in marriages because of their pleasantness, a characteristic that would have won them first place in any congeniality contest.

The other two Swensen brothers, identical twins, would not have even considered entering such a contest. Nor would they have been allowed. Their dispositions were laced with gunpowder which exploded in barrages of nasty remarks, grumblings and sneers whenever they were displeased with something. This happened often, and if the Smithsonian Institute would ever display an example of such personalities, waxed figures of Les and Lo would be in the showcase for all to see.

Lo, whose Christian name was Lowell, and Les, who always insisted that his full, official name was merely Les, were especially handsome and did manage to wile two fairly nice women into marrying them. During their courtships they intentionally imitated George and Nell, and by the time their wives realized what they were really like, the women were knee-deep with six children each and too uneducated to run away from their situations.

Their marriages, however, did take the twins away from George and Nell, and there were many years of peace for them on their parents' farm. Then one late Saturday morning, a few years after the twins' last children were grown and gone and settled as far away from farming as they could manage, the peace ended.

The wives decided they could beat the train to the crossing and save themselves a boring ten minute wait. They had succeeded before and there was no reason to think this day would be the exception.

It was. And they paid for this exception with their lives. So when the already badly dispositioned twins became widowers, and in such a gruesome way, their crabbiness became almost incontrollable. They gave up farming and took up drinking and within a year had become the most obnoxious men in Iowa. No one could match them. No one wanted to be near them. No one cared if they recovered from their sudden losses or not. The community grieved for the dead wives, but not an ounce of this concern went to Les and Lo.

But good old George and Nell did care—it was the kind of caring for each other that some parents build into their offspring's upbringing. They took them in with the promise they would help farm the land and share expenses and chores. After a few of Nell's hot breakfasts, hearty dinners, and refreshing suppers, the obnoxious ones let go of their constant drinking and confined it to the weekends. But they didn't let go of their precious unpleasant ways. Their sullen attitudes were their emblem of identity, and they held onto it with all their strength.

***

Jake was not aware of or interested in any of the Swensens' past private affairs. He only wished he could quit thinking about his present mental affair with Nell and her blankety-blank green and brown checkered dress. The breeze that day, maybe if it hadn't been for that slow, almost-not-there breeze, his mind would still belong to him.

Jake came out of his reminiscing when he saw the light on his back door shed; he was glad to be home. He was too tired now to realize, as he frequently did lately, how alone he was. He mused about how, long ago, he had slowly accepted the idea that he would probably never marry. Over the years the tall women turned him down for tall men, short women for the same reason.

Tall, tall, tall, the whole world was tall. Midgets were tall, babies were tall, everybody was tall. Everybody except him. He was short, and his peers of childhood and the town gossips of adulthood didn't want him to forget it. One time he heard some kids in town giggling as he passed them on the way to Barney's about how it was a good thing he didn't have a horse because he would need a ladder to get on it. And that was not the only time he heard shifty remarks here and there all over town.

But Jake was not without sympathy on the subject. The Tollivers of the hardware store once expressed their scorn to Jake for all these loose tongued people, and the three devised a plan to put them into their foolish places. The plot was in the form of a rumor, a rumor that went as far as the town council who seriously considered its value until Harold stepped in and explained the matter. Jake invented the story, the Tollivers spread it around: the story that Jake was suing the township, suing it because the town fathers had built the sidewalks too close to his hindquarters.

Although Mrs. Tolliver softened the word 'hindquarters' to 'backside,' she did a very effective job of planting the seed into one of the town gossip's head while Mr. Tolliver was snickering in the back of the store, snickering and admiring his wife's nerve. And for that, Jake always considered Mrs. Tolliver to be the consummate proprietor—always aiming to please the customer.

His height was not his only drawback. "His voice sounds more like rasps than speech," one woman declared to her best friend one Saturday afternoon over hot fudge sundaes at the corner drugstore.

And that is how the years went by, with both the attractive and unattractive women turning him down for even something as casual as a date. He finally gave up on them and eventually his passion for women waned, and he filled what leisure time he had from farming with visits to Harold and Dolly, and at home, a close kinship with his pets. So by the time Jake retired, he had accepted life without a woman. Until Nell.

If she were a spinster, which Dolly had indicated when she offered an introduction, then she was a spinster in name only. Surely, Jake decided, her quiet pleasantness that he had observed from a distance was not compatible with the sharpness of the word spinster. Old maid certainly didn't fit either because she appeared to be barely middle-aged and far from the wretched condition that old maid implies.

Her five-foot eight inch unmarried height did not keep jockey-height Jake from eyeing her at the barbecue. But tonight at the Hallgrens, the height difference did keep Jake from letting Dolly know he was attracted to her. She was only a painting, the kind that should be viewed from a distance and not touched.

Jake finally came out of his reverie, so he thought, and parked his pickup, absentmindedly leaving his pets inside the vehicle while he unlocked the back door. But Prince howled, a sound he rarely used, to let his master know he had no intention of bedding down inside this cramped vehicle overnight. And like a robot temporarily distracted with information about a new program—which in this case was The Nell thing—Jake went back to his truck and released his prisoners. They went into the kitchen where Jake stepped out of his shoes and his jeans and finally his shirt, after which came the bed. "Oh boy," he sighed as he sank into it. "Oh boy."

Mitzie jumped onto the kitchen table for her nightly nap, and Prince crawled under Jake's bed. Household activities were turned off for the night. Loneliness, for the moment, was forgotten.

***

The next morning while Jake went to the emptiness of his kitchen and to its almost bare refrigerator and poorly stocked cupboards to decide what he would have for breakfast, Dolly and Harold were engrossed with a new project.

"Dad, what do you think about re-upholstering that wingback of mine and that easy chair of yours?" Dolly asked over the French toast and leftover cinnamon rolls.

"I knew you'd get around to that someday, Mama, and I

55

have only one request. Do them in matching material this time."

Dolly glanced in at their chairs in the living room. "Don't you think we should each pick out what we want?"

"Nope," Harold's eyes opened wide. "You pick for both of us. We're the same person anyway after all these years."

Dolly turned around and put her hands firmly on her hips. "I hope not, dear old man. I hope we are not the same for goodness sakes. We have learned to live with each other over the years, but that's tolerance, not sameness."

"I want another cup of coffee, please," Harold stalled.

"And I want you to approve of my chair idea." Dolly left the kitchen and went into the living room. Harold followed— might as well get this over with.

There was silence. Dolly glanced at her husband on and off; she knew this subject would not be resolved with a snap of her fingers this time. The cuckoo clock cuckooed, and Proudflesh scratched at the door.

"Well, okay, Mama, how about a compromise?"

"What kind of a compromise?"

"We'll get two different fabrics for the chairs, but you pick them both out. You may not be the same as me after all these years, but I am the same as you. And, woman, you know that."

She knew that, and she laughed. "A compromise it is then. I already have yours in mind."

Harold sat back in his chair. "You are right, Mama, you're not like me at all. You're too shrewd." He frowned. "No, shrewd is too nice a word. You're devious."

Dolly ignored the remark. "I found some really nice material at the dry goods section of Tollivers last week after the quilting session. Your chair will have swirls of rose, blue, and green on a gray background. Mine will be blue with orange birds drinking out of birdbaths."

"Birdbaths? Orange birds? What's got into you, woman? There's no such thing as orange birds and you've got them drinking out of birdbaths on top of it all."

Dolly went back to the kitchen to clear the table. "Yes,

there are orange birds, the female cardinal has an orange tinge to her. What do you know about birds anyway? How many have you noticed on your way in and out of the barn? And when you were still out plowing and planting and all that farmer stuff, how many lady cardinals did you see?"

"Dolly, are you getting smart with me?"

"Are you getting smart with me?" she snapped back. "Do you question my judgment?"

Harold went over to the stove, his steps deliberate as if on a mission. He was looking to change the subject, and he noticed a kettle on the back burner. He lifted up the lid. "Applesauce?"

Dolly had gone to the kitchen's bay window to look over her violets, and she turned sideways to her husband, her eyes twinkling. "I'm making it a new way this time, a special recipe I think you will like."

"What's new about it?"

"I'm going to add orange food coloring."

Harold backed away from the stove and back to the table. "Mama, I know all about female cardinals and all about everything outdoors. You know I know all about that stuff. Now, is your poking fun at me going to stop, or should I go milk Brie again?"

He started to go to the back door when Dolly hurried over and put her hands on his back and then slipped her arms around his waist; she nuzzled her chin to his shoulder, and the two stood there briefly, like children lost in the wilderness and not wanting to admit who had gotten them there.

The stove timer bonged loud for the applesauce, and Dolly went to it. "After this cools, Dad, I will make apple cake. How's that sound to you?"

"Do you have enough ingredients for apple cake?" Harold asked.

"I always have enough ingredients for anything."

"Do you have enough ..."

Dolly interrupted. "Don't you dare finish that question, Harold Hallgren." But she was too late.

"... orange food coloring?" Harold winced as he hurriedly went through the back door and to what he considered the quiet safety of the outdoors; he knew that when he came back inside, their bantering session would be over. They had had a lot of them since they first settled down together. The orange applesauce razzing would not be the last one, but it would tide them over for awhile.

Years ago, even while Harold was still in the lower grades in school, the neighboring farmers referred to him as a ladies' man and hardly the type to marry so young and to be so devoted to it. From the time he learned to dance in the school's gymnasium facility, Harold was more conscious of the girls than any of the other boys were. He had his first date at twelve and didn't stop until he met Dolly.

At college he arranged dates on his calendar with as much importance as class schedules. Sometimes he had two dates in one evening. He continued to think of girls as 'no big deals,' as giggle parcels of fluff to flirt and hold hands with and to kiss with all his might. The more he dated, however, the more he decided all girls were alike, and that he would probably never marry, but instead spend his entire manhood going from one skirt to another. He boasted loudly of this one time to his parents because he didn't want them to expect any grandchildren from him, and the sooner they accepted this, the less nagging he would have to endure.

It may have been a coincidence, but one weekend after a week of heavy exams when Harold and Jake came home to dramatize their ordeals to their respective parents, Harold opened the door to a well-proportioned, old-fashioned hourglass figure of a young woman. Harold's initial amazement of 'did I come to the wrong house, who are you, pretty lady?' was quickly explained by his mother who rushed from the kitchen to introduce her cousin's stepdaughter from Omaha, Dolly Robertson, to her one and only skirt-chasing son.

Dolly seemed older to Harold, she was by two years. And maybe this maturity is what caused Harold to literally stand back and take a concerned look. What was this lovely lass with enormous green eyes and wavy brown hair and a bit of a bite in her conversation and smile doing in his parents' house during one of his infrequent visits home?

His mother explained later that Dolly had just been in the neighborhood, but Harold and Jake decided nobody drives two hundred miles just to be in the neighborhood. It was a deliberate act. Jake teased Harold that his own dear sweet mother had gone wife hunting for him, and after Harold digested this possibility for a few weeks, he decided to investigate the lady.

He did this with a call to Omaha for a date, and on their second encounter—they seemed more like encounters than dates—Harold learned that all girls are not frivolous pieces of nothingness.

Dolly had substance; she also had the desire to be a farmer's wife because she loved the quiet of the country, she admired the fortitude of men who dared to challenge the ravages that nature could cause, and she thought these men special for making a livelihood from that challenge.

As for Harold, after years of dating empty words, he was awestruck by a woman who asked him what kind of fertilizer his Dad used, how often the county elected a road commissioner, and how do you tell the difference between male and female corn? When he replied that the female corn was bagged in sacks labeled female and the male sacks were stamped male, he held his breath that she wouldn't pursue him to answer how the baggers knew. When she didn't, but instead laughed at his reply as though to say it was all right he didn't know, Harold knew Dolly was interested in more about him than just his kisses, although she certainly did not hold back on that.

He was comfortable with her, she was a brace that gave him strength to his weaknesses, and she also did not mince words about marriage. So when Harold decided that Dolly was more of a support for him to begin farming than all the knowledge he could gain in college, he quit school and married her. Gradually over the years he realized more and more that he not only had a woman to love, but a woman who cared for him in a hallmark-enduring way, a woman who took deep breaths rather than scold, and who cried for a month when she found out she could only bear him one child and not give her husband the son that most men demand.

Whenever Harold came in from the field he saw more than Dolly tending to the stove, he saw a rock there, a soft, squeezable rock that didn't giggle silly when he patted her bottom with affection, and who didn't whine or berate him for the clods of soil he sometimes forgot to leave outside the shed. He long ago decided that Dolly's one-upmanship on their disagreements was little to pay for her solidness. He always eventually gave in to her. And the twinkle in his eyes at the end of these episodes was his thank you to her for being an otherwise perfect wife.

**

Jake and Harold rarely got drunk. In college they did, but not frequently, and the drinking episode during the last rain storm was their first since those reckless days in school.

Although the Saturday afternoon trips to Barney's Beer Palace was a faithful meeting for them both, and although they came to Barney's sometimes during the week after their retirement, they no longer got so drunk that Barney was unable to correct the situation quickly with hot coffee which he forced on all his patrons who might occasionally drink to excess. He watched them all like a parent watches, like first grade all over again.

If the matter went beyond salvation by coffee, Barney would go to his back room apartment and make a liverwurst sandwich which he forced down the throat of the guilty one. This was not easy for him to do because, not only was the inebriated condition of the party concerned in such a state that made swallowing a wedge of liverwurst difficult, but Barney dearly loved the sausage himself. To share it with someone who overindulged was something his occupation simply had to endure.

This endurance was never used on Jake and Harold until the weekend following the Saturday afternoon cloudbursts. That week in-between, Jake experienced more loneliness than ever, and Harold experienced another verbal episode with Dolly over orange food coloring. It was then that Barney encountered the exception to their 'rarely-got-drunk' reputation.

These three incidents of the week before, however, is not what brought about Jake's and Harold's frame of mind that would not only call for Barney to brew an extra pot of coffee, but to also force him to the back room for the liverwurst.

For Jake it was the reminder of his bachelorhood and the anticipated library search to end it, plus the mention of Nell Swensen's availability, topped off by his helpless feeling to do anything about it.

As for Harold, the orange food coloring and the female cardinal never entered his mind again, but the rain did. He hated rain, he hated overcast, and both of these conditions prevailed the entire week. Of course he never told anyone this, a farmer is not suppose to hate rain, and he was always grateful when it rained enough for good crops, but he didn't like the stuff falling all over him, and he didn't like the day that didn't have sunshine. He told Dolly this, but only once because he wasn't proud of it. If Jake ever found out, Harold realized their friendship would end. For a farmer to hate rain, with the exception of flooding, was blasphemous, at least it was for Jake who worshipped not only the land, but anything that sustained it.

So with Jake thinking that Harold was upset about the wingback chair, and with Harold thinking Jake was upset about probably everything, they met as usual, gloomily, at Barney's with the intention of getting drunk. Beer drunk. Beer and pretzel drunk. Hang the hangovers, hang the rain, hang the pretty blondes. Hang everything—there were defeats to be celebrated, frustrations to languish over, and complaints, complaints, complaints.

"Barney. BARNEY. Spin those beers down our way," Jake

called out. "Keep shoving those mugs along the counter until my buddy and I get our fill. We are cattle at the trough."

Harold hoop-howled at the anticipation. "And we won't fill up until sometime tomorrow."

Barney opened wide the tap lever. "I'm closed on Sunday, you know that." He put the mugs of ice cold beer on the slick countertop and let them go, one right after the other.

"Where's the pretzels, Barn?"

"Your elbow is in the bowl."

Jake and Harold threw back their heads and let out with matching guffaws. L-o-n-g matching guffaws.

"Come on, buddy friend of mine," Harold exclaimed to Jake who was sitting elbow close to him, "come on, let's get us a table."

They drank deep into the mugs of biting beer and signaled Barney for another round. Barney complied.

"Hey, Harold Tough Guy," Jake sang out, "which table should we take?"

"I don't know, they're all so pretty."

Jake plunked his freshly filled mug down on the yellow table. "How about here?"

"No, no, no," Harold asserted. "I don't like yellow."

"Okay, okay, then how about that green one over there?"

"It's too much in the corner—too far to go for the beer."

"Then you pick one."

Harold stood in the middle of the room and twinkled his eyes and wrinkled his nose like he was one tall slender Santa Claus. "Right here, buddy, right here. No table, I'm just going to stand up in the middle of this room until I fall over." He scooped his hand into the pretzels. "Another one of those ice cold beers would be nice, Barney. Slide me another."

Barney shook his head no. "Eat all the pretzels in that bowl first."

"After my next beer," Harold bargained.

"Before your next beer," Barney insisted. He hoped to save his fresh supply of liverwurst for himself.

Harold laughed low. "What's wrong? Think I'm drunk?"

Barney took a towel and wiped the counter. "Both of you need a good swift kick. You came in here just to get drunk. You're acting like zoo animals at feeding time. Settle down."

Harold went over to Jake with his empty mug and whispered: "Buddy, let's sit over in the corner while Barney cools down."

The pair sat quietly until Barney decided his liverwurst was safe and then he replenished their mugs. It wasn't safe, though. Jake pounded Harold on the shoulder, and Harold pounded Jake on the shoulder. They stood up in a leaning fashion, crept over to the bar for toothpicks to chew on, and when Barney stooped under the counter to look for more pretzels, they sneaked to the exit, banging the door as they left.

They were suddenly in the parking lot, and neither felt any the worse for their over abundance of beer. Any the worse, that is, until they started their engines. With their vehicles side by side, Jake turned his wheels sharply to the left, and Harold turned his wheels sharply to the right; they both shifted into reverse and gunned backwards. It was a synchronized modern dance that went wrong.

"Hey—what the hell?" they both shouted.

Their pickups had stopped themselves upon rear end impact, and the two drivers sat motionless with his own private thought.

Jake got out first. "It is awful back here. Harold, you get out and look at this mess."

Harold got out. The pair, by this time weaving instead of walking, went toward the saloon and to Barney who had left his counter when he heard the metal crunch. He opened the door, peeked out, and shouted to the two inebriates who were by this time almost stomach to stomach to him. "I thought you guys were sober. Git back inside and stay until I tell you to go." Barney's voice went into a screech: "For crying out loud."

"We were sober when we left," Harold stated.

"It was the fresh air," Jake added.

"Oh no," Barney steamed, "it was a couple of jerks who didn't eat enough pretzels."

Harold plunked himself down at the bar. "You won't tell the sheriff, will you Barn? And for pity sakes, a man can eat only so many of your blankety-blank pretzels. Why not popcorn or sandwiches? Where was your liverwurst when we needed it?"

"Shame on both of you." Barney reached for the coffee pot.

One hour and four precious liverwursts later they went out to the parking lot again. They looked at how the back ends of their vehicles were bowed together.

Jake cleared his throat. "We'll have to get drunk oftener."

"Oh really?" Harold smirked, ready for an argument.

"Yeah, we've forgotten how to drink. We can't handle it anymore."

They leaned over to see if their trucks were locked together. Harold stood up and nodded to Jake's wise thoughts on their disastrous afternoon drinking spree and then said, "Remember our freshman year in college? We had drinking down to a science. There were no bent fenders then."

Jake stood up and screeched, "Harold, we had nothing but jalopies then. They came with dents. Remember?"

Harold looked the other way. Darn Jake won't even let him say something even though it wasn't true. Everything for him had to be exactly just the way it really was. No imagination. No stretching of the truth. Everything black and white. "For pity sakes, Jake, can't you let me make a remark and let it go at that?"

"I did," Jake said back. "I let the one go about drinking in college—we didn't drink in college except for a few beer busts. That's not enough to get it down to a science."

"Okay, okay," Harold shook his head, he'll never change.

After the two decided their friendship was worth more than quibbling and derogatory remarks, they inspected the pickups. Even though they would need repairs, their bumpers were not locked together.

They slowly drove apart from each other with adeptness of sober men, which they almost were by this time. Harold fussed over what he would tell Dolly and decided he wouldn't tell her anything. He would hide the damage until he could sneak around for repairs. Dolly never rode in it anyway. She'll never miss what she referred to as his toy. Lucky Jake, he didn't have a wife, at least he was lucky for this time.

"Oh," Dolly exclaimed when Harold walked in the back door. "You startled me. Where did you park, old man? I didn't hear you coming."

Harold cleared his throat. "Out back, behind the barn. I thought your ladies would need the space for parking when you play bridge again."

Dolly frowned. "That's not until next week. Besides, you never accommodated my ladies before."

"Well, maybe I'll never do it again. So enjoy it now." Harold brushed past Dolly and went into the bathroom. He didn't like to keep secrets from his wife unless it was for Christmas or birthday or anniversary. He felt he was cheating her now, and she didn't deserve that. He closed the door, brushed his teeth wishing he had sandpaper for his tongue, washed his face, and shaved with the lather he had left in the mug from the morning. Dolly never cleaned his shaver if he failed to do it which he usually did; she left it as a reminder of him when he was out in the fields, a habit she retained even after he retired.

Harold came back to the kitchen. With his mouth shut tight, he brushed his cheek against Dolly's.

She stood back and looked straight into his guilty eyes. "Why are you pursing your mouth so much, Dear? Afraid I'll smell the liverwurst and coffee?"

Harold also stood back. "How do you know about the liverwurst?"

"Harold, dear sweetheart, between my quilting circle and bridge club, I know everything. All wives know everything. It's in the wedding contract, it's in the genes, it's in the soul."

Harold pulled on his suspenders until they were extended way beyond his stomach, and then released them with a gusto. He loved the feel of their snap against his meager potbelly of old age. "Mama, remember how we taught our daughter to never deceive us or anybody because it might turn into a habit and she'd end up dishonest?"

Dolly put her hands on her hips. "What did you do, Harold?"

"I dented the pickup."

"Are you hurt? Were you hurting in the bathroom all that time?"

"No, neither Jake or I got hurt."

"You mean you ran into Jake? What did you do—run him over?"

"No, no, for pity sakes. We back-ended each other."

"Why?"

"Why? For crying out loud. You know why. We were drunk."

Dolly didn't answer anymore—she had her confession—and proceeded to shake her head as she turned to the cream sauce on the stove.

Harold sat down at the table. He looked out the bay window and then at the cuckoo clock. It would soon be time to milk Brie and then this confession ordeal would be over.

"Jake needs a wife," he said to break the silence.

Dolly stirred the sauce more vigorously. "Is that what you two were celebrating?"

"No, we weren't celebrating anything. We were just a couple of bums getting drunk together. We thought we were sober when we left. Jake's lonelier than hell. I merely thought I'd help him out a little. If he had a wife, he wouldn't be so lonely and stuff like that."

"Are you lonely, Harold? You got drunk too." Dolly shut off the burner and sat across from her husband.

"Hell no, I'm not lonely. I got you."

"But what if I die?"

"You'd better not." Harold leaned over the table towards

her and stared her in the eyes. "You're not, are you? Is something wrong?"

"No, old man, I'm fine. But I hope that if I do die, you won't spend your idle time drinking. I'd prefer you found another woman."

"Nope, no way." Harold shook his head with jerky no-no motions. "I couldn't ever marry again after you. I could never replace you."

Dolly jutted out her chin straight back at him, a mannerism she showed when she wanted to be more clearly understood. "Harold, if you ever get so drunk again that you can't drive decently and get killed as a result, I won't wait five minutes for your replacement. Okay?"

"Okay."

***

Jake drove home slowly to make up for his carelessness in Barney's parking lot. He wondered how Harold would tell Dolly about the accident. He wondered how he would tell his own wife if he had one. Would he not say anything at all and act like it's quite an ordinary event to crash your pickup in a parking lot? After all, being a husband was not like being a child. A man shouldn't have to answer to his wife like a child has to answer to a parent. Or does he?

The night was starting to fall down on Jake as he held his own conversation. He pressed on the gas pedal. Nothing was as lonely as coming home to an empty house at twilight. With neither sun nor moon in sight, the world is in a holding pattern, a limbo, and it's nice to have someone there to distract the silent void.

He had his pets, of course, and this helped the empty situations. Prince was really a prince in his affection if not in his looks. The three brown spots on his otherwise white body didn't make much sense as to the breed of dog he was, not even mongrel, but the companionship he gave made up for this visual fault. Jake had found him as a pup wandering all over the road nine years ago, an obvious discard not even weaned. Dolly found an eye dropper in her drawer of throwaways, and Jake carefully fed him drop by drop until the young dog became quite robust. He felt a kinship to his new dog that was stronger than he had felt for any of his previous dogs because this one looked like a reject just like Jake always looked. Prince's only drawback was his panting. The least little disturbance was cause enough for his eyes to bulge and his panting to start.

Harold couldn't stand it. "I'd rather have an overly barking dog than an overly panting one. Why don't you tell him to shut up for pity sakes?" Jake didn't have to tell Prince to shut up, he wouldn't have anyway, because he only had to stroke the top of his companion's head, and he would immediately settle down.

Mitzie's entry into his life was not as dramatic as Prince's. Jake merely went to a neighboring farmer and hand picked what he considered to be the gentlest kitten from the mother's fifth litter. Jake originally named the female kitten Bitzie because she was so tiny, and he thought that if it were possible to have a feline as a blood relative, then this kitten was related. But as she grew, Jake realized her name was a mockery to her very large body, and so he replaced the B with an M, for monster, and ever after called her Mitzie.

Occasionally before Jake's retirement, she perched on top of fence poles and stared down at her master who was inspecting the ground for weeds and the crops for infestations. She was a calico and proud of it, or so it seemed, the way she strutted around Jake's kitchen like she owned it, which she did, and not just because she was a cat, but because of her queenly appearance of three coat colors reverently placed in an evenly marked symmetry that only an artist would choose and which most calicos do not have the privilege of displaying.

He had let her have two litters, all grabbed quickly by town people. Barney had two of them whom he secretly fed liverwurst to whenever he indulged himself. Jake had taken her to Omaha to be fixed; the county vet had had a recent heart attack and Jake didn't want to wait until the doctor recovered or was replaced. He took her into the first veterinarian sign he saw and stayed in a rundown motel that allowed Prince to stay with him for the two nights Mitzie was indisposed.

After Mitzie recovered from the insulting ordeal, she was more attentive and affectionate to her master; now, every time Jake mended his fences, she followed along with Prince. Jake found a joy in seeing her straddle two fence posts with her rump resting on the higher post as if to show it off and let the world know it was the most important part of her body, which at one time it was. She would stare at Jake for as long as it took him to do the mending, and then continue to stare until he was no longer in sight. The uneven posts were her favorite high spots, along with the table in the kitchen.

She acted like a Mitzie, according to her master, and when Harold once asked what that meant, Jake explained that a Mitzie is a cat who acts like a dog, who stays in the back of his pickup instead of leaping out while he is in Barney's. Harold, amused, dropped the subject as he did whenever Jake and his pets made no sense to him.

The twilight had turned to darkness by the time Jake and his thoughts arrived home. Prince and Mitzie were probably wondering what happened to him. He had left them at home, which he rarely did, and when he did, he never knew why— he just did. He would have been happy to have only this thought to think about now, but there was more complicated things to muse. Does Dolly know about the bumper mishap yet? Does a wife have the right to know her husband got so drunk he couldn't back out of a parking lot without crashing? Would a wife scold or comfort? Dolly would probably do both. What would his wife do? Wife, wife, wife.

Jake was glad it was dark when he drove up to his shed because he wouldn't have to look at his smashed bumper now until morning. If he had a wife, she wouldn't be able to look either. Then he would have all night to figure how to tell her. That's probably what Harold planned to do. Wise Harold.

Mitzie greeted him with many sassy meows for leaving

69

her cooped up in the house all afternoon, and Prince sloshed kisses all over his nose, and panted several welcomes. This contrast in his homecoming was what Jake needed—a complainer and a comforter—just like a wife, Harold's wife, every man's wife, and even his wife, if he had one. What would Nell Swensen say? Nell Glorious? Nell Blackburn?

Since the barbecue he thought mostly of her. Since last weekend with the rainstorm ordeal at Barney's, he thought only of her. There were not too many county or town events in the near future, actually there were none, where he could see her again and hopefully have the courage to approach her. Although Jake had never courted a lady before, he knew the procedure started with an introduction and a willingness afterward for the woman to go on that first date. Jake also knew that the best method to win a woman's love was to be as natural as possible under the circumstance. But would Nell Swensen Glorious like what came natural to Jake Blackburn?

He told all this to Prince and Mitzie. Many times he not only talked things over with them, but he answered for them too. These conversations filled his head with noise, a human noise that the television could not provide.

Occasionally when it was time for Prince to eat, Jake would call: "Prince Blackburn, bring me your dish or they'll be no supper for you tonight," after which Prince would answer, 'go get it yourself.' Jake would then reprimand: "You lazy, no good varmint, why do I put up with you?" and Prince would look at his master and pant and possibly really think 'the man's crazy.'

One time when he got up earlier than usual and saw Mitzie stretched out on the kitchen table, he feigned shock. "When I sit down for breakfast, young lady, I don't want your be-hind in my face or your tail on my forehead. Get your body the heck off the table," to which Mitzie would reply, 'that's no way to talk to a lady of breeding,' with an answer from Jake of: "No lady sleeps on top of a table, what would the town people think?"

Sometimes Jake held each animal tight against his chest to

gently squeeze them as though to ooze their bodies into his for more strength to survive the loneliness. His three nights a week for supper at the Hallgrens and his Saturday afternoon sessions at Barney's was the only close other companionship he had. After Jake saw Nell Swensen at the barbecue, however, he decided this wasn't enough.

Besides, he had to do something about those thoughts that kept going around and around in his head with the intensity of a race car going around and around a track, his feelings changing lanes of thought about whether Nell would ever look at him once, let alone twice. What if she was another one like his blond girlfriend in the first grade, or, what if she was crazy about him and waiting for his approach? What if a dozen other men, at least that many, were courting her silly? What if there was something wrong with her and that's why she never married? What if, and would he care, if she had twelve children tucked away in her house ready to pounce on the first suitor?

There were too many 'what if's' to consider. He had to get control of this thing, and right now. Stop thoughts, stop brain thinking, cut it out, go watch television, take a walk. But Jake knew his head would not turn off until he did something about that woman. Something. What? He was lost in the helplessness of inexperience. But he couldn't let that get in the way anymore because he was confronted with more than his loneliness, his wife-lessness, he was confronted with the fact that he was plainly and simply attracted to her.

He could shove away his boredom frustration again, as he had many times in the past, by seeing Harold oftener and going for longer walks and talking in greater detail to Prince and Mitzie. But another conversation with Harold or more silly chitchat with Prince and Mitzie would not bury his desire for Nell Swensen. It was there. It wouldn't go away. The barbecue had shown him someone who entered his heart as well as his mind and made relinquishing that fact as impossible as surviving a ten year drought. Jake's entire emotional being was in an arid, cracking uproar now, and he had to find a way to quench it.

***

Regardless of how much thinking and worrying and rehashing of a problem that one engages in, there is a force out there that unexpectedly comes to resolve the problem, but that unfortunately or fortunately, does not announce itself beforehand.

Sometimes when this resolution presents itself, the person who has been thinking and worrying and rehashing reacts in such a sudden manner that all thoughts of the problem leaves the head and action takes over, action that couldn't possibly have been planned because it is usually so clumsy.

As for Jake constantly fussing over his Nell problem, probably not even God would retain interest in the number of times his head hashed it over, over, over. And sandwiched among all his thoughts of Nell, he remembered the old gossip about how he was so short that he had to use a ladder to mount a horse, a horse he never ever had, but the tall people had to laugh about something, he guessed. The little blond girlfriend opened her mouth again and again, and the number of times grown girls turned him down for dates grew to the thousands by the time his rehashing subsided.

So on that certain day in the last part of summer and two weeks after the barbecue, Jake's mind was ready for a rest. A rest that was not to come.

The Courtship

J ake rounded the corner of Main and Elm with his red
pickup, his newly repaired red pickup, which was muddy
again from another heavy rain the day after he brought it
back from the Boone County Auto and Bicycle Repair Shop.
Prince and Mitzie sat beside him.

Nell Swensen walked around the corner of Main and Oak
and appeared to be heading for the hardware store in the
middle of the block.

Then it happened. Jake's newly repaired, muddy red
pickup and Nell's clean and newly pressed green and brown
checkered dress passed each other in opposite directions.

Jake saw her. He shifted down to second gear and
tightened his hands around the steering wheel so tight that if
the wheel had been human, he would have choked it to death.
There she was, all alone, walking toward, yes and better yet,
walking into Tolliver's Hardware. For pity sakes, the fact of
Nell's appearance finally reached his heart and it pounded
until the thuds reached his eardrums, and he could no longer
hear. He could, however, still think.

But too many thoughts at once, so he circled the block
twice until he realized Nell Swensen did not go inside the
hardware to wait until he decided his best plan of action. Nell
didn't know, for instance, that he had put on a clean shirt that
morning, that he had pulled on a fairly new pair of jeans, and
had reviewed his mud-caked vehicle with a promise he would
get his pitchfork to it soon to remove the chunks of earth
baked on by the sun after the recent storm. She didn't know
he came to town to buy stamps at the post office, a tiny facility
in a tiny building next to the drug store. She didn't even know
he intended to come out of his malaise of recent retirement
and do something about his loneliness, whatever that might be.
She didn't know any of these things or of anything about the
man in the red pickup who, if she had looked his way, would
have seen him having some trouble with the steering wheel.

And there were a few things that Jake didn't know either— the main thing being how he would approach the Great Nell, the lady, the all-in-all wonderful person he had seen only once before. Then the second thing in this morning of surprise happened. All the thinking and planning and reasoning stuff that was in turmoil inside his head suddenly stopped. Action took over.

He slammed his pickup against the curb which resulted in Prince and Mitzie sliding right off the seat onto the floorboard. Prince started to pant, and Mitzie meowed several insults. "Sorry, sorry, sorry." Jake almost fell off the seat himself from leaning too heavily on the door in his haste to get out. He leaped up and onto the curb adding extra strain to his already rapidly pumping heart that wanted to burst out of his chest.

He swallowed hard and ran his fingers through his mass of curly hair. Better slow down. Good thing for deodorant, wonderful invention. He took long, slow steps to the door and tripped on a display of cracked pots just inside the entrance. He was down on his knees now, but not completely down, when Mrs. Tolliver came over to him.

"Hello, Mr. Blackburn, Jake," she said. "Can I help you find something? Interested in a pot?"

Those dumb pots. What were they doing cluttering up the entry? How can a nervous person get by so much congestion? Were the Tollivers begging customers to buy them before they became even more cracked?

Jake stood up as tall as he was able and thrust out his chest which wasn't hard to do because his pounding heart had expanded it somewhat. He chose his words carefully. "No thank you, Mrs. Tolliver." What do I mean, no thank you? Your dumb meddling pots should be thrown out as fodder. I'm trying to court a lady, not get tangled up in a barricade of pots. For pity sakes. For pity, pity sakes.

Jake smiled. "Nice display in your window." Unnecessary display is what he really meant. Tolliver's was the only hardware in the town of Boone County, Jake's anger rambled on, and they were sweet people, but they didn't seem to realize that if someone wanted hardware, they would have to come here, fancy display or not. No competition. That's probably why they get by with tripping up nervous customers over blankety-blank cracked pots.

Jake looked past Mrs. Tolliver, clear to the back of the store where Nell Swensen was. Thank goodness that wonderful woman was far enough away, and with her back turned, so she probably didn't hear and see the commotion over what an ordinarily routine entrance into a store can sometimes turn into. She hadn't tripped. No sense in her seeing him trip. She'd probably wonder how anyone whose eyes were so close to the floor couldn't see the objects on it.

Mrs. Tolliver went back to where she came from, and Jake sighed relief. She was a nice lady, but kind of naive. What did she mean, do I want a pot? Sure, I'll take them all and throw them through the window at that unnecessary display. Jake calmed down at that idea and also at remembering how Mrs. Tolliver had helped spread the rumor about him suing the city. She was all-right and not worthy of his wrath; he was overdoing his anger and needed to get control of himself quickly, so he locked his knees and thrust his hands deep into his jeans. Relax. He had to relax. He did it with a leap over the pots and a jump into aisle one. Now he was himself again.

Okay. Now, a slow, casual walk down the aisle with a look to the left, a look to the right. If Jake were a dancer, he would have done that. God put that woman in the hardware store just so Jake could settle his tangled mind and heart over her once and for all. And God had better help him now because the more aisles he went in and out of, and the closer he got to the back of the store, the more jelly-like his legs became. First his heart, now his legs, what next?

Hiccups. Might as well, everything else has gone wrong. And if Jake hadn't been so full of fear and so busy addressing God for help, he would have remembered how a college classmate once remarked in the middle of an exam that Jake was proof that size had nothing to do with the loudness of one's hiccups.

Jake put his hand over his mouth until he realized this technique might strangle him. Deep breaths. Pray some more. How much more before it works? Please God don't let anything else happen, hold on to me, I'm falling apart. Keep me standing. Spare my throat. See me through this, and I'll never fuss over anything again. You put her into the hardware, but You didn't give me enough notice on how to handle it. Do it for me. Please. Finally, God and Jake managed to calm the hiccups.

He was now at the furthermost part of the store where unattractive things like nails were stocked. She was there, looking down at them where they were tossed and scrambled in a barrel once used for wine. He went to the other side of the barrel to face The Nell although he really wanted to stand next to her like they would when they got married. Big plans, huh, God would probably say. Don't push your requests, Jake scolded to himself. Remember, all you asked for was courage to talk, the ability to keep standing while you did it, and no more hiccups. The wedding can wait.

There was a pause. Jake cleared his throat. Her tall, slender frame looked up from the nails and then down at his short, slender frame.

"It's tough to be out of nails, isn't it?" Jake's voice, not the remark, sounded exactly like a band of guardian angels tugging on his cords and enabling him to speak even though the angels needed to practice a little on getting rid of the strained and accompanying high pitch. As for the remark, he did this all on his own and wished he had asked for advice on that too. Tough to be out of nails? What a stupid thing to say as the first thing to say to the woman you love. Where is Charles Boyer? Where is that famous Casbah? Certainly not in Tolliver's Hardware today.

Nell Swensen stared down at him. She didn't say anything for an awful moment, but then she smiled. What a smile. Maybe the lady doesn't have a voice, but she sure has a smile, and it went from her face to his.

Jake gasped, like one does just before a first kiss. Then he heard the sound of hard-soled shoes on wood floors. It was Mrs. Tolliver again. That's great. She was coming after him.

"Mr. Blackburn, are you sure you don't want any of those pots? They're almost free, you know. I'll just have to throw them out if somebody doesn't buy them soon." She motioned to her husband to come over from the cash register. Although it was Mr. Tolliver who operated the store at quite a profit, it was his wife who busybodied herself around it to make sure the customers found whatever they were looking for and to feel guilty if they didn't. Mr. Tolliver ignored the signal, his receipts needed more attention now than a seasoned customer who knew his way around. Fortunately, the proprietor averted a big deal scene over nothing, at least nothing to him.

Jake shook his head no rather vigorously, and Nell turned her smile to the interruption. Mrs. Tolliver looked at the unmatched pair. "Oh," she said. "Oh." She left as quickly as she came.

Nell reinforced her smile. "I'm not out of nails, it's my brothers. I love hardware stores, and the boys need nails, so I volunteered while they are at the tavern."

Tavern? Jake thought. Saloon was more like it. What a nice way to refer to Barney's and everything in it. She is certainly a real lady. "I know your brothers," he lied. "Met them at the barbecue. Know them by sight anyway." He continued to muse. One couldn't help but notice their taller than six foot bodies on which were attached huge heads and hands and arms.

Nell picked up the nails one at a time. "They like their Saturday afternoon beer. Do you ever play checkers with them at Barney's place?"

Checkers? Jake thought. Where did she get that information? The only things her brothers did at Barney's was drink beer at two separate tables—the one with the particularly thick neck that blended into his shoulders like a prize football player usually sat off by himself. He was the nicer of the three, he didn't belch intentionally. Jake supposed they wouldn't tell such a nice sister they were something other than genteel checker players, that they were really pool shooters and pinball machine pullers. And neither did he himself want her to think Barney's was anything but a sedate place to sit while the beer went down the throat.

"I don't play checkers." Jake looked away. What a fantastic statement. Should he also tell her he doesn't eat candy and chew tobacco and that he absolutely hates oatmeal? Those angels were pulling the cords for sound, all right, but he needed someone to tell him what words to say. Words and sentences so really profound that she would want to spend the rest of her life with him.

Nell found a scoop for the nails and dug in. Then Jake realized action might be better than words. "Here, let me, this is a man's job." He took the scoop from her in about a gentle a fashion as picking up a pitchfork and gouging it into the ground. He stopped. "I hope I wasn't too rough, excuse me, I was pretty rough, excuse me, I'm used to handling tools roughly." Roughly? Was that a word? She was tall enough to kick him out of the store, so why didn't she? Dear God, kick me out of this store, but please don't let her do it. Oh God, I need You, where are You anyway?

Nell laughed. "They told me one bag would be enough. Thank you for your help—your rough help."

He worried about her last three words. She agreed that he was rough. But she laughed about it and then said thank you. Maybe she thought only his hand was rude and that the rest of him was okay. He handed her the full sack. "This should do it, although your brothers won't be able to build a barn with this amount, will they?" Another wonderful statement. That one was especially good, fifth grade level.

Nell smiled again. "No, the barn we have is in pretty good shape. These nails are probably for fencing repair, don't you think?"

"I have a fence too, along the road. City people think corn is free in the country. I'm sure your brothers have a good barn. Most people in these parts have a good barn." Jake continued on with one remark after another hoping something intelligent would eventually come out.

"My name is Jake Blackburn. I suppose you have a name also." He forced himself to laugh and that sounded awful too.

Nell folded down the top of the sack and looked toward the cash register at the front of the store. "Nell Swensen," she stated as she started to walk away.

He had to strike now; he followed behind her as he kept up with more remarks. "Well, well, I should drive by your place sometime, mine is by a creek, I rent out my land now, I'm retired." But Nell kept on toward the register, there wasn't anything about what he was reciting that interested her to inquire more. She didn't seem to care he regretted retiring from the vigor of working the land which left his mind free to be lonelier than he had ever before experienced. Jake's entire body grimaced in pain. Why doesn't she turn around? He had to think of something to get her attention again. Maybe he could say something about being madly in love with her. That ought to stop her for awhile.

But Nell stopped without that last remark, turned around and plainly, simply looked at him. There was a lull, he had to make use of the lull.

"May I escort you to the cash register?"

She nodded, and Jake puffed up with encouragement. He soon deflated, however, when he realized it would have been better if he had kept the full bag of nails instead of handing it over. Carrying the bag to the door would have been a real gentlemanly thing to do. It would make up for his roughness. Rats. That was dumb to hand it over. Rats. Millions of rats, rats, rats. He had to get that fool bag back. Maybe he could take it when she put it on the counter to pay. She already knew he had a grabby hand, and she didn't seem to mind. But maybe she would place it out of his reach. Maybe he should ask for the bag. Ridiculous. How far could he carry it now? Two or three steps? He would just have to seize that darn sack off the counter even if she put it out of reach. He was agile, he could do it. Then he would offer to take the bag to his pickup and drive the three of them home. That would be a bigger gesture than merely holding the nails while she paid, and it might also make her feel more akin to him.

She placed the sack on the counter out of his reach, and suddenly, the next minute filled with a moment of action that people try to avoid. And even if Jake had thought about it beforehand, the episode would have happened anyway. Some embarrassments in life are meant to be, and Jake's embarrassment was not to go unsatisfied. At the time Nell paid and started to pick up the bag, Jake's unthinking portion of his brain—a description Harold used when he couldn't figure out why someone did something bad or stupid—grabbed for the precious object, and he tripped.

Nell's waist dug into the counter from his shove, and the nails spilled, crashed, sprawled from aisle one to aisle two with some sprinkling onto the array of cracked pots.

Jake's mouth dropped open. He was in that vacuum again with the silence that only death brings. He looked at the lady he was trying to court with a pleading stare as she straightened herself up from the assault. He looked down at the nails. He thought of coffins—one at least—his. These nails would do nicely for his coffin. They would seal him in forever and away from the Tollivers and Nell Swensen and any further attempt on his part to win the lady over. He closed his mouth, and the angels rasped and then left him speechless—they probably wanted to find someone with a little more grace than he to help.

Mr. Tolliver shook his head in a tactful, this-happens-all-the-time manner. Mrs. Tolliver came running from the storeroom. And Nell laughed.

She laughed? Jake looked at his Venus in disbelief as sound returned to his world. His mouth opened again, a little less obviously than before, and it was at this moment that he really and truly fell in love with her. It was an unexplainable surge of warmth that enveloped him, it was probably her laugh.

"I'm sorry about laughing," she said as she put her finger

on her mouth to quiet her reaction to the woeful scene. "But comedians get paid for doing things like this, and we did it for free."

We? Jake thought. She's taking part of the blame? He definitely had to pursue her now, she was too good to be true. Nell's remark had swept away the tension, and Jake's heart returned to normal size. His voice returned as well. By the time Mr. Tolliver swept up the nails, Jake was able to speak to his prey again. "I'm sorry about ramming you against the counter. Real sorry." He couldn't say anymore, he might cry, especially when he realized the word 'ramming' was not very fitting for a lady to hear.

"Oh, don't worry, I have a strong waist."

Jake took a deep breath. "You are a kind person, Nell Swensen, and I am a clumsy person," and for the first time since he entered the store, Jake heard himself say something intelligent. The pair left Tolliver's side by side with Nell's waist intact and Jake's face red, a blush-red, and not from humiliation anymore, but from accomplishment. He felt like he had been through an eternity with Nell Swensen. And he had.

**

"Can I drive you somewhere?" Jake asked as soon as they were out of the store.

Nell didn't think so. Her brothers expected her to wait until they were through with their beer and checkers.

"I can drive you home now. You can call Barney's and tell your brothers you are home and they needn't bother. They'll be glad, they won't have to rush." Jake talked fast, he didn't need the angels anymore, but he didn't want to lose his foot in the door that he had so valiantly and awkwardly placed there. If Nell went to Barney's, her brothers might ask about the nails and then she might start laughing and then they would ask why she was laughing and then the whole county would know. Besides, he wanted Nell all to himself. And so far things were going so well in spite of the cracked pots, hiccups, grabby hand, and near assault.

Jake gently touched Nell's elbow with his hand and guided her toward the direction of the pickup. "It's over there," he pointed.

Oh for pity sakes, he squealed to himself, the cursed thing is caked with that blankety-blank mud from the last rain. Why hadn't he cleaned it? He hadn't anything else to do. Now it would take a ton of water and a pitchfork to get through that dried-on earth.

"It's the red one," he continued. "I'm washing it tomorrow. I wash it every week, hose it down real good."

Nell took the direction Jake's hand offered. She smiled. "My brothers never wash their trucks. They're caked with mud like this all the time."

She knew. He knew that she knew he was lying. Now what? He took a deep breath, and before he could figure out how to come up with a story to cover up the lie, he saw right before him something worse to worry about: Prince and Mitzie. There they were sitting shoulder to shoulder looking out at them and probably leaving messes all over the front seat although they had never done that before. They always rode up-front and went to the back only when Jake was at Barney's for a few hours because their master thought they could stretch and breath better there.

Jake blanked out for a moment; then he felt an urge to run away—the panic he felt inside Tolliver's had returned. No wonder he was a bachelor. How many other men have had these awful things happen while trying to court a lady? If either of my animals left anything more than fur and hair on his precious seat, he would sell them to the glue factory. Oh no, Jake's skin tingled, what horrible thoughts for his pets, forgive me, help me, they love me, I love them. Oh please, let Nell like them. I need you again, God. Oh please let the seat be clean.

Of course the seat was clean. What a silly thought.

Nell reached out to Jake's perfect pets and firmly stroked each one like they had been friends for years. "I love them, and I don't even know them. My brothers won't allow house pets, they think all animals belong outdoors. We don't even have a dog anymore since we moved. They left behind the only one we had when we sold the farm with the excuse the new owners wanted him. Are your two allowed inside the house? That's where I think pets belong."

Oh wow and super-delooper, she approves of inside animals. Jake's confidence surged. He puffed up, turned sideways from Nell and started to spit between his teeth when he realized she wasn't Harold or any of the other saloon men and that spitting was not the thing to do right now. But it was too late, the spit had formed and when he tried to reverse its direction, he gagged. "Gaw-ga-ga-a-a-w."

Nell turned around quickly and abruptly lifted up both of his arms high over his gag-stunned head. His lungs responded, and he calmed down. But his heart started to pound again, and he hardly heard Nell explain about the First Aid class she had taken in Iowa only last year.

Although Jake stopped gagging and coughing and clearing his throat, he still wanted to die. Would his goofings never end? How much longer would she put up with him before she ran away in disbelief that such a person existed? God, are You there?

Nell lowered his arms. "Next time," she reprimanded, "spit it out, Mr. Blackburn ... Jake. Being a proper gentleman isn't worth dying for."

Jake couldn't look at her. It was his boyhood all over again when his mother would rescue him from foolishness. He was glad, this one time, that he was shorter than the woman—he didn't have to look her in the eye.

And that is how Jake and Nell met—over nails and swallowed spit. As Jake watched the woman he wanted to marry stroke his pets, he wondered how many more of his ways Nell would tolerate before she found him disgusting. He had never thought of himself as disgusting before, but he had never acted so foolish before, what an oaf he was. His conduct in Tolliver's showed no evidence that he had ever been out in public previous to the ridiculous nail-spilling scene. Nincompoop. That's what Dolly Hallgren would call him now, her favorite insult word. A real ninny.

He had to get his mind on something else, and quickly, because Nell had finally tired of stroking. He had to do what he ran into the hardware for one hundred purgatories ago. He had to ask Nell Swensen for a date. Now. Do it now.

"So. You seem to like animals. That's Prince and Mitzie. Prince is the dog and Mitzie is the cat."

Nell laughed.

Jake turned redder than royal purple. Of course Mitzie is the cat if Prince is the dog. You dunce ninny simpleton. Now you're talking to Nell like she is as socially dumb as you are. You didn't have to tell her the remaining animal is a cat. If one has a dog and a cat and if you point out the dog, it's not necessary to say the other one is the cat. It's obvious. Ask her for a date now, that is if you can do it without oaf-ing through that too.

Nell nodded. "Nice names. Did you choose them?"

"Oh sure, there's nobody else that could have done it."

"Oh?"

"Uh-huh, I've been alone for about forty years now since my Mom died. My Dad too, a few years before my Mom. I've never married. No time, I guess." He chuckled a little.

But Nell laughed. "Isn't that what we all say? That's my reason too."

Jake relaxed. So far she hadn't run away. She was keeping the conversation going. And she sure liked Prince and Mitzie. He signaled for them to get out and jump into the back. He climbed in himself and smoothed out the old green padding he had provided for the times they rode in the rear which was never. They obeyed like robots, good. Maybe Nell would see that although he may not be able to conduct himself properly in a hardware store, he must be capable of something if his pets behaved.

When he was through impressing Nell with the back of his pickup, he went to the front where the animals had been and slapped at the seat in a frenzy to rid it of their hair. "I guess that's clean enough," he said and opened the door wider as a welcome for Nell to enter. She did, and Jake was one step closer to the bravery he needed to ask her out.

He slammed the door shut as gently as a door can be slammed shut and ran around to the driver's seat before she changed her mind. He started the engine and slowly backed away from the curb and away from Barney's and away from that ridiculous hardware store.

"Well, Nell, so you bought your brothers some nails. Are you real busy now, this time of the year?"

"Busy? I'm a housekeeper, Jake. I cook and wash and clean for three men. Yes, I'm busy." Then she turned her head to him, smiled, and said quietly, "Why do you ask?"

Jake darted a look at her and then down at the road she had pointed for him to take. He inhaled his lungs up as high as they would inflate, and as the air slowly released, one word after another came out until he had a complete sentence. "Are you too busy for supper and a movie?" There was silence. He inhaled again for more words. "With me?" That was it, the question was out in the air for her to stomp on or to grab at. There wasn't anything more he could do, please God, make her say yes, make her mine, keep me alive while I wait for the answer.

"I'm not too busy for that." A short answer to a short question. It was that easy, it was that hard, and now it was over. This lady thought him all right in spite of everything, even though, when looking down at him all cushioned and sunk into the driver's seat, she surely realized their difference in height.

"I'm shorter than you are, you might have noticed."

"A lot of people are, Jake."

He straightened up as tall as he could. "Yeah, okay, well anyway, you just said you aren't too busy, so how about supper? This Friday."

"Any time after six. How nice of you to ask."

This was too much. Not only did the lady say yes without coaxing, she's darn polite too. Jake glanced over at her once in awhile like one does to a chosen prey to make sure it stays put. "There's a spy movie at the Grand. We can eat around six and go there around eight." Two date events in one evening— he was closing in on Harold's college record.

She smiled. "Turn right at Binder Post road. You'll see the Swensen place in a few minutes."

Jake obeyed. "I think I know which one it is, a little off the beaten track though. Harold and I, Harold is my best friend, my best man friend that is, we used to drive our beat-up cars all over this area when we were fifteen, sixteen, and pretend we owned every blasted inch of it. I'll never forget how pitch black it was at night with only headlights to break into it. We were pretty senseless then. Up and down and around all these hills after the Friday night movie. Our folks worried, but we didn't. Kids, huh?"

Nell laughed that wonderful, comfortable laugh. Jake caressed his fingers around the steering wheel. Thoughts exploded in his head. Was he to actually have her all to himself for an entire evening, alone? Super-delooper time again, he shouted silently. That joyous squeal returned again and again and popped inside him like hot kernels of corn. It was time to celebrate, it was rivers and rivers of fish begging to come out, it was a price markup on summer crops. It was, yes, it was truly super-delooper time. And Nell smiled as though she heard his excited thoughts.

Jake didn't say anymore after he excused himself for not being a friendlier host at the barbecue. "I should have introduced myself." Nell didn't say anymore either after she apologized for keeping to herself at the event when she usually didn't. They smiled at each other, they seemed satisfied with each other, they were shy as kindergartners with each other. And, as it was years ago with Jake and Harold, one short and one tall—it was that way again.

Jake carried the precious bag of nails up to Nell's back porch shed door and tucked them in a corner for her brothers to see. He confirmed their date on Friday at six and then took long, hurried steps back to his pickup before he passed out from joy. He didn't do this, but he hopped into the seat as lighthearted as a general winning a battle without a fight. He hoped Sam's Clothier and Miscellaneous Store still had that navy blue and black bow tie he had eyed in admiration for months now. He hoped his navy blue suit would still fit. Of course it would, wouldn't it?

**

After Jake purchased the bow tie, and after his mouth let out a few more ecstatic expressions on the way home from the purchase, he continued the tirade by pounding his fists on the steering wheel and lifting his backside up and down on the seat in rapid motion; this emphasis of joy continued until he screeched his dirty pickup to its stop near the barn; then, while shouting more obscenities of elation, he emotionally crashed in front of the television.

He didn't think about fixing himself a lunch, and he didn't think about feeding Prince and Mitzie, although they had thought about it, and he didn't think about Brie's milk that had soured in the refrigerator waiting for him to get rid of. He had let out all his pent-up fear of dealing with Nell Swensen by afterwards being noisy and silly; now all that was left was a very weary Jake who, at the moment, was unable to move.

He was stunned.

He looked at the television picture, but didn't see. He listened to the television voices, but didn't hear. His mind was preoccupied with the memory of his brother Alvin's ha-ha remarks about Jacob's Ladder. 'You can use that ladder to climb on a horse because you'll always be too short to do otherwise,' Alvin would sneer. His mind was wondering what his runaway brother would say now. Alvin's peewee brother hadn't used a ladder to ask Nell Swensen for a date, and he hadn't climbed up a ladder to scoop out the nails in the bin, and he hadn't even used the ladder to climb away from embarrassment after the clumsiness he experienced throughout the entire Tolliver Hardware ordeal.

But all those years of belittlement by Alvin, the rejection of his blond grade school girlfriend, and the turnoffs by grown women had been diluted out by the many times Jake's mother had held and hugged him, soothed, and told him how important he was. And it was the positiveness of his mother's assurances that Jake was now able to think for a split moment he was tall enough to jump out of his pickup, run into the hardware store, and stand opposite a woman by a nail bin who might not turn him down.

Consequently, after Jake recovered from the verbal celebration of super-deloopers and other words of ridiculous joy, and after he spent the evening of silent limbo in front of the television, he awoke the next morning taller than Harold and weighing only thirty pounds. Little irritations didn't bother him. The kitchen colors sparkled with cleaner and richer tones. The bird chirpings were extremely loud and pleasant. His beloved pets walked rather than ran through the house and then politely waited by their food dishes while Jake filled them more abundantly than usual.

God had given him a preview of Heaven which his mind finally soaked up. On his way to Harold and Dolly to tell them the big news, he turned his pickup around and went back home. Jake had forgotten something. "Wait here, you guys," he said to Prince and Mitzie, "I'll be right back." He ran through the shed, through the kitchen, and into his bedroom. He knelt by the bed's side, clasped his hands high above his bowed head, and rasped out: "Thank you, God, thank you."

***

Jake stood in front of the living room mirror looking at his reflection of navy blue suit and new bow tie. He put two fingers in his mouth and exhaled until the whistle noise was loud enough for Prince and Mitzie to hear. He had recovered from his nervously executed shave and a session of throwing up stomach acid, and he was ready to embark on his date of a lifetime.

Prince came lumbering in from the shed, a gait he acquired from a bump on his hindquarters as a pup when he hadn't run fast enough to avoid an unusually fast pickup from the next county.

Mitzie didn't come in lumbering or in any other fashion. She was satisfied to be where she was. Jake went into the kitchen.

"All right, you two," he commanded as he placed Mitzie on the floor to let her know, again, he didn't approve of her tabletop lair. "All right, all right, all right. I'm taking a pretty lady out tonight." He leaned back and looked up at the ceiling in an emphatic gesture. "An exquisitely pretty lady." Then with hands on hips, he looked straight into their eyes. "And you two are not coming along. Understood?"

Prince looked up and yawned, a jaw-cracking yawn. Mitzie licked one paw, stretched one leg out in front, then slowly started to lick the other paw.

"I see you two are heartbroken over this. Stay off the table, Mitz, and Prince—try not to pant." Prince did not pant, Mitzie did not stay off the table.

***

George Swensen opened the door almost before Jake knocked on it. It was the kitchen door that Nell had entered when he dropped her off three mornings ago. It was the only door most farmers use.

Jake stood still and looked up at the massive body of Nell's younger brother and felt like a rowboat next to the Titanic, although this titanic didn't look like it was about to sink. Maybe the rowboat would.

"Here," George said, "have a seat at the table. That's Les over here and Lo over there."

Les and Lo were leaned back in their chairs, each with one leg from their huge bodies on the table and staring down at their empty plates. Jake, thinking about how Mitzie helps herself to his kitchen tabletop, lost all concern over it when he saw that two grown men, with powers of reason a cat doesn't have, violate the politeness of a visitor present. At least Mitzie jumped off when an outsider came into her master's kitchen.

George went to the stove for the coffee pot, poured, and offered the mug to Jake.

91

Jake took the hot container although he wished he didn't have to. He knew his hands would shake, and they did, so he clutched the mug with the might of all his fingers and sat down at the table. He was out of place with three oversized men and a mug of coffee he didn't want. Where was Nell? Was he early?

"You're early," Lo said.

Jake felt short. He knew he wouldn't have cared about Lo's remark if he were tall like them. It is okay for tall people to be early. It is also okay for tall people to make a smart remark back. Jake was silent.

"I saw that bow tie at the store awhile back, it's ugly," Les monotoned.

Jake nodded and took a slow sip of the coffee. "Yes," he said. He noticed Les' faded shirt and wondered why someone so poorly dressed would ever look inside a clothier's to make a judgment on any of its contents. He was glad to now have the mug to hold on to.

George cleared the dishes from the table, apologized for the mess, and then sat opposite his guest who hoped his host would sink down in his chair as low as he. George, unfortunately for Jake, couldn't possibly have sunk down so low; he was the tallest of the three brothers, six feet four, and he had a thick bone and muscle structure. His neck was almost the width of his head, a football player's neck and head, but without the helmet and shoulder pads. The foursome looked like three bulls and a calf having after-dinner coffee together.

Jake's body weight, that dropped to thirty pounds due to the euphoria he had felt after Nell said yes to a date, now rose to fifty pounds of displeasure after the insult of the bow tie and finally came up to three hundred pounds of agitation in general. And he had been in the Swensen kitchen now for at least nine hours. He looked at his watch—it was not quite six.

Lo left the kitchen and yelled for Les to follow. The television went on. Jake felt a little relieved after two of the three great chunks left.

"You're new to these parts, aren't you?" Jake asked the remaining brother.

"Yup," George replied. "I saw you at the beer joint last week. Go there often?"

"Nope," Jake answered in the same casual way. "Just once or twice a week. Maybe three times or so. Never stay long, maybe a few hours. I'm retired. Do you know Harold Hallgren?"

"By sight, by sight," George replied.

"We're best friends, have been for years. He's retired too. We started school together." Jake began to relax. George didn't seem so big anymore.

George grinned. "I would have taken you into the living room to wait, but we're mostly kitchen men."

Jake grinned back. "Most farmers are, I guess. Who has the time and strength after a day in the hot fields to get past the kitchen anyway?"

George leaned back on his massive neck and gave out a sudden burst of laughter. After that he got up from the table, almost knocked it over onto Jake, and went to the cupboard. "How about a quick shot of booze, Jake?"

Jake looked up. "I'd rather rain check it. I'm taking a lady to supper tonight."

"Sure, sure." George shut the cupboard. "You are certainly right about my sister. She is a lady. Nice, nice, lady."

"That's why I asked her out. And I'll be a gentleman with her, you needn't worry." Jake would have wagged his tail if he had one. Better get a few good words in here now.

"I'm not worried. Heaven knows we're all old enough to do what we want. Les and Lo don't see it that way though."

"What do you mean?" Jake sunk down into his chair—he felt secure and snug with his body half under the table after he heard that remark about the unfriendly brothers.

"I mean that those two lugs, twin lugs, expect our sister to be here at all times. Their wives were there for them all the time—that is, until they both suddenly died two years ago.

Nell is their substitute mother and housekeeper."

Jake stared into his empty mug. That was just great, wonderful, a possible obstacle on his way into Nell's heart. "Have you ever married? I heard you haven't. Neither have I."

"Neither has Nell."

"Uh-huh."

The conversation and exchange of their marital status halted for awhile. Then George slapped the table. "What's keeping that gal anyway?" He left the kitchen and Jake heard him climbing stairs, one heavy foot after another. Jake looked around the kitchen. How pretty. Just like his mom had kept hers. He wondered how often Nell had to scrub it with three gigantic men trampling all over. The curtains were probably handmade by Nell, the windows clean as though they were open.

Twins? Did George say twins? Two lug nuts alike and vying for first place at rudeness? Jake sighed. Maybe they were only bashful.

All of a sudden Nell came into the room, and her appearance put flowers on the table and songbirds in the window sills. Her wavy blond and gray hair, short and flowing, reached over to Jake and said hello. He forgot about the unwanted mug of coffee and the twins' unnecessary remarks and the oversized neck of George. But he didn't forget to look at her feet—thank goodness, she had on flat-heeled shoes.

Jake got up from the table and folded his arms over his chest because he didn't know what else to do with them.

She smiled. "I like your bow tie."

"Thank you," he answered. Then he went to the living room entry and called thanks to the twin blockheads because he didn't know what else to say to them. He waved at George as he and Nell turned to the back door. "Thank you for the coffee."

"Sure, sure," George said. "I'll get the dishes, Sis, you two have yourselves a good time."

Jake wondered if George meant that remark—because his kitchen visitor was taking away the only lovely thing in the house.

***

Calhoun's Restaurant was the only restaurant in town. It was always busy, and it never took reservations. But Jake knew the owner better than anyone else, he thought, because in grade school and high school they had always sat next to each other in alphabetic kinship; Jake decided that this childhood coalition would get him the best table with minimum waiting.

The owner was not in, he was home buried under blankets of a sneezing cold and coughing flu.

"I don't mind waiting," Nell comforted.

Jake pulled at his bow tie and felt burdened under his navy blue. "Well, it's just that we might miss the movie."

"Maybe there will be other movie nights," she said as she sat down in a chair in a row of ten other people.

Nell's remark didn't sink in; it sat right outside Jake's ear like oil on water, unable to penetrate his brain and tell him that his present date had just hinted about a future date. His thoughts were too occupied with the delay in eating, with the harshness of the twins, and with the ever present shock that he was really and truly on a date with Nell Swensen. And even though Jake said "Oh, of course" to Nell's suggestion, he didn't hear himself say it, he was too much in a fog with thoughts narrowed to only what he had planned for the evening and not with anything Nell might offer. He stood over her as she relaxed in the chair and felt as hulking as her brother George looked.

Nell was tall, but she was small boned and slender. Almost fragile. Jake mused how such a delicate creature came out of a family of giants. Maybe she was adopted. Maybe the brothers were. No, not the twins anyway—surely the parents would have returned them.

The crowded waiting room was quiet. It was Friday night and the noisy people were at Barney's. Jake didn't like noise

95

unless it was his and Harold's. That's why he went to Barney's on Saturday afternoons when the loud ones were either at home, subdued from the night before, or resting to gain strength to do the noise all over again Saturday night.

Tonight at Calhoun's, Jake not only had his quiet, he had Nell too.

The hostess came to the waiting area and most of the patrons got up and followed her. Jake relinquished his feeling of towering height and sat down next to Nell.

She turned sideways. "Is your real name Jake, or is it a nickname?"

"Jacob. Jacob Robert."

"Oh, how noble. I have a real name also. It's Eleanor Adele. My father didn't like that name so he called me Little Nell when I was young. He claimed that Nell was the proper nickname for both names, which it is if you stretch your imagination. Anyway, I was Little Nell until I grew taller than Dad. Then I was just plain Nell."

Jake sat up board-straight. Noble, she said? And she mentioned her father was shorter than she. What a lady. He wondered if she found something good in everything. Good, good, good, Jake decided, Nell was plain and simply good in every way and with everything and all the time.

"I've never cared for my name," Jake said. "My brother teased me when I was very young about climbing a ladder. 'Where you got your ladder hid today?' he would taunt every chance he got. He left home before I was old enough to know that he would leave forever, but I never forgot that ladder question because that was about the only thing he ever said to me."

Nell laughed. Her entire face sparkled with a low, clear, gentle laugh. "My brothers thought my nickname was something you gave to a horse. The twins let me know, too. I used to wish I was a Diana or a Rachel or something that was real girl.

Jake got up and stood in front of her again. He liked standing in front of and over her. "Well, at least my name is better than my brother's. He was named after our two grandfathers, you know, obligation names."

"Oh no," Nell laughed again as she looked up at him. "Dare I ask?"

"Alvin. Alvin Fester. Alvin Fester Blackburn."

Nell quietly whooped. "Fester? Is that a name or a condition?" They laughed together. Jake felt so proud—at long last, his older brother had done something good for him.

Neither of them noticed their food much after they finally got a table. It was no longer important as they sat opposite each other, a contrast in appearances. Nell's smooth, clear skin and almost unblemished hands belied her fifty-seven years. She took such small bites of food and started to chew only after the morsel was fully on her tongue and her mouth closed. Jake noticed her delicate manner and worried she might be too demure for him until he realized she had accepted his date even after all his goof-ups, especially the strangled spit part. He quit worrying, but only about that.

He didn't think about how much older he looked than she, although he wasn't much older. Every crease in his face, every line on his brow, was further emphasized by the permanent brown patches of skin haphazardly placed by years of summer suns. His manner of eating matched his physical demeanor as he carelessly dug into his food as though he had never eaten in public before.

Neither of them said anything once they started to eat except for an occasional 'this is yummy' from Nell and a few brisk chin wipes and one 'excuse me' from Jake. Unlike teenagers new to dating, Jake and Nell were not stiff with each other. They were like a pair of leather gloves fitted loosely over hands, gloves soft and worn, hands still and warm.

"How about some apple pie for dessert?" Jake offered after he and Nell at last put down their forks.

"No, not apple pie, but I will have some of the rhubarb," she answered.

"Rhubarb?" Jake questioned. Nobody ate rhubarb pie

unless they had to. He remembered how his mother complained it took a ton of sugar to make it sweet enough to eat. A surge of bitter taste came in his mouth just at hearing the word. "Rhubarb? I don't think they have it here. Don't you want some apple?" Jake was mighty pushy for someone who, less than a few days ago, was weak with fear that the lady wouldn't even talk to him.

"No, I make apple at home. I want something I don't make myself."

"Oh sure, of course," Jake said after he saw it on the menu. "I guess they do have rhubarb. I wonder why. I don't think anyone eats it." He grinned. "Except you. I hope they have some left."

Nell turned her face aside and smiled just a little, the kind of smile that comes when someone is trying to prevent a laugh.

"How about some ice cream ala mode over the rhubarb?" Jake continued.

Nell turned her face back to her suitor. "No thank you, Jake, you are a very good host, but I don't want to mask the taste of the rhubarb."

Jake swallowed a big bite of his apple pie brought with haste by a waitress who had too many customers. He noticed that Nell's rhubarb portion seemed too large for someone so daintily seated opposite him. But she kept up with Jake who wouldn't let the subject of rhubarb rest.

"If you like rhubarb so much, why don't you make it at home?"

"Too much sugar. It takes too much sugar. I don't want to know I'm eating that much sugar." Nell cleared her throat. "I guess people are like that, aren't they? If they don't have a hand in something, they think it doesn't exist."

"That's for darn sure," Jake replied and then looked down at his empty plate. It was almost time to leave and too late for the movie. That meant he would have to take Nell home now. And how would he manage that? Should he kiss her goodnight on their first date? She was taller, for pity sakes, why hadn't he thought of that before? He should have had it all worked out, how he would do it—and if he would do it. Maybe he would merely take her to the door and kiss her hand like an English gentleman.

Maybe he shouldn't kiss her at all, he would wait until she made the first move—if she made it, that is. If not, there would be other times if he behaved himself now. No sense in being pushy.

Jake paid the bill and escorted Nell to the pickup which was as clean on the inside and the outside as a two-year-old red vehicle could be. "Would you like to do something else? It's not too late, but I guess there's nothing else to do is there?" He laughed to himself. Except necking. He didn't say that though.

"I guess not," Nell replied. "We did enough for one evening anyway. That was a lovely meal, Jake, you are a good cook."

There went his chest again, all puffed up. He opened the door and supported Nell's elbow while she climbed in. When he got in on his side, he noticed she sat a little closer to him than she did on the way there. Things kept getting better and better.

"I'm not a good cook, you would think I would be after years of being alone, but I'm not. It's too easy to go to the Hallgrens." He had to let her realize that after they were married, he would not encroach on her territory.

"Well, you may not be a good cook, but you certainly know how to pick a good restaurant."

"It's the only one in town."

"In this town," Nell answered.

Jake looked over at her. Up, and over at her. Those happy, but heavy clouds lifted a little, and through the clearing Jake started to finally hear what Nell might be hinting at. Was she suggesting another date in another town? He certainly couldn't let this conversation die down. He cleared his throat. "Have you ever eaten in Omaha?" Might as well go for something big, the city was less than two hundred miles away, that would be plenty of time for them to be alone.

Nell returned his look and pointed to Binder Post Road. "You may not believe this, but I've never been to Omaha."

"No kidding?"

As Jake turned the wheel in the direction that Nell gave, the pickup hit a chuckhole, hard, and his beloved passenger bounced up to the ceiling. Jake slowed almost to a stop. "I'm sorry, my gosh but I am sorry, did your head hit?" Jake wanted to shout an obscenity at himself for hurting the one person he wanted to be the nicest to.

"It was close." She hesitated with adding 'but that's all right' until she saw Jake's open mouth and pleading eyes crouched down behind the wheel. She smiled in forgiveness.

"It won't happen again, not that hard anyway," his words tumbled out like marbles rolling on ice, "I'll slow down and pay more attention, I hit chuckholes a lot because I'm not tall enough to hit the roof." There, maybe that remark about his shortness would be punishment enough for his carelessness and Nell would forgive.

She changed the subject. "What is Omaha like? Is it dusty and smelly and loud and big?"

"Bigger than here. Bigger than any place in Iowa. But otherwise not too big. It's a good-looking town... city. Clean and hilly. Man, is it hilly. I go there a lot. Harold has some friends in the west section, and he and Dolly visit them now and then. Harold, he's my best friend I think I mentioned before, he once said that the place is so hilly you can't even walk across the street without going up or down a hill. Maybe that's what makes it so good-looking. Lots of trees too." He turned on the high beam lights to cut through the evening's approaching blackness. "Didn't your brothers drive by there when you moved out here to Boone County?"

"I was half asleep. It was night."

"It's only a few hours from here. About three hours. I go there a lot." Jake hoped she wouldn't ask how much 'a lot' was because he didn't go there 'a lot.' Twice a year, maybe three.

Binder Post Road was deserted. Jake became frustrated. The evening was too late for them to do anything but go home, but it was too early for the Friday night revelers to be out. He and Nell were caught in-between, it was like a date ending before it was over. He had spent more time than he ever had before, bathing, shaving, and dressing just for this evening; he had even talcumed his feet and lotioned his hands and face. And now the date was all over in two hours. A measly two hours. He hadn't planned things well. Next time he would phone for a reservation, beg for one, insist on one, demand one, so they could go to a movie also. Maybe next Friday or Saturday.

Jake was still a bit numb over Nell's acceptance of him or he would have thought more clearly about timing. He would have realized he could take her to supper one night and the movies another. His planning ability was still on high school level when young people were only allowed one night out a week and so, consequently, were able to get in many activities in just a few hours. Not that he had had any experience with dating then, but he knew how Harold had functioned because Harold always told Jake about his dates and eventually Harold's dating encounters became Jake's in thought.

Nell moved closer to him. Surely she would say yes to next week and maybe he had better get a yes to that before he tried to kiss her goodnight. He turned on the radio. Thank goodness for the Friday night musical oldies. The rich music calmed him, and he started to think about the goodnight kiss possibility again. Why not kiss her while they were still in the pickup where he could anchor his feet against the floorboard and stretch until their heights were almost the same? Nell would have to scrunch down a little, but not as much as she would if they were standing. He had to assume she would scrunch down to meet his stretch, he had to assume she would react in exactly this manner, because without that assumption he would have to worry about another way to get in that goodnight kiss, and he didn't want to worry anymore.

Good. It was settled. First he would ask her out for next week while they were still driving home. Then, after they arrived, he would kiss her goodnight before she had a chance to slide over to the door.

The radio played a love song from Jake's teen years. He hummed along quietly, remembering the melody but keeping the words to himself. It was a slow tune for a slow evening. He wondered if Nell was also thinking the words. Probably not—she wasn't droning along with him.

He stopped humming. He had better slow down with the romantic stuff. He didn't want Nell to scoot away from him. Instead of humming, he would concentrate on how he would kiss her. If they remained in the pickup for this event, it would mean he would have to stretch and then lean over slightly until she did the same. But what if she didn't lean? It would look pretty dumb for him to lean and not do anything with it. A clown might do something like that and not appear foolish, but Jake didn't think of himself as a clown. Not yet.

It might be best if he took her to the back door and kissed her hand. No, the kiss would have to be in the pickup because he wanted her mouth. No, he would have to figure a way other than the pickup because after they married, they couldn't go to a vehicle every time they wanted to kiss.

The sofa. Of course. They would have a sofa to sit on, and he could kiss her there. The bed. Another place for kissing. Maybe that was the best place because in bed he wouldn't have to stretch and she wouldn't have to scrunch. But then they would have to wait until they got married. He didn't want to wait, and besides, who waits until their wedding night to kiss? Probably nobody. Jake sighed. What a burden of thoughts.

"Did you have a busy day?" Nell asked.

"No, the usual. Why?"

"Because you have been quiet, and now you just sighed."

"Oh, no, I'm quiet a lot, and I sigh a lot. Always have. Even when I was a kid, my mom asked me why I sighed so much."

Nell laughed. "Come on, Mr. Blackburn, you are teasing me."

Jake smiled and looked over at her again. "Yeah, but only because I didn't want you to think I am tired. Actually, I'm raring to go again next Friday. How about you?"

"Oh my," Nell replied, "I'll be in Iowa."

"Oh?" Jake stared straight ahead. What happened to his fairy tale? An oncoming car flicked on its high beams as a signal for Jake to reduce his, and Jake was so irritated by what was ordinarily a common event, he mentally cursed the driver. High beams, low beams, what does it matter when Nell turned down next Friday with him? How could she go to Iowa? How could she go anyplace? He had counted on next week. He had counted on forever.

"Why are you going?" he asked quietly, which was quite a feat for his screaming anguish to disguise. "How long will you be gone?" His palms started to sweat. His palms never sweat, he was not a palm-sweater, but Nell's announcement turned him into one.

"I don't know how long I'll be gone," she answered in a matter-of-fact tone. "But I do know I leave on the six o'clock bus. In the morning." She became silent.

Jake was silent too, he drove in a numbed serenity, until his mind started to think again. Of all the lowdown, blasted, unfair, crummy things. "I'll take you there," he said.

He would let Nell decide where 'there' was: to the bus in town or to Iowa itself. He cringed. What if she said Iowa and when they got there, a boyfriend would be waiting? Maybe he was making a fool of himself. He hardly knew Nell. Maybe he had gone too far out on that limb. Hurry up and answer me, darn it, please don't end this date forever. Please don't let tonight be just one of those blips that happen on television. Please say something real quick. Tell me where you want me to drive you. Hurry, hurry, I can't stand it. What's the big deal about Iowa anyway? Iowa is Iowa. No need to think anything romantic about it.

Nell smiled. "Thanks for the offer, Jake, but I can't ask you to drive to my place and then to town and then back to your place. It's too much for me to expect."

"Oh no, no, no it's not. Not at all, it's nothing. Uh-huh, nothing. Absolutely no problem. I'll find something in town to do afterwards. I won't go straight home."

Nell laughed. "Isn't six o'clock in the morning a long time to wait until Barney opens up?"

"You know about Barney's?" He had to hedge about that subject because he couldn't decide whether to act innocent of the Beer Palace's activities or whether he should simply come out and admit it. He had avoided the subject in the hardware store because the gentleness and quiet of Nell was so incongruous to the occasionally rowdy times at Barney's; he didn't want Nell to think he was rowdy.

Nell became talkative again. "Dolly Hallgren told me how you and her husband go to Barney's every Saturday for lunch and a beer. Yes, I know about you and Barney's."

Jake looked over at her. Lunch? he thought. Where did Dolly come up with this lunch business? Pretzels isn't much of a lunch. And a beer? Does Dolly think Harold comes home late Saturday afternoons all red-faced and boisterous on only 'a beer?' I wouldn't deceive Nell like that if she was my wife. I'd tell her everything. Then Jake realized that perhaps Harold did tell Dolly everything, and for the sake of her dainty women's bridge club she turned the truth into something nice.

"So you've heard about our Saturday afternoon beer?" Jake smiled as he temporarily forgot about the tribulation of Iowa. He was instead thinking relief that his activities at Barney's no longer had to be hidden, that all the time spent there and all the occasional drinking catastrophes could now be put to rest under the cover of one beer and a bowl of pretzels.

Nell side-glanced Jake. "I bet it's more than one beer, isn't it?"

Jake couldn't look at her. She was wise to the ways of men in beer joints. His right ear started to ring and his forehead sunk into deep furrows. "We're not drunks."

"Of course not. I wouldn't have gone out with you tonight if I thought you were."

Jake sat tall again. "Don't worry about what I'll do after your bus leaves. I'll go to the Hallgrens for breakfast, which I do a lot, and then at noon Harold and I will come back to Barney's. We will drink to your return." He hesitated because his mind went pitch black again. "You are returning, aren't you?"

"Oh my, yes. It's only a visit."

"Probably have a bunch of girlfriends there, huh?"

"A few friends."

All right, so she wouldn't say whether the friends were girls or boys, all right, all right, all right. It was time to change the subject so he wouldn't appear anxious. "You'd like Barney. He's not your usual type person, but you'd like him."

Nell didn't say anymore. Maybe, Jake thought, she was thinking of Iowa. Maybe he overestimated her congeniality. He cleared his throat. "How about it? How about tomorrow? May I escort you to the bus?"

"Escort?" Nell replied. "What a gallant way of putting it. And yes, I would like that." She laughed. "Now my brothers won't have to draw straws."

Jake smiled as he drove into the Swensen driveway. He turned off the engine and noticed a back porch light on. Although the light would help him walk Nell up to the house, it would also help everyone see a goodnight kiss if he decided his courage was great enough.

It wasn't. But as Nell stepped to the ground, he squeezed her hand a little, put his arm around her back, and held her close to him as they walked to the door.

"I'll be here at five tomorrow morning."

She nodded and opened the door. Jake turned away without attempting a kiss. Tomorrow, tomorrow, sometime tomorrow, he would give that kiss to her right smack-dab on the mouth. Tomorrow.

***

Jake set two alarms, one on each side of his bed. The setup looked like bookends with him sandwiched between ready to jolt upright the instant the blaring sounded. Even when he farmed, he was not used to a three-thirty wake-up, so he fixed himself with twice the waking power—he must not miss that bus. Everything must be perfect for Nell. What woman would marry a man who missed buses? Although he didn't want her on that bus, he didn't want to be the one who didn't get her there. She would go the next day or so anyway, without his help and with thoughts of his incompetence.

Both alarms went off at exactly the same time, and the ensuing shock rolled Jake out of bed. His heart pounded loud enough to hear as he sat upright, stiff, like a board. He took a deep breath and opened his eyes wide to the dark darkness; he yawned of course, then stretched to make himself feel taller. He wanted to be tall today.

Prince continued to sleep through the alarms and through his master stumbling over him on the way to the bathroom. Jake shaved, showered, dressed, and then nudged Prince's underbelly with his foot. "Come on, come on, get up, rise and shine, be happy."

Prince rolled over, opened his snout in a big yawn, and went back to sleep. It was too early to rise, shine, and be happy. Jake went to the kitchen, lifted Mitzie off the table, and put down food and fresh water.

He had only forty minutes left to get to Nell's so he decided it would be better to return for the animals later, after Nell was gone, on the way to Harold and Dolly's for breakfast. No sense in their being in the pickup until later. Nell might think it strange, riding to the bus with two sleeping pets. Jake slammed the back door and fumbled with his keys to unlock the pickup, squinting under the dim light over the shed. He wondered if Nell thought Barney was strange, he wondered if she thought he was strange. What will she think of Harold? What did she think about anything? Maybe nice people don't think about people very much. Maybe that's why they are nice.

Nell stood on her back porch stoop, a suitcase at her feet and an apple pie in her hands. The sun wasn't nearly high enough yet to reflect its gold on her hair, but Jake knew it was there. He reached for the suitcase and eyed the pie. He wondered if the recipient of the pie would be an Iowa man friend or an Iowa lady friend. Do women bake pies for other woman or only for men? Why doesn't Iowa just simply go away? They can make their own pies. Maybe the friend was a banker, and if so, he could afford to buy his own pie. By the time Jake and Nell reached the pickup, he was sick of pies. Even Dolly's lemon creme had lost its appeal.

Jake heaved the suitcase onto the back of the truck. He wanted to heave the pie also, right up into the air for a thousand birds to catch and devour.

Fortunately, Nell interrupted his evil-thinking spell. "Is there a place for this pie back here or should I leave it up front so you won't forget to take it inside the house after you and Harold are through with Barney's for the day?"

Jake simply stood there while he choked up and stared at the pie. Dear God, that thing is for me. And Dear God, she mentioned Barney's in a matter-of-fact way like it was okay to go there with her pie, and Dear God she is permitting me to take her to the bus, and Oh God, what a wonderful lady she is and what a wonderful day this is and Thank You, Thank You. Thanks.

Jake also thanked Nell, but a little less profusely because he didn't want to overdo it. But he did continue to Thank God all the way to the bus stop. He glanced many times at the pie sitting so perky on Nell's lap; and each time he looked at the prized pie, his heart smelled the juicy aroma.

The gift of the pie took him to the bus stop with happy thoughts, but after he shoved the suitcase onto the side of the bus, he turned to reach for Nell's hand and she was not there. She had hurried up the steps to find a scenic seat, and now Jake had only empty space standing next to him. No Nell, no Prince, no Mitzie, no Harold and Dolly—he was there on the street with no one on it but himself.

He began to realize the quickness of Nell: quick to accept a date, quick to return that invitation with apple pie, and quick to leave town. He decided he had to act quick too. He got on the bus and sat next to her. "We have a few minutes, the bus isn't running yet," Jake said, and before Nell could reply, the driver came back on, raised himself up onto his seat and started the engine. Jake knew that time and noise were against him now, so he didn't say anything more. He stood up, and with no further fuss, bent over and kissed Nell's mouth with forceful tenderness, her sparse lipstick smearing his lips and her fresh smell penetrating his nose. Then as quickly as he had moved toward her, he moved back. Nell looked up at him in a startled way, but with a suggestion of pleasantness. She smiled, took a Kleenex tissue from her purse, and wiped Jake's mouth clean. Neither said anything; the bus gasped exhaust; and Jake hurried off and down to the lonely street.

He looked up at Nell's window. Thank goodness she smiled, nodded, and waved. The bus rolled forward. She was gone. Jake stuffed his hands deep into his pockets and backed away. He wished Prince and Mitzie were with him now. He wished he had insisted Nell tell him why she was going to Iowa.

***

"I wonder why Nell went to Iowa," Jake said to the Hallgrens over the breakfast he walked in on.

"Have another pancake, Jake," Dolly offered as she stabbed the last one with her fork and slapped it onto his syrupy plate. Dolly didn't want him to leave before she and Harold had heard every word of what Jake had said and then what Nell had said and then what Jake had answered and then what Nell had answered, until every detail of the date and Iowa departure was told.

"Thanks, Dolly, but my appetite is subdued this morning." Jake closed his eyes and remembered how he had kissed Nell. Too sudden, too pushy. Maybe Nell thought that too and would never come back. Maybe he hadn't scrubbed his teeth enough and had offended her. Maybe she didn't like short men after all. Maybe he had better think about something else for awhile.

"Eat up, Jake," Harold said as he went to the stove for his pipe and matches wishing that his buddy would tell more.

"Get used to it. Your Nell probably has all sorts of delicious surprises for you when she comes back. Are you really going to eat that pie of hers all by yourself?"

"I shouldn't have told you about the pie. Now you will think I'm selfish—especially with me eating your breakfast."

"That's what I'm thinking, buddy ... selfish."

Dolly pooh-poohed her husband's remark with a wave of her hand. "The first pie in a courtship is never selfish." She turned to Jake. "If Nell's first gesture toward you had been a necktie, would you have given part of it to Harold?"

Jake laughed. He pressed his thumb on the table, a sign to Harold, a sign the two shared that no one else understood, a signal that meant one of them had bested the other.

"That's more like it, pal," Harold replied. "You've been acting kind of quiet for someone who should be on a roller-coaster right now. Even your hair doesn't look as curly as usual. You want to know something? You are coming along better with Nell now than I did with Dolly at first. In fact, Dolly didn't make me a pie until after our honeymoon."

Jake leaned back on his chair and looked Harold straight in the face. "Dolly didn't abandon you for Iowa either."

***

As each day passed, Jake regretted more and more not knowing why Nell went away and when she would be back. Surely she must be thinking he wasn't interested enough to even hint for answers she had avoided on that night of their one and only date, that all he wanted from her was a quick, smeary kiss.

Where was she staying? If he knew that, he could write. Her brothers must know. He would ask them, easy enough, but what would they think of him for not knowing? A simple man, they would chant? Simple minds don't think ahead. The twins, for sure, would gag laughing on that. He had to think of a brilliant, casual way of asking, a way that would tell them that it was perfectly normal to not know everything about your date. He would think about it for a few days, something appropriate would pop into his head.

The next week the pie was down to a crumb, and Jake's mind was still muddled. Ordinarily he would have eaten the pie in one day, but he wanted it to last as a reminder. Even if he didn't love Nell Swensen, which he did, her baking alone was worth her return. What a tangy sweet feeling he had of her with each bite of the pie as it crunched and squished around in his mouth and slid affectionately down his throat. I must not lose her, he agonized. Pie or no pie, I want that woman.

Two weeks after Nell left, Jake became very concerned. He wasn't ready to face the brothers with his stupid question so he thought of another plan, a plan that would keep him from missing Nell's return.

He drove early to town, when no one would be around to witness his foolishness, and looked at the bus schedule in the postoffice. It was glued to the announcement board on the front of the building as though the arrival and departure times would never change. The one room postoffice had a counter in the middle to separate the customers from the attendant, and the room was always open to accommodate the town people and occasional farmer who had a postoffice box. The town gossips liked to come to the post boxes more often than most others, and they always lingered, maybe in hopes that someone would drop a piece of mail they could pick up for the purpose of casually reading the return address, or maybe because they wanted to be near the source of news and feel it surge through their bodies.

Jake needed to avoid such an encounter. The morning after his brilliant idea, he arrived at seven, parked his pickup one block away, and nonchalantly walked past the schedule. The departure bus left at six in the morning every third morning and the arrival bus came at two in the afternoons on the same days. That meant he could go to Barney's at one o'clock every third day, have a beer and some pretzels, and then drive his pickup past the bus. If Nell got off, he would drive his pickup one time around the block to give the impression he wasn't overly eager, and then offer her a ride home. He had to remain calm, no screeching of the brakes and leaping out of the truck, no nothing that anyone else would not do.

After Jake determined how he could meet Nell's return without asking her brothers, he decided he needed to prepare for even more. Future dates together, future movies and suppers and driving to Omaha, and of course, future marriage. The future was full of Nell occupying the front seat of the pickup, and consequently Prince and Mitzie would have to learn a new routine concerning the riding arrangement. From now on, the front seat was Nell's.

After a quick lunch of baloney on bread thickly spread with mustard and catsup, Jake rummaged through his shed until he found a brush and rag. He swept away the animal hairs on the front seat, dusted and washed the upholstery, hosed down and waxed the outside, and hoped no one would notice and ask why he did it.

He went to the attic where his mother had stored old rugs and unrolled each of them until he found the special one, special because it was for his beloved, soon-to-be displaced pets. He threw out the old beat-up rug and put the memory-laden one with its deep green piling in the back end of the truck and ached with a surge of remembrance that went through his body like a streak of lightening. The rug had once been by his bed, placed there by his mother who realized her son's love of the earth and the things on it; the day the dry goods had displayed a rug of varied shades of rich green was the day she bought it, and then waited until his fifth birthday to lay it by his bed; she had told him to stay on the rug until he pulled on warm socks before dashing over the cold bare floors to the bathroom. Now, Jake mused, a memento from his past would do him a service in the present. He ran his hand over the rug's remaining softness and wondered if Prince and Mitzie would appreciate it as much as his young boy's feet had.

He whistled for his animals, and they came right away— even Mitzie, who usually ignored any idea that wasn't hers.

He opened the front door of the pickup, and just as they were about to leap up, he carefully slammed the door. That should give them the message, but it didn't. Prince started to pant and Mitzie started to walk away. Jake picked each one up and shoved them onto the back end. He pointed to the rug, he ran his hand over the rug, he bawled them out for not going to the rug, and then he cried.

This was no little event. This was a new era. His pets were never in the back unless Jake was stopped for a long time, like when he was at Barney's. "All right, you two, this is a new era. No more front seat riding. And no jumping out of the back, either. Understand? Mitzie, do you hear me? None of your independent ways while we're driving about. You save it for when we are at home. Okay?"

Mitzie yawned and licked her paw. Prince continued to pant although he did sit on the rug to do it. Jake worried. Right now they seemed all right, but would they be when the pickup was bouncing up and down on the hard dirt and gravel roads? Would their feelings be hurt? Would things never be the same for them again? Jake decided to make a test run of their reaction to the change in their seating. He would drive a few miles with them in the back to see if they would stay there and not jump out. This had to work, even if he had to train them by stopping the pickup every time they leaped off and putting them back on. The front seat was Nell's and it had to remain clean. They would know this after a time. They would know.

Jake's heart pounded as he slowly drove the pickup out of the driveway; this had to work; it was unpleasant now, but he wanted both Nell and his animals; he wanted an addition to his life—not a replacement.

So far it was working. They hadn't jumped out yet. By golly, it was working. Jake increased his speed to ten miles an hour. Still working. Twenty miles now. Everything okay. Better stay at this for awhile. Then as Jake's stiff body relaxed, his mind started up. He had to know more than every three days when Nell would return. Of all the dumb things. He had asked her once after the date, why oh why didn't he ask a second time—like quickly right after the kiss? He had thought about it, but didn't think it important, didn't think she'd stay away so long; he had taken her quick return for granted, as though he owned her actions and didn't need to know the details.

He was up to twenty-five miles an hour when he decided it was the pie. The pie made him take Nell's feelings for granted. That was it. The pie. And it was gone. And so was Nell. It was time to worry again.

Thirty-five. Maybe he should go to her brothers and make a full confession of his dilemma. No, better yet, he would invite them to Barney's for a treat. Saturday night would be a good time—Harold always spent that time with Dolly playing checkers or something like that—and he could get them drunk on whiskey and then he'd get them into a poker game and he would talk about things to distract them from the game and they'd be so distracted from conversation and bleary-eyed from the whiskey that they wouldn't later remember he had asked about Nell.

Forty-five miles now. But if they were drunk and distracted enough to forget his question, maybe they would give the wrong answer. Besides, maybe they never got drunk when playing poker. He rarely played poker himself or got drunk while playing, so why should they? Solitaire maybe. Can you make bets on solitaire? Surely they knew how to play solitaire. Everybody else does. But possibly not. His only knowledge of them was that they usually came to Barney's an hour after he and Harold did, drank one whiskey and one beer, pulled on the pinball plungers a few times, waved at the room—at least George did—and left.

Jake's passion for fussing and worrying brought his pickup up to fifty miles an hour which included two chuckhole bumps and a lean to the left. It also included a return to the present time which meant: are Prince and Mitzie still with me? They were not in view of his back window. He turned the vehicle around and sped back, looking to the left and to the right and straight ahead. His throat as well as his heart pounded. Dear God, where are they? What have I done? I don't deserve to have Nell. I can't even care for two trusting animals properly. I am a beast, I might as well be living in a cave and come out once a day with a club and stalk my prey. He had forgotten that his pets had survived their back seat ride home from Tolliver's that precious day he confronted Nell.

They weren't anywhere near the road. Maybe they were dead of fright on the floor of the truck, in a pool of red blood on the green rug. He stopped. They were there. Mitzie licking her stomach on the rug, and Prince standing on the side with his paws on the sideboard. Jake felt relief, although he didn't have the slightest idea how they—especially Mitzie—had handled the chuckholes at fifty miles an hour. His old mattress. He would drag that out of the attic and put it underneath the rug. His brave pets deserved that.

Once the concern over Prince and Mitzie subsided, Jake started in on Nell again. What if she was already home? What if she only stayed away a few days, maybe she came home before he had finished the pie. His heart and throat started throbbing again, and he rushed back to his seat and drove away like a racer out to win all the bets. Prince and Mitzie would have to hold up awhile longer—he would apologize to them later. Nell was the most important thing now.

***

"What brings you here?" Lo Swensen asked in a frowning manner after Jake drove up to within a few yards of the back door stoop.

Jake's fingers curled tight around the steering wheel. "I was out for a drive, thought I'd stop and say Hi."

"Hi," the brother replied. "Bye."

Les Swensen shouted from behind the hen house. "Who's there?"

"Jake," Lo shouted back, then spat from the side of his mouth, never taking his eyes off the intruder.

"Jake who? Oh, you mean the squirt?" Les continued.

Jake's eyes widened and darted over to the hen house.

Surely the twin knew he could hear that insult. What was it with these bums? There was no letup with remarks that made a person feel totally unwanted. He certainly couldn't ask them about their sister now.

"Where's your other brother?" Jake questioned after deciding he had worried too much about Nell to give up in the middle of nasty remarks. George, though ridiculously oversized, was at least friendly. "Where's George? I came to talk to George," Jake said although he really wanted to say— get out of my way you slimy, spitting beast—but the possibility of the other beast coming from behind the hen house to help gang up on him kept Jake's tongue still.

Lo spat again. "He's on house chores. The place finally got unlivable, according to him. That's why he's inside and we're outside doing the work." He blew his nose hard, unnecessarily. "He still has to do his share out here though. He'll probably be through around noon. You probably won't want to wait."

Jake's heart thumped. What does that mean: 'not want to wait?' Am I unwelcome inside? He leaned out of his window and looked at the hard, bare ground underneath and then at the flower bed trimming the side of the house. What a contrast between the two areas. But there was even more contrast on the inside, especially if Nell were there.

Jake got out of his truck, stood as tall as possible, and pierced Lo's somberness with his eyes. "I have something funny to tell George."

Lo turned and shouted again. "George, can you take visitors? There's a big shot out here with a joke. No, I take that back. He's the joke, and he wants you to look at it."

George didn't answer. Jake went to the back of the pickup and stroked Prince for assurance of something friendly. Prince panted in return, and Jake visualized bullets coming out with each pant and spraying on the twin.

"Uh-mm," Jake said. "Uh-mm. Actually, I don't have something funny to tell George. I have something to ask that he might think is funny." Blast it. What was this? Why did he think he had to explain everything to this bozo?

Les came from the hen house. Now there were two of them. Great joy in the morning. David only had one Goliath, and he at least had a weapon. He wished Prince would attack instead of pant. He wished he was at Barney's with a big beer and a big pretzel. He wished he was dead and then he could wait for Nell in Heaven. But none of that was possible now, so what the heck, tell them what you came for, get it over with. "It's about your sister. I don't know when she's coming back from Iowa. Thought I'd give her a ride home." Jake's face got hot. If the twins were insulting before, they certainly would let him have it now.

The pair didn't say anything. They smirked and walked away. They were probably out of fresh remarks. They probably had a quota for each day, and they had just used it up. It was a good thing, that the quota was up, because so was Jake's endurance.

George came to the door. "That you, Jake?" He opened the screen and heaved the dirty water from a pail onto the flower bed. "Why don't you come in? I'm doing Nell's chores, and I'm almost done."

Jake finally had an ally. He scurried inside before the twins thought of some other unwelcome thing to say.

"How have you been?" George asked as he picked up several wet and dirty rags scattered around the kitchen and slung them over the backs of the kitchen chairs.

"I need some information," Jake said.

"Want a cup of coffee?"

Jake hesitated. If he drank coffee, he would have to sit on one of those chairs with a wringing soppy rag hung over it. But he didn't want to refuse and make George think he was unfriendly.

"I'd love a cup, thank you."

George turned up the simmering tea kettle and scooped heaping teaspoons of coffee into two mugs. His thick neck turned to Jake. "What do you want to know?"

"I'd like to know when Nell is coming back."

George poured the hot water straight down the middle of the mugs. "I don't know."

Jake's body jerked in embarrassment. He had made himself foolish by asking something he should have the answer to, and for that, there was no reward.

"She never told us," George continued. "She said she didn't know for sure. I figured she just wanted some privacy. Why didn't you ask her on your date?"

Jake took the hot mug of coffee and continued to stand. "I did ask. She didn't know how long." He couldn't tell George he hadn't pestered Nell for details of her trip because he had been too busy figuring out how he would kiss her, and then after he decided he would do the kiss the next day on the bus, he was too busy slobbering all over her mouth to leave room in his head to think about anything else.

"I wonder why she didn't tell you?" George went on. "I would think she would have told you."

Jake swallowed the hot coffee. The heat burned his throat and George's remark seared his heart, sharp and clean like a sword through a young bull: maybe Nell didn't want him to know; maybe she would never be back. He looked around the kitchen, Nell's kitchen, and sensed the hollowness her absence brought. Oh, if only she would come in right now. He was used to happy kitchens, his mother always provided one with her quiet cheerfulness and comfort; and Dolly and Harold's large bay-windowed room constantly sparkled with friendliness. But right now the Swensen kitchen was empty of any of this because Nell was not in it— and all the cheerful Georges and all the fine curtains and all the apple pies in the world could not fill it up.

George pointed to the chairs. "Why don't you sit down?"

Jake forgot about the sloppy rags and sat down. Why was George being so nice to him? Did Nell instruct him to be extra polite as a comfort? Probably not. George was friendly the night of the date. The one date. Maybe Nell was going to tell him how long she would be gone after he got on the bus with her, but was so overwhelmed with his glorious kiss that she forgot. But why didn't she send him a postcard and tell him now? Does Iowa not have postcards? He thought about Prince and Mitzie whom he had banished to the back of the truck, perhaps needlessly.

He leaned back against one of the detested rags and looked down at his coffee. "Why didn't she tell me?" he carelessly said out loud just as Les slammed the door on his way in from the porch. "Because she doesn't want to see you again," he boomed out.

Jake's head swelled and turned hot red. He froze to the wet chair.

"Hey, big brother, what an awful thing to say," George frowned as he turned to Jake. "Don't pay attention to him, he knows nothing about nothing."

Les went to the living room and turned on the noontime news. George filled the tea kettle with more water.

Jake remained motionless. Of course. That apple pie was a goodbye gesture. Although what Les said was rude and ugly, it was probably true. Why would a lovely woman like Nell be interested in a man so many times rejected by women who were not nearly the prize she was?

George said something, but Jake didn't hear. He left the kitchen, went to the back of his pickup, and shooed his pets into the front seat. He shaded his eyes against the sun's sharp reflection on the newly waxed pickup, a reflection that seemed to mock his effort to establish an acceptable courting vehicle. He drove home faster than a high speed police chase, screeching this way and that with Prince and Mitzie cowering on the floor. He held on to the steering wheel with all his strength, and when he arrived home, he hit the brakes so hard the pickup slid across the gravel along with all his hopes of a life together with Nell Swensen and with no apology to his dog and cat. Life was rough on everybody, on everything, and even on beloved pets.

He turned off the motor and sat still; he heard the vacuum of silence, and not even Prince's panting relieved its stagnant echo. He went to the living room and turned on the television but could not hear its sound. It started to rain, and he didn't hear that either. He sat crosswise in his easy chair, his legs dangling over the side, and looked blankly at the screen. He was swallowed up in the chair that never before had been so enormous; and he cried silently with only the tears as evidence of his grief until he blew his nose into his last clean handkerchief.

Prince put his snout on Jake's thigh and looked as mournful as his master. Jake put his hand on the dog's head and slowly the numbness exchanged places with a heavy pain. He glanced over at Alice's picture. There was a fine spider thread running from the frame to the wall. The spider was gone, it had left its habitat for now, and Jake sighed. He had better get a cleaning lady in before the winter holidays began. There wouldn't be anyone to enjoy the effort, but it was the polite thing to do.

***

Jake was not the only one in Boone County who needed a ladder of angels with God at the top booming down reassurances and hope and promise.

Billy and Angela Charmley could have used one too. They were like a pair from a Charles Dickens' novel, packed full of rejection, dejection, and consequent heartbreak.

Like Jake who gradually realized his shortness was the factor in how he felt about himself, Billy and Angela gradually realized their parents' neglect left them like hollowed-out trees. To make up for this oversight of parental love and acceptance, the children especially good about completing homework because the results were praise by the teachers, recognition of their worth, and sometimes a hint of love.

They were, by far, the best students in the history of Boone County, and not because of a higher intelligence. Besides all the completed homework assignments, they were quiet and polite and accommodating. Their way of surviving and of receiving attention was to not make anyone angry.

While Jake compensated his childhood of low self esteem

with jokes and quick remarks, Billy and Angela did no such thing. One might say these two had a personality arrest.

This trio of despair could have come over on the Mayflower together—they were miserable, and they had an uncanny ability to survive heart-hurting hardships. Jake tried to overcome his hurt by wooing and hopefully winning the prize of Boone County. The children, however, had no options for overcoming anything.

The youngsters only had each other, and that was not enough. Jake had proved that with his friendship with Harold and Dolly— but it just wasn't enough.

***

"I'm bored," said Harold.

"Me too," Dolly replied.

It had rained for two days without stopping, not even for a little while, a quiet rain that soaked deep into the ground. Farmers stay indoors a lot when it rains, especially retired farmers. Although the Hallgrens enjoyed being alone after their daughter was raised, they appreciated other people, almost all other people, and the activities they brought. The long rain finally made them want those other people.

"Why don't we go to the Samuelsons?" Dolly suggested during a commercial break on television.

Harold looked over at his wife, his mouth dropped open in disbelief. "The Samuelsons? We're not that bored, are we?"

"Yes, we are."

"I wonder what Jake's doing? I mean, I wonder what he is really doing?" Harold got up and folded the day-old newspaper he had read the second time.

"Why don't you call him once more, Dear? Maybe he would like to go to the Samuelsons with us. He seemed a little down when he left us last."

Harold swallowed hard. "I'm tired of calling him and hearing him say he's busy. It's his turn to call me. I wonder what he is so busy with? You don't suppose Nell returned and they're haying it up, do you?"

"Harold." Dolly exclaimed his name so sharply, it hit the wall and stayed there.

Harold didn't let that outburst stop him. "Maybe he really is busy, like he says. You know, re-al busy."

Dolly got up and went toward the kitchen. "How would you like it if Jake accused you of such a thing?"

"He couldn't. I'm married."

"Oh? And what does that have to do with it, Sweetheart?"

"It means that because Jake and Nell are not married, they are free to do as they please." Harold swatted at a late season fly that flew sluggishly low and buzzed around him.

Dolly came back to her chair. "I wouldn't be too sure of that. Jake may be free, but I'm not so sure about Nell anymore."

"Uh?" Harold asked. "Uh? Is Nell married? Is one of those huskies from Iowa her husband instead of her brother? How did Jake manage a date in front of her husband?"

Dolly picked up the rolled newspaper and tapped his arm with it. "Stop it, Harold, don't be cute. You know that's not what I meant. You can be so irritating at times."

"But I am all yours, dear wife. Maybe Nell isn't all Jake's. Maybe she went to Iowa to get married."

"No, she didn't go to Iowa to get married," Dolly stated as if with authority.

"Then why did she go for pity sakes woman? I really can't stand this conversation anymore."

"I don't know why she went. To visit. Possibly to get away from her brothers. You know what, Harold? I think her brothers are the reason she's not free. I think they pretty much expect her to kowtow to them. Jake may have to court them as well."

Harold shook his head no. "I still think my theory is the best. They're in the hay. Why don't we visit Jake instead of the Samuelsons?"

"Doggone it, husband, I want you to give up on your nonsense thoughts."

Harold pulled out his suspenders and snapped them back. "I'll forget about Jake if you'll forget about the Samuelsons."

Dolly looked straight into her husband's eyes. "I wish it would stop raining."

***

The constancy of the rain and the subsequent absence of sunshine always put Jake in a sad mood. He never told anyone though, except Prince and Mitzie, because he didn't want to complain about that element of nature that grew his crops for so many years.

This ordeal of rain, however, was more than Jake could tolerate, although his heavy, dark mood was probably due more to Nell's mysterious truancy from him than to the rain itself. He called Harold.

"Well, I don't know if I should go to Barney's," Harold said to Jake's request. "Dolly's getting pretty fed up with the rain too. Why don't you come over here?"

Neither Jake nor Harold kept much liquor in their homes. They were social drinkers only, and if there wasn't anything to be social about, they didn't drink. That is why they enjoyed their sessions at Barney's so much—they liked being social.

Dolly knew about their sociability and that their tongues were so loose during this time that they would have fallen out of their mouths entirely by now if they hadn't been attached. She took the telephone from Harold to encourage his and Jake's visit to Barney's; she knew Jake would tell a lot to Harold after a few beers. She had to ease her mind that there was no scandal between Jake and Nell, even though she would have given it her blessing anyway, and the best way to get this information out of tight-lipped Jake was to get him relaxed. "Hello, Jake," she said, "Harold will be at Barney's as soon as he finds his rain boots."

"Thank you, Dolly," Jake answered.

"Thank you, wife," Harold said. "Jake sounds pretty down. We men should be alone for awhile. Why don't you bake us a pie for when we come back?"

Dolly put her hands on her hips and looked intently at her man who sometimes overstepped his boundary of nerviness. "Maybe," she replied slowly, "you should concentrate on getting the truth out of Jake's situation with Nell and let me decide about the pie. Remember, you just got out of a visit to the Samuelsons. Don't push it."

Harold decided to push it as he leaned over for a kiss. "Don't make it apple, it might remind Jake of what used to be." He bent over to give Proudflesh a long stroke and saw Dolly's startled look from the corner of his eye. "A pie is a small price to pay for all the juicy stuff I'm going to squeeze from Jake. I've got you on this one, wife. You can throw that look of yours away. Or better yet, put it in the pie."

Dolly nodded. "Yes, you do have me this time. Enjoy it because it will be a long time before it happens again. Now go. And don't come home drunk."

***

"We need the rain, you know," Harold said to Jake who sat leaning forward on the bar stool, arms outstretched on the counter, with his left hand clutching a mug of beer.

Jake stared straight ahead. "Yeah, sure, and it couldn't have come at a better time."

Harold didn't answer. He knew by that sarcastic remark that Jake didn't want conversation—he wanted company, a body to sit next to. They drank deep into their mugs and simultaneously wiped foam from their upper lips. They looked like a pair of lonely drifters setting the scene for a John Wayne western.

"Hey Barney," Harold called out. "How about two more beers?"

"Sure enough," Barney replied as he gave the glass he was drying an extra swirl with the dishtowel. He went to the tap. "Have you two heard any gossip lately?"

"Nope," Jake hurried to say. Although he thought Harold wouldn't say anything about the Nell problem, he wanted to emphasize to him that the subject was off-limits.

"Nope," Harold added.

They drank into their second beers.

Barney took the quarters from the wet counter and polished them dry with his apron. "Are you sure there ain't no gossip?"

123

"Yep," said Jake.

Barney persisted. "How about you, Harold? Do you know any gossip?"

"Nope."

Barney rung the quarters up on the cash register. "You two have a secret, I can tell, both of you are too quiet."

"Nope."

"Nope."

"Yep. You two know something." Barney pointed his eyes at Harold. "Why don't you tell me what it is?"

Harold straightened up on his stool. "Okay, I do have some gossip."

Jake suddenly sat up on his stool and turned to Harold with a sharp look.

A smile came on Harold's face. "The gossip, Barney, is that you know something you want to tell us, but you want us to tease it out of you. Right?"

"Maybe," Barney answered.

"No maybe's," Jake shouted back with the strength that two quick beers bring. "Get on with it for pity sakes, and don't tell us that the gossip is that we're going to have more rain."

Barney laughed. "That wouldn't be gossip—that would be rumor—there's a difference, you know."

Harold nodded.

Jake scoffed. "And what is that difference?" Anything, he worried, to steer Barney away from what would make a real juicy piece of gossip: he and Nell.

"Well," Barney hastened, "rumor is about something that is a possibility, and it is not told in a vicious way. Gossip is also a possibility, but it is meant to be vicious."

"Isn't that refreshing?" Harold said.

Jake relaxed. "All right, Barney, if gossip is vicious, then why do you want to tell us your gossip?"

"I used the wrong word. What I have is not gossip. It's rumor. In fact, it's something that is downright nice."

"Okay," said Harold.

"Okay," consented Jake. He perked up, it couldn't be about him if it was downright nice.

"Well," Barney hesitated briefly, "it's about you, Jake."

It was a good thing Jake was sitting down.

"Yeah? What about me?" Jake spoke as nonchalantly as he was able under a circumstance that he thought might explode him angrily into a million pieces.

"The town mouths say that you and Nell Swensen have something going."

Jake clutched his hand tight to the beer mug until his fingers blanched white. "So?"

Harold rearranged himself on his stool. "Which gossip mouths are you referring to, Barney?" Although Harold wanted to protect Jake, he was also eager to get the story. For Dolly, of course.

"You know, the usual ones. Agatha Anna Jensen and Fern Schmitbauer."

"That explains it then," Harold said.

"Yep, that sure explains it," Jake added, still trying to be nonchalant.

Harold pulled on his suspenders. "Dolly told me once that Agatha Anna and Fern keep their hearts beating and their mouths lubricated by talking about anything they can get their ears and eyes on. You know, we haven't had any real juicy gossip, rumor, or whatever you want to call it, since that cowboy from Montana came down here, romanced, and then left town with that young miss from the beauty parlor. That's been a few years ago, and those two biddies and their big flappy mouths are dry. They're latching onto every little thing."

"Then it ain't true?" Barney was disappointed.

"Listen, Barney," Harold continued, "I once noticed that Schmitbauer woman at the grocery store. Every fiber in her body is held together with strands of gossip. The one time I shopped for Dolly, I happened to be standing behind that gossiper in line. Her torso vibrates. Quick, short vibrations. That's because it is always ready to pick up even the tiniest remark by someone. She's a human radar device."

Barney shook his head. "They say Jake took Nell Swensen dining a few weeks ago. Hey, Jake, I think it's great if that's true. Somebody should romance that woman. That Nell is a real lovely lady."

"How do you know?" Harold asked. He noticed Jake staring into his empty mug, motionless, frozen with his nonchalance. How did Barney know? When had he seen her? The barbecue?

"I saw her at the barbecue and asked someone who she was. She was new to me. She seemed so quiet, and her smile, well, that's quite a smile she has, a really sweet smile. If I was older, I'd sure do more than just look at her."

Jake cleared his throat in place of screaming. Barney's description of her reminded him of their one date, and if Barney thought the same thoughts, then how many other men thought the same thoughts? How many other eligibles would take her to dinner? How many others already had? "It's only gossip. Don't pay any attention. Besides, she left town, and she's never coming back." Jake slid off the stool and turned his back on Barney and the gossip and went to the blue table and green chairs. "That bar stool is too high for my legs—they're falling asleep." He wished all of him would fall asleep. Forever.

Harold knew when Jake hurt, and Jake hurt now. This knowing came from a memory of Jake right after the birth of his and Dolly's daughter, when Jake pounded on their door and told how he had found his mother dead in front of the television. Jake had stood there, his arms hanging limp and his shoulders hunched over, reciting: "My Ma is dead." Today in Barney's Palace, Harold sensed that same hollowness about Jake, a cover-up for anguish, as he followed him to the blue table. He noticed how sunken-in Jake's body appeared, and he wished he could sink down with him. But Harold couldn't do that, so he did the next best thing. "Want another beer, buddy?"

"No, I just want to sit here for awhile."

"Everything's going to be all right."

126

Jake blew his nose although it didn't need blowing. It was a gesture of distraction. "You don't know about things like this. Everything's always gone okay in your life."

Harold nodded. "You're mostly right about that, but only mostly. My little girl suffered a lot with her first marriage, and Dolly suffered when we couldn't have anymore kids. And when they suffer, I suffer."

"Are you suffering now?"

Harold looked away. "No, I don't have anything to suffer about now, but I am concerned about yours. You assume too much. You assume you'll never see Nell again. Personally, I think she will come back and have a reasonable explanation for why she left."

Jake looked at his friend, the whites of his eyes burning red with anguish. "I feel like a child with a first grade love."

Harold looked back at Jake. "And you act like one too. You've got to think positive. How do you really know she's not coming back?"

"Because," Jake answered slowly, "because, when you have a lot to lose, you think the worst."

***

Jake liked to walk. When he was young and farmed the land, he enjoyed using his body for more than the planting and harvesting. After a long day's work, he would walk a mile or so along the oak-laden road near his house. While his hired farm hands sped away from their work, looking forward to an evening of not moving their bodies anymore than necessary, Jake would be walking.

He liked the firmness that hard ground gave to his feet. Some of the people in town, usually the tall women who appeared even taller when standing next to him in a store aisle, would snicker that maybe if he didn't walk so much, he wouldn't be so short. Harold knew about these snickers from the gossip Dolly brought home after her quilting sessions; he wished he hadn't stopped the story the Tollivers and Jake sent out about Jake suing the township for building the sidewalk too close to his hindquarters—his best friend was entitled to revenge.

127

Undaunted by his past mistake of interfering, however, Harold decided he might stop the critical tongues if he could get Jake to quit walking so much. "I don't know why, for pity sakes, you'd want to walk after you're all worn out from the field." But Jake's reply was final: "It's God's blessing. It's a freedom, a way I have to know I can walk away from the whole world."

Harold had laughed at that statement. "Jake, old buddy, I happen to know you'd never leave your farm." And then Jake had laughed back, "No, no, not the farm—just the world."

***

The rain stopped, but the gloom persisted. Early in the evening after Jake had tried and failed to find consolation from Harold and a number of beers, he left Barney's, drove home, went inside his barn, removed the pitchfork, and walked along the road with the implement by his side.

He had walked one half a mile before he realized what he had done. What was this mud-crusted tool doing in his hand? He didn't have anything to dig. It certainly didn't look like Nell. So why had he brought it along? Harold would have said 'for pity sakes.'

All by himself, he felt foolish. He wondered if his peculiar behavior was due to the remark Harold made at Barney's about how he thought Jake's recent busyness was due to he and Nell making out in the hay. That was a pretty dumb thing to say, Harold, even for you. Jake threw the pitchfork to the side of the road. He felt ridiculous; he was angry; his head filled with tears that wouldn't come out.

He stopped walking and leaned up against an oak. More thoughts came to him: maybe a bunch of acorns will fall all at once and hit me on the head and kill me. Or maybe some maniac will come along and stab me to death with the discarded pitchfork. Maybe the whole world will blow up in one more minute. Maybe Harold and Dolly are having a fight right now and will get divorced. Maybe then Harold will know what real misery is.

A small airplane flew low over Jake and tipped its wing.

Jake raised his arm in a return gesture and hoped the pilot hadn't seen the pitchfork. Surely he would know that Jake had thrown it there and was now slightly crazy, and the pilot would fly to the nearest insane asylum and report him. Then a bunch of men would come, strap him down, and fly him away. And all because he took his pitchfork for a walk and, worse yet, threw it away—sane farmers don't throw their pitchforks away.

The cloud-hidden sun suddenly dropped. Jake retrieved his pitchfork and walked back home; he hoped Harold and Dolly hadn't heard his thoughts; he felt ashamed for leaving Prince and Mitzie closeted in the pickup; he hoped the sun would show up better tomorrow; he wondered if he would notice.

***

The sun came out a little at a time, in spurts, and glowed through the Hallgrens' bay window and onto the kitchen table. As it reached its full early morning potential it spread across the room and touched the geraniums, the violets, and cactus.

Dolly leaned over the plants to enjoy the sun's warmth on her arms. She felt like a fresh bun on a Sunday buffet table, and it put her in a mood for asking her husband a nonsense question. She loved to do this, Harold always seemed so vulnerable when she was silly. "Harold, how many farmers do you think have cactus plants in their house?"

"Probably not any," he accommodated, "unless the Samuelsons do. They have everything else jammed in their house. Yes, the Samuelsons definitely have cactus—if not real ones, then artificial."

Dolly straightened up her body with the slow motions of beginning old age and tilted the slats on the window shutters to deflect some of the sun's sharp intensity. She dabbled the plants with water instead of giving them a good soak. This way, she could attend to them oftener—they were important to her, and she showed this by giving constant attention. One time Harold suggested she drench the plants once a week or less and forget about them in-between. He suggested that only once.

But this morning Dolly was like a kitten who needed to play, and Harold thought of how much Jake was missing by not having his own kitten. He loved Dolly even more when she was playful with conversation, and he always tried to keep her in this mood as long as he could with a few questions of his own. "Why don't you put me in a pot and spoil me like you do your plants?"

"I'll put you in a pot, all right, but not to spoil you, although I think we should breakfast on the lemon cream I made for you and Jake yesterday and which you said Jake was too depressed to come and eat. The sun is so bright and promising this morning that I think we should celebrate with a special treat. How's that sound?" Dolly opened the flour bin and scooped out a portion of its contents. "But let me get a cake in the oven first just in case Jake changes his mind and comes by later. How's that sound, old farmer?"

Harold poured himself a cup of coffee and chuckled over how his wife sometimes referred to him as old. He didn't mind because she was two years more than he. The vaporous steam and the intangible aroma of the hot liquid flowed into his entire being, its aura penetrating his senses, and at that moment, with Dolly vigorously stirring the sugared dough, he let out a gasp of joy. Jake was right—Harold Hallgren had been lucky with his life—and this morning he was lucky again.

"Wife," Harold exclaimed, "we're pretty lucky to have each other, don't you think?"

Dolly scrapped off the wooden spoon and poured the bowl of gelatinous dough into the cake pan. She had done this many times over the years, but Harold hadn't noticed it much before now.

"I mean," he continued, "I think we are suited to each other. Don't you think?"

Dolly put the pan into the oven, wiped her hands on her apron, and sat down at the table. "Would you pour me a cup of coffee now? Thank you."

Harold hurriedly got up. "We've been married forty years almost, and we still like each other and enjoy talking to each other. Don't you agree?" He poured the dark brown coffee into her 'MOM IS GREAT' mug.

"What are you getting at?" she asked.

"Nothing. I'm glad we're married. I feel sorry for Jake, that's all."

"I don't agree, Dear." Dolly smiled as she got her strength back from beating the cake batter.

Harold almost dropped the coffee pot. "You mean you're not glad we're married?"

Dolly took hold of her husband's rough, chapped hands. "Yes, Dear, I am. I meant that I don't feel sorry for Jake. Nell will be home soon."

Harold sat down. "Not according to Jake. He was really depressed at Barney's yesterday. He made me depressed. Especially when you decided I had no right to the pie because Jake was suppose to eat it with us. He thinks Nell is gone forever."

Dolly blew on the steaming coffee and sipped its heat with caution. She wasn't cautious, however, about what she said: "Nell will be back, and she will go right for Jake."

"What makes you know that?"

"I'm a virtuous woman and so is Nell Swensen. She knows a good man when she meets one. And she definitely has met one."

Harold leaned forward as though he had a secret to tell. "What does virtue have to do with it? She is taller than him."

"No, old man. Jake is shorter than Nell. He is short and mighty. You know what? The ladies at the quilting club think he's a John Wayne cut in half. He does have beautifully broad shoulders and such slim hips. They may poke fun of his height, but they sure don't smirk at his figure."

Harold had never thought of his friend as anything but short, so it took him a moment to answer. "I guess he is pretty much mostly muscle. His hair is that way too—all curly and thick. If it wasn't for that one pox scar on his forehead and his darn shortness, he'd cut a fancy figure, just like you said." He reached over and patted Dolly on her shoulder—he was so proud they had given Jake such a boost for his ego.

Dolly turned down the oven and shook her head in disapproval at both the negative part of the remark and the curtness of its tone. "I doubt if Nell has noticed the scar or cares about his unruly hair. I think she appreciates a man who doesn't tower over her like her brothers do. She is a very delicate and gentle woman, Harold. She needs a gentle man."

Harold laughed, he was still proud of himself. "Well, I don't know how gentle he is. He can get pretty roughhouse at times."

"He is gentle," Dolly insisted. "He moves gentle."

"Oh?" Harold raised his eyebrows. "Aren't I gentle? Don't I move gentle too?"

Dolly shook her head no again. "I love you, dear husband, but you do not move gentle when you walk."

"Yeah? Then how do I walk, Miss Priss?"

Dolly waited, then looked the other way. "Sweetheart, you walk like a lumberyard." She then cut quickly into the lemon cream.

***

While the Hallgrens pitter-pattered about virtue and cactus and walking and chickenpox scars, Jake was stretched out on his bed like a figure in a coffin, completely disinterested in getting up. He fantasized that as long as he lay still like that, the world would pass over him and take all the heartaches with it. His in particular.

Mitzie's meows were so loud, a passerby might think someone was torturing her. Prince nuzzled Jake's hand, then his face, then his entire body. Finally he had had enough neglect too and let out a sharp, loud bark right over his master's head.

Jake sat up straight like someone had inserted a hinge. That single bark was the one command Jake always obeyed. "All right, all right, give me a chance, you two can hold it a little longer."

Prince couldn't, and with his next bark and wag, something else came with it. Jake stumbled down the stairs with eyes half shut and pajama bottoms half open and two distressed animals in pursuit. He ran through the kitchen and jumped into the shed and out the back door. No farmer ever ran as fast from a tornado as Jake ran now. And no farmer was ever as shocked at the morning light as Jake was now. He staggered around barefoot on the cold ground until it and the sun's intensity finally woke him up.

Where had ugly yesterday gone? White clouds pranced around on a blue playground, glad to be back. For an instance, oh, how he loved this world. Oh, why wasn't Nell here right now, next to him in her bathrobe and sharing this massive wonder on display in the sky? Oh-oh, maybe she really was looking now—but with a tall, strapping man in Iowa.

Jake closed his pajama bottoms and went back to the kitchen. The room needed fresh paint. Was it worth his effort? Should he even consider painting it now, with Nell gone forever? Of course. She'll come back. The first chance he got he would go to Tolliver's and buy some bright, cheerful, Nell-type paint. He had to believe in something.

But for now, with the new sun, he wanted to walk around his land and chat with the young farmers who coddled the rich soil much like he had when he was young. He decided, again, he had made the right decision to retire because now he could share the love of the land with four new spirits named Leutzinger working it—working the pick of God's earth, Jake's earth.

Although Harold had almost abruptly stopped interest in what his renters did, Jake did not relinquish so easily. "I'll never completely let go," he had stated at the barbecue to the other retired farmers. "My body may have called it quits, but I'll always be in that land—I'll be in it and on it and around it. No, sirree, I'll never let go."

And every morning since his retirement, Jake walks a portion of his land; and every now and then when the

133

weather is especially beautiful or when his mood is especially unhappy, as it was last night, he will venture the oak-lined road in the early evening as well.

But now is now, and somewhere between his thoughts on walking and on Nell and on fresh paint, the phone rang.

***

Jake whistled long and very loud for Prince and Mitzie to return. He put two fingers in his mouth, closed his lips around them, and whistled. A train at its most shrill sound could not have been more intense.

Prince came loping back, panting of course, and happy. Mitzie was not with him, and she wasn't expected to be—there are things a cat must do that takes longer than what the master has to do—finding mice takes time, deciding on fresh paint does not.

"Come on, boy," Jake called to Prince. "Come on, we've been invited to breakfast."

The two arrived before Dolly had her special cake out of the oven. Prince jumped out behind Jake and ran over to Proudflesh who was licking his paw after another minor aggravation; they ran off together.

Jake opened the door without knocking and walked into the warmth of the Hallgren kitchen. He heard laughter and slow chatter bounce off the walls and into his being, a hubbub that seemed to always be there even when it was quiet. The brightness of the room and the slight lessening of Jake's dark mood was quite a contrast from yesterday's rainy darkness and slow turning movement of Barney's ceiling fan. Jake usually relished going to the saloon for sessions with Harold, but this morning he needed another atmosphere; this morning he needed Dolly's kitchen and her strong voice.

They ate the hot cake and drank the warm coffee and sighed when the lemon cream caressed their tongues and slid down to waiting stomachs; Dolly studied Jake's silent face, and she worried about it, and she hoped Harold was wrong about Jake's gloomy thoughts on Nell.

"More coffee?" she asked him.

"Sure," he replied. "Thank you." Then Jake almost ran to beat Dolly to the coffee pot. "Excuse me, Mrs. Hallgren, I should be waiting on you." He poured for Dolly and himself.

"Hey," Harold exclaimed, "what the heck is going on here? My cup is more empty than anyone's. And what is this 'Mrs. Hallgren' stuff? You've never been formal before. Am I going to be Mr. Hallgren from now on, Mr. Blackburn?"

Dolly shook her head. "Dear, when someone calls someone in a formal way, like Mr. or Mrs., it sometimes means affection and respect. It's sort of an acknowledgement of one's worth."

Harold turned to Jake. "Then it's Miss Swensen?"

Jake turned red.

"Harold," Dolly stomped with her voice, "what's got into you? It's none of our business."

"It's not? Well, I think it is. I'm sick and tired of Jake glooming around here. Gloom, gloom, gloom. He comes to breakfast but doesn't speak except for this Mr. and Mrs. stuff." Harold put his hands flat on the table. "Put it out right here, buddy, right here on the table. I want all that gloom on the table now."

Jake got up. He felt hot, and his chest billowed slightly in and out. He started to pace back and forth in front of the sink.

Harold beckoned with his hand, motioning for Jake to come over to him. "Come on, come on, out with it. Let it out, buddy, don't keep it all to yourself. You're hurting."

Jake came over and yanked out a chair next to Harold; he sat down hard and clenched his teeth, straining the words through: "Are you referring to my problem with Nell?"

Harold stood up and hovered even more than usual over his friend. "Well, sweetheart, I'm not referring to Aunt Sarah down the lane. You know darn well who I mean."

Jake clenched even more. "This really isn't the place for it. This is just between you and me—Dolly doesn't have to be bored by my problem. I am embarrassed."

Harold chortled. "Oh, come on now. You know perfectly

well that anything between you and me is always and only between you and me—and Dolly."

"Take it easy." Dolly went to the sink and ran hot water for the dishes. She hoped her husband would shut-up for now.

"No, I won't take it easy. I'm mad at both of you. My wife tells me my best friend has nothing to worry about, and my best friend tells me his life is over. What's going on here anyway?"

Dolly turned around, ignoring the foamy soapsuds running down her arms and dripping onto the floor. "What do you mean— Jake thinks his life is over? I figure it's just begun." She talked as though Jake were not there and she and Harold were merely having a conversational spat.

But Jake was there. "Oh?" he shouted. "Oh?" he repeated as he walked toward the door. "How can a romance that ended before it started be called the beginning of anything?" He was usually tight-lipped, but now he carried on like the Hallgrens weren't there either. "Unless it's the beginning of the end. Sure, that's it. You were right, Dolly, you usually are— it's the beginning all right, of the end."

Dolly's voice rose. "I don't understand you, Jake. Nell has shown every indication to me that she is definitely interested in you. What more do you expect?"

"Indications? What indications?" Jake mocked. Dolly was unaware that Jake was not looking for indications. He was looking for Nell herself, not an indication. He was looking for her at the bus station, he was looking for her in a postcard, he was looking for her to return, he was looking for her to marry him. Today. Any day. Tomorrow. He was looking for one bird in the hand, not the two or more in the bush.

Dolly, nevertheless, thought indications were sufficient. "Her piano."

"What piano?" Jake returned to the table and sat down like a little boy ready to receive a treat. He was momentarily satisfied with an indication.

Dolly dried her hands and arms and poured more coffee.

"Hasn't she told you anything about herself?"

Jake was silent.

"Well," Dolly lowered her voice, "I guess I've been with her more than you have. The bridge club. We women talk, you know. Some of the bridge players can get more information out of a person than a news reporter. I was at the same table as Nell on her first bridge party. I heard a lot."

"Yeah, yeah," Harold egged on, an eagerness for gossip that Dolly responded to with a sharp look of disapproval.

She turned to Jake and softened her voice even more. "I figured you knew. I figured you knew as much or more than I do."

"Yeah, old buddy, how about that?" Harold interrupted, ignoring another of Dolly's facial reprimands. "What did you two talk about on your date if it wasn't about each other?"

Jake picked up his coffee; he cleared his throat; he was ready for that big-deal indication. "What do you know, Dolly?"

"I know why she went to Iowa and probably why no one has heard from her. She's busy arranging to get her piano shipped here. She's also saying goodbye to Iowa because I have a feeling she wasn't ready to say goodbye when she moved. You see, Jake, she almost as much as announced she might move out on her brothers and take an apartment in town. This town."

Jake stood up as though he had been given a football and needed to run with it. "You mean she really is coming back?"

Dolly patted Jake on his shoulder. "I'll tell you everything. I had invited Nell to linger awhile after her first bridge game with the girls so we could get better acquainted. It's surprising how much information a person can get from someone when an extra cup of coffee is involved. Anyway, she told me that even though George was a peach of a man to keep house for, she couldn't stand living with the twins. She couldn't stand it when they were children together, and she still couldn't. She and George took them in, you know, only because the twins went slightly crazy over their wives' deaths and they didn't want their family name to be tarnished by their grieving brothers' sometimes unsavory actions.

Jake felt weak again. "So she hates her brothers. I hated mine. But how does that tell me that she will come back? Maybe she wants to get far, far away from them, like to Iowa."

Dolly sighed, just as she sighed many times years ago when her young daughter asked the same question over and over. "Because at the last bridge party she didn't say anything about staying in Iowa. She indicated she only wanted her piano"— there was that indication word again. "She asked if anyone knew of an apartment in town, our town I'm sure, where she could live and do housekeeping and teach piano. She'll need to work, that's all she's ever known."

Harold slammed his hand on the table. "See, buddy, see? Didn't I tell you?"

Jake smiled. "Excuse me, Dolly, but Harold, you're a liar— you didn't tell me a thing. Your caring wife did, you liar, excuse me again, Dolly."

Dolly went back to the sink and the soapsuds. "My goodness, I would have told you sooner, but I figured you knew."

Harold looked at Dolly and made a face of reprimand just like she had done earlier to him. He made sure her back was to him though. "I told you he was down and out and in the dumps, but no, you kept saying there was no way he could be. You never told me any stuff about an apartment and a piano. Why didn't you tell me? I tell you everything."

Dolly turned around with the soapsuds again. "Because Nell confided in me, it's as simple as that. The only reason I said anything now is because I thought Jake knew and he didn't and he should. Anyone who cares as much as he does for someone should know things."

Jake rasped amen as Dolly continued. "Although it's been a long time since I've been courted, I do remember that when a man is interested in you, you don't tell him everything."

"Oh, is that so?" Harold commanded.

Dolly nodded. "That's so. At least not everything of any importance. I guess a woman is afraid she might scare the suitor away if she talks of serious matters in her life."

"That's awful," Jake replied. "I wonder if that's why no girl would have a second date with me, or even a first? I tend to not say much, and if the woman doesn't say much, then nothing gets said. Do you suppose that's why women have shied away from me—because nothing important ever got said? Do you suppose it was that, and not my shortness?"

Dolly and Harold didn't answer. Proudflesh barked to come in, Prince pawed at the screen. Jake didn't say anything anymore either except that maybe Harold should take off the screen door and put on the storm. Harold said something about changing his door after Jake changed his own darn door. Jake then waited for Dolly to say something smart about the possibility that his shortness was not the thing that kept women away, but she didn't. So he decided to settle for her 'indications' as he signaled to Prince, said thank you, and left.

***

Jake now had a new worry. It wasn't as bad as the old worry of giving up on Nell completely, but it wasn't that much better.

He mulled it over and over on his way home from the Hallgrens that morning. Once in awhile he interrupted his mulling to stroke Prince under the chin, which cheered up Prince, but didn't do much for him.

That indication, that hint Dolly spoke of: the apple pie. Did it really and honestly and truly mean that Nell was interested in him? Maybe she made a lot of apple pies for a lot of men. What if their first date didn't mean anything special to her? She skipped town afterwards. Right afterwards. Not even a postcard.

On the other hand, Jake continued with his brooding, maybe she thinks I'm not interested in her. After all, I didn't insist on why she was going away or when she would be back. I didn't push anything, just went along with the entire episode as though it was another ho-hum supper date in my life. She probably thinks I date a lot of women and consequently don't care how long one of them will be gone.

Jake slowly curved the pickup onto his driveway. There was Mitzie with her usual no-expression stare waiting for him to feel guilty for leaving her behind. Jake returned her look with his own no-expression stare—he also had been left behind. He slowed the vehicle even more, rolled down the window, and Mitzie leaped onto the steering wheel, then his lap, and finally next to Prince; she licked her paw as if to say that she was good at jumping through small openings and what a bore it was. Jake wished he had her confidence.

Then, like in a spell, he kept the pickup moving until he had circled the driveway and was headed back to the Hallgrens. This time he would ask Harold to demand that Dolly tell him everything. Everything. She had held back on information before, and she was probably holding back again.

Harold was in the barn with Brie, not to milk her, but to give her sleek body a few affectionate slaps and to put down more unneeded hay. Harold's feelings for Brie and the barn were akin to Jake's feelings for the land. Jake never paid any attention to this fact, he was always too involved with his own passion, so when he returned to further interrogate his friend about Nell, he expected him to still be in the kitchen.

Only Dolly was there, sweeping up Proudflesh's hair into her tiny dustpan.

"Hi, Dolly," Jake said casually as though he always came back immediately after he left.

Dolly was just as casual, she was used to Jake in her kitchen. "Why is it that it's always the kids and the pets that make the messes in a house?" Dolly answered not caring it was Jake there instead of Harold. She walked past him and emptied the dustpan into the slight breeze outside.

Jake folded his arms across his chest, he was on a mission. His words came out in staccato fashion. "I guess Harold is not here. Where did he go? Is he in the bathroom?"

"He's out walking Brie to the backyard and talking too I'm sure. You know how he loves that cow. Can I help you?"

"Well ..." Jake looked out the window and didn't see Harold and Brie outside, and he would have then gone and looked in the barn, but Dolly seemed so endearing at that moment, so full of help and comfort.

"Come on, Jake, let me help. It's about Nell, isn't it?"

"Yes."

"You seem worried. I thought you would be relieved to hear about the piano and her wanting to leave her brothers."

Jake shook his head no. "Has Nell ever talked about me to your bridge club?" If he had ever in his life taken the time to not believe he was so bold to ask such a blunt question, this would have been the time.

Dolly hung up the broom and dustpan. "Why would she talk about you? You just had your first date."

"Well, I mean, did she say anything about me in general? She did know I existed before our date. She didn't go out with a complete stranger, you know."

"More coffee?"

"No thank you. Dolly, I want information. I came here to ask Harold to go to Barney's so I could ask him to ask you for more information. I'm embarrassed about this whole thing, but I can't help it. I want to do everything in my power to win Nell over, but don't tell anybody. Please."

Dolly sat down and told Jake to do the same. "I would never gossip about you. Your secret is my secret—except for Harold. I tell him and he tells me and you know about that." She patted Jake's hand. "But I would never tell the bridge club anything about people close to me. Harold is close to me, and all my complaints about him go into the sink when I wash dishes. The same for you. You're close to me."

Jake thought he might cry. Dolly continued. "Nell has never talked about you or any man, but remember, she's new to the club, and I don't always play at the same table as she."

By now Jake no longer felt he might cry, but he should have, to relieve his heavy feeling because his thoughts were getting dark again. "I bet she thinks I'm better than nothing, huh?"

Dolly smiled. "Jake. Doggone it. You and Nell haven't been together long enough to get serious. What's the rush?

Besides, don't assume that a woman always feels she needs a man in her life. If Nell goes out with you, it's not necessarily because she will settle for any man." She felt ashamed of her words. It was easy to comfort Jake in such an unconcerned way, but she knew better. She knew that a lot of times when a man and woman meet they know right away that's it. She wished she could have said something that would definitely assure him. Was there such a thing?

Jake felt as bad about Dolly's remarks as she did. "Sixty years old is my rush. I'm sixty years old. Besides, I don't want to lose her to someone else. You say that all women don't want to get married. Then how come they all do? There are other single men out there, you know, and when they find out Nell will date a man shorter than she, they'll surround her like sassy geese."

Dolly tried to smile. "I don't mean to be so blunt, but first of all, all women do not want to get married. You know better than that, although I guess you can assume for now if it will help—that when a woman accepts a date she is interested in a possible marriage. Tell me something ... what is it about Nell that has you so fired up and so sad at the same time?"

Jake leaned back in his chair; he looked puzzled. "Well, why, well ... it's her. It's just plain her. Her everything."

Dolly tilted her head back in a soft laugh and sparkled her eyes to Jake. "You are in love, you are certainly in love." Then she became quiet and took Jake's hand. "Hold on to that love, and she will sense that. She will realize, if she doesn't already, there is something you have that no taller man has for her."

"You mean I can love her but not tell her?" He was like a little boy asking for direction.

"Not until you're fairly certain she loves you also. Don't rush her, Jake, please don't. She'll run. She says she has never married and maybe that's why. Your feelings for her will get through merely by your being there. Love kind of spreads out—like a halo over a head. Give her a chance to respond to it without any shoving."

"Is that how Harold courted you?"

"No, that's how I courted Harold."

They both laughed, a relief had come, and Jake forgot how he had wanted to cry just a few minutes before.

Harold came in from Brie and stumbled against the milk pail which he bawled out for being in the way when he didn't need it. He blew his nose and came into the kitchen.

"Back again?" Harold pretended to be surprised. He knew when his friend got onto a subject, he wouldn't let it rest until it was all talked out, which it never was. He knew the subject of Nell would never end, at least not until she either married Jake or someone else. And maybe not then.

Jake nodded. "You knew I'd be back. There's nothing new about me. I'm still your nuisance."

Harold laughed. "No you're not, you've never been that, but I do get a kick out of you. Why don't we go to Barney's and hash over how to get you a wife. Then you'll have someone in your own kitchen. Like I do."

Jake looked over at Dolly. She winked, and Jake bowed. "All right, sir, Mr. Hallgren, companion, advisor, let's go." His body stood erect as he walked out of the kitchen like a soldier going to battle; and he had no idea of the battle that was really out there.

***

Barney was decorating his saloon with Halloween stuff when the pair walked in. "Hey," he called to them, "hey, do you think this skeleton is a little too much?" The corpse, made of what looked like real bone, rattled as Barney hung it on the coat rack.

"I didn't even notice," Jake said.

Barney stepped back and looked at the scary addition to his saloon. "How about you, Harold, what do you think?"

"I think it's in poor taste." Harold evidently had forgotten his childhood when he thought a skeleton at Halloween was the greatest thing to hang anywhere.

"What? What'd you mean?" Barney muddled.

"Jake and I want some beer. Got anything else today besides pretzels?"

"What do you mean, it's in poor taste?"

Harold took off his jacket. "I mean this is no place for childish antics. What if one of your customers just lost a loved one or even a pet?"

Jake put his hands inside his jeans pockets. The last thing on his mind was concern for someone else now. He felt gloomy again. He didn't care if Barney's feelings were hurt or if some customer had just lost a loved one. All he cared about was Nell and where in the dang, darn, blast was she anyway? He did, however and out of habit, muster up a compromise: "Come on Harold, let's quit this fuss over those unimportant bones. It looks fine, Barney. Keep that dumb skeleton there, anybody who has just had a death in the family will probably not come to a public place anyway. Not to this one I should hope."

Harold frowned. What happened to Jake's good mood? What had happened to his own mood? Jake used to be happy all the time, but now it was happy, unhappy, happy, unhappy. "How about something stronger than beer, buddy?"

There came that feeling to cry again. Jake's throat rasped, his eyes closed. Oh, if only this misery would end.

"Come on, Jake, let it out." Harold went to the farthest corner of the room. "Here's a table as good as the one Dolly and I have at home—we'll sit here to talk things over. Just let it out here on this table," and Harold placed the palm of his hand gently on the firm green top.

Jake sat down. "Keep it down, please, I don't want everybody in town to know."

Harold went to the counter for the fresh beers Barney had just drawn while he was eyeing them for possible news. "Come on, Jake old buddy, we're alone now. Barney can't hear from way over there."

Jake swallowed the cold beer slowly because he had to think slowly about what to say. Finally. "Since Nell left, I have been homesick."

"Huh?" was Harold's wise reply.

Jake pushed his beer aside. "I said that I feel homesick."

144

"Okay," Harold conceded. "Okay."

"You have probably never felt homesick. You are probably just laughing yourself to death right now."

"Oh yeah? I do so feel homesick now and then. Sometimes when I stay at Barney's too long, I miss Dolly and Proudflesh and my warm bright kitchen. The bedroom too, of course."

"Okay then, you know how it feels. But you can cure yourself by going home. I can't. Nell isn't in my home. She's in Iowa."

"I'm aware of that, buddy. Someday she'll be in your home." Harold hesitated while he thought of something Dolly would say. "Just have faith." There, that ought to do it.

Jake stared straight ahead. "In just one short date, she established a home for me, a home in my heart. Now, how much more cornball can you get? I guess when you're young, you're romantic, and when you're old, you're cornball. But I don't care—just don't talk about this to anyone else."

Harold reached for the basket of pretzels at the next table. "You are right. It's getting too much cornball. Let's talk about something else for a change. I think you dwell too much."

Jake clenched his fists. "I'm going to her brothers again. I'll ask George for a phone number I can call. I'll get this misery over with, and if it doesn't work out, I can always shoot myself."

Harold snapped a large pretzel in half. Its sharp crack made Jake jump. "That's what gunshots sound like, kiddo, are you sure you want to do that to yourself?"

Jake smiled. "No, of course not, at least not until after Prince and Mitzie die. They'd be heartbroken."

"Me too."

Barney came to their private table and sat down. "Business is sure slow. Wait till the hunting season gets going and every drifter from the city comes to brag about their expert shooting. I'll just rest here with you two until it starts."

"So," Harold shifted sideways to accommodate Barney's

presence. "So, Barn, what's new with you?"

"I have more gossip, or should I say rumor?"

Jake turned away. He supposed Barney would riddle his patience with questions about him and Nell.

Harold finished his beer. "Gossip is okay if it's new. Got any new rumors?"

Barney looked down and nodded his head like a parent whose child had just brought home all F's. "It's about those kids, you know, the ones who come in after school to talk to me over a bottle of orange soda pop."

Jake turned to face Barney. "You mean Billy and Angela? The Charmley kids?"

"Yeah. Anyway, they have been coming in oftener and staying longer. They never say much except thank you for the soda. Billy sweeps the floor to pay for it. Anyway, I finally asked them if they weren't expected at home. Nope, the boy answers me. But the town gossips say there is trouble in their house. Big trouble."

Jake sat up straight. He remembered what Dolly had said about the kids' parents having such awful fights. But he had pushed that rumor aside after Billy had bicycled over to his farm one afternoon after school to talk about things that kids talk about. "They're such nice children—who would ever think their parents are bad? I thought the reason they didn't go home right after school was because their parents both work, and not because it is unpleasant."

Barney shook his head. "We tend to forget about irksome things, don't we? I agree, when the two are around here, I figure everything is okay. But it's not. There's big trouble in that house. Getting bigger. The little girl used to smile a lot. Now she just drinks her soda and stares straight ahead— and at nothing that I can figure."

"Isn't that something," Harold said. "The kids have never come to Dolly and me, so I don't really know who you're talking about, although I do know there are a lot of sad children in the world today."

"Their parents beat each other up," Barney leaned back on

146

his chair, settling in like a customer. "The kids seem to seek out single people, Harold, they probably avoid couples because they might think that couples means fighting. I bet that's why they haven't come around to you."

"I like to think only city folk beat up on each other, what with all that congestion and noise that wears on one's nerves," Harold said. "So what city are they from? Omaha?"

"Denver," was Barney's reply. But it didn't matter where the Charmleys were from because something new to think about had suddenly come into the saloon, mixing in with the beer and pretzels and worried concern over Nell.

This abrupt something hovered over Jake and then spread over his thoughts of Nell until it covered her up; the concern over the boy and girl from Denver became important now. Gossip can sometimes do that. It can distract from one's own problems, although briefly, and give the worrier another direction. Gossip, one could then suppose, is not always a bad thing.

At least not in Jake's present situation, where the Billy and Angela eye-opener worked to bring his mind away from his own sadness and onto someone else's. Jake wondered if there was another kind of abuse besides beating because there was no signs of the kids being beaten that he noticed. He wondered if neglect could be considered an abuse. According to Barney's latest description, the children needed attention and love—when there are beatings in the home, healthy love is not there.

Ignored. The kids were most likely ignored. He knew what feeling ignored was like; he also knew what feeling love is like. He had been loved by his parents, and it was this basic love that made life tolerable for him when his pretty blond girlfriend of first grade chose to ignore him. In between his swallows of beer and chitchat with Harold and Barney, this wise thought of basic love came to him, and it resulted in a pang of concern for the brother and sister.

Jake got up and went to the bar. "Mind if I draw my own?" he said as he replenished his mug.

147

"Nope," Barney replied. "I'm wondering too much about what is really wrong with those bad characters from Denver to think about drawing beer right now." He sat there, still, like this would indeed bring the answer to Billy and Angela's problem.

Harold brought his mug to Jake for another beer as though more beer would solve the problem. "Why don't you ask the kids about their home life, Barney? You're not shy about other peoples business."

Barney looked startled. "What do you mean, ask them? I may not be shy about wanting to know everything that goes on, but I don't want to come right out and ask. Especially two little kids, for crying out loud. Besides, I don't necessarily want to get involved, unless of course, they are being beaten, which they aren't."

Jake came back with the beers. "I'll ask them. The next time I see them, I'll ask. Maybe they need some help. I can help." His twinge of concern for the children relieved his pain of concern over Nell, and he felt a little more comfortable with life again.

The saloon door opened with three customers and Barney went back to the bar.

Jake looked at Harold. "Do you suppose there are some people with bigger problems than mine?"

"There sure are, there sure are. And now, have you changed your mind about shooting yourself?"

There came a sudden puzzled hush into the room. Then Jake almost shouted. "Oh dear God, Harold, you know I really wouldn't do that."

"No, buddy, no. I really don't know that."

***

They cut short their stay at Barney's. Jake wanted to get home in case the children came by. "If those kids come in here, send them to my place, will you Barn?"

Harold took a deep sigh of relief. Thank goodness Jake is starting to think of someone besides himself and Nell and her blankety-blank trip to Iowa. Maybe those three kids can help each other. He laughed. Yes, there were indeed three kids involved here—Jake was surely one of them.

"What's the joke?" Jake asked.

"There's no joke. I don't only laugh when something is funny. Sometimes I laugh when I'm happy."

"Oh," Jake replied, "I'll have to remember that."

***

Harold kicked at the leaves that had started to fall; he slowly opened the shed door and went into the kitchen; he heard the television and knew Dolly was sitting in front of her four o'clock quiz show. He hated quiz programs, the questions were too fast and answers sometimes even faster. Dolly had told him once that if he would listen to the shows, he would learn. "You don't have to know the answers, dear old man, nobody in the world will know you don't know." But Harold couldn't stand himself knowing that he didn't know.

He sat down in his chair next to Dolly who only glanced briefly at him while she continued to give all attention to the questions and answers. Then her concentration wandered. Why is he sitting here? He never sits here during a quiz show. He may not be interested in a movie she would pick for evening viewing, but he would sit there anyway and read a magazine or make remarks or give Proudflesh a belly rub; but the minute a quiz came on, he would leave and feisty around with his dog in the kitchen or go to the barn and slap Brie on her hind side and ask her how things were. So why was he here now?

Dolly leaned forward and turned off the set in the middle of a question on somebody's wedding in the White House. "Okay, dear, what is it? What's wrong?"

"Nothing."

"Come on, husband Harold, I turned off my quiz program, and I expect an answer now."

"Wife Dolly, there's nothing wrong. Jake found something else to worry about now, so let's not worry about his problem with Nell's vacation for awhile and start to think about his other problem."

149

Dolly sighed with concern. "We don't need quiz shows to be puzzled about—we have Jake. That is what you want to discuss, isn't it?"

"Yeah." Harold shifted sideways to his wife. "Jake is heartbroken, I think you know that, and we can't imagine how he feels, so we shouldn't criticize. Besides him, there are now two kids whose parents ignore them—that's Jake's new problem—and we can't imagine what those kids feel either. We're lucky, you know, we always have been."

Dolly nodded in agreement. "But what are you getting at?"

"I mean, are we always going to be this lucky? I don't mind dying, but I don't want you to die."

"I'll do as I please." Dolly picked up her knitting.

"Don't joke, Mama."

Dolly put down her knitting and laughed a little. "Do you remember when we were first married and absolutely blind with love, and how we vowed, I mean really positively vowed, that neither of us would marry again if one of us would die?"

"Oh dear God, we loved each other, didn't we?" Harold smiled at the memory of their first years alone before their daughter was born.

"We still do, sweetheart, but it's different. Our world has gotten bigger. Our little girl grew up, and then the grandchildren came along, and they all helped us realize there are other things on this earth besides two people clinging to each other for dear life like we have a tendency to do."

"There is a lot more," Harold agreed. "But let's not talk about that now. Let's talk about what you will do if I die first, which I had better do."

Dolly mulled over their promise of never marrying again. Over the years, after their first thrust of romantic love had simmered down to a more practical relationship of thoughtful considerations, they had talked about a possible situation where there would be no Harold or no Dolly. They had dismissed the thought then, but Dolly realized they had better not dismiss it now.

"What would you want me to do?" she asked quietly.

"I want you to do whatever would make you happy. So you'll probably have to get married again. That is what I would want you to do."

Dolly picked up her knitting, balanced a needle on each thigh, lifted up her chin, and turned to Harold as if to make an official announcement. "Okay, dear, I will marry again if you want me to, but that wouldn't be the first thing I'd do."

"Oh?" Harold wondered. "What is the first thing you'd do?"

"I would travel around the world."

Harold frowned. "What do you mean, you would travel around the world? I don't want you ending up with some foreigner."

Dolly tilted her head. "You mean you don't want a sheik eating at our kitchen table?"

Harold grabbed his pipe and headed toward the kitchen. He turned around at the doorway and pointed a finger at her. "Maybe you'd better not get married again—I'll just have to take good care of myself."

Dolly turned the television back on to the final quiz questions, but she could still hear the shed door slam hard. She mulled again over the remarriage topic and decided the idea should be dismissed forever.

***

Jake let Prince and Mitzie out of the pickup—he had returned them to their place up-front—and looked up the road. Maybe the children would come this afternoon, it was about time for school to let out.

He decided to walk down the road for about fifteen minutes and hoped they would be coming on Billy's bicycle by the time he returned. They hadn't come, so he called Barney.

"Hi, Barney," Jake shouted over the phone as though the saloon owner was hard of hearing.

"Yeah? Who's this? Jake?"

"Yeah, say, are those kids at your place yet?"

"They're drinking their orange pop like good children,"

Barney laughed.

Jake was taken aback. That Barney could really be weird at times.

"Say, Barney, if you can quit laughing, would you ask them to come over to my place?"

"What for?"

"To say hello. Maybe they need somebody to talk to."

"They can talk to me, but they're not. If you want somebody to talk to, you'll have to look somewhere else."

"Oh? And are you their protector? Get Billy on the phone for me."

"Sure, Jake, sure. But if you could see these two sitting here at the table like soldiers with the soda pop in front of them, you'd laugh too."

Jake doubted that. "Just get me Billy on the line, will you please?"

Barney left the phone, and all Jake could hear was silence. He didn't even hear Barney call to Billy. For pity sakes, Barney acts like the kids belong to him, which is sure nervy considering he didn't want to get involved. Weird, weird, that Barney is so weird.

Barney came back to the phone. "They're gone, Jake. I told them you wanted to see them, and they got off their chairs and walked out. No, they ran out, and the boy was smiling."

Jake grunted. Barney wasn't so weird after all. Good old Barney, you could always count on him. "Hey, Barn, thanks. Thanks."

***

The sun broke out in a late afternoon effort to claim the diminishing day. Jake could see the reflection of the steel bicycle as Billy, with Angela on the bar seat behind, pedaled as fast as he could. The boy stood up on the pedals and bore down hard, although he needn't have. Jake would be there this time. Jake even called them at Barney's, that must mean something special because he had never been called on the phone before. Billy didn't know what a command performance was, but he was able to react to it. His speed picked up, it was especially helpful to have a lightweight sister and level ground most of the way. The features of the mountain bicycle gave him the added strength he needed as his agile body glided it around the curves with Evel Knievel determination and dexterity. The bike was the one luxury the Charmleys afforded their children—it meant they wouldn't have to accompany them to school or extra events.

"Hi, kids."

Billy skidded to a stop and waited for his sister to awkwardly maneuver her legs off the bike. The pair squinted their faces into the day's remaining sun and hesitantly came over to Jake. The speed that Billy used to get to Jake's farm and the speed he used to walk to where Jake was standing was like a well greased wheel, but that now at confrontation, had suddenly lost all its lubricant. Inside himself, Jake felt the same way.

"Hi."

"Hi."

They stood there, the three of them, like rejects in a toy factory, looking at each other and bashfully saying hello a few more times.

"How are you two kids today?"

"Fine."

"How would you like to be finer? How about a big glass of ice cold milk from a real cow and some cookies from a real oven?" Jake had never before offered a treat to a child, except at Halloween when they demanded it, and it made him feel good to do so. Besides, these children needed something healthy in them, something other than that orange soda pop. It also gave him a chance to get rid of Brie's excess supply before it spoiled.

Billy's and Angela's faces really brightened now. The three went into the kitchen. The children stopped just inside the room, motionless except for their heads which surveyed the surroundings.

"Come on, come on," Jake urged. "Pull out a chair. There

are cookies in that pig jar right over there on the counter next to the stove. See it?" He pulled the jug of milk from the refrigerator, grabbed two glasses from the cupboard, and set it all down on the table.

Billy removed the pig's head and handed one cookie to his sister. He took one for himself and offered a third to Jake who declined with his left hand as he poured the glasses full with his right in an easy manner that looked like he did this all the time.

"Now, this is what's good for you, not that soda pop. You kids have to quit drinking that stuff all the time. Tell Barney to lay off it. You can come here for milk instead." Jake didn't want to yank the children away from Barney, even though Barney didn't want to get involved, but he was tired of hearing that all they did at the saloon was drink orange pop. "Nevermind," he continued, "I'll speak to Barney about the pop—he's a good man, a good man, let's not hurt his feelings."

Billy nodded. "And these are good cookies, sir. Did you bake them?"

Jake smiled. "No, Dolly gives them to me. She's Harold's wife. You've seen Harold before, haven't you? He's always with me at Barney's. Harold Hallgren. He's a good man too most of the time."

The children gulped the milk, and Billy wiped his mouth with his rumpled sleeve. "We don't know many people around here," he said. "Our folks work a lot."

The corners of Angela's mouth turned down on that remark.

Jake noticed both the sleeve and the turned-down mouth. He felt awkward, he had never seen, close up, such ragamuffins as these two appeared. Their necks were soiled, not smudged like it had happened recently, and Angela's hair barrette hung loose in amongst tangled hair. Their clothing ill-fitted them, and their shoes were scuffed beyond recognition of the original color.

He handed them another cookie and decided the next time they came, he would lead them to the sink to wash their hands first. "So," he continued, "what kind of chores do you kids do at home?" He thought another cookie and some conversation would cheer them up, but Angela's mouth went down further. Please don't cry, Jake urged to himself, I'll give you all the cookies in the world, but please don't cry.

Billy moved closer to his sister, and her face lightened up a little. "We make supper and do the dishes."

Jake sat back in amazement. Their clothing and Angela's sadness was enough for his mind to adjust to, but now the addition of making supper was beyond his knowledge of what goes on in other worlds. "You make the supper? Your mother must be very busy."

"Yeah," Billy answered. "Real busy. We don't see much of her, or our father either."

Jake poured more milk. He didn't care if he spoiled their appetite for supper, which he probably wouldn't because by the time they got the meal on the table, they'd be hungry again. Also, the milk would be a substitute mother. "Oh well," he tried to talk as casual as possible under the circumstance of his shock, "at least you see them at eating time."

Angela shook her head, almost in anger, and spoke for the first time. "No we don't, we ..." and she stopped when Billy nudged her under the table.

Jake looked at one child and then the other. "Let her talk, Billy, let her talk and tell what she wants to." But Angela shook her head and trembling, bit into the cookie.

Billy stood up, he evidently needed to do that to get the courage to explain. "Okay, sir, the truth is we eat supper alone. Our folks work until six or seven or eight, and we're too hungry to wait."

Jake felt dumbfounded on that one. He looked at Billy like one looks at someone who has said something hard to believe. Six or seven or eight? What kind of jobs did they have, and where? The next county? And if so, why didn't they live there? His own parents would never have made him prepare supper, and then eat it alone. The most his mother had ever asked of him was to set the table and help dry the dishes, and then not always. She was there all the time, she never went away at supper time, and supper was always at six o'clock. None of the kids he grew up with made their own supper or ate alone. He knew children like Billy and Angela existed, but not in Boone County, Nebraska, unless, oh my, the orphanage also housed kids whose parents had beaten them.

He visualized Billy and Angela at their kitchen table, alone, by themselves, just the two, every night, no big people around like there is suppose to be. Even parents who work far from home manage to have at least one of them there for supper. The more Jake visualized no parents at home, the more he felt that echo of aloneness he experienced sometimes in the evening, but at least that feeling waited until he was grown up.

"You kids are joking me, aren't you?" He tried to smile.

"Nope. No, sir."

He hoped they had been teasing, even in the light of their neglected physical appearances, he thought they might be fibbing about their supper time situation.

"They go drinking after work," Billy added to what Jake considered to be enough amazement already. "They go someplace in the town next to us and sometimes in the town next to that one. It all depends, sir."

Jake didn't ask what it depended on. "Why don't you call me Jake instead of sir? I don't like being called sir, never call a farmer 'sir'. Not in this part of the country anyway."

"All right."

"My full name is Jacob Blackburn, but I go by Jake."

"All right."

All right? That was as bad as 'sir'. Jake began to sense he wasn't really here, that maybe this was the Twilight Zone like on television awhile back. He plain and simply didn't know what to say to two children who were on their own. He felt almost put down. Billy and Angela were like adults. All they needed were jobs to buy food and pay rent and they would be equal to him. Well, almost equal—they did need to learn how to clean themselves up a bit.

156

"Do you two sit at the table when your folks eat even if it is later?" Jake couldn't reconcile himself to their unusual existence.

"No." Angela's voice was loud and strong this time. "We're not allowed."

Jake sat back. He had been slapped again. "You mean they don't want you there?"

"Nope," Billy confirmed. "Nope, sir ... Jake."

Jake scratched his head, and his fingers got tangled in the mass of curliness which was not unlike the mental tangles in his brain over what he considered two very deprived children. He had heard and absorbed all he could at this time. He needed to tell Harold and Dolly. Maybe they would have something wise to say. Of course they would.

"I want you kids to feel free to come here anytime you want. There will always be milk and cookies." This invitation was all Jake could handle at this moment. He had never met a neglected or abused child before, he had never seen them in the flesh and blood. And even though he had given milk and cookies to these two flesh and bloods sitting at his kitchen table, it would take him awhile to fully adjust to the reality of their situation.

***

Jake's preoccupation with thoughts of Nell returned shortly after he put back the pig's head on the cookie jar and washed the two empty glasses of milk. If he had continued to think of the children, he would have perhaps realized there was more to their neglect than tired, faded clothing and aloneness at supper time.

Jake didn't know there were holes in the underclothing of the brother and sister. If he had, he might have also been aware of how these holes matched the defects in their parents' marriage, and that the holes seemed to get bigger after every fight and every warning by the sheriff.

Billy didn't tell Jake about the night a week before when he was undressing for bed and noticed a small hole in his underwear that got larger and larger as he studied it and finally showed an image of his father's face coming through. He didn't tell Jake that he blinked in disbelief to make the image go away, and it did, but there were other signs and images in the past and present that didn't go away.

Billy was too young to know about hints and signs and indications that can mean something is amiss. Otherwise he would have realized the image in his shirt hole was another signal similar to the lumps in the oatmeal, lumps that tried to go down his throat in a choking manner while his mother scolded in a strained, flat voice. She never greeted her children good morning, and because she considered breakfast as only a necessity, she mostly turned her back to them as she cooked what should have been a thick, creamy, tasty oatmeal feast into a tasteless, lumpy morning nightmare.

Eventually the holes, both the imaginary ones and the real ones, became bigger until they could no longer be hidden from the town people. Slowly, like a novice with a camera, the picture of the Charmleys came into focus, and people started to talk: why were Billy and his father never seen together? Why not Angela and her mother? It was always only the two children with each other. There was no family unit, no association, not even a suggestion.

One of the town gossips sharply claimed she knew for a fact there was no family portrait on a piano or anywhere else in the house. There weren't even any snapshots of the kids. And because the town had no other abusive or neglectful parents that result in unkept children, Billy and Angela sort of stuck out. Mothers know that limp, faded, and tattered clothing are to be freshened up and mended or thrown away—not left out in plain view for the whole town to see.

Eventually everyone started to notice the physical appearance of the children because everyone was paying attention. That is, everyone except Jake—until that one afternoon at the cookie jar, and then only briefly. He had his own feelings to control and change, feelings that were limp, faded, and tattered.

***

158

"If God were a Christmas tree, He would be that one," Dolly said to Harold as she pointed to the tall, perfectly symmetrical blue spruce in the Dittmer's front yard as they drove by on their way to town.

Harold smiled. "It's a little early for such thoughts, isn't it? It's only October, you know."

"I know. But do you remember last year when the Dittmers had to crawl out on their roof so they could string lights all the way up to the top of that tree?"

Harold grimaced. "Please remind me to not come to town if and when they do that again. I don't want to be anywhere near if they should call for help."

"I don't agree," Dolly said. "I think this entire community should help them with the lights. Everyone always oh's and ah's over that tree, especially when it lights up in the pitch black, and so everyone should pitch in. That includes you."

They both remembered last year when the Dittmers decided to string lights on their spruce. The conifer extended above the second floor, and the family decorated it with brilliant white lights arranged in Maypole fashion from the very top to the very bottom. Then when the winter's vigorous winds danced the tree back and forth and up and down in graceful sways and dips almost to the frozen ground, it looked like God's hand was caught painting a moving picture of holiday beauty.

Harold shifted his burgundy-colored Buick into second gear and turned the corner of Main and Sycamore. He would let Dolly out at Jensen's Dry Goods and then drive up a little further to Barney's; while the women stitched remnants of cloth together for a bed comforter, he would stitch together some beer and pretzels for himself.

The women quilted bedspreads and sold them to shops in nearby towns and even to places in faraway Omaha. They chatted and laughed and ate cookies and gave their profits to the town orphanage. The orphanage was not really an orphanage—the children in it were sometimes unwanted rather than orphaned—but the sisters, who offered the second floor of their overly big house to care for the children in need of a home, thought it more genteel to call it the town orphanage than a home for unwanted children; the sisters were retired, spinster school teachers and a bit genteel themselves in everything including their wish to be called spinsters instead of unmarried old women.

Dolly got out of the car with great difficulty because a wind had come up that slammed the car door against the curb and held it there. "I hate wind," Dolly shouted to Harold as he started to get out to help her. "Stay there for goodness sakes, old man, I'm not completely helpless."

Harold sat back and waited while Dolly grunted and groaned in an attempt to get the door shut. He moved the car forward a little to relieve the door and finally she got the job done. He looked around and hoped there were no witnesses to how he had permitted his wife to struggle. Next time he wouldn't allow her to be so assertive, at least not in public.

Dolly turned quickly and hurried into the store. Harold yelled, "I'll be at Barney's, you know," but Dolly was opening the door to the dry goods—no need to hear something she already knew. While the women diligently sewed and talked for four hours every Friday afternoon, their husbands drank beer and ate pretzels at Barney's. Jake always joined the men and always wished he had a wife in the dry goods store sewing away also. Sometimes Nell's twin brothers came, coincidentally, and kept to themselves. They always came together and always left together; they were one person, a package, that walked into the saloon, ordered beers, drank them, wiped the foam with their sleeves, pulled the pinball, and left. Nobody paid much attention, nobody cared.

Harold drank his beer slowly, he usually did, and daintily wiped the foam from his upper lip and nose—in public he was dainty. He looked over at Jake. He enjoyed his buddy's company, but the thing that warmed him to his innermost self was that after he was through at Barney's and after he had said goodbye to his friend of many years, he would have Dolly to go home to— Dolly with her warm remarks, Dolly in their warm kitchen.

Jake didn't have that. He was working on it. On the way to meet Harold at the saloon for conversation and companionship, Jake went to the bus stop to check for Nell. As he waited for the bus's arrival, he thought of Billy and Angela and how empty their lives were also. After the children left school for the day, they had only an empty house to go to. Their lives were centered on those outside sources, like him, that would provide them with some meaning. There was no friendly kitchen for them to sit in, there were no welcome home smiles and hugs and what-did-you-do-in-school-today questions.

Jake turned off the motor and settled in. The bus was late. He thought again about moving to town where an occasional street noise would give him a connection to other people while he sat alone in front of the television or laid in bed with a book opened on his chest as he slowly dozed off to sleep. He shook his head no. He couldn't leave the land; he couldn't leave the ground he had scampered on as a young boy, the earth he had plowed as a young man. He decided to make do with Prince and Mitzie and an occasional meal with the Hallgrens. Unless, of course, Nell would someday get off that blooming late bus and walk into his arms forever.

By now the bus was really late. Forty-five minutes late. Jake left his pickup and stomped into the postoffice to demand an explanation. "The bus came early," the mail attendant said in a tone as disinterested as Jake was interested; and he sorted the mail and slid letters and bills into their respective boxes in the same monotone way; then he sighed and looked more intently at Jake and finally hum-drummed further information because he could see by Jake's immobility that more information was needed: "There was no one waiting to get on, so the bus went around the corner to Sam's for gas."

Oh well, Jake decided, she wouldn't have been on that bus anymore than any of the other buses he had checked faithfully. He drove by Sam's to make sure she wasn't still on the blasted bus or standing nearby. She wasn't, and he knew she wouldn't be even before he looked, so he went to Barney's and hoisted himself up on a stool next to Harold. As his legs dangled, he wondered if anyone at all in the whole wide world was as sad as he was today.

"I think we'll have an easy winter this year," Harold finally said in an effort to bring some optimism into the beer palace. "A lot of snow for the spring planting, but not much cold."

"Isn't it funny," Jake answered and turned to Harold so that Barney, who was at the other end of the counter, couldn't hear. "Isn't it funny that I can't stand to have Nell in Iowa? I want her with me all the time."

"At your beck and call?" Harold teased.

"No," Jake frowned. "You know me better than that. I don't beckon, and even if I did, Nell wouldn't answer. Does Dolly?"

"She says so."

"Well, maybe if Nell and I were married ..." Jake hesitated.

"You'd better find out before you marry her if she'll come when you beckon." Harold reached over for a pretzel.

Jake sat up indignantly. "I don't want her to come when I beckon, for pity sakes, I have Prince for that. I don't need a wife to do it too. In fact, I can't think of anything more demeaning than to expect a woman to come when you call. That expression: bring me a beer Mabel, is only a joke. No one really says it."

Harold nodded. He didn't want to go into the fact that some husbands really say that. He let Jake think he had made a point and went back to the original line of conversation. "So maybe that's why you're not married—you're not willing to beckon."

"What do you mean? I never notice you beckoning Dolly."

"That's because I did it so much when we were first married, she anticipates my calls and comes without me having to beckon every time."

"You are really full of it, aren't you?" Jake answered, and he almost laughed as he slid his empty mug along the slick counter for Barney to refill.

Harold sent his mug after Jake's. "Yes, I'm full of it. Always have been. I've always been full of it, and you've always been empty of it. That's why you're so serious about things all the time. Why don't you learn to be full of it a little?"

"It's not my nature, old true and full friend of mine. One is born to that kind of nonsense."

The two, like in a symphony, grabbed at their mugs of foam dripping beer that Barney scooted back along the counter. The chime over the saloon door rang, but the pair ignored it as they usually did, especially on a Friday afternoon when it chimed a lot. Jake was about to say something to Harold about coming over to his place for the Saturday afternoon Nebraska football game on television when he felt a hand on his shoulder.

Jake turned his head around, and his eyes looked straight into the eyes of Nell. He looked at her, and he looked at her. He was in a kind of shock. He swirled around on the stool and slid off. He removed his cap and fingered it in his hands with quiet expectation. He turned to look at Harold whose eyebrows were raised and frozen that way. He knew by that expression of his buddy's, that Nell was real, she was not a mirage or anything else illusionary. Now, what was he suppose to do? Finger his cap for the rest of the day? Throw his arms around her in grateful relief? Do something, Nell, I'm up for suggestions.

She did. She smiled in a brightness that could blind, and Jake joined her in silent celebration of each other's presence. Is there really a twilight zone? If ever angels were to sing to him, now was the time. Now was the time for Santa Claus to appear, now was the time for the Easter bunny, for a million dollars to fall from the ceiling, for his father to come out of the cornfield and his mother from the kitchen. He was in a vacuum, no noise—none—except for the thumps of his heart.

Jake cleared his throat as though to speak for the first time in many years. "Were you on that bus that came early? I didn't know it was going to be early, or I'd had been there. I didn't know you were coming."

"Yes, Jake, thank you for your concern. I thought I would check the tavern for a ride home. I just left the quilting session, I'm too weary to join in today and hoped you or my brothers would be here. My suitcase needs to be moved from the postoffice before it closes."

Jake touched Nell's elbow in a gesture for her to sit down at a table. He stared over at Harold until Harold quit staring, then he sat next to the woman who had no idea how much she was missed. "I'll take you home, Nell, I'll surely take you home. How was Iowa? You've been gone a long time."

Harold turned back around, away from them and finally lowered his eyebrows. Barney nodded at him a few times, made the okay sign with his fingers, and started to whistle something about there's no tomorrow. Harold nodded back, and the only noise other than the background of the other patrons and Barney's subtle whistling was the swallowing of beer and the faint thud of mugs and ding of glasses striking together as Barney wiped them dry and put them back on the shelf.

***

Jake kept sneaking glances at Nell as he drove her home. He noticed the corners of her mouth turned up, cemented that way. He wondered if Iowa put that upward curve to her mouth or if maybe, hopefully, he did. He remembered how willing Nell had been to date him, how she had fussed over him with an apple pie, and how her lips had pressed soft and then firm against his when he kissed her on the bus for Iowa several weeks ago. But she hadn't written him, and she had given Harold an equal smile when she walked into Barney's today. So how would he figure out her feelings for him, that is, if she had any?

Maybe not. Maybe Nell smiled at everyone. Maybe that bus kiss was a polite return of his, or worse yet, a curiosity to determine if he was any good at kissing.

Why doesn't she say something, anything, like: Will you marry me? or: I came back to Nebraska because I can't live without you. He would even settle for: You're the nicest man I have ever known.

The pickup bumped over a few ruts. Jake apologized and looked at her again. "Whoops, sorry about the rough ride, didn't mean to be so wobbly."

"I missed you, Jake."

And with that, the pickup slam dunked into a deep rut—poor Prince—the vehicle weaving helplessly back and forth to get out. It was a bad thing to happen, but a good thing for it to happen then because Jake needed the time to figure out how to answer a remark he couldn't believe he heard. It was time to be clever, to say something wonderful that never in the whole world had ever been said before. "I missed you too," was all he could manage to say. And although it was appropriate, it was neither wonderful nor clever.

He bore down with all his strength on the steering wheel, hoping this would get him on ground level again. His thoughts did what his pickup could not do—they raced. Why was he fighting this machine? Why didn't he stop the engine and open his mouth?

The motor finally died. God must have killed it to force him to continue a conversation that said something more profound than a ditto of Nell's remark. Then, as Jake restarted the motor, something more profound did come from his mouth, and it spilled out like excess gasoline in a fuel line. "I couldn't stand it without you. One date, and I'm crazy. Why didn't you write?"

Jake's veins pounded against his skull, his heart thumped like it wanted out, and his digestive tract growled during which he desperately prayed for it to not go any further than the growls.

"You didn't ask me to," Nell answered.

Jake stared straight ahead, his thinking so gnarled he couldn't sort out what she had said and what he had said and what answers, if any, either had given. What was her 'you didn't ask me to' remark in answer to? Oh yes, it was the 'why didn't you write me' question.

"You mean you didn't write me because I didn't ask you to? Is that why you haven't married me yet—because I haven't asked you?"

Jake wanted to slide down under the steering wheel, way down where even God couldn't find him and cause more embarrassment, but he was already down as far as driving visibility allowed. This lovely, lovely woman was at his mercy as he emotionally jumped all over her. He wanted to scream out in tears—Dolly had warned him to take it easy with Nell, and he had goofed with a question that one mere date does not call for.

"That's right," Nell laughed.

That's right? What did she mean by that? He wished the pickup would find another rut; he needed another diversion; what was he suppose to say now? What did her 'that's right' mean? He might as well be talking to Shakespeare.

He turned off his thinking and opened his mouth. "Well?"

"Well, what?" Nell asked. "Are you asking me?"

"Well, of course I am. I'd be a fool not to." He hoped she was referring to his proposal, his mind was still a little jammed.

Nell frowned. "What do you mean that you'd be a fool not to?" Her voice was hurt and probably her heart too.

His flannel shirt was getting too tight; he had buttoned it too close to his neck. He moistened his lips and thought maybe he should throw his darn tongue away. "I didn't mean anything by it. I only want to propose. I don't know how to do it. No other woman has ever let me get this far before."

Nell's smile came back. She turned her head to Jake who was looking down at his left thumb hangnail. "All those women must have been fools. I would love to marry you."

Stunned. Jake was stunned. One minute he was dangling his legs at Barney's, and the next minute he was engaged to be married. His mind was no longer gnarled or jammed or panicked. He knew exactly what Nell had said just then. He knew exactly because he had wanted her to say yes, and she did, and that was that.

He felt an instant camaraderie with her, a closeness that one feels beside a crackling fireplace with a bowl of popcorn on the lap and a rerun of a favorite childhood movie on the television. He wanted to tell everything about himself, every dark, silly thing that he ever experienced or thought or spoke.

"Um-m," he started, "speaking of those other women, you know, the ones who never let me get close enough to propose? There weren't that many of them. I mean, there haven't been that many women in my life at all."

Nell nodded and continued to smile. "Me either, not many men in my life either."

The pickup was having trouble with the ruts again, so Jake steered it off the road. He turned off the ignition, looked at Nell, and slowly whispered to her: "Wh-oop-ee." He raised himself higher on the seat cushion than he had ever been before. He stared straight into her face, threw back his head, and this time gasped loud: "Whoopee."

Nell laughed. "Aren't you going to kiss me?" She moved closer.

Why of course. Why hadn't he thought of it? Too much stuff going on too suddenly and all at once. He took her face into the palms of his hands, tilted his head sideways, and kissed her. He kissed her mouth, her chin, her eyebrows, her cheeks, and her mouth again. "God, woman, I love you. Thank you for loving me back." Then he remembered, yes and thank goodness, he had brushed his teeth before he had left for Barney's this morning.

Nell put her head on his shoulder, and they sat there in a calm repose, cradling each other. Jake wanted to utter whoopee again, but he didn't want to break into the silence. For pity sakes, she said yes, they would get married, they would live together and love and laugh together. He had stepped into a brand new world where there would be lots of love and talk and breakfasts. This was not the time to emit another whoopee—he could yell that later when he was alone—now was the time to relish this new reality. They leaned against each other, motionless, finally speechless, barely breathing.

How long? Long enough for Harold and Dolly to come whizzing by thirty minutes later and notice them. Harold even stopped his car and backed up under protest of Dolly to mind his own business. He merely wanted to make sure this wasn't an accident at the side of the road. This was not an accident. Harold decided it was best to move on.

Jake and Nell remained in limbo even after they noticed an onlooker or two. Prince's patience, however, wore out. He barked from the back of the pickup and pawed at the window. He probably wished he had stayed home with Mitzie.

Nell raised her head from Jake's shoulder, and Jake started the engine. "Stay right next to me, Nell, don't move away. I'll get you home so you can plan our wedding. Okay?"

"There is just one thing, though," Nell hastily said.

"Uh-huh." Jake held his breath. Just one thing. Of course. This event had been too easy. There would be a stumbling block in the way. Of course, why not?

Nell continued. "I want to tell my brothers myself, alone. I'll do it tonight or so."

"Oh?" Jake responded, still on edge. Although he was relieved that Nell didn't ask him to ask the brothers for permission, he felt a little left out of the family unit. As rotten as the twins were, he still wanted their blessing, that is, if such a thing from them was possible.

"I hope your brothers like me. At least George seems to."

"Jake, they hardly know you. They probably neither like nor dislike you. But when I leave them to get married, they will have a big adjustment to make. None of them have ever been without a woman around the house. George has always had me for housekeeping and cooking, and Les and Lo went straight from widowhood to me." Nell took a deep breath. "It will be quite an adjustment for them."

Jake said nothing. He gripped the steering wheel and looked in the rear view mirror at Prince who had positioned his body sideways against the window as a reminder to his master of his presence.

Nell put her hand on Jake's knee. "You asked me to marry you. I will, and with great joy. But remember that my

168

brothers are used to having me around. They may not take kindly to you at first. I will be cleaning and cooking for someone they hardly know."

"Sure, Nell, sure," Jake answered with the uneasiness that comes when a person starts with no hope, then has a lot of hope, then has no hope again. Once Jake's world opened up with Nell's acceptance, he expected even more. He wanted everything to be smooth sailing, he wanted nothing bad to ever happen again. But this business about the brothers— that they might act unfavorably to him—well, it took that hope away.

Jake knew he had to say something, anything, to hide his fear, his inability to understand at this moment of sudden happiness that everything might not be okay. "I don't expect you to go from working for your brothers to working for me. I'll hire a cleaning lady. High school girls are good at that. I want you to save yourself for me."

Nell leaned her head back and laughed.

Her cheery response put Jake back into his mental vacuum again. What was so funny? All he wanted was to let her know that he didn't want marriage just to gain a housekeeper. He had better say something more promising than a cleaning girl. "You don't even have to cook, we can eat out all the time." Oh-oh, maybe he shouldn't have said that. That apple pie of hers, and no telling what other goodie she was capable of making. Maybe this pre-wedding promise wasn't a good idea.

Nell laughed again.

Why did she laugh? Was it because she was relieved she would never have to cook again? He had better say something to ease that idea out of her mind. "Well, I mean, you don't have to cook all the time. What I really mean is that I don't expect you to get on your hands and knees and scrub the floor. Okay?"

"I don't do that now. I use a long handle sponge mop."

"Fine." Jake no longer knew where he was in this involved communication. He felt like he was interviewing a

169

woman to take care of his house and groceries rather than discussing with her a lifetime of love and devotion.

Nell turned and tapped on the window at Prince. Then she tapped Jake's shoulder. "The future men in my life. I'll be more than happy to cook and clean for you both. I was laughing because you are so doggone sweet to say what you are saying."

Finally Jake got it, and then he laughed too. He had hope again. "Okay, if you think that's sweet, how about a brand new washer and dryer? How about anything at all that will make your life easier? I intend to help you with all your chores."

Nell reached over and gently twitched Jake's nose. "For awhile anyway, right?"

"Forever. Just don't tell your brothers." Jake squeezed Nell's hand and slowed the truck. There was no need to rush away from this perfect moment. Even without a ceremony, he felt they had become one person on that chilly October afternoon inside the red pickup so recently made new by the Boone County Repair Service.

***

Dusk was heavy overhead as Jake drove off the main road and onto the gravel of the Swensen driveway. The formidable body of one of the brothers silhouetted the barn door as he went from one chore to another.

"That must be George," Nell said. "Friday is his turn to milk and that's probably where he's going next."

Jake braked the vehicle and turned off the motor. "How about another kiss, Nell, like the one you gave me back on the road?"

"You don't have to ask permission. I respect you, Jake Blackburn."

Jake Blackburn. Nell Blackburn. For pity sakes, Jake mused, less than a day ago there was no evidence of even a Nell in his life again, let alone a Nell Blackburn. He felt like someone who had not only entered something in the County Fair but who had also won first prize. Nell. He even chuckled how this afternoon's activity was a lot like putting a thumb into plum pie and pulling out not just one plum, but the whole darn pie. He could have mused on and on about his good fortune, but decided he had better quit and get on with the kiss. He could gloat later.

"Excuse the stubble on my face," Jake babbled, "I didn't exactly shave well this morning. Didn't you notice it earlier? I would have shaved better if I had known you were coming home today, and I certainly would have if I had had the slightest inkling that today was the day I would propose."

Nell scooted over and kissed him. "You talk too much when you shouldn't and don't talk enough when you should."

Now it was Jake's turn to laugh. "I guess after we're married, I won't have to apologize for my whiskers because you'll only feel them bright and early in the morning. I promise to be well groomed for you at all times."

So they kissed again, paying no attention to the stubble, and were still kissing when George came out of the barn and walked toward the back door shed with two buckets of warm and bubbly milk. He was too busy watching his footing in the late afternoon sun of autumn to pay attention to the presence of a pickup or the romance it held. He walked right into everything and slopped milk down its side.

Nell noticed because it was her side of the pickup that got hit and slopped. She tried to pull her mouth away from Jake's to tell him about the interference, but Jake wasn't through kissing; he was so engrossed he didn't notice George back away and look down at the ground even more intently than he was looking before. So Nell put her hands on Jake's chest to push away, but he took hold of them in a loving caress and kept on with the kiss.

"Air, air, I need air," Nell gasped.

Jake let go. He saw George walking away and frowned. "How long has your brother been watching us?"

"Brothers, Jake, brothers," Nell laughed. "You missed the two at the kitchen window."

Jake was bewildered. What kind of brothers did Nell have? Why were they looking? Wouldn't a glance have been enough? After Nell explained that George had accidentally walked into the side of his pickup, he was still left with no explanation for the two at the window. Not too many people accidentally walk into windows, especially if they are inside a house. Those twins were deliberately looking. Surely tactful adults don't stare at two people kissing, surely they know it's none of their business. If Jake had taken the time to reason out the situation, he would have remembered that Les and Lo paid no attention to social graces that considerate adults pay attention to, that they did whatever they pleased, which was usually never associated with anything thoughtful.

Jake got out of the pickup and went to assist Nell. She glided off the seat, and Jake squeezed her hand again. He looked up at her. "Your twin brothers must be quiet versions of our two town gossips."

Nell patted his hand. "You'll get used to them. Everybody eventually does. And as far as George goes, you will like him— he's my baby brother and my buddy."

Jake finally smiled at the thought of George being a baby anything. "Will you call me when your session with your brothers is over?"

"Yes. Goodnight, Jake."

He started to walk her to the house, but she shook her head no.

He walked back, grasped the steering wheel and hoisted himself onto the seat without touching the side step. Nell stood by while he started the engine. He looked down at her. "Woman, the first thing I'll buy after our wedding is a peek-proof window shade."

Nell waved and shouted. "What did you say?"

Jake leaned out the window. "Heavy shades, blackouts, like in World War II."

"What did you say? Louder," Nell insisted.

Jake backed up quickly, forgetting about Prince in the back end who lost his footing and fell onto the blanket. Thank goodness for the blanket, Jake thought as he realized he had ignored his pet and hoped the dog would forgive him.

Jake wasn't through with Nell, however, and decided he could apologize to Prince later.

"I said shades, real heavy shades. Okay?"

Nell called back "Okay," and Jake yelled back "Whoopee," and Prince panted back disgust.

Jake drove home shaking his head back and forth almost all the way. He plain and simply could not believe it. He really and truly could not believe it. Nell was going to marry him. For weeks he had worried and sulked about whether he would ever have another date with her, and now he would never have to worry about that again because this special lady would be his date forever.

He smiled, and then he laughed, and then he cried, all the while continuing to shake his head and pausing now and then for another shout of whoopee. It was probably best that Prince was in the back and away from his master's tirade of love—the dog's panting in response might have been too much for Jake to bear.

***

Nell walked slowly to the house. She was no less surprised than Jake at how the day had turned out, although she had expected something like that from Jake eventually. The visit to Iowa had been emotionally grueling, a chance to let go of the past and think of a better future.

Jake was there for her at just the right time with the right kind of question, the proposal, and she had responded with the intuition of a person deprived of love for too long.

He was the first humble man she had ever dated, the first man who tried so hard to please, and the only one who didn't expect her to fuss all over him. She was glad of her visit to Iowa because it gave her a chance to think about and appreciate these qualities in him.

Maybe he was a little fast with the proposal, but what a proposal it was. And although she had decided on her return trip to Nebraska that she could live a lifetime with a personality like Jake's, it was when he proposed in such a bungling manner that a flood of affection for him surged throughout her entire being, filling every inch of her being in a previous existence of want. Oh Jake, she mused as she opened the shed door, you dear, dear man.

Then she went into the kitchen and her brothers.

***

Jake stopped his pickup halfway home and whistled to Prince whom he was still ignoring in the back end. "Come on up front, you hound," he called to his dog as he leaned over and opened the passenger's door. "Give me a hug, a big slush on the mouth, we're getting married. You, me, and Nell—and Mitzie too of course, if she'll have us."

Prince jumped and barked and then panted his way next to Jake's side. After the slush, he settled down with another bark, which probably meant yes.

"It's been a long day, hasn't it pal? Well, from now on we will all be happy." On the inside though, Jake's thoughts weren't that definite. He knew better than to illusion a 'live happily ever after' idea. He worried a little about the brothers. Surely they wouldn't give him trouble. This wasn't a hundred years ago when families had sole say-so about who was to marry who. And this was Nebraska, not some undeveloped country with old world ways. He had read about these things during his long stays in the library in college. Things like that don't exist here, not anymore. But how about Iowa? Na, same kind of people, he'd be all right, no trouble, no need to worry, all's well that ends well, and this will end well.

Maybe not. Why didn't she want me to come in with her? She could have waited until morning to tell them. Of course, sure, she wanted to bawl those bozos out for peeking. That was it. Jake said whoopee again, but this time without much exuberance.

***

Les and Lo sat at the kitchen table, each with a newspaper raised in front covering everything but the fingers. George walked in behind Nell who was over by the sink putting away the dishes, a comfortable routine which would calm her down before she made the uncomfortable announcement.

"Welcome home," George said.

Les and Lo continued to stare at their newspapers, ignoring her, or perhaps they were dead.

Nell turned around and smiled at George. "I suppose you did all the housework, right?"

George didn't answer.

"Oh," Les said as he peeked out from behind the newspaper's list of hog closings, "you're home."

George sat down at the table. "I just mostly cooked. There wasn't much time for cleaning."

"That's a woman's work, anyway," Lo added.

"That's right," confirmed Les. "George was our woman."

The twins put down their papers so they could laugh more openly about what they considered to be very clever remarks.

"Yes," Nell said pointedly to the twins, "your housekeeper is home, boys, but don't either of you rush me with a welcome." She didn't expect them to acknowledge her return, but she did wish they would be more cheerful to make up for their hawking out the window at her and Jake. She wished they would have a guilty conscience over it, although they never had one in the past. It would make her telling the news easier, to them at least—it would still be hard to tell George.

She poured herself a cup of coffee and joined the trio at the table.

"Hey, Sis," George asked, "where's your suitcase?"

Darn it, she realized, it was in the back of Jake's pickup along with the dog hair, cat whiskers, and one mud-caked shovel. She got up and pretended busyness at the sink. Her announcement should come out now, but she didn't know how to begin. Like Jake with his proposal, she had never done this before either.

"Where's your suitcase?" Lo repeated. "George will get it for you, he's our baby brother. He'll do anything."

Nell drew a deep breath. "It's in Jake's truck." She took an even bigger breath and raised her voice, this was it: "It's in Jake's pickup where it belongs. I'm going to marry him."

It was done. All that was left was to survive the response. George got up and stood still for a moment. He walked over to the door and nudged it shut a little tighter. Nell took a glass from the cupboard and turned on the water. Les and Lo folded their newspapers in a very deliberate, precise way, a manner that had a message of disgust in it.

"Why?" Les asked dumbfounded. "You have a home here, right here in this kitchen."

"When?" Lo asked after he had unclenched his mouth.

"Soon," Nell said with a relieved sigh.

George came back from the door. "How soon is soon? Tonight? Tomorrow? Next year? Next year will be good."

Nell turned around and put her hands on her hips. "Soon is right after I get over my ecstacy that Jake asked me." She had forgotten about not wanting to hurt George. She dug her fingers deeper into her waist.

"Ecstacy?" Lo shouted. "For him? He's shorter than you for pete sake. How can you get excited about a short man?"

"You got excited about a short woman ... you married her, remember, Lo?" Nell hardly moved her lips while she made the remark to him that opened up a wound never fully healed; and it hurt her to hurt him.

Les laughed. "She's got you there, brother. Boy, isn't she quick with the replies?"

"You're quick to fall in love, too, aren't you?" George said quietly.

"Yeah," Lo recovered, "yeah, yeah, yeah. And how quick are you going to get married? You could have let us know you planned to leave. You didn't even tell us why you went back to Iowa. You didn't even tell George. What kind of a sister are you, anyway? We're supporting you, you know." He went over to the door, opened it wide, and slammed hard—a gesture that had nothing to do with anything but a tantrum.

Nell swirled her body around to the sink, away from them. How dare he say that. She gasped and clamped her fingers onto the counter's edge; she managed to hold her head high while her heart thumped anger.

"We'll hire a woman," George said after he recovered a little from the suddenness of the announcement.

Nell turned to him:

"I went for the piano." That was part of the reason.

"I also went to have some time away for myself." That was almost true.

"I decided awhile back to leave here and take an apartment in town and give piano lessons and do housekeeping. Then Jake proposed." That was completely true.

She took another deep breath. "I'm sorry, George, but with or without Jake, I would have left."

Les folded his arms across his chest and dug his feet into the bottom rungs of the chair. "That's a bunch of hooey, sister, hooey, phooey, blooey. Your problem is that you're ungrateful."

"That's enough, enough," George intervened. "Jake is a likeable man. He's friendly and appears to be very interested in our sister." He turned and nodded at Nell. "You have my blessing, but oh boy, what a shock." He went to the door to nudge it again. "I'm going to bed ... it's been a long day."

"It's hardly dark yet, little brother," Les shouted as he followed Lo's example at the door, opening wide and slamming. "You stay up and figure out who we're going to hire to do this crud around here." He hesitated just long enough for his remark to sink into Nell, then he sunk it further: "Cheap crud."

Nell's voice snapped back. "I didn't realize my job was so reviling and cheap, and anything else demeaning you can find to call it."

George raised his arms in an attempt to orchestrate peace. Then he quit. "I'm going to bed. Let them be, Nell. Just let them be."

Les got up and went to the door.

"Stop," Nell demanded. "Don't you dare open or shut or

slam that door again." She paused. "At least not until I'm gone."

He didn't wait.

**

The words, 'we're supporting you,' rang like grating chimes in Nell's ears. She went to bed without calling Jake about the suitcase. She cried and pounded her fist into the pillow. 'We're supporting you' kept seeping steadily into her thoughts, slowly, like a creeping vine that finally envelops an area until it overruns and becomes the only noticeable thing.

How cruel. She kept house, she cooked, and she washed their mud-stiff overalls. She could go to any farmhouse and earn a living doing this. A job was a job, whether at home or away.

Nell turned over on her side and took her umpteenth deep breath. Why did the twins who had had their chance at marriage begrudge it to her? Life certainly wasn't a fairy tale, although she thought this for awhile right after Jake proposed and kissed her: she would live happily ever after. Then she laughed a little. Perhaps her 'ever after' would come after she left Les and Lo. Poor George. Maybe there is some nice woman in the county for him. She would look into that possibility after her wedding. Sleep would come easy now.

Then, just before deep sleep came, Nell woke suddenly and bolted straight up in bed. The creeping vine had returned to unsettle the peace. Perhaps she was living off her brothers after all. Maybe she would only be moving from them to Jake and living off him instead. Would Jake consider himself as supporting her? Of course not, it was different—she would be his wife. No, it wasn't different; she would merely be another housekeeper and eventually Jake would be another brother.

She laid back in bed, but she couldn't sleep. The creeping vine became more tangled: maybe in a few years Jake would accuse her of living off of him also. Life certainly isn't perfect, for every something good there is something bad. She drifted off to sleep again, not out of relief, but out of exhaustion.

**

The Buick that had stopped briefly on the road to look at the occupants of the red pickup finally arrived home. Harold and Dolly got out.

Harold opened the shed door, and Proudflesh ran into him in his eagerness to get out. The dog barked several times, decided that was enough to let his master know he had stayed away too long, and then ran toward the field and his relief.

Dolly walked past them both and into the kitchen. Harold followed, passed behind her, and meandered toward the television in the living room. Dolly hung up her hat and coat, asked Harold to do the same as she always did to no avail, and sat down in her chair next to him.

"Well," Harold said.

"Well, what?" Dolly replied.

"Well."

"Why don't we just talk about it? Or would you rather call Jake and ask him?"

Harold looked up at the ceiling. "It's none of our business."

Dolly turned down the sound on the television. "Do you want me to call and ask him?"

"Yes."

"All right. I'll call tomorrow morning and invite him to breakfast. That is, if he's free."

Harold nodded. "Call him now. I can't stand it any longer."

"You will have to stand it. Remember, dear heart, Jake took the suspense a lot longer than overnight."

"If that little so-and-so didn't ask Nell for her hand, I'll crush his little body to the size of a pea."

Dolly raised her voice. "Little? Did you call your best friend—little? He doesn't need to have that come from you. Shame."

"He knows I know he's little," Harold returned. "For crying out loud, we're best friends. He calls me plenty of things."

"Like what?"

"Well, he called me a dummy once."

"But you aren't a dummy, so that doesn't count. Jake, however, is little. You called him something he really is."

Harold looked askance at his wife and raised his voice also. "No, no, no, Jake isn't little. He's short, but he's not little. So there. You just said it was all right for Jake to call me a dummy because I really am not—so-o-o it's all right for me to call Jake little because he really is not. It's just a figure of speech for crying out loud."

Dolly got up and went into the kitchen and the stove. "Want some coffee with your sandwich?"

"Sounds good to me, thank you," Harold sighed with relief that Dolly had decided to give up on the tiff concerning Jake's size. "What kind of sandwich are you making me, good woman?"

"It's something new, you just invented it."

"Oh?" Harold replied, "I did? What is it?"

Dolly came back to the television. "Crushed pea, dear, I made you a little crushed pea sandwich."

***

Jake sped home, hitting every rut on the way; the deep grooves bounced Nell's suitcase up until it hit the back window. "Doggone it," Jake hissed as though someone was there. Now he would have to return the darn thing and possibly walk in on Nell's announcement to her brothers.

He turned the pickup around and started back to the Swensens. One mile later he changed his mind; he couldn't go back now: he visualized himself standing in the midst of three oversized men while their sister told them she preferred the company of a little, sawed-off runt to them. His previous moment of bliss over thoughts of a new life with Nell was replaced with this frustration. He stopped the vehicle to give himself more time to think. Then he turned off the ignition to give himself even more time to think. But he decided he needed more than time, and so he leaned toward Prince until his face was almost on the dog's snout. "What should I do, pal, go back or not?"

Prince whined and barked right into Jake's face. It was hard to distinguish whose expression was the most forlorn.

Jake rubbed his dog's ear. "What's wrong? Is it something I said?" He laughed. "For pity sakes, dog, I'm actually afraid to go back there. Is that why you're whining—you know something I don't?" That was it, his Princie knew something. He turned his truck back home again.

He would call Nell in the morning and tell her he forgot the suitcase; and he would have been satisfied with that excuse, but his conscience stepped in and nudged him to be ashamed of such blatant dishonesty to the woman he loved, the woman who would give him her trust and devotion and concern. He decided he had better practice some of that himself, and he started with thoughts of her nightclothes. She would need them, and also her toothbrush. Her comb? How about aspirin? Aspirin, for sure, after she told her brothers the news and they yelled at her.

Yelled at her? Of course, they would yell at her. Why wouldn't they?—especially those twin lummoxes. He had better go rescue her. He turned the pickup around once more, and Prince let out a heavy sigh of accepting the fact he would probably spend the entire night in this seat next to his master bouncing up and down on the unkept roads.

The thought of a heroic rescue didn't last long because Jake again brought his pickup to a quiet stop several yards from the Swensen driveway entrance. He thought once more of turning back; he thought once more of calling Nell on the phone in the morning with his previously well-thought-out, inconsiderate lie; he thought once more of how wishy-washy he could be at times.

A flock of low flying, southbound geese honked away as they looked for an overnight spot to rest. That's what he needed to be right now—a goose. Then he wouldn't have a choice of whether to go on or to turn back; he would have to follow instinct. People don't have instinct to decide things for them, too bad, because now he would have to use what people do have: choice. Should I do this, or should I do that? Choice.

Jake recalled reading about George Custer in the college library on one of those many Saturday nights he was alone. George Custer never hesitated. He made a lot of daredevil decisions, fast ones, and they all worked out all right, well, except for the last one. Should he take a stand against Nell's brothers? Should he walk right into the kitchen and let those twin lugs beat him up? Why couldn't he be a flying-south goose instead of a George Custer?

While his brain asked why, why, why, his hand shifted to second gear, his foot pulled back on the clutch, and he and Prince gunned the Swensen's dirt and gravel driveway at an unheard of speed for such a short distance. A cloud of dust surrounded the brave man, his dog, and pickup, and the shattering noise sent the geese up to a higher plane of flying safety.

Nell bolted straight up in bed for the second time that night; George ran into the kitchen in only his long johns; the twins almost dumped over the table in their clumsy scurry to the window.

"Hey," they all shouted as the quiet of the country was penetrated with a fearsome sound, none of which were the honking geese. "Somebody's coming after us with a fierce pace." "Get the shotgun." "I already have it."

Every light on the inside went off, and every light on the outside went on; it was a team effort, something rarely done in this family of disagreeables.

"It's that damn pickup and that damn elf inside it," Lo screamed. "Who ... in the hell ... does he think ... he is?"

Nell hurried into the kitchen.

"Your lover-boy has returned," Les sneered.

"And with a great gusto," George laughed.

Nell held her head high, walked past them, and opened the back door. It was Jake, all right. His truck stopped as abruptly as it had started, and the suitor jumped out equally as fast. He reached into the back compartment and set the suitcase on the cold, hard ground.

"Hi," he smiled.

Nell shook her head. "Jake, you didn't have to return my suitcase tonight, but thank you so much, it is late, you'd better go home now."

Jake quit smiling. "What? Go home? Something wrong? You told your brothers? The news didn't settle well, did it? How about George, didn't he approve?" He fired the questions rapidly, like machine gun bullets, to disguise his worry that things were turning out unfavorably.

Nell pulled her robe tight around her middle. "Jake, we need to talk more about our marriage."

There, in the early dark with only a dim light over the shed to show two tired people in conversation, Jake felt the same way he had when he discovered his mother dead in front of the television. He felt suspended without anything to grab on to. "What's wrong? Do they really object to our getting married, or is it me? It's my height, isn't it? They think you should marry someone taller."

Nell shook her head back and forth in a reassuring motion of no. "Oh for goodness sakes, Jake, your height has nothing to do with it. Sure, the twins put up a big stink, but I expected it. The real stumbling block is not my brothers. It's me. Lo said something nasty to me, but it's true. I need to support myself for awhile. I need my own place and my own income. Lo said they are supporting me, and I feel bad all over my entire being about this."

While Nell stood there telling Jake how badly she felt all over her entire being, Jake was feeling tingly all over his head; then his hands became clammy; his heart, or course, started to pound. "You mean you don't want to marry me anymore? You said yes, are you sorry now?"

The corners of Nell's usually upturned mouth went down. "Yes, I do want to marry you, but not right away. My brothers support me now, and when I marry you, you will support me. Do you know how that makes me feel?"

"No." Jake said. "I've never been supported by anyone

since I took over my Dad's farm right out of college. But I don't understand why you suddenly feel this way. My Dad didn't support my Mom. Harold doesn't support Dolly. It's like a team, the wife earns her so-called support just like a regular job. Why can't you and me be a team like my folks were and like the Hallgrens are? It would be my pleasure."

Nell blushed. Yesterday, this reasoning of Jake's would have been flattering and comforting, but tonight it was not— Nell needed a support from Jake other than money and a team offer. "Will you accept how I feel even though you don't understand?"

"It's my height. You suddenly realized you don't like short men anymore than your brothers do, and you've giving me some excuse about independence and stuff."

Nell came closer to Jake, her chin resting on his shoulder as she slowly embraced him. She waited for him to return the hug.

"Not here, Nell," he replied to her affection. "They're watching from the window and probably laughing at how short I am against you. I bet they are laughing themselves to death. Ha, ha, ha, ha-ha-ha."

Nell stepped back and frowned. "So. Is that why you never married? Do you think so little of yourself you can't even hug the woman you love and want to marry? Do we have to sit down whenever we want to smooch?" Nell took a deep breath of the night air. "I'm the same person, Jake, standing up or sitting down."

Jake continued to look up at Nell, but from a distance. He felt like a puppy dog who had misbehaved because it hadn't yet learned how to behave. In other words, Jake didn't know what to think or what to say about Nell's remark.

Then suddenly the guardian angels from the hardware store came back; they filled him with the essence of Nell's remarks, and Jake's former thoughts of the instinctive geese and the daredevil George Custer went away. His grief simply puffed out of his head, and he saw Nell now as she really was, and he cried out loud. "Oh my, oh my." He reached for her hand and brought her to him; he raised up and kissed her. "Woman, woman, woman, where there's a will there's a way, isn't there?"

Les and Lo watched from the narrow window, jammed together like fryers in a coop. Their insensitive gawking reflected their lifetime of tactlessness. Although they were industrious at farming and knowledgeable about it, their attitude of life, especially after their wives sudden and violent deaths, was not one of good cheer and caring and camaraderie of anyone, not even themselves. They existed because they thought it their duty to exist, and after years of their children away and silent, the twins functioned only on gut feeling and daily survival. It was this attitude that neither George nor Nell could penetrate, it was this immaturity that finally brought them to peeping windows and caustic remarks.

Nell knew this, and consequently she didn't care about what the twins thought of Jake; but she did care about what she thought of herself.

Jake put the neglected suitcase on the back porch stoop. He felt limp again, his bravery over for now. "How long will it take you to support yourself?"

Tears came to Nell's eyes. "I will rent an apartment in town and when my piano comes, I'll give lessons and do housekeeping. I have some income from my inheritance that will pay some of my way." Then the tears ran down her face. "You see, my parents left me money instead of land."

Ordinarily Nell's remark about her inheritance of money instead of land would have horrified Jake—land was much more valuable than money—but he had sunk too far into his own complaints to realize anyone else's. When he said he would help her move, he didn't mean it as a joyous offer. He wanted to take the whole rotten world in his hands and shake it. What if Nell wouldn't want to marry him after she had been on her own for awhile? Maybe she would think differently of him.

He thought that possibly he had already lost her.

***

Jake leaned forward on the steering wheel and looked up and out at the faded, dark horizon. There were a few stars to keep him company, but he longed for something to recite from memory to fill the void in his mind. A poem from his childhood, a joke or two from his teen years. It was too late to go to the Hallgrens, and besides, they were probably sick of his whinings anyway. Maybe his latest complaint would be resolved before he saw them again; maybe Nell would rush into his arms tomorrow and marry him immediately and everything would be good forever and ever.

But for now he knew better than to think such Walt Disney thoughts. He first learned of what reality was when his father and then his mother died. He also knew he had to return to the real world so he would be able to do something to keep Nell before she decided that the company of her piano was as good as his. He needed Jacob's ladder and all the angels on it.

Prince no longer sighed, panted, barked, or yawned; he slept, and he was still in this trance when his master arrived home. Jake leaned over and pressed his face against his dog's belly; Prince stirred, and it was this movement of his trusting pet that stirred Jake also. Something had tossed down that ladder, and Jake suddenly realized how far down on it he was. He was too weak for any angels to comfort him—he needed help straight from God.

He sobbed and covered his face with his hands in humiliation. "Please tell me what to do. I love her, help me, don't let me lose her. Please don't, please don't."

Prince nudged his snout under Jake's hand and licked the distraught face. Jake's tears really came then. "Oh God, thank you for my pets. For my land. For Harold and Dolly. And probably Barney too. But please, I want more. I want that woman."

Peace, like the calm after a grueling battle, came to Jake for a little while. He scooped the waiting Mitzie up in his arms, and with Prince close by his side, he opened the kitchen door and turned on the light.

He decided he would have to court Nell, starting tomorrow, brothers or no brothers. He would just have to put up with them until Nell moved out and he would have her all to himself without the worry of nasty twin remarks.

George seemed okay, so he really only had the twins to contend with. He merely had to figure a way for a David-sized man of some refinement to ignore the presence of two Goliath-sized men with no refinement.

Should he walk into their kitchen, crammed from wall to wall with their presence, and pretend to be blind and deaf? Or should he acknowledge them with his mouth and somehow dismiss their remarks from his mind? Would it be possible to drink in all of Nell and at the same time spew out the distaste of Les and Lo? Thank goodness, he thought, Nell and I are too old to have children—what rotten uncles those twin lugs would make.

Jake sat down at his own kitchen table and pounded his fists. He would not tell the Hallgrens about what happened tonight; he would remain sophisticated, like he really knew what he was doing, and spend all his energy and time with a master plot to get Nell away from her brothers, her apartment, and her anything else that came up as an excuse to delay their marriage.

He would buy those magazines he occasionally eyed and envied in the drug store, magazines whose covers shouted all kinds of advice for men and women in love and what to do about it.

It was time to go after Nell and to do it with all his might.

***

Jake was so busy concentrating on getting Nell to marry him right away, he hadn't taken the time to think through the events that happened since he declared his love for her and proposed. His mind was so jammed with getting Nell into his life, he hadn't really thought about anything she had said except she wanted to wait until she established independence before they married. If he had thought about everything she had said, he would have realized something she had not said.

She had not declared her love for him. Her joy, her respect, her happiness, and a surge of warmth that could have been love. But she had not told Jake of this surge. She had not declared love. She had declared only that she would marry him.

***

Nell went back into the Swensen house carrying her one lone suitcase. She dropped it on the floor, not because of its weight, but because she was tired of the entire ordeal.

What slobs, she thought, and her eyes opened wide at the word she finally admitted was the best to describe Les and Lo. Slobs. They gulped the meals she cooked for them in less than five minutes, tearing the meat portions apart with teeth instead of knives, wiping their mouths with one heavy swipe each, belching, and then abruptly getting up from the table; there were never any comments of thank you, or that was delicious, or sorry, we have to rush off to our chores. No nothing. They thought of her in the same sense as rain and crops and sun: that she would always be there for them.

In the two years since the grieving brothers moved in with her and George, their rudeness overpowered her younger brother's gentle manner until all Nell noticed was them. And perhaps George was a slob too because he never made them conform to his and her household. It was time to get out. It was time for sweet, gentle, bungling Jake.

But first, she had to be alone.

***

The following day started as usual for the Swensens. George went to the barn to milk the two cows. Les went there also to untangle some barbed wire for mending the fence in the back section. Lo turned on the radio loud and pulled the shotgun off the living room wall. He took pleasure in inspecting it now and then, especially after he heard the coyote howl early in the morning. Although he knew the coyote was friend as well as foe to the farmer, his meanness liked the feel of control over them.

Nell awoke in response to the radio noise and carefully, slowly positioned her feet on the floor in a deliberate manner as though she was on her way to a mission or cause and she had to first make a plan; then she hastily threw her housecoat over her shoulders, slid into her slippers, and rushed into the bathroom; she brushed her teeth, combed her hair, and stood looking at herself in front of the mirror. After awhile she started to move again and by the time she walked into the kitchen she had decided the plan for the day. Cook, clean, launder, call Jake, find an apartment, look for a job. Hopefully Jake would bounce around with joy at her ventures. Actually she knew he would not.

Lo left the living room and the radio and came into the kitchen. He gingerly held the stock of his rifle with the barrel pointing down. Nell followed him as she came out of the bathroom and wondered if Lo would ever think of being as gentle and caressing with her feelings as he was with his shotgun.

"Who's going to get our breakfast after you leave?" Lo asked as Nell went to the egg bin.

"You boys can take turns, like you do now with milking, plowing, and stuff," Nell answered with satisfying mischief in using the word 'stuff' to refer to other farm activities. She thought this might make up for the mean housework remark from last night. She was relieved, however, that Lo admitted by his question that she was moving out.

"Maybe we just won't eat."

Nell shot a side-glance and narrowed her eyes. "What did you boys do after your wives died and before you moved in with George and me?"

"We didn't eat."

"You know that for sure?" Nell was amused.

"Well, we can't cook, so we must not have eaten."

Nell shook her head. She couldn't worry that her brothers would turn into skeletons after she left. "Who cooked while I was in Iowa?"

"Nobody."

"What did you eat? Frozen dinners?"

"Nope. We ate nothing."

Nell took a dozen eggs out of the bin and cracked one open. "Lo," she sighed, "either you are trying to be funny or you need to grow up."

"Well," he answered with a smirk, "it must be that I'm trying to be funny because if I don't eat no more, I won't be able to grow up, will I?"

Nell cracked open the remaining eggs, one after another and dropped them, splat, into the hot frying pan. She was glad to be distracted by the sizzle and smoke.

George and Les came back from the barn; George dumped the pails of warm milk into a large container in the small refrigerator kept for only that purpose in the shed; Les slapped at his trousers, walked around the throw rug, and slowly lowered his body onto his chair by the table.

"Oh boy, I'm getting old," Les said. "I don't think I'll be farming much longer. Don't have the strength anymore."

Nell scooped the eggs out of the pan onto a platter, covered them with a paper towel, and set them inside the oven.

"I'll have an extra toast this morning, Nell," George called from the shed as he cleaned out the milk pails.

Nell took out another slice of whole wheat and turned to the coffee pot.

Les looked sharply at his sister. "Are we having real coffee this morning or will we have to drink that instant stuff we were forced to use when you skipped town?"

Nell tilted her head back. "I have never made instant coffee for your first coffee of the day, and you know that."

"Well," Les continued, "I thought maybe you'd changed, that maybe going back to your roots gave you fancy ideas, like the one you had yesterday of marrying that short man."

Lo slapped his hand on the table. "That ain't fancy, brother, that's stupid. She knows we don't like her so-called man, she'll come to her senses." Then he added as though this would matter to Nell and she would change her mind,

"There's more about Jake Blackburn we don't like besides his shortness, you know."

"What's that?" Les asked.

"His raspy voice. Raspy, raspy, raspy."

Nell turned her back to the two hecklers; she cleared her throat, took a deep breath, and took the platter of eggs out of the oven.

"Here's your breakfast, boys, eat up kids, I don't mean you, George," and she tipped the platter toward Lo's plate and gave his four eggs an extra scoot with the spatula which resulted in the eggs missing the plate and ending up on the table.

"Whoops," she said and turned to Les. "How many eggs for you?"

Les sat up straight, no longer really that tired. "None, if that's how you serve them. Did that little toad of a boyfriend teach you how to serve breakfast? Huh? Huh?"

"How about three eggs?" and the spatula overshot the eggs onto Les' lap. "Whoops."

George came from the shed and sat at the table. He looked up at Nell who looked down at him with a face that appeared renewed. "How about some eggs yourself?" he said ignoring the display of his sister's disgust with the twins.

"No thanks, I'm not eating this morning," and with that, George set the platter in front of himself and devoured the remaining eggs quicker than Les could clean up his lap.

***

Jake ate his breakfast of cold cereal flakes and mushy applesauce; he didn't want to call Nell and hear more bad news from her until he had at least one meal in him for the day. With every bite he put off any future reality—he had had enough of that for awhile.

He even washed his dishes, fed Prince and Mitzie, and made an especially neat effort at folding the dish towel. This all took time.

Finally, "How are you doing this morning?" he asked Nell who answered the phone before the first ring was complete.

"Ready to move out of here," was her reply.

They hardly spoke as he drove her back to his house. "I thought you could have coffee with me while you go over the ads. How's that sound?" Jake couldn't believe he managed to be so accommodating about the ads.

"Okay," was all Nell managed to answer.

"Uh-huh, okay, do you still want that apartment in town?" Nell shook her head yes, an unhappy yes.

The pair might as well have been in earthquake country for the chasm that was between them now. Sitting close together does not necessarily put a couple in the same area of agreement, and Nell and Jake were definitely on either side of a gap.

Jake turned into the driveway and swerved around Mitzie who was rolling in the gravel to relieve her dry skin.

"You're mighty quiet this morning, Nell."

"I'm always quiet when I think and hurt and wonder about something."

"Well, we're here." That was the only thing Jake knew for sure right now as he got out of the pickup and hurried over to Nell's side to help her out; but Nell had already opened the door and her feet were almost on the ground.

Jake felt apart from her, as apart from her as he had felt close the day before when he proposed and they held each other like a ceramic of man and woman embracing forever.

They went into the kitchen. Jake offered her a chair. She sat down. Jake went to the coffee pot. The flow between them was gone, and all Jake could think to say was something obvious: "I put a pot on just before I came for you. So it's fresh. The coffee I mean, not the pot."

"Where are your ads, Jake?"

He opened the door under the sink and reached for yesterday's newspaper. "Are you sure I can't talk you into answering my ad instead?"

Nell blew on the steaming coffee as she took the paper from him.

Jake sat down and warmed his callused, used hands on the mug. "You know what?" he said to Nell although her eyes and mind were behind the newspaper. "You know what I miss right now?"

Nell put down the paper and tried to smile.

Jake continued. "I miss your smile."

"Do you have a pencil? I need to circle some of these ads."

Jake went to the utensil drawer and brought back a pencil. "There can't be that many ads in our small town ... you are going to stay in our town, aren't you?" Please make her stay.

"I don't know, Jake, I'm looking at the other towns around here so I can get the best situation."

Nell circled; Jake looked; he opened his mouth and closed it again; Nell sipped the coffee; Jake looked at his watch; nobody said anything about anything until Nell was through penciling.

"Good coffee," she said.

Jake stood up. "I'd make you coffee everyday if you would stay here and marry me and live happily ever after."

"I'm sorry, Jake, but I can't marry you when I feel so low. I want to be a good wife and not some dependent, whiny leech."

"Oh no," he almost screamed, "you're not any of those things."

"I have to prove that to myself."

Jake started to pace. "There is such a thing as being too independent, you know. Like Billy and Angela. Has Dolly told you about them? Their parents don't look after them at all. Those kids are on their own—at least as far as they feel anyway. And you'd better believe they don't feel one bit good about themselves either."

He paused, pulled up a chair opposite Nell, looked down at the floor and asked, "Do you care that I hurt too?"

Nell put her hand under his chin. "I care."

"Then what happened to your smile? I think I could stand waiting for you if you would only smile again."

Quick tears came to her eyes. "Is that what you love

about me, my smile? Is that all your love is for?"

Sudden panic came to Jake. "Of course not. For pity sakes, your smile is what caught my eye. You seemed so content and wonderful the first time I saw you. You see, I only smile at people I like. So I figured you do the same and that you smiled at me in the hardware store because you approved of me. That's all I meant about your smile, nothing else, just approval."

Nell shook her head. "No, Jake, that's not all there is to it. My smile doesn't necessarily mean I am happy and approving. My smile merely means I'm not unhappy at the moment. Right now I'm very unhappy."

Jake went to the refrigerator, took out a jug of Brie's milk, and quietly placed it on the table; he went to the cookie jar, looked in and saw he was out of Dolly's cookies, and reluctantly reached for the store-bought ones in the cupboard. He placed them in front of Nell and hoped she wouldn't mind they weren't homemade.

"You mean you smile on the outside but not on the inside?" He opened the cookie package and the crackling of the cellophane echoed his sharp remark.

"Sometimes." Nell seemed to brighten up somewhat as though she was relieved of a burden. "A lot of people do that, Jake. Especially women. We are taught to smile, to be pretty is to smile. After awhile it becomes a habit."

Jake didn't know what to say to that. The cookies and milk sat mute. Prince barked, Mitzie meowed, Jake let them in, and more silence followed. Some couples think that if a man and woman can be in each other's company for a period of time without saying anything to each other, then they are compatible and comfortable with each other. This wasn't necessarily the case with Jake and Nell right now.

It was Nell who broke into the hurting quiet of the room with, "Jake, do you like piano music?"

He looked over at her. "Yeah."

"Then you will be the first one I play for when my piano comes from Iowa. Now, will you help me find a place to put it?"

"...Yeah." And he wished it would be his place. And he wished she would smile, even if it were only on the outside.

***

November is not the best month for a person to be unhappy in because the brightness of October's colors are gone: and gone was Jake's confidence that he had won Nell over.

After the harvesting is done, November is the month when farmers and townspeople gather around their televisions and telephones more: but this was the month when even visits to Barney's Beer Palace did not bring joy to Jake.

November is the month of distrustful weather for trips to large towns and cities like Kearney and Omaha for entertainment and shopping; so, any unpleasant episode in a country person's life will seep in deep to the spirit and leave it with a hollow feeling: and this was the November that Jake was a recipient of this void.

November is the month when a minister might pray at the end of a sermon that all heartbreaking events wait until spring when nature shows the goodness of being alive: this was the November that Jake had no patience for the long wait or for the goodness or for just plain anything.

November is not the time to feel unrequited love: this was not Jake's best month.

***

Harold's eyes popped open in amazement at what he had just read in the Boone County Chronicle. The news took his mind away from constant thoughts of Jake and Nell in the red pickup the day before. "Can you imagine that, wife?" he called to the kitchen at Dolly. "The town orphanage is going to be richer than we are, richer than the entire county."

Dolly slammed the cupboard door shut as though this would get her quicker into the living room and by her husband to hear what sounded like remarkable news. "What are you talking about, old man?"

Harold put the newspaper down on his lap, rapped his

knuckles on the leading story, and looked up at Dolly. "I'm talking about this article here, see, on the front page, this little news item that leaps out at you like war news does."

Dolly took the paper to her chair, and her eyes popped open in amazement too but, unlike Harold, she followed her reaction with a broad smile. "Can you imagine that? I knew we had a few rich ranchers west of us, but they might as well be in the next county. I never thought of them as being a part of us. Can you imagine that?"

Harold stood up and pulled on his suspenders. "We always wondered what rich old man Jenkins would do with his money after he died. No heirs, none at all is what Barney said. Long ago, Barney said that long ago."

If Dolly had been the type, she would have sat in her chair for awhile in a trance. But she wasn't that type, so she kept on: "Now we know something unbelievable. I guess my quilting days are over, or at least until the girls and I can think of some other charity."

Harold kept pulling on his suspenders and kept talking as though the Boone County Chronicle had hired him to explain it all to his wife. "It says that Jenkins willed almost a million bucks to the old maid school teachers so they can expand that old, tired home of theirs and hire more help to run their orphanage for now and for a long, long time after the ladies die. That rich son-of-a-gun was raised in an orphanage in Omaha and his Will includes that particular one as well as a few others west of his spread in the Plains region."

Dolly squeezed her hands together like a little girl pleading that the new doll that had unexpectedly been given to her would not be taken away. "Oh, I hope the money will be handled right so nobody can abscond with it and put it into their own selfish pockets."

"Jenkins set it up, a long time before he died, in a trust with one of those big shot banks in Omaha. He was a good business man, right?"

"He was a good man, period, for caring about children like that," Dolly said as she went to the phone.

"Wait a minute, good woman, whoa. Before you spread it all over town, let me tell you the rest."

Dolly frowned, her good mood suddenly gone, and not because Harold thought she hadn't read the entire article but because he had accused her of something she took pride in not doing. "What do you mean, 'before I spread it all over town?' I'm not a spreader, you know that. Everyone knows the news by now. I merely want to talk it over with the girls. Repeating a joyful story over and over makes the joy last—it rubs it in forever."

"Okay, okay, don't get excited, settle down, woman. As long as you have to gab about something everyone already knows, the article goes on to say that Boone County has to share the orphanage with the immediate surrounding towns, and that's why the home will have to expand. Okay, that's all, now you can phone your girls."

Dolly lifted up the receiver. "If you say so, dear, you know best. Is there anything else you would like me to tell my fellow gabbers, like maybe the sun won't set in the west tonight?"

Harold guessed not.

**

Jake took Nell from apartment to apartment, there were only two to choose from, and from job to job offer with his hand supporting her elbow and his head mostly bent down, looking like a trainer walking his animal through its paces.

The paces, actually, were not many because besides the lack of apartment availability, there weren't a lot of jobs either. And to Jake the ordeal lasted more than one day; it seemed like a year ago, an unhappy year ago, when he and Nell left his kitchen and the cellophaned cookies and walked every inch of the small town over and over.

That night when they returned to the restaurant where they had their first date, Nell said the thing that Jake was afraid she would say: "I'm afraid I'll have to leave this area. I'm either not right for the job or it's not right for me."

Jake slouched down in his chair and stuffed his hands

inside his pockets. His eyes slowly scanned the restaurant room, and he noticed, for the first time, a picture of Herbert Hoover on the wall. What, for pity sakes, was a picture of Herbert Hoover doing on the wall? Where were George Washington and Abraham Lincoln? Why Herbert Hoover? No wall he had ever seen before held a picture of only Hoover. But then, nothing in his life made sense anymore anyway, so why should this choice of a president's picture come as a surprise?

All the while Jake was deep in thought about one of his country's many dead presidents, he was not responding to Nell's statement that she needed to look into another town for her independence. And because Nell didn't know of Jake's momentary obsession with an explanation for Herbert Hoover's picture, she guessed his silence was his way of saying he would no longer help her.

"I won't ask you to take me to the next town, Jake, I'll ask George."

If that had been Jake's picture on the wall instead of the former president's, it would have crashed to the floor. Jake did not like at all what Nell had just said. While he was sulking, she was moving on, moving on and away. His body reacted before his mind as he got up from the table and took Nell's hand into his; he paid the bill; he escorted her to the pickup; then he asked: "Can we talk some more about this?"

Nell's mouth puckered. "I bet you hate me, don't you?"

Jake opened the door. "No, I don't hate you. I hate me. I figure I blew our entire future together by rushing you. I bet I'm the one you want to get away from, not your brothers."

Nell put her finger on Jake's mouth to erase his illogical thought. "If you love me, if you trust me, you'll let me do this."

How many movies, Jake thought, had he heard those exact words from a lover who was trying to break up the romance? What was he suppose to say now? Okay? He knew it wasn't okay, he knew he was reaching down to her as she was falling to the bottom of a barrel whose darkness would hide her forever; he had to reach her with the right words before that happened; he had to wiggle his way to her with words. Words of guilt: "All I know is that I love you and you said you loved me and so why aren't we moving closer together instead of further apart?"

It didn't work because all Nell answered was "I am so very, very weary, and all I want now is to go home and go to bed."

They drove back without talking, and the evening's eerie howl of coyotes and yelping hoots of owls moved into the silence.

That night Jake blankly watched television while sitting on the floor so could hold onto Prince. Tears came on his face as he wondered about Herbert Hoover again, wondered, but no longer cared.

***

"Why don't you kids go visit Jake at his place?" Barney said to Billy and Angela as they sipped on orange soda pop.

"It's too far to go, and it's cold. Besides, he won't be at home," Billy answered.

"Well, Jake told me his door would always be unlocked for you and your sister and you were to help yourselves to milk and cookies. He don't like me serving you soda pop. Thinks it ain't good for you all the time."

Billy reached over to his sister's chin and tried to wipe off the orange stain. "We went there yesterday and two times before that, and he wasn't at home, and the door was locked. So there will be no more trips over there for us."

"I'll talk to him, kid. I'm sure it was an oversight, you know, he plumb forgot."

"Don't bother," Billy blurted out. "It was a dumb idea anyway. We have milk and cookies at home."

"No we don't," Angela piped up.

"Yes we do. We have milk anyway. And we'd have cookies too if I baked some. It's no big deal."

Barney came out from around the counter to the orange table with the orange pop and the orange stain on the young girl's mouth. "Yes it is a big deal. You just hold on to your anger for awhile, young man, and give us big people a chance to show our concern. Some of us are new at this sort of thing. So. Jake blew it. Maybe he has problems too."

Billy stood up and reached for Angela's hand to leave. "All big people have problems."

"They sure do," Barney grinned.

"Then why do all these big people with all their problems want to add more problems by paying attention to us kids? Why do outsiders care about my sister and me? I know why, Mr. Barney. It's because some of these big people who are nice to kids are nice to them because they have a big supply of milk and cookies they want to get rid of. That's all—that's the only reason."

***

"Here I am again," Jake said glumly to the Hallgrens as he walked in on their breakfast the next morning.

Harold pulled over a chair and motioned for Jake to sit. "Okay, buddy friend, we want to hear everything up to and including now. When are you and Nell going to get married?" If tact had been taught in school, Harold would have flunked. Dolly hit her husband's foot with her own. "Harold, stop that, quit being so snoopy."

"I can't stand it anymore," he answered. "Jake has to tell us everything." He hoped that would include the red pickup incident on the side of the road the day Nell returned from Iowa.

Jake poured himself coffee, straddled the chair, and told the Hallgrens he no longer feared going to Hell when he died because he was putting in his time right now. "First there was victory," he said directly to Harold to satisfy his friend's overly zealous curiosity. "First the victory, she said yes." He turned to Dolly. "Then the defeat. She is putting me off about a wedding date, and I think I will lose her."

Harold frowned. Not openly, but to himself as he thought: here we go again, more mournful trips to Barney's for the purpose of discussing unpleasant things rather than enjoying an exchange of insults.

"You told me not to rush her, Dolly, but I did. And she accepted. I almost exploded out of my truck, no Harold, not for what you're thinking, but for pure joy and surprise." Now Harold knew what Jake knew he wanted to know, and maybe he would shut up.

Jake continued. "But now, n-o-w-w-w, she's looking for an apartment and a job and anything else instead of making wedding plans. She talked to her brothers about getting married, and afterwards she put me on hold. I think it was her brothers who scared her away from me. They would be losing a great deal because she does all the cooking and cleaning for them. I should have courted the brothers also."

"Yes, you should have," Harold answered curtly without being asked.

"Now, now, now," Dolly said, "let's not cry about what we should have done. Jake, I think you need to make some of your own decisions. We are here to comfort, but from now on you need to do your own thinking."

Jake swallowed hard. "Won't you even give me some hints?"

"No." Dolly insisted.

"How about if I come up with an idea, and you then approve it or reject it?"

"No, no," Dolly quickly intercepted before Harold could say yes. "We are only here for comfort."

"I don't want comfort, I want a solution."

Harold stood up. "If we help you again, buddy-buddy, and our ideas don't work out, will you promise not to shoot yourself?"

Dolly gasped.

"Is that a promise, buddy?"

Jake turned red. "I'm embarrassed. Why do you think I'd kill myself. It's degrading."

"But you are in a very degraded state right now, and you have been all this season. You can't have white, fluffy clouds all the time, you know."

"I have never thought that," Jake barked defiantly. "It's just that those gray clouds hover closer to the earth than the white ones. That's why, when I'm unhappy, I am unhappier than I am happy when I'm happy."

"Sure," Harold returned.

"It's just that I keep thinking that when Nell gets her own apartment, a million men will come out of the walls and propose to her. They will all be tall and better, and she will realize how much easier it is to get a proposal in Nebraska than Iowa, and she'll pooh-pooh me altogether. That's why she never married in Iowa, you know ... men there don't propose as easily as they do here."

"Oh?" Dolly said. "You have statistics?"

"I know what I know," Jake stated.

Dolly said "huh?" and shook her finger. "Just because a woman isn't married doesn't mean she has never been asked."

Harold looked over at his wife. "I don't believe that, woman. I was the first man to propose to you, and you accepted." He snapped his fingers. "You said yes ... just like that."

"You know that for a fact?" Dolly chided.

"Well, you're my wife, aren't you?"

"Yes."

"And I was your first proposal, wasn't I?"

"Yes."

"Then how can you tell Jake otherwise?"

It was Dolly's turn to stand up. She took off her apron and folded it deliberate and neat over the chair. "I can tell Jake otherwise because I was lucky to have a good man come to me so early in life. Some women I know didn't say yes to the first suitor. And there is one woman in particular I know who finally said yes to her fourth proposal."

There was a quiet in the Hallgren kitchen with its bay window jutting out like new ideas do at first.

The silence didn't last long. "Who was that, who are you talking about?" Jake said as he held his breath.

"Nell. It was Nell, that's who. Jake, you were not her first proposal." Dolly waited until she thought he had digested that bit of news that some men do not want to hear. Then when she noticed the cake might crumble, she smoothed it over with frosting: "You were, however, her first yes."

There was more silence, and even it sounded embarrassed.

"Is that why she changed her mind about me? Because she forgot she always says no?" Jake poured more coffee, shaking with concern over what Dolly might reveal next; it wasn't the caffeine that triggered his hand to tremble—it was the conversation.

Dolly put up her hands in exasperation. "Jake, it almost seems like you are the one, not Nell, who wants out of the proposal. You are so negative, maybe you don't truly love her."

Jake's eyes became like saucers, glistening, ready for tears to fall if further provoked. "I love her. I know I love her. I know the difference between a crush and love. I've had plenty of crushes. Anytime I thought I had a chance with a woman, I'd get a crush. But not love. I didn't really love any of them. Why am I telling you all this? I can't stand it."

He became quiet, and Harold and Dolly permitted him to remain that way while he smoldered on the idea of maybe not really being in love.

Then he started up again. "With Nell, it's different. I love her merely by looking."

Dolly sat down again, relieved. "It's her smile, isn't it? All the girls at bridge think she has such a nice smile. Very winsome."

Jake shook his head. He remembered what Nell had said about smiling and was filled with pride that he knew a part of her that no one else did—a secret. "No, I used to think that, but not anymore. She told me her smile doesn't show her insides. And I still love her without her smile. I guess I love whatever is inside her, whether it's a smile or a frown."

"Personally, I think you should court her brothers," Harold said as though it was his own idea. "That is, if you have the stomach for it."

Jake nodded yes. "I'm fighting for my life. I have the stomach for whatever it takes. Besides, George isn't too bad a fellow."

"Then concentrate on him," Dolly blurted out. "What Nell has told me about the twins is a disgrace."

"Oh?" Harold perked up. "Tell us please."

Dolly went to the pantry and pulled out a cake pan full of doughnuts she had made two nights before and forgot. "I've told you already, Harold, and I wouldn't gossip like this, except I think it will benefit Jake. Besides, it's an interesting and awful story.

"The two older boys, Lowell and Lester, they are twins you know, were married for many years and, according to Nell, had good marriages. George's only sweetheart married somebody else because he didn't want to have children, and so he and Nell set up housekeeping in their deceased parents' home. George farmed the land and gave a portion of the profits to the twins as sort of an inheritance-sharing.

"Then one morning at a railroad crossing, the wives of the twins were hit by a train. Lowell's wife was killed instantly, and Lester's died a month later ... or was it the other way around? Anyway, the one whose wife died right away shut himself up in his house while George and neighbors worked his fields. Then when the other one's wife died, George went to the rescue again. Nell said the grieving widowers spent a lot of time banging things around, shouting, and not listening to reason."

Jake interrupted. "They must still be in mourning."

Dolly gave him a reprimand look and continued. "It was because of this double bereavement that George and Nell took their brothers into their home. After a few years they sold all their properties and came here to claim their uncle's land. Personally, I think Nell and George made a big sacrifice to come here, although they claim their Nebraska farm is richer."

Harold looked puzzled. "I wonder what they base that on? Iowa has mighty rich dirt."

Dolly passed out the doughnuts that had patiently waited until she was through with the Swensen saga. "You know what I think? I think they came here to get the twins away from their grief ... you know, a change of scenery."

"They probably all needed a change of scenery," Harold offered.

"From each other you mean, don't you?" Jake chortled, after which he bit half the doughnut off and rapidly chewed it into a pulp for swallowing. A big gulp of coffee helped it down. "That's really a terrible story, good doughnuts Dolly, and I don't think I can fight through all that grief to convince them Nell is better off with me. I think I'd better concentrate on courting only her. I wonder why she never told me all that stuff? Thanks for the information, Mrs. H, now I'll only despise the twins instead of hating them. I wonder why she didn't tell me about something so awful."

Harold cleared his throat. "Grief can do strange things to people. Nell probably doesn't want to think about cheery you and un-cheery them in the same breath. But I bet those two icky brothers were mean before their wives' demise."

Dolly nodded in agreement. "Everybody reacts differently to sudden shocks in their lives. Jake, do you remember what you told us about how your mother reacted to your young sister's sudden death? You said she told you, after you were grown up, that the tragedy made her love you more, that she no longer took motherhood for granted."

Jake's eyes swelled with tears at the memory of his mother's constant, comforting love. He blew his nose, some of which was for Nell also. Harold and Dolly sat still while Jake recovered. Then he said, "You know what? I benefited from my mother's grief, but Nell has suffered from her brothers'. So has George. I'm going to take her away from that bad atmosphere and help her get an apartment. I hope she will eventually think I am better than that apartment and whatever job she finds." He took a deep breath as though he was about to begin a crusade. "God will have to look out for George."

Dolly smiled, but she didn't say anything. She didn't have to—she was satisfied that Jake really loved Nell.

***

Nell stood by the long, skinny, kitchen window holding back the cream eyelet curtains, transfixed and looking like she was a part of the embroidered pattern. She was waiting for Jake whom she had finally located at the Hallgrens. "Teach me to drive," she had pleaded to him over the phone. "If I know how to drive, I won't be so dependent on others."

Jake left Harold and Dolly as quickly as he had come that morning.

"He sneaked in here and then he sneaked out," Harold shouted to Dolly. "What in the hell is going on around here anyway?"

Dolly laughed. "I hardly call it sneaking. More like rushing." She pointed to the phone receiver that was dangling loose and bumping against the wall.

In fact, Jake left in such haste after he answered the call from Nell that not even habit made him hang up the receiver. He engined his pickup and took off in second gear, leaving not only the swinging phone, but Prince and Mitzie as well. For pity sakes, he sputtered, now she wants to learn to drive. She'll just get further away from me. She'll get too blasted independent. And why am I in such a hurry to help her do this?

Jake slowed down and thought about the positive side to Nell's driving. There had to be a positive side. Okay, if Nell did learn, then after they were married they could take turns driving to California or New York or Boston where all that history was made. Also, if Nell could drive, they could invite Billy and Angela to stay late into the evening and listen to Nell play the piano, after which they would all get into the pickup, and Nell could try to drive around the ruts in the dark to get the kids home. She could even drive to get them on a Saturday morning while he walked around his land, and when they were all together, they could drink milk and eat cookies and talk and hopefully laugh a lot.

206

Suddenly Jake's mental rambling stopped. The kids? Where were they? He had forgotten about them; had they forgotten about him? He speeded up the truck as though this would make the forgetting go away. It didn't because he remembered even more: Prince and Mitzie. Those precious two things were still at the Hallgrens.

But that was okay, he fussed, they would learn along with Nell and the children to be more independent. Everybody independent, nobody needing anybody, we can all live in this enormous world separate from each other and relish our independence. It would be the Fourth of July all year round. Everybody would have their own firecracker to toss without any help from anybody, heaven forbid that, and celebrate one long independence day. Thank goodness for the Founding Fathers—what foresight they had.

Jake screeched to a stop and looked toward the barn. The brothers were not there. Perhaps they were dead. Independently dead. Maybe that's why Nell needed to learn how to drive: all her drivers were dead. I wonder how they died, Jake's scrambled thoughts asked. Maybe I killed these sons of bucks yesterday and blanked it out. I hope I didn't get George.

Nell took Jake's hand and led him into the kitchen. "The boys all went to town. I'm so alone without a way to get around. Please teach me to drive, please."

Jake stopped Nell's lead and put his arms around her. Although she had asked for another favor so she could become more independent and then perhaps leave everyone behind, including him, he felt closer to her now than he had ever felt close to anyone before. He had a woman who needed him, even though it may be temporary. He hugged her closer and sensed her whole essence penetrate him, like a ghost would, if there had been one hanging around.

Nell didn't move; she hugged him back and started to cry; she pulled away and blew her nose. "I am closest to God when I cry, Jake." She sat down and motioned him to do the same. "Whether I am happy or whether I am unhappy, I feel

207

God when I cry. My wet face must really tug at His heart because I feel such a strong presence of something very near me. I think it's God."

Jake cleared his throat. That was really something, what she just said. All he ever felt when he cried was a stuffed-up nose. "You felt God? Didn't you feel me? I'm the one who hugged you."

Nell laughed and blew her nose again; her smile returned. "Of course I did. God gave you to me, you know. You are wonderful for me, my dear man, and I do appreciate you. But you are not God."

"I suppose not," Jake replied. "But thanks for putting me second." He hesitated. "I am second, aren't I?"

Nell went to the stove for coffee. "Jake, you must think I'm wishy-washy, that I'm using you for my own satisfaction. That's not true, it only seems that way. But I feel something now besides my desire to marry you. I feel hemmed in, like I will go from one frying pan into another. I am fifty-seven, and I have yet to be alone and fend for myself." She heaved a big sigh. "Getting back to why I called this morning—I need to be able to drive. What if something happened to you and I couldn't get you to a doctor?"

There was that blankety-blank independent thing again. "You don't look fifty-seven," Jake said. "I'm sixty, but I think you know that."

"Will you teach me to drive?"

"Right now this minute?"

"Whenever you will, I'd appreciate it."

"How about after we get married?"

The living room clock chimed the half hour. Jake's head turned to it, and he recalled how his father had wound his own clock with a key every week like it was an occasion. He had wound it a few days ago himself, but usually forgot, so he was used to not hearing chimes, and these startled him and added to more things to be uneasy about.

Nell didn't say anymore. They drank the coffee as though they had done this many times before, together, without talking.

Finally, Jake put his empty cup down and rolled it back and forth between his hands. "I figure it will be more convenient after we're married." Ha, now she'd have to marry him. "We can be private about it, your brothers won't see and jeer you. How about it, Nell?"

"I just don't know." Her mouth turned down again.

"Will you at least give me a chance to court you before we do this driving thing? I never courted you—one date—and then pow, I hit on you for marriage. I'll slow down. I want to bring you roses and buy you chocolates."

Nell smiled again. "Find me an apartment, Jake, help me get a job, and you can court me all over the place. I can't wait to have you over to my own home for supper."

Jake heard the brothers returning. He took out his keys for a quick exit. "Then it's settled, we'll have a few dates, you can cook me a meal or two, and then we'll get married. Right?"

"Something like that," she answered.

***

One week later Nell had an apartment, a job at the orphanage, her piano, and a vague promise from Jake to teach her to drive.

"Oh Jake," she exclaimed the first evening they ate together in her small apartment, "the orphanage will be my salvation. The maiden sisters hired a lawyer who will hire a builder to expand their home. There is excitement all over. Just the other day we got another child, and this one is from another county. We hope everything will be settled by spring so building can start before we get too crowded."

***

Fortunately and unfortunately it appeared neither Jake nor Nell had considered taking the time to think through their sudden decision to marry. When Jake came to Nell in Tolliver's Hardware, Nell was no longer looking for a husband, no longer much interested in marriage. Her last heart-breaking encounter in Iowa had almost switched her mind away from men as potential romances or husbands.

So, Nell's initial impression of Jake was not of husband

material, but of a short man who had the courage to think she would respond to his helpfulness at the nail bin. This first uncertain impression of him, however, did not last long. She knew as soon as his fumblings started and his persistence in making the purchase of nails an important event, that this man was pursuing her. And after years of the predictability of George and the verbal sneerings of the twins, she was ready for a treat.

That treat came in the form of an eager, almost bashful, bungling, short-statured Jake. The way his eyes looked into hers, as though to plead for mercy to pay attention to him, stirred her feelings into a smile and a response to his intentness. She probably would not have considered Jake as anyone other than a passing hello when she was young. But she was no longer young, her years of living and learning what life really is all about had changed her man requirements from the tall, stately, muscular type to the qualities that can reside inside anyone regardless of the outer packaging. These qualities, she had recognized, were friendliness, caring, and an awareness of the other person.

Nell's trip to Iowa was in haste, and for two reasons: she knew during their first date that Jake was a fast mover, and fast movers don't give their targets enough time to decide whether to encourage or to shoo. Nell wanted the time to decide. The other reason was something she didn't want to admit even to herself, a hopeless something she had not been sure of before her move to Nebraska.

So she left. She intentionally did not write Jake, thinking that if they were meant to be a couple—like an item in a store—he would still be there when she returned. As the weeks passed, she thought of him more and more. He soaked in; his short height was something to be aware of, but not to take issue with; he gradually became more important than an item in a store.

She actually started to miss him. She needed attention, and Jake had given it to her in a most gentlemanly, however nervous, manner. No smart remarks, no manhandling, no assumptions—only kindness and gallantry that she used to think was a trait confined to tall, handsome men with deep, smooth voices. So by the time Nell got off the bus and walked into Barney's, she was ready to be plucked from her tree of famine and put into a simmering pot of fragrant spices.

As for Jake, he had lost enough of his fear of approaching another woman for romance when he saw Nell inside the brown and green checkered dress. The breeze that blew her skirt in his direction also blew the essence of this too-tall, very slender woman into his heart.

Although the immediate courage Jake needed to approach Nell was not there at the barbecue, it did come later when he finally tired of wondering about her, when he finally decided he had to know now whether she would pay the attention to him that he paid to her. When he saw her in front of the hardware store, he didn't see Nell. He saw a stalk of corn, a wavy patch of wheat, a clump of potatoes, all waiting for him to harvest. And it was this impression of Nell—that she appeared as important as the land—that finally gave him the courage to pursue her.

Jake's marriage proposal was not in haste, and neither was Nell's reply. The makings for the 'will you' question and the 'yes' reply were planted by both of them years ago; and the makings stayed buried until they finally matured on the road back to the Swensen farm when Jake clumsily asked, and Nell bluntly answered.

**

Billy stopped his bicycle on the road and pushed backward on the pedals to brake; he leaned forward and put his weight on the handle bars to rest; he looked straight ahead at the house several yards away, and no part of his outside body expressed anything of what his inside was thinking; he was as motionless and silent as a scene from a picture of still life. His eyes focused on Jake's house and pierced through it with a stare as forlorn as a puppy taken from its mother.

Angela slid off her place in the basket rigged onto the back of the bicycle and started to pick up and drop small

211

stones one at a time in her gentle, ladylike manner.

Jake came out of his house with Prince by his side and headed for a walk in a direction opposite the children. The late afternoon sun was almost gone, and the deep pink streaks of sky with a man and his dog walking toward it would have made a nostalgic postcard scene except for one gloomy image. Billy.

He was too young to realize that Jake had actually not seen him and his sister; he was too young to understand that Jake always went for a walk in the same direction without first checking to see if a young boy and his sister were on the same road staring at his house. Billy was simply too young to know a lot of things, but he thought he did, and as a result of Jake's oversight, he knew for sure now that adults merely existed, that they weren't something special that kids could look up to or depend on for promises made. If it hadn't been for Angela's distraction of dropping stones that plink-plunked in his head, Billy would have sat down on the hard-packed road and cried his heart out.

But he didn't have to sob out loud for Prince to sense a presence of someone other than his master's somewhere in the distance. The dear dog let out a rather loud, sharp bark, and Jake turned in Billy's direction.

The two separate clumps of rejected humanity, Jake and Billy, looked blankly at each other for less time than it takes to blink, and then Jake waved Billy to come, come here, welcome, how have you been?

Billy whistled sharply for Angela to remount the bicycle; he pedaled fast toward the scene, leaning forward with his head almost on the handle bar because this would surely get him there faster. "It's just me, Mr. Blackburn, me and my sister, we were out for a ride after school." Billy was too young to be sophisticated about hiding eagerness.

Even though Prince knew the children, he felt obligated to bark one more time and, of course, start to pant. Jake gave the dog some pats on his backside and motioned for Billy and Angela to get off the bicycle. "Would you two like some milk and cookies?"

"No, it's getting dark fast. We have to go pretty soon. Thank you though, Mr. Blackburn." Billy had evidently lost his memory of his disgust about the milk and cookie offer, his mouth watered for them, but he didn't have a light on his bicycle bright enough to find his way home after darkness on a deserted country road.

Jake laughed at Billy's formality of the thank you and the Mr. Blackburn reply. "Where did you learn all those manners? Did your folks teach you something after all?"

Billy's face winced.

Then Jake's did. He looked straight into the young boy's face and apologized. "I'm sorry, kid, I guess I need some manners myself. Why don't you two get off the bike and go on a walk with me and my pal?"

"It's too dark late, it's too dark pretty soon," Billy fumbled for words.

Jake put his hands on the handle bars. "No, it's not too dark late. You walk with me, and then I'll drive you and your bike home. Okay?"

Billy slid from the bicycle like butter off a hot ear of corn. "Oh sure, okay, come on Sis." His hands shook as he leaned the bicycle up against a tree, and if he had had on short pants instead of long corduroys, his knees would have been seen knocking together.

The four walked side by side in the middle of the seldom driven road, with Prince making sniffing side trips into the dead autumn foliage and weeds. Crackle noises pierced the quiet country as the animal dashed from one area to another.

"You have such a nice dog, Mr. Blackburn," Billy said with a slight quiver in his voice, a quiver that comes when someone is overwhelmed with a sense of feeling a part of someone or something other than oneself.

"Thank you, son, but call me Jake... I think we've covered this subject before. It's all right to call me by my first name. You can leave all that formal stuff for your teachers and people like that. Okay?" Jake wondered why he unthinkingly called Billy 'son.' It was such a grown-up thing to say 'son.' No, it was not grown-up, but rather an awkward way to refer to a boy almost unknown to him. Awkward, yes, that's what it was. But then, these were awkward times.

Billy answered "okay" to Jake's second request on calling him by his first name.

Jake recovered from his awkwardness and asked Billy about how his parents were.

Neither child answered.

"Well, okay then, how are the two of you these days?"

Billy picked up a stone and hurled it forward on the road. Although the boy had stopped quivering and shaking, he remained silent, and between this silence of the children and Nell's idea for independence and Prince scurrying about, Jake felt he was the only one in Boone County, the only one in Nebraska, the only one in the world. He had been alone most of his life, but he never experienced its impact until now with the children quietly next to him and Nell busily tucked away in her apartment.

He cleared his throat. "You two aren't making much conversation today, are you?" Jake said as he hurled a few stones of his own.

"Nothing to talk about," Billy answered.

Jake picked up another stone and handed it to Angela. "I usually don't talk much today or any day except when I have something to complain about. I complain a lot. How about you, Billy, do you have any complaints?"

"Na. I do get scared sometimes though."

"Like when?" Jake pursued.

"Like ... anytime."

Jake whistled for Prince to rejoin the group. Then he chuckled. "Life is a scary place to be, isn't it?"

"Yeah," said Billy.

"But not always. Right?"

The solemn silence came back.

***

While Jake, Billy, and Angela were busy throwing every

stone they could find in Jake's area of farmland, Nell was sitting in front of her piano.

She touched the keys lightly, and the soft noise filled the small apartment. Then vigorously, until the entire town would have heard the outburst if windows had been open.

But the townspeople were closed in for the coming winter and had started to fuss over Thanksgiving.

***

"That little runt, that little bastard runt," Lo mumbled to Les over their beers at Barney's.

"What's that?" Barney asked. "Did you say you wanted another beer?"

The twins turned their backs on the proprietor and took their drinks to a table far in the corner.

"What are we going to do?" Les asked. "We will have to hire somebody."

Lo pounded the table. "That little bastard runt took away our housekeeper, and I bet they're shacked up together. Don't you think it funny, brother? I haven't got any wedding announcement. Have you?"

Barney swiped their spilled beer from the counter and frowned at the brothers. He didn't trust them. He worried they might burst into a saloon brawl any minute; he brooded about their odd personalities which consisted of stomping in, yelling for beer, yanking on the pinball machine knob a few times, and throwing quarters on the counter. Their mouths always had toothpicks in them, soft from saliva and rammed between bottom teeth; they walked slow and cleared their throats a lot in lieu of a decent conversation, and their faces were always bland nothings of expression whether they were upset or not, which they usually were.

"Bartender," Lo yelled. "Bartender. We want more beer and we want it now."

Barney winced. He was used to more respect from his regulars who knew he was the owner of the saloon as well as the barkeeper. No one else would ever refer to him as a bartender, anyone of age could be a bartender, but not anyone could own the place. "If you bring me your mugs, I'll fill them up for you." He was taking a chance on that request and he knew it.

Lo belched, but he did get up and come to Barney with his mug. "You need a dishwasher so you can give customers clean refills."

Barney eyed the blob of breakfast on Lo's bib overalls.

"Ask for clean glasses," Les yelled from across the room. "What kind of a joint is this, anyhow?"

Lo put his head back and laughed obnoxiously loud. "A second rate joint, that's what. Small town, small town."

Small town? Clean glasses? Barney angered. A lot of nerve those beady-eyed belchers have about his place. Any customer could see they were perfect examples of spigot drinkers—the type who bend down under a beer barrel and drink from its faucet. Barney filled the mugs without looking at his accusers who strutted words like flunk-outs from the big city of charm—he was afraid he might throw the filled beers into their offensive faces.

"Hey Lo," Les yelled again. "Ask Mr. Bartender if he knows any housekeepers. He should, in his line of work. Ha-Ha."

Barney took a deep breath. He wanted to avoid saying anything to them, even if it was a simple no.

"How about it, beer slinger, do you know anybody who can keep house for three men?" Lo swiped a pretzel and crunched it all at once between his teeth. "Do you know any broken-down woman who would be grateful for a job?"

Broken-down woman? Barney looked up sharply at his belligerent patron.

Lo laughed again and opened his arms in gesture of something. "Hey, hey, saloon man, don't be offended. You don't think a pretty young thing would want to keep house for three old farmers, do you? We need a woman who will be grateful. All right? Wow—touchy, touchy."

Barney felt a little better about the brusk man's roundabout weak apology. Besides, the Swensens would be lucky to get anyone who knew about them to come to their farm and be constantly insulted; and he licked his wounds with that thought. "You can post a notice in the drugstore window, everyone reads the drugstore window. Maybe within a week or so, everybody will have seen it." Barney turned away, he didn't want to be too helpful.

"Oh hey, all right," Les yelled from the corner table. "Got any paper?"

Barney ripped a sheet off the yellow pad he used for inventory. It was a 'begone with you' kind of rip. He thought of the tape he had in his back room apartment, but he didn't mention it. If the brothers could afford a housekeeper, they could afford tape.

The twins settled down, scribbled an ad, and walked out without further remarks; they left their empty beers on the table, and so did Barney. Nobody ever sat over there anyway except once in awhile when Harold and Jake had some secret they didn't want anyone to hear. It could wait until closing time.

***

The widow Clara Bruggeman stroked each of her six cats on their backsides and shooed them outdoors for the day.

The cats were all she had left of her marriage and motherhood; as a young girl she had taken in strays, and now she had generations of their offspring to keep her company on what city people would describe as the lone prairie.

Her husband Claus had objected to her cat menagerie, but he deferred when Clara told him that when he chose her, he chose the cats too. Claus' resentment was not the cats as such, but that Clara let them have the run of the house. Eventually he deferred on this also as their marriage union produced more and more children, eleven, during which Claus realized an occasional cat here and there was not the congestion problem.

Clara's creased face and leather-tough hands proved her thirty-five years of drudgery starting with marriage at sixteen and her first child the following year. Although Claus was a highly productive farmer with enough hired hands and eventual help from teen-age sons, he relied on Clara to raise the children, to cook, to clean, keep the farm records, and to rub him down after a day in the hot sun. Her cats were the only creatures who did not drool, grunt, sass, or complain about the school's homework. She treasured them.

After the children left the farm—not a single one of them took up farming, a fact for Ripley—and after Claus died, Clara was finally alone with her cats. Besides keeping company with them, which was much of the time, she whiled away the deserted winter months by shoveling snow away from a portion of her backyard and putting down sunflower seeds, a cache of acorns, berries and suet. The squirrels, birds, and rabbits who came to this oasis were additional company for her.

Like her wildlife friends, Clara also lived hand to mouth. Although Claus had owned his land and had sold it for a comfortable profit after all the children were gone, his expertise as a farmer did not apply to any investment ability; he put all his money into local oil ventures which never produced, and now all that Clara had left of an otherwise productive life was her home.

She lived on money sent by the children which mainly paid the taxes for her house, food for her stomach, and gas for her dilapidated station wagon. She was still physically and mentally agile at fifty-one years, and she gradually acquired a desire for more things to do as well as more money to spend. She was also the first and only one to answer the Swensens' drugstore ad.

***

"I'm Clara Bruggeman, and I'm asking about your housekeeper job. How much do you pay?"

The three brothers asked Clara to step into the kitchen where most of her work would be done.

"We want you here early enough for breakfast, and then we want you to leave right after you get through making supper. In between time, you'll clean all over the house and make the beds. You can wash the supper dishes the next day so you're not here waiting for us to finish eating and getting paid for doing nothing." These directives, of course, came from the twins.

Clara raised her arm like a traffic cop, a gesture she had used many times with her eleven children. "Hold on there, whoa, just hold on. You want me to clean the house everyday? What for? How about the washing? That's what you'll probably need done everyday, not the cleaning."

Lo crossed his arms. "We want you here everyday, all day, and we will pay minimum wage by the month."

"No deal," Clara answered as though she didn't need the job. "I might as well still be married with kids all over the place. I'll work by the hour starting when I get here unless I grocery shop for you. Then that time will be included. And I want to be paid in cash every week." By this time Clara turned her attention to George who was the only brother not rolling his eyeballs up at the ceiling or making a pouting face. "I will clean once a week, wash clothes three times, and do the supper dishes before I go home. You fellas can eat while I scrub the pots and pans, don't worry, I'm not one to sit around and do nothing. Then I will expect to take my supper home."

Les walked out of the kitchen, and Lo stomped into the living room after which the television came on loud.

George smiled at Clara. "We'll let you know. Give me your phone number and some time to talk to the twins."

Five days later the drugstore still displayed the ad, and Clara knew she had the job although George had not called.

"She certainly is an ugly woman," Lo said after two days of haggling over everything imaginable about the widow.

"Ugly and old," Les contributed.

"Old? She said she is fifty, that's not old," George said.

"Fifty what?" Lo snorted. "Fifty million?"

"Yeah," Les kept on, "she is just awful looking. She looks dirty."

Lo laughed. "Yeah, like she needs dusting. How clean do you think she'll get the house when she's so dirty herself?"

"She's not dirty," George defended. "She's leathery. She

probably had a hard life. Remember, she said something about a dozen kids."

"Eleven." Les shook his head in disapproval. "No wonder she's widowed. Probably worked her man to death inside as well as out."

George raised his voice. "Then she's the one we want. A good worker. Right?"

On Thursday the twins argued about the bathroom facilities because Lo thought maybe her leathery skin was due to a social disease.

"Right," Les embellished. "What if she leaves germs on the toilet? Maybe she even spits inside the house. That's how you get tuberculosis, from spit."

On Friday Lo worried she would gossip in town about their underwear, and Les further debased this possibility with the thought that maybe she didn't know what underwear was.

Late Saturday Lo suggested she didn't have any brains, and Les seconded that and then added maybe no sense either.

One week later, with no one else applying for the job, George called Clara and hired her. "Under your terms, start tomorrow if you will."

"What do you boys eat for breakfast?" Clara replied.

***

Jake always took Prince and Mitzie to the Hallgrens to stay whenever he wanted the freedom of a trip to Omaha. Mitzie didn't care as long as there were mice to find, and Prince played with Proudflesh so well, that Jake thought nothing of leaving his pets behind. Occasionally Jake sacrificed leaving Prince with Harold and Dolly so the animal could enjoy companionship with one of his own kind.

Now there was a new reason for leaving Prince and Mitzie at the Hallgrens: he didn't want his two treasures in the front or in the back of the pickup while he courted Nell.

"I love your pets, Jake, it's all right if they come along with us," but Nell's permission was to no avail; Jake wanted to concentrate on Nell and not have to worry about a panting breath or scratching paw.

On the same day that Les and Lo Swensen voiced loud concern about Clara Bruggeman's dusty skin, Jake dropped off Prince and Mitzie at Harold's and drove to town to have lunch with Nell at the drugstore in another attempt to woo her into his arms, his house, and his bed.

The only ones without special worries for the day were Harold and Dolly. Or so they thought.

Dolly bent over the oven door and removed the hot, bubbly casserole of baked beans covered with scoops of brown sugar and mustard. "Harold," she shouted, "Harold, Harold, Harold."

Harold's dim voice returned his wife's verbal ruckus. "What's so important? I'm in the attic."

"Prince is in a barking fit. Take care of it. Now."

Harold thumped-thumped down the attic stairs and went to the back door. "Hey, Prince, shut up, your master would be ashamed of you." Then Harold's heart skipped a beat. Proudflesh was not with Prince who continued to bark, his snout in vigorous motion, eyes wide open and penetrating, after which he started down the driveway in the direction of the road.

Harold rushed back to the kitchen. "Dolly, help me, I think something's happened to Proudflesh, I'm going to look."

Dolly put down the steaming, odorous casserole and inhaled deeply, but not for the beans. "Oh God, Proudflesh, please be okay." She ran after Harold.

They found him where Prince led, on the side of the road, his breath in short pants, his eyes bulged out in fear and pain and helplessness. There was blood.

Harold let out a cry and waved Dolly to go back. "Get the wagon, I need the wagon, hurry Mama."

Dolly ran back up the road; she hadn't taken time to fasten her sweater, and it flapped in the wind as she hurried to the porch. "Please God, don't take that dog, it will break the dear old man's heart."

Five years ago, shortly after losing his German shepherd to old age, Harold had found Proudflesh wandering helplessly

221

in town. The ribbed-shrunk puppy was not yet weaned; Harold took him home and treated him like a human being with eye dropper feedings and warm blanket bedding. The two became like father and child.

Dolly thought about Proudflesh's entry into their lives as she dumped the load of logs from their daughter's childhood wagon and hastened back. The wagon bumped and snagged on the gravel with Prince running up to it, barking even more. "Shut up, Prince. Thank you, but shut up."

"My boy's in pain, Mama, but I think he will be all right. His back leg has a pretty deep cut, but I think my handkerchief will hold the blood until I can put my own pressure on it."

Dolly stooped down and hugged Prince who finally quit barking, and the three carefully walked back to the house with Proudflesh awkwardly inside the wagon. They lifted the substitute stretcher up the steps and into the kitchen and then lowered the injured pet onto the shiny linoleum floor. Neither of them complained about the wagon being too small or the floor too clean for this unhappy emergency; neither of them said anything, but both felt guilty for thinking it.

Dolly opened her drawer of clean rags, ripped one into strips, and tossed them over by Proudflesh and Harold; she rinsed another rag through her fresh, sudsy dishwater and flung it at Harold who caught it in midair and gently, quickly cleansed the torn leg. Blood continued to come out, but it was only a trickle now, and Harold felt safe with the snug cloth wrap in place of his heavy hand clamped onto the injury.

"How about some iodine?" Dolly asked.

"Not yet," Harold answered. "I want the gash to come together first. If it starts to fester, I'll soak the bandages with it later."

Dolly complied. Harold knew more than she about mending torn flesh, just as she knew more than he about soothing fevered brows. She patted Prince on top of his head who barked once more before settling beside Proudflesh.

Next, she knelt beside her husband's companion, hugged his face with her hands, and whispered, "Get well for goodness sakes, your master loves you, and so do I." Finally, after considerable whining and panting, both dogs went to sleep in exhaustion.

Harold sat at the kitchen table and drank the hot chocolate Dolly made as a treat for his anxiety over the possible loss of his favorite dog. When Harold was young and working the fields, he relied on dogs and cats to keep away coyotes and mice— they were a part of his work team. But in his retirement, and especially because of Proudflesh's scrawny condition as a pup, Harold cherished this animal of his old age. Cherished and needed.

"Mama," he said, "Mama, I don't want to lose that dog. But when I do, I want it to be in the middle of the night when he'll go peacefully. One big sigh and it's over."

"That's the way we all want to go, dear."

Harold continued being pensive. "I'm more aware of suffering than I used to be. Take those two kids, the ones who hang around at Barney's and who bike to Jake's once in awhile. They're suffering from neglect."

Dolly nodded. "You mean Billy and Angela Charmley? I understand their parents are not the usual kind of people. You're right, neglect can hurt just like a cut finger or stomach ache."

"Especially now, Mama. I meant to tell you and forgot. Their parents, the ones with such a charm-ing name, skipped town and left the children. The kids are at the orphanage now. Probably much better off."

***

Mr. and Mrs. Charmley. The townspeople joked that there should be a law against the Charmleys having such a lovely name, because they certainly were not charming.

Their marriage had started out like most people's, but somehow they quit loving each other, and the passion that produced two children faded until it became like a robot. And for some unusual reason, when they quit loving each

223

other, they quit loving their kids.

That was the rumor, anyway, and a lot of gossip time was spent guessing why the Charmleys ignored their children. One of the townspeople suggested calling County Welfare. "These kids, they're like paper dolls without a face drawn in," the druggist's wife complained. Others joined in, but the welfare office said they could do nothing as long as the children were fed, clothed, and intact. The fact that Billy and Angela were grungy and expressionless did not count as violations.

The eventual move of the sad brother and sister to the orphanage did not come about by a neighbor's complaint; it precipitated when Mrs. Charmley went back to Denver and directly into the apartment of her former boyfriend. Although this change made the mother happy, it worked the opposite on the father—not because he missed his wayward wife, but because he was stuck with the kids. He didn't want them either.

So he left. One late afternoon Mr. Charmley called on the sheriff and told him he didn't want his children anymore, "will you arrange for a foster home?"

When the sheriff shook his head no, the father started to talk a continuous spiel, crowding out anything the sheriff wanted to say further, using one long sentence after another with explanations here, heartaches there, a few measly excuses in between, until all of the words became like garbage stinking up the room; the sheriff stood up, put his hands flat on the desk, looked his antagonist straight in the eye and said, "It's not that easy to get rid of kids."

At the same time the sheriff's ears heard himself say that, his face cringed over the possibility that maybe the father would get rid of the children in another way besides giving them away, a way unfavorable, such as leaving them in an area of rain-parched Death Valley where no human being had ever been before or would be likely to go in time to rescue them. Or maybe the father would just plain and simply kill his offspring.

The lawman quickly decided it was no longer appropriate to give a lecture on parental responsibility. With the townspeople's complaints fresh in his memory, he decided to make a deal with Billy and Angela's remaining parent. "Run away, run off, and leave your children behind. I'll call County Welfare, but please, let me know when you do it so the kiddies will not be alone for long." Then the sheriff pounded his fist on his desk and jabbed a finger onto the father's nose. "And you had better, you had re-ally better, leave this area for good. For always. Forever."

The father left town the next day when Billy and Angela were in school, honking his horn with a thumb up at the sheriff who was strolling by Tolliver's Hardware store. The sheriff called the County Welfare office, and before the two forsaken children had a chance to go to Barney's for orange soda pop or to Jake's for milk and cookies, he led them up the front steps of the orphanage. The quiet, well behaved pair of siblings, unwanted, unneeded, ignored, and dressed like rag pickers, arrived at their new home with no luggage and a hollow gaze of abandonment on their faces. There was no crying and no questions on their parts—things like that don't happen inside a vacuum.

Even when they looked up into the friendliness of the two spinster sisters, the forlorn boy and girl did not feel the happiness they briefly had when Jake offered them milk, cookies, conversation, and stones to toss as they walked along the road together. Not Jake nor Barney or anyone else who paid extra attention to them were in their thoughts at this frightening time because these people were not inside the vacuum they were in now.

***

Clara picked up the bucket of water she had used to scrub the kitchen floor and threw its dirty contents over the dying summer flowers Nell had tucked in close to the house for safety.

"Oh my golly gosh," Clara exclaimed. She had accidentally drenched her favorite cat, the one she brought to work with her everyday. The cat screeched and ran into the barn scattering squawking chickens all over the place and evoking a loud, mournful moo from the cow George had started to milk. The cat continued to meow and shake water from its coat, and the cow continued to moo.

But the milk flowed, and George concentrated on it so he could ignore Clara's embarrassment as she hurried into the barn. "I'm sorry, Mr. Swensen, truly sorry. I know better than to raise a ruckus in a barn. I guess I was too hasty to get rid of that dirty kitchen floor."

"George, call me George." He laughed. "So that's how the cat got doused? That's okay. Just be thankful the twins weren't around. You probably would have owned one less cat."

"No kidding? Are they mean? I thought they were just sassy."

"They're everything unpleasant. I think they probably never will recover from losing their wives. Thank goodness the children were raised before their fathers got even more contrary than they were before that horrible accident. The women were killed by a train, you know, killed like teen-agers out for a joy ride."

Clara asked for details, and after she heard them, she wondered how she could think that dousing a cat and upsetting a barnyard was such a big deal. She looked for the wet, meowing form even though she realized it would be hours before the feline would forgive and return.

She went back to George to talk more about his family tragedy. "Do their children ever visit?"

"Na. They came around a lot when their mothers died, but that got to be old hat after awhile." George looked up from his milking stool at Clara. He noticed she didn't appear to be so haggard today, and the little sun that angled into the barn shone on the housekeeper's hair displaying a tinge of red, a tinge of life on her otherwise colorless appearance.

"Well," Clara continued, "I won't keep you, but I will put on a fresh pot of coffee if you'd like. There's a chill, it'll warm us up."

George nodded. It would be nice to have a gentle person to talk to for awhile before Les and Lo returned from town and their too-many beers.

Clara nodded also. Then she walked around the barn on her way back to the house in case her cat was sulking nearby.

***

Jake got up from the dinner Nell had cooked for them in her apartment and took the dishes to the sink. They had eaten like hard working farmers do—heartily—and their dinner plates looked like they had licked them clean, just as a dog does when pleased with a feast.

Nell laughed softly at seeing Jake's gesture of help. "You know what, my dear gentleman caller, do you know what I think?"

"What?" Jake turned and smiled back.

"You are truly a gentleman."

Jake squirted soap into the sink and turned on the water. "Oh, I don't know about that. You made this delicious meal, and I'm only thanking you for it."

"Jake, please sit down, let's have coffee. I can clean up later."

Jake obeyed. He wondered if after they were married—that is, if they ever got married—Nell would prefer conversation before the evening meal cleanup.

"Remember our first date," she continued, "when you told me what a loving mother you had?"

"Sure I do. She watched her only daughter die at her feet while she still carried me. I never knew my sister Alice, but I bet that little girl would have grown up to be a wonderful mother too." Jake lowered his head in bashfulness at sharing this thought.

Nell took his hand. "Jake, I didn't bring this up to stir sad memories. I brought it up because I have something to ask you."

Jake sat up straight, suddenly, puzzled. He wasn't embarrassed anymore, but he was concerned, and his thumping heart told him so.

227

"First of all, I have to tell you something sad: Billy and Angela Charmley were abandoned by their parents."

Jake's mouth dropped and his eyes opened wide. "Huh?"

"You like those kids, don't you?"

"You bet I do. I'm proud to be nice to them, they always seem so deserted. Where are they? They'll need somebody. W-h-e-r-e in the blasted bits a-r-e they?"

Nell laughed lightly at Jake's intense response. "I guess I won't have to ask you after all. I know what your answer will be."

"Where are they, Nell?"

"At the orphanage. But they are sleeping on the floor in sleeping bags and will continue to do so until the new addition is built."

"That may take years. Jensen's money will have to go through probate or something like that, won't it? And even if not, those kids might be grandparents before the new addition is in. They'll go from sleeping bags to an old peoples' home."

Nell shook her head. "I don't know about that, but I do know it's crowded at the orphanage now and will probably get more crowded before everything is settled."

Jake frowned. "What are those kids doing on the floor? Dogs sleep on the floor, at least the ones I know do, most of them anyway. Aren't there any sofas?" He remembered his mother's description of how his sister died, on the floor of the cellar, and he grew up thinking the floor as a sad place for a child to be. "We've got to get those kids off the floor for pity sakes."

Nell almost clapped her hands, the orchestration was going so well. "That's what I want to talk to you about. I can take them into my apartment. We may be a little crowded too, but at least I have an extra room, and we can get two beds from somewhere, Omaha, the Salvation Army, and maybe you can put up a partition in the room and give the kids a little privacy from each other and still keep them close."

A partition? Jake thought about the movie with Clark

228

Gable and Claudette Colbert where they slept in separate beds with a blanket partition between to assure propriety. A blanket? What would Nell be turning her extra bedroom into? A motel? What happened to wedding plans?

Jake decided to postpone any further unpleasant thought concerning his role in the matter. "Where are their parents?"

"They went back to Denver. The version I heard and believe, which is not the only one, was that the father took the children to the sheriff's house and said 'here' and then left."

"Those awful people ought to be arrested."

"I heard the sheriff was going to, then decided to do something better. He had the father sign a paper saying how the mother had deserted and that the father relinquish the children to the townspeople with them as temporary guardians. The druggist witnessed the paper signing in all seriousness, although both he and the sheriff knew it wouldn't stand up in court. The sheriff did this charade to give himself more time to obtain a legal arrangement; he figured the father couldn't care less about it being legal, he only wanted out as quick as possible."

Nell took a deep breath and continued before Jake could interrupt with remarks like, "Charmley must be stupid or without a soul or something unpleasant like that."

"The sheriff said I can house them for now, and that's why I'm asking this big favor and understanding from you. Jake, the sheriff knew about those kids long before the father left town. He told me he investigated their house more than once after the neighbors complained about the loud arguments—he was a little afraid for the children. He checked up on them all the time."

Jake rubbed one eye until it squished; he blew his nose hard enough for brains to come out. "I'll get them the beds this weekend. How about it if we all go to Omaha, and then we can buy them some clothes too? Let's do something for those kids besides bed them down."

Nell put her hand up to her mouth to prevent a scream of

joy, but she couldn't hide her eyes of glistening tears. "I'll ask the sheriff and maybe he can sign some kind of permission so we can get things for them at the Salvation Army."

"No, no, no," Jake hastened. No Salvation Army, they're for the poor. I have money. The bed and clothes are on me. I'll foot the grocery bill also."

As though she hadn't heard Jake's offer, Nell walked to the back room and motioned Jake to follow. "I think a partition in the middle here will give the kids a little privacy from each other, but also keep them together during their adjustment. Will you do that for us, Jake?"

Jake wished he had a beard to tug on now, a distraction and delay from feeling what he started to feel, a feeling he didn't care for, a beginning of thought that didn't fit in with his original plan for himself and Nell. She was so enthused and engrossed with the children, was she getting further and further away from marriage? She had two children now, maybe she wouldn't want a husband too. He loved Nell, and he cared about Billy and Angela, but separately. Yet now when he thought of his woman and the children, he thought of them as a package. There would be no more of Nell alone with only him; there would be no more of milk and cookies with only the children. Was he no longer necessary?

Nell waited for his answer, but Jake didn't respond. She repeated the request for the partition and added how much she would appreciate it, she really would, and so would the kids.

Jake looked around the meager room. Why didn't Nell suggest they get married right away, and then the kids could each have a large room upstairs in his house? He so wanted to ask her this, but the question died in his mouth from fear the wrong words would come out, words like "marry me or we're through." Besides, there was no way he ever wanted to be through with Nell; he would take her in any amount she was available, anything at all, so he could at least have a part of her abundant niceness. Dolly had warned him to take it easy with Nell; now would be a good time to start, a good time to be silent.

The silence made Nell walk away from the room, but Jake could see her eyes forming tears before she had a chance to turn around and hide them. She went to the kitchen sink and the dishes; suddenly her tears dropped all over, and she grabbed for the Kleenex tissues. "I don't understand you, Jake, you're so sympathetic and helpful one minute, and then the next you act as though you don't want any part of this."

Jake went over to the sink; he looked at Nell's wet face, then his tears came too. Like two kindergartners, they leaned against the sink and sobbed their hearts until they were exhausted and blew their noses until they were out of the tissues.

"I think, I think," Jake stuttered, "I think maybe we are both pretty much mixed up."

"Oh yes, Jake, we must be. But we can't cry and carry on. We have a responsibility to Billy and Angela."

"We?" Jake's face brightened. "We?"

"Yes. We. That's what life is all about. Responsibility. Both of us."

"That sounds better, my dear woman. You kept talking about you and the kids, you and the kids, never me and you and the kids. It seemed like you had put me in the dugout, you know, the sidelines, where one watches but doesn't play."

Nell nodded the way a woman nods when her man refers to everything in terms of sports. "Is that why you cried?"

Jake stood up to his full height and put his hands in his pockets. "Partly."

Nell nodded again. "Is the other reason because you don't know how to install a partition?"

Jake blew his nose again. "No. The other reason is because it would be so easy for you to marry me now, and then we and the kids could be one united family that lives happily ever after. I'm losing you, aren't I, Nell?"

Nell went to the pantry for another box of tissues just in case. She pulled Jake's hands out of his pockets and pulled on them until the hands and they were at the sofa. "We need to talk."

Jake shook his head no. "I don't want to talk if you're going to send me away forever. I don't even want to go away for a little while anymore."

"I will never send you away, my dear man. But I think you are working on doing that yourself."

Jake shifted his eyes back and forth and finally focused on his accuser. "What'd you mean?"

"I mean that we have, and especially now, shared life together—the good and the bad. So far we have survived your hurried and harried marriage proposal, and Les and Lo's ridiculous insults, and my deceptive smile. We are pretty strong together, young man."

Jake sat on the edge of the sofa and placed his hands over the edge of his knees like Harold used to in grade school when he was told to settle down and behave. "You mean you will actually marry me someday?"

"I have never felt so good since I left my brothers. I am getting further away from willy-nilly Nellie. But I need to get more distance from them, and I'm afraid you won't give me that time. I am afraid you will start to hate me because of my delays. But, and please hear me out before you clamp down on only half of my explanation, when I accepted your proposal, I did it out of frustration and hate for my twin brothers, not out of love for you."

Jake stiffened before Nell finished. He couldn't help but stiffen.

Nell bent down on her knees, placed her hands over his, and looked up into his face. "I love you now. No more frustration and hate—only love. I feel different about a lot of things now. And I know I have been courted by the nicest man in Boone County and in any other town. None of my movie heroes with their tall, sleek bodies and sexy smiles can touch you and your special charm. What more can I say, dear Jake, you have won me over."

Jake was still stiff, Nell's first words of marrying him out of frustration rang in his ears. He cleared his throat, sat up straight, and looked right at Nell. He frowned. "Did you just say you have only recently fallen in love with me? You didn't love me when you got off the bus and tapped me on the shoulder at Barney's?"

"I never told you I loved you, until now, did I?"

"I don't remember. I assumed it when you said yes. I assumed it with the apple pie. I assumed it like you were saying it all the time."

Nell got off her knees and sat next to Jake. She was worried. Jake looked over at her.

"I feel foolish," he said. He felt betrayed.

"I don't deserve you," she said.

A stranger walked in the room then, a presence that had the strength to push them apart with such force that none of the king's horses or men would be able to bring them together again.

Jake thought about what Dolly had said— don't rush her.

Nell thought about Jake's betrayed feeling. She went over to the window and looked down at the street, then back at him. "I started loving you shortly after I moved in here. I was finally away from my past. I guess I was not capable of loving you while you were tied in with my brothers and a farm that really belongs to only them. We are independent of them now. Please forgive my deception."

Jake took a deep breath, and the stranger left the room. When a woman, whom a man already loves, asks forgiveness over something she could not help, well, that sometimes makes the man love her more. Jake was that man.

Jake reached over to Nell and kissed her. "Will you marry me someday?"

"Yes. Someday soon."

The next afternoon Jake went into Nell's back room and put in a partition between narrow beds the Tollivers gave on loan. That night he went to get Prince and Mitzie from the Hallgrens, Prince and Mitzie whom he had dropped off at his best friend's the day before. His elation at Nell's renewal of her marriage promise fell a little, however—he had forgotten his pets.

***

"Oh my golly gosh," Clara exclaimed to George as they each finished a third cup of coffee. "Look at what's coming up from the road."

George turned to the window. Les and Lo and their pickup were having a time of it driving in a straight line along the driveway.

"How did they ever make it home so far in one piece?" Clara added.

George didn't hesitate to answer. "Probably because God didn't want anything to happen to the pickup."

Clara shook her head. "This isn't the first time, then?"

"Nor the last."

Les and Lo somehow stopped the truck several safe yards from the house and slowly weaved their bodies up to the back door. Clara rushed to put on a fresh pot of coffee while George went to the door to assist. The twins went right for the table and pounded on it for coffee.

"I just put on a fresh pot. You two should have phoned you were coming home drunk. Didn't Barney have any coffee for you?" Clara had never experienced drunkenness in her family, but she knew it existed on Friday and Saturday nights when her young sons came back from town and described how an occasional weekend celebrator had helped himself to too much celebration. Her Claus had never indulged, even though she thought it would have been all right now and then for him to go to town and drink with his fellow farmers; maybe if he had, they might not have had so many children.

But enough of the past and its drinking habits, Clara realized, because now she was concerned that Les and Lo would probably be even meaner. She decided to say no more and to do their every bidding until they sobered up.

After Clara poured the coffee, George signaled for her to follow him into the living room. "This is unusual," he said as a prickly feeling went up his arms. "Barney always soaks them with coffee and sandwiches before they leave his place when they're drunk. I can't call him on the phone with them sitting there, so I'm going to town to check things out." George took a quick look into the kitchen. "And you'd better leave for the day."

The prickly feeling transferred to Clara. "Do you think something awful has happened?"

"I don't know. Those two will fly off the handle if I ask if anything happened, so I'll check it out in person. Besides, I don't need to be around here while they sober up. I need an excuse to get away—far away."

"What about supper? I haven't even peeled a potato yet." Clara started back to the kitchen. George grabbed her arm.

"No, Clara, go home. I'll deal with that later. They may come swinging at you."

Lo pounded on the table. "Where's our supper? There's no supper in the oven. Where's that woman leech who gets paid for not making my supper?"

George opened the front door and waved for Clara to follow. "Get your cat and leave. Now."

Clara obeyed, and so did her cat who was sitting at the back door to be let in; as Clara went around the house to retrieve her animal, she sensed a presence at the long, narrow window. She knew better than to even glance that way and chose instead to sprint to the steering wheel of her car and its ignition.

George slid himself into his brown and white trimmed truck and drove around the abandoned pickup resting just inside the road.

Clara did not go home; she was afraid the angry brothers would come after her to make their supper; so she followed George all the way to Barney's.

***

"George Swensen," Barney yelled as soon as he saw the third brother enter the saloon. "George Swensen, your brothers are no longer welcome in my Palace, and as far as I'm concerned, neither are you."

George didn't have to have Barney explain to him the reason for his outburst. He could see the moment he opened the door; he could see the destruction. Of all pitiful things,

235

how could this be, even though he had suspected such?

It was obvious the plastic chairs of every color had been thrown against the walls; it was obvious that most of the tables were upside down and scuffed, and it didn't take much imagination to know that if the furniture had been of wood, an uncountable number of splinters would have been strewn everywhere.

Beer was still wet on three of the wall pictures; the bar mirror was shattered at the top, the bar counter covered with the broken mirror glass after it slid down Lover Doll's giant eyes which miraculously were still intact.

George was silent, not only because he was angry, but because he was ashamed. If he had been Jake, he would have cried. His own kin had committed this crime and left it for everyone to see. Their atrocity of passionate contempt had trashed Barney's only existence.

Barney, however, was not silent. "The sheriff has been here, and I told him to leave those bastards alone until they sobered up. Then I'll get my revenge. I want them to be awake when I spill my guts all over their faces." He took a deep breath. "They hit my moose."

George nodded in sympathy and turned red with shame. He walked over to Barney who was screaming all sorts of words by this time, words that flew through the air like the furniture and beer had. He knew that saying I'm sorry, they will pay for all this, I promise, was meager for the occasion. But he said it anyway.

Barney slapped some of the glass off the counter with a wet towel. He continued to shout at George who was now only two feet away. "I hope they have insurance that will come to me in the mail because they will never come in here again. They had better not even step onto the parking lot. Or the sidewalk in front. Or any place else within my sight. And my eyesight is awfully good."

George saw that Barney had been crying in-between all his shouting and screaming. He wanted to clamp down on his shoulder with his big hand and comfort him, but he knew that wouldn't be the thing to do right now. Instead, he stepped back and started to pick up the fallen furniture and take the severely damaged ones out to his truck. He went in and out of the saloon until the worst pieces of the angry scene were in his pickup. He then climbed up on the counter and wiped Lover Doll clean.

He noticed the beer-stained pictures of Clark Gable, Humphrey Bogart, and Marilyn Monroe, and he wondered if Barney was crying for them as well as his beloved moose head. Marilyn Monroe should never have beer thrown at her. He took the pictures down. "I'll replace these," and hoped Clara or Nell would know how.

Clara came in and stopped George as he left with the pictures. "I tell you what," she said to him, "my day isn't up at your place yet, so I'll work in here until five or six. Okay?"

George nodded approval because he couldn't talk to Clara now; even though she was no Queen of the May, he was humiliated nevertheless when he saw her gasp at his brothers' treachery to Barney and the saloon and its precious contents.

"Whew," Clara said after she viewed the full impact. "I hope you Swensen folks have insurance." But George only had enough strength in him to shake his head to her remark as he drove off to the dump. She turned to Barney. "Is there such a thing as insurance against meanness? I hope you will let me clean up a bit. Would it make you feel better if I told you those two crazies will have no supper tonight?"

Barney looked at the leathery woman's reflection in the remaining part of his mirror. "No supper? I wished they would have a supper, a last meal before they're electrocuted." Barney wanted to shut up, he didn't even know this woman, but he couldn't. "They won't go hungry. They'll kill the nearest cow and then set fire to somebody's barn to roast it. I don't believe I know you."

"Bruggeman. Clara for short. Maybe you knew some of my boys. My husband never came here, but my boys did and always had a good time. They're all gone now to those faraway places like Omaha and Kansas and wherever. My husband Claus died a few years ago. Why don't you find me a bucket, and I'll scrub down your walls."

Clara's presence and her firm, quiet strokes as she washed the beer-smeared walls, calmed the saloon. She should have done this to Barney as well, because every time he picked up pieces of broken mugs and pitchers and glasses, his face turned red and his voice let out a moan.

Because Barney had run outside at the beginning of the twins' brutal attack, and because Clara had come in after it was all over, only the room and its contents knew that the first chair Les threw against the wall was for his anger at loosing his sister as housekeeper and cook. And that the second chair thrown was because he realized he hadn't broken anything with the first one. The third chair he threw at a table, and that was for the train that killed his wife. And the fourth chair was deliberately and meanly pounded into his wife's grave.

Lo joined in with the same vigor once the example was set. He used, instead, the tables to show his disgust with the world and pitched them at the long mirror above the bar and Lover Doll. The image created in the mirror intensified the already destructive scene.

Barney had ducked, then stood up, ducked, then crawled rapidly to the door and out onto the sparse gravel. He reacted to the outburst on his property in an as gentlemanly a way as he could: he went to the twins' pickup and kicked the sidewalls. This satisfaction completed, his anger then turned to panic at the reality of what was happening, and his breathing became like an empty-tanked semi-truck gasping for one more drop of gas. Finally he ran for the sheriff.

The Swensens had hurt Barney as much as if they had picked him up and thrown him along with the tables and chairs. The destruction was an example of their lack of respect for anything or anyone, and this included gentle Barney and his multi-colored furniture. They not only demolished the innards of the saloon, they also shattered a bit of its owner. And another sad part to this event was that

Barney had no intention of getting revenge as he had promised George. Barney wasn't like that.

***

While Proudflesh limped around the kitchen on his healing wound, Jake apologized over the phone to Harold and Dolly for leaving Prince and Mitzie with them for so long without calling. In fact, Jake had never forgotten his pets before, and especially never as long as overnight.

The next morning when he walked into the Hallgren kitchen, he felt uncomfortable. Sometimes he walked in nonchalantly or sad or angry. But never uncomfortable. "I forgot them. I plain and simply forgot them. I'm in love. So. I heard my Princie saved your Proudie's life? I guess he earned his keep."

Harold's smile would have gone from one end of his ear to the other if his mouth could have reached that far; he was still elated over finding his dog in time to stop the bleeding. "Of course Prince did—those two dogs love each other, you know. I love Dolly, you love Nell, Brie loves me, Mitzie loves you, and the whole world loves the whole world."

Dolly interrupted with a laugh. "When Harold is happy, he is really happy. He's also silly."

Harold continued. "My dear friend, it's all right to call your pooch Princie once in awhile if you like, but what's this 'Proudie' business? What kind of a nickname is that? Does that mean I can call Mitz to your cat? We're not much on that cutesy stuff around here, Jake-ee. But if that's what you want, do you think Nell will adopt those two kiddies?"

Jake no longer felt cute. He shook his head. "I don't know. What I do know is that I will keep on courting the socks off that woman even though she has assured me with another yes. She is certainly full of excuses for not marrying me right away, but I'll keep courting, and eventually my proposals might sink in."

Harold clucked. "You're doing it all backwards, you know that, don't you? The courting comes before the proposal. You're suppose to ask a lady for a date first. Now that your

239

woman knows you really want her—I mean, Jake old buddy, you're even showing a little desperation—she can delay on you until doomsday."

Jake frowned. He worried that Dolly didn't voice an objection to what Harold said. Why didn't Dolly slap him down? Wasn't she listening? Dolly, not listen? There was no such thing as that; Jake knew he was without support, he knew that with Dolly's silence, Harold might be right; he realized Dolly's continued muteness might mean he had been putting words into Nell's mouth all this time, words that possibly didn't want to be there and one day would leave. He worried again about Nell's confession about not loving him until now.

He had to say something in Nell's defense and for his own assurance. "You don't know Nell. She wouldn't taunt me like that. She's a good woman."

Dolly still didn't say anything, but Harold sure did. "A lot of women are good. But they can be real coy when it comes to a man courting. How about if Dolly speaks to her?"

"No, no, no. Not anymore." The thought of his struggle wore him out, and he didn't want to be worn out anymore. He felt like everything was ganging up on him. All he wanted was to marry Nell—why did there have to be such a siege of events? "Nell and I have been through a lot of bad things with each other, and we're still together. She reminded me of that yesterday. That's why I forgot Prince and Mitzie. Nell does make a lot of sense about wanting to be on her own for awhile. It's all right. Really it is."

Jake started to walk away, hesitating for Dolly to defend him. She didn't. It was not over, his battle with Harold's opinion about his courtship conduct was still not over. He had better say something more. "I care about those kids. Nell and I have another thing in common now." He stopped and turned to the Hallgrens—this was a moment he didn't want to walk out on hurriedly because this was a moment, not of convincing his best friends, but of convincing himself.

He cleared his throat and finally opened the door. "See

you in church." That was the only thing he could think of to say because there was no way he would reveal to anyone what Nell had just told him.

***

Church was not where Nell headed after she found out about Les and Lo's episode at Barney's. She didn't even bother to call Jake first, she was too much in a flutter to get to the farm; she hurried in and out of every store until she found a neighboring farmer ready to leave for home. If her mind had led her heart, she would have called and then waited for Jake to take her there, but her mind was not functioning at the moment—her sense of shame was. Besides, and although she didn't want to admit it, the twins might make hamburger out of Jake; if they could destroy non-provoking furniture, what would they do to something that provoked them?

She stomped into her former kitchen. Clara was by the sink and turned to see an otherwise gentle-faced woman look angrily around the room. The two women looked at each other.

"Oh," Nell said as she relaxed her grip on the doorknob, "you must be Clara. I see you are still alive."

Clara laughed and held her hand out to Nell, a gesture that didn't fit in with a woman whose life had concentrated on several children and a husband, but a gesture Clara learned to use to negotiate credit extensions. "So far I am, anyway. George protects me I guess."

Nell took Clara's handshake, and her graciousness returned. "Thank you for calming me down. I came to beat up on the twins, but I can do that later."

The two women started to chat as though chatting was something new, and within two hours drank two pots of coffee, ate an uncountable number of cookies, exchanged a few stories of their present life, and shared an occasional event of their guarded pasts. Snow started to fall, but the two were locked in a session of words and expressions that only time could wear out.

241

"Jake loves me so much, and he is so afraid of losing me. He kowtows too much. I don't like that. He is a good man, and I love him more every time we are together, and I hate that he thinks I have the upper hand. I don't want the upper hand. I want both our hands in the same place."

Clara laughed. "That won't ever happen. What will happen is that you'll take turns at it. Claus and I did. But mostly I let him think he had all the say-so. He didn't, but he needed to think that, and that was my say-so contribution."

Nell raised her eyebrows. "Didn't you need him?"

"Of course. But women are suppose to need men, they're used to it. Men aren't, they like to think they can go through life on their own, and it's best not to remind them they can't."

It was Nell's turn to laugh. "You mean that one hand washes the other although one of those hands thinks it's not dirty enough to wash?"

"You will have a happy marriage, you know the rules already."

And that remark of Clara's would be the last remark either would make for awhile: Lo had come into the room.

He removed his heavy boots at the door and heaved his wet, cold body into the kitchen. "I thought you were here to work," he pointed at Clara, ignoring Nell who had stood up and stretched to full height with hands on hips and slow, deliberate words coming out of her throat: "Who do you think you are—you and Les? Who in all of creation do you two think you are? You are no longer welcome in any shop in town. Nowhere. No Where. You slobs, you."

Lo turned his finger to his sister. "And you are no longer welcome in this house. You never were. Never were." He went into the living room pleased with his last remark and convinced it was quite appropriate.

Les came in from the shed. Nell put her open palm on his chest and shoved him as far as she was able, as far as anyone could shove a tank. "You pompous idiot. You criticize my Jake because he is short of stature, then you go out and destroy a man's place of business."

Les stepped back and looked away. Nell continued. "What I want to know, Big Man, is this: what is the most de-si-ra-able trait in a man? A big physique or a big heart?"

"Yeah, yeah, yeah," Les smirked as he loped to the living room in a fashion that said his sister's anger was due to women's hysteria, an attitude he nourished with every female confrontation.

Nell turned to Clara and smiled. "Well, that's that. A few months ago, I couldn't have done this. But I keep thinking height has nothing to do with strength. We think of Napoleon and short and strong all in the same description. And that's how I feel about Jake, short and strong, but with the addition of sweetness. This is why I can shove on my brother's chest and why I can call them jerks. Happy Thanksgiving."

***

"Speaking of Thanksgiving," Clara said as she drove Nell back to town through the snow that had stopped falling at about the same time Nell pulled the pedestals out from underneath her twin brothers, "George gave me the day off. Some of my kids invited me to Omaha, but my car is not too steady and neither are my cats when I leave them overnight. Why don't you and George and Jake come to my house for the turkey feast?"

Nell nodded. "You mean, George and me and Jake and Billy and Angela?"

Clara slapped the steering wheel in a display of joy. "By all means. I'm used to lots of people around my table. Let me know how many others you can think of, and I'll grab one or two of those fresh turkeys in the grocery."

Nell's face brightened. "Okay. How about George and Jake and me and Billy and Angela and Harold and Dolly?"

Clara's beat-up, rusting car entered Main Street; she glanced over at the saloon. "How about Barney?"

"Sure."

"Do you think they'll all come?" Clara asked. "Who are Harold and Dolly?"

"I'm not sure of anyone but Jake and the kids. I won't

spend Thanksgiving without them, especially not without Jake. And I know he certainly won't spend it without me."

"The kids? How about them?"

"Oh, they'll be there. They're used to eating meals alone, without adults, and this should be a wide-eyed treat for them. Thank you for asking, Clara. I didn't mean to be pushy about your invitation, but I guess I am still turned on after shouting at the boys. I need to calm down. Also, let me check with Jake first before I give a definite yes. I'll let him take the lead for awhile. Right? Of course."

"Greasy guns, I think you have it," and Clara laughed all the way to Nell's apartment.

***

Nell spent that evening, the one after her kitchen outburst with the twins, without Jake; she told him what she had done and that she needed to calm down by herself.

That wasn't the real reason she wanted to be alone; she wanted to think through some of the things Clara had said; so after Billy and Angela went to their room to listen to second-hand records on their second-hand record player, Nell sat herself sideways on the sofa and looked at one wall and then at another.

She was thinking, she was feeling, she was deciding. It didn't take long because all the information she needed for her future was well inside her head—it merely needed sorting out.

The next afternoon—with her duties at the orphanage completed for the day, a fresh batch of cookies cooling, and the children doing homework at the kitchen table—the blare of Jake ringing the doorbell sounded a lot like music to Nell.

"Let's go to the sofa," was the first thing she said to him.

Jake nodded and sat down, automatically, without thought.

"Please don't get comfortable yet, Jake, I have something to say."

Jake looked up. He sensed how exceptionally gentle and pleasant Nell appeared; he was suspicious. "What is it Nell?" Hurry up and tell me, he moaned inside. He was afraid she had changed back to not loving him again.

She sat down next to him, on the edge of the sofa, and turned until her knees touched his. They looked straight into each other's faces. Nell knew what she was going to say, but Jake didn't, and for a moment his mind and heart blanked out. This was going to be something awfully good or awfully bad.

"I love you, Jake, and I want to marry you,"—that was an awfully good thing— "and I want us to share a kitchen, a couple of lonely kids, and a bed,"—another awfully good thing— "and I thank you for loving me,"—more awfully good stuff.

But why was she telling him something they had already discussed and settled? Oh, oh. Was the awfully good stuff over and the awfully bad stuff coming?

"That's all, that's everything I wanted to say. After yesterday's fiasco with the twins and after a long talk with a woman who knows more about marriage and children than I do, I decided I needed to tell you how much I appreciate you and your patience and willingness to take two kids into your heart."

It took a few seconds for Jake's mind to understand everything Nell had said. In a daze, his thoughts reached up to her face and her lips; he kissed her as though it was their first time, hesitantly, like maybe she would slap. His mind cleared a little after she returned his halting kiss with a generous one. Then it happened, he suddenly got it, at last Nell's message sunk in; it was the generous kiss that did it, that made him know, really know, that she merely wanted to emphasize her feelings for him, that she had only awfully good things to say, that she loved him as much as he loved her. Well, probably as much.

Now all he had to do was say something in return. Something cute right now would be appropriate. "Kitchen? Children? Bed?" He nodded his head up and down and smiled as far as his mouth could go. "Sounds mighty fine to me. But what about the cookies? I smell something sweet. Will we share them too?"

"You will have to marry me first," Nell teased in return.

Jake scooted deep into the sofa, threw his head back, and let out a very loud howl. "Well, I don't know. This is so sudden."

Nell slapped his knee, the children looked up from their books, and if Nell's piano had been a player piano, it would have played. Nell stood up. "You rushed me into marriage, and now I'm rushing you. Please go to the kitchen and greet your children. They miss those walks with you, and they want to marry you too."

Some things take so long to happen, and then they happen. Now, at this moment, it happened for Jake and Nell.

***

"So, that's how you two want to spend your profits and inheritance?" George said to Les and Lo after their demolition of Barney's. "So, you want to spend it on furniture for a saloon?" He took the mug Clara handed to him. "Well, to each his own, I guess. How about the tavern across the county line? Maybe you could do that one in too."

The sheriff waited three days before he called the twins into town. It took him that long to simmer down, and besides, he wasn't dealing with desperados—only a couple of lunkheads.

He snapped his fingers when Les and Lo appeared in the doorway; he snapped his fingers a second time and used one of them to point with great thrust at the two chairs they were to sit on; he spit into the spittoon, which he usually didn't do because he was the one who would have to clean it out, but he needed to create an atmosphere of toughness—the Swensen boys loomed a good four inches over him—and so he used every John Wayne type of mastery he could think of.

He cleared his throat, it was time to begin. "You two ought to be ashamed of yourselves," he finally decided to say. "Barney's a good friend of mine. Everybody who is decent is a good friend of mine. You attacked my friend's property which is against the law to begin with, and to end up with, it is against human decency. Look at me, you two, look at me. I want you to see the anger fanging out of my eyes. At you."

Les and Lo sat on the other side of the desk and stared at the out-basket.

"I could put you in jail, I would love to put you in jail, but Thanksgiving is almost here, and I don't want to have to attend to you two nuts. I don't want my appetite spoiled. Have I said enough to make you feel bad?" He struck a match on the heel of his boot and lit his pipe. "I will exchange your time in jail, which should be 100 years, for something else. An apology to Barney and complete restitution of everything you destroyed or damaged or looked cross-eyed at. I want the Palace in tiptop shape within a week."

"An apology?" Lo challenged harshly.

The sheriff spit again, might as well, the spittoon was already messy from his first spit. He wiped his chin and nodded and decided to leave the spitting to the outdoors after this. "Yes, yes, indeedy-do. You did more than wreck the saloon, you damaged Barney. He has never, ever hurt a fly, and it's hard for him to understand how two hulks could lash out at him like you two did."

"Are we free to go now?" Les sulked with a sneer.

The sheriff stood up and spit again. Doggone it, he forgot to stay away from the spittoon. Too much anger to get rid of. "One week, you get one week. If you don't do as I say, I will have to send you to the bad boys farm." The sheriff almost laughed at what he considered not only a funny remark, but one that probably soaked in as an insult like none of the others had.

Les and Lo no longer needed to worry about who would cook them Thanksgiving dinner; while everyone else in Boone County would be chomping down on various parts of steaming turkey, they would be driving back from Omaha after the pre-holiday sale at the state's largest furniture market. They hoped, in their sarcastic manner, that this furniture store would be large enough to carry all the saloon replacement necessities and offer them a couple of rebates and several discounts as well. They then decided, in more sarcasm, that they would not apologize to Barney.

"If that saloon keeper is such a nicey-nice, he won't be running to the sheriff when we don't apologize," Les boasted, and then added, "if the sheriff asks him, we'll say we forgot."

"Oh for crying-out-loud," Lo returned, "we're not kids anymore. We don't have to apologize. I'm not worried. Bad-boys farm? I think we're just been insulted, brother. I think I'm going to remember that."

"Don't," Les said, "just because the sheriff is uneducated is no reason we have to be."

***

At the same time the sheriff was spitting in his spittoon and reprimanding the twins, Jake was frozen in rapture over Nell's marriage proposal, a mood quite different from the mood of the angry sheriff and his two antagonists.

Jake got up from the sofa and bustled his way into the kitchen where Billy and Angela were pondering over their homework, doggedly pondering over it, in an atmosphere quite different than the one they were used to with their parents. The children hadn't heard anything of Jake and Nell's conversation because they hadn't tried to hear anything— their parents never said anything they wanted to hear.

When Jake appeared, however, Billy and Angela looked up at him and into the seriousness of his expression; his cheerful humming didn't help relieve the stare on their friend's face; they were awkwardly afraid again.

"If it's all right with the law," Jake blurted out to the studious pair, "would you kids like to become our kids? Nell and me? We're getting married for sure now."

"December 20th," Nell called from the living room.

Jake's reaction to what Nell said was like he was deaf and suddenly heard something. "Oh? December 20th?" He sat down on the nearest chair and shook his head back and forth, up and down. "Oh my God, did You hear that?" Jake was not exclaiming in vain, he was actually addressing God. "That wonderful creature you created some fifty years ago has set the wedding date."

248

Nell laughed and came to the kitchen.

Billy started to smile. In just a few days, he and his sister had gone from a memory of living with bad characters to a future of living with a real character. "I don't know about God, Mr. Blackburn, but I heard you. Did you hear him, Sis? We have a new home."

The little sister looked up at Nell, and her mouth quivered. She put her hands over her face. She cried, but she didn't know why.

Even though Billy had shown some recognition of happiness over Jake's announcement, neither child had ever experienced emotion filled with something wonderful; they remained in their chairs, neither knew how to jump with joy or how to hug and squeal with delight.

Jake and Nell hugged each other, and the children merely watched; were they suppose to do something? Jake and Nell squeezed each other's hands, and the children continued to watch; were they suppose to say something? Jake and Nell gave each of the children a hug, and the children sat still; were they suppose to hug back? They didn't know what they were suppose to do. So they went to their room; and that was what they knew how to do.

Jake and Nell sat down at the table and tried to make light of Billy and Angela's somber reaction. They knew it would take some time before the children would join in to a family situation like ordinary children do. But there was some hope—each of them had grabbed a cookie on their way out.

***

"We're a little awkward with each other right now," Jake told Harold while they sat one late afternoon on Barney's bar stools with the shattered mirror hideously in view. "But things will relax after we all get used to what's happened."

Harold shook his head. "I don't know about adoption. I doubt if you can adopt. The parents didn't officially surrender them to the county. Maybe they'll be back someday. I think they're both too dumb to know about the legal repercussions of abandonment but at least one of them may come back and block adoptions."

Barney dumped more pretzels into the basket between them. "The sheriff ain't looking for them. He doesn't want them found. Thinks they'll want the kids back. A lot of rotten parents do."

"Maybe they went to Hollywood to become movie stars," Harold said. "The sheriff said they are darn good lookers."

Jake slid off his stool, leaned his body against the counter, and finished his beer. "Those kids should go to Sunday School. Every Sunday, not just now and then like when their rotten folks had the urge to do something right for them."

Harold turned on his stool to Jake. "So should you, buddy. You don't exactly set the world on fire with your own church attendance, you know."

Jake pointed to his chest and his head. "My church is right here and here and that is where it belongs. Churches don't care about short, unmarried men. And you know that."

Barney refilled Jake's mug. "You met her at the barbecue, didn't you?"

Jake wiped his mouth with the palm of his hand. "I saw her at the barbecue. But I actually met her at the hardware."

"I guess that's as good a place as any to meet someone." Barney turned his attention to another customer who not only needed a short whiskey, but an explanation of the obviously dilapidated saloon condition.

"How about your intended?" Harold persisted. "What church does she go to?"

"She doesn't go either."

Harold raised his eyebrows. "That's hard to believe. Churches are usually full of nice women like Nell. Are you sure she doesn't go?"

"No, actually, I'm not. But she has never talked about church. I figure if she was a church-goer, she would have had me there by now."

"Maybe she isn't a Christian," Harold continued. "Two of her brothers certainly are not."

"Maybe I'll ask her."

Harold raised his arm for another beer. "You can't marry somebody if you don't know their religion for pity sakes. Where will you get married? In the middle of the Sand Hills where there aren't that many people around to criticize?"

Jake frowned, and Harold received the full impact of it. "Nell will make the plans, and I don't care what religion she is. I know she is a woman of God because she follows all the rules I learned in Sunday School when I was a kid, and she's awfully nice, and she looks like a Sunday School teacher, and she is sweet and comforting and a lot of other nice things. Even without all that, I still love her, and that's what counts. Not anything else." Jake's eyes raced around the room like he was looking for someone, a somebody who would tell Harold to shut up and quit making trouble when there was no trouble there.

"She's either a Dane or a Swede," Barney boomed across the counter as though the conversation belonged to him. "So she's probably Lutheran."

Harold started on his second beer. "I don't know, Jake, it seems there's a lot you don't know about your lady."

Jake plunked his quarters on the counter, zipped his jacket, and made an exaggerated motion to leave. He got as far as the door before he decided more must be said; he got as far as opening the door before he felt anger at having to defend his and Nell's love; he went out into the parking lot and back in again before he got the courage to put Harold in his place and let him know everybody's world isn't pat and dry like his. He cleared his throat and raised his voice—he wanted everybody in the whole blaming saloon to know this. "There is something you left out, dear friend. Something that I do know."

Harold waved and smiled, embarrassed that he was giving Jake a hard time for no valid reason. "What's that, buddy, what is it you do know?"

"Love. I know love. No church, no nationality, no nothing has a monopoly on it. It's just there. For everyone."

"Who is Clara?" Jake asked Nell over the phone.

"You remember, my housekeeping replacement. George thinks a lot of her, and so do I." Nell cradled the phone between her ear and shoulder—it was the next best thing to having Jake there in person.

"Nell," Jake responded, "wherever you will be for Thanksgiving, I will be too. It's my favorite holiday. What time do you want me to pick you guys up?"

In only two weeks following Nell's announcement of the wedding date, Jake had settled into his new family situation as though it had always been. He referred to Nell and the children as 'you guys,' and although the expression puzzled Billy and Angela, Nell was pleased that Jake had finally relaxed about their impending marriage. Jake was so relaxed, Nell began to realize her choice of husband was becoming more choice every day; Jake's irritating aspects had decreased and his charm started to come through; her fear that maybe he would be bitter about the delay in their marriage didn't happen, and she hoped someday she would have a chance to reward him for his patience. If there is such a thing as a woman having a rescuer, Jake was it.

It had snowed three inches the week before the holiday, and on the day of Jake's favorite celebration, the sky was scrambled with large and especially white clouds. The blue that managed to show between the thick clusters was especially blue, and Jake's pickup was especially jammed with two adults and two children on their way to Clara Bruggeman's for Thanksgiving dinner.

Jake's joy would have burst his body if that was possible. He looked over at Nell. "In the summer the kids can ride in the back, but I don't know about the winter. Angela will be getting too big for your lap pretty soon, and if Billy's shoulders get any broader, he will be pushing all of us out the front seat."

Billy beamed, and Nell hugged Angela.

"We'll manage somehow, my dear," Nell said.

Jake looked over at her. "You are really something, aren't you? You say we will manage somehow, when what you really want to say is ... Clunkhead, why don't you buy a regular car. That's what you're thinking, right?"

Nell laughed. "Why, of course, that's what I'm thinking. But that's not what I'm saying. You're in charge of transportation." She hesitated, during which she cleared her throat twice. "It would be nice to learn to drive a regular car."

"Drive?" Jake grasped the steering wheel tighter, losing some of his recently acquired relaxation. "I thought you had forgotten about that. Billy here will learn in a few years, and then you'll have two men to escort you to wherever you want to go."

The pickup hit a rut, and Nell hugged Angela tighter. "I'd like to learn how to drive around these ruts."

Jake's face turned red.

"I'm sorry, Jake, that was a terrible thing to say. I guess it was my motherly instinct talking."

Jake shook his head no. "You are right, Nell. I've driven only myself for so many years, it's hard to adjust to passengers. I'll have to shift the gears in my head as well as the ones in my hand and try to drive more polite." He looked at Billy. "That was a pun, young man. Do you know what a pun is?"

Billy's heart pounded because he didn't know the answer and he was afraid he should; he was also confused; but he thought he had better say something. "No, I don't know what a pun is. But I do know what a good time is, we have those at recess, and that's what I'm having right now. My little sister and me aren't used to having big people talk to us like this."

Big people? Jake thought as he turned the wheel away from an unusually deep rut. Big people? This kid will work out well in my new family. He mused that, of course, anybody shorter than he would refer to him as big even though he wasn't. To Angela he must appear gigantic. Nice feeling. Nice kids.

Two rut maneuvers later, Jake came out of his reverie,

enthused to bring the children even closer to him than their shoulder to shoulder sitting arrangement at the moment. "You know, one way to have a good time is to have a conversation."

Billy shrugged his shoulders. "I don't have anything to conversation about—what is conversation?"

Nell put her hand gently on Angela's pale cheek, and the fragile girl leaned further against her. "We'll teach you, both of you. Jake, let's have a conversation about something ordinary."

"All right. You pick the subject." Jake was enjoying this so much.

"Thanksgiving." Nell was enjoying it too.

"What can I say? It's my favorite holiday."

"Why?"

"Because it is. It just plain and simply is."

"But why?"

"I don't know."

If there had been a Christmas tree in the pickup, Billy's face would have been the star lighting up the top. "I get it. Conversation is a bunch of questions with no answers. Like in school, although the teacher makes us give answers."

The big people laughed.

Nell replied, "Not quite. Sometimes conversation is thoughts. For instance, one person makes a statement of some kind, and another person either agrees and enhances the statement or disagrees and refutes it."

Angela looked puzzled up at Nell. The words: statement and enhance and refutes were not in her vocabulary, and not much in Billy's either.

"I don't get it," Billy sighed. You big people are too smart for me. I don't get what you're saying."

Jake cleared his throat real long on that remark. Not only was he big now, but he was smart too. Why didn't he think of getting a kid years ago?

"Okay, Jake," Nell said hurriedly, "let's give them an example. I'll make a statement: Jake likes Thanksgiving the best, and I like it the least. The reason is because I always do all the cooking, and the men do all the eating."

She nodded to Jake. "It's your turn."

Jake didn't respond. He couldn't. His brain stopped functioning right after Nell said she didn't like Thanksgiving. Harold was right—he didn't know everything about Nell. He could live with someone of a different religion or no religion at all, he could love someone who was taller than he, but could he survive Thanksgiving with someone who didn't like it? It was a good thing Nell said why she didn't like it; there was hope he could remedy the reason.

He recovered because he didn't want to give an example of family disagreements. "Okay. I like Thanksgiving because Dolly always does all the cooking, and Harold and I always do all the eating."

Nell laughed, unaware of her traumatic statement and the fact that Jake had lost all of his relaxation by now. "We agree on so many things, don't we? Now Billy, that was an example of a statement followed by an agreement or enhancement."

"I get it," the boy said, although he still didn't know what enhancement meant. "But I want to know why Jake likes Thanksgiving more than any other holiday. I don't like any of the holidays."

"You don't?" Jake shouted. "Why not? All kids like holidays. You get to stay home and play."

The four in the pickup became very quiet. There was no reason to explain why.

Nell cleared her throat. "Why don't we change the conversation for now? We can continue it later."

"Sure," Jake said. "Billy, you don't have to answer my little outburst. But if you ever decide to like holidays, I hope it's Thanksgiving."

All the passengers relaxed again, all except Jake. He had to find a way to make Nell like Thanksgiving, a way other than promising her she didn't have to do all the cooking—he certainly didn't want to do that because he doubted if Thanksgiving would be anything without good cooking.

Angela interrupted his worry session as she bolted up straight and exclaimed, "I know why you like Thanksgiving the best. It's because everybody talks to everybody."

"Oh my dear God," Nell said.

Oh my dear God, Jake thought. That little girl told him his answer. He slowed the pickup and said as softly as his raspy voice was able: "Angela, do you know why I like Thanksgiving? It's more than talking and laughing and cooking and eating. It's a celebration of the land, and I love the land and every smidgen of dirt on it."

Nell's eyes glistened. "And I bet you have always taken good care of it, my dear man. I guess you're entitled to have someone cook a feast for that. Someone like me."

Jake nodded yes. Now he would have something more to be thankful for on his Day, a something he hadn't known before—a woman who appreciated his passion for the land. He wanted to burst out to Nell again, but the children sat between, so he held back. They were family too, but they didn't have to get in on everything. "It's getting kind of thick right now. I'm not sure I can take much more thickness."

Both children looked puzzled, and Billy said, "What kind of a conversation is this called?"

"Love," Nell said.

They drove into Clara's rutty driveway with the echo of Nell's last word. Jake decided it would be all right for her to not like Thanksgiving—as long as she loved him and recognized his love for the land. After all—not everything in the world is perfect.

***

"Golly gum gosh, dear God, thank you for your blessings," Clara prayed very loud and with much enthusiasm as though she had never prayed before and she needed to make up for it.

George patiently waited for Clara to end the prayer so he could start the carving of what looked like the largest turkey ever bred for Thanksgiving. He and the stove were flanked by the three women, a request Clara had made because there was more reverence to slicing the bird on the stove's top with only the cooks there instead of at the living room table in front of everybody. "Claus always made me carve the turkey on the stove in the kitchen. He didn't believe in dining room ceremonies where the man carves the turkey. He said it was silly to carve a bird at the table regardless of those Thanksgiving pictures to the contrary."

The hot juices trickled down the leg of the bird, and the dressing steamed hot as Clara scooped it out and plopped it into a bowl.

"Claus used to make me, and then our sons when they got old enough, cut the turkey," Clara reminisced. "He said I could choose between whacking off its head or carving it up later." She laughed. "One year when I was feeling particularly feisty, and when he asked which job I wanted, I told him that I would be the butcher as well as the carver if he would give birth to our next offspring. He didn't get my point that there are some things in life for which there is no choice." She took a deep breath, hoping no one would interrupt. "I told him whacking and carving the turkey was all his job, just like mine was to carry and deliver babies."

Nell grimaced. She wondered if the children had heard Clara's tirade about killing and cutting and birthing. She hoped not; the conversation attempt of Clara's was starting to become uncomfortable; Billy and Angela might ask later what that was all about, and she and Jake would be left with explaining.

Dolly cleared her throat unusually loud. She pulled her hot casserole of broccoli out of the oven and sat it next to the mashed potatoes and sweetened yams. Nell arranged carrot sticks, green and black olives, sweet pickles, and her special concoction of cranberry sauce onto Clara's ornamental tray.

Angela followed Nell's movements with eyes of wondering how so many different foods could be on one table at the same time. Billy tried to coax his sister into the living room with the men; he wasn't used to not being her center of attention, and he wasn't a bit interested in pickles and olives. It didn't work — Angela had found something besides him to cling to: a kitchen full of people moving here and moving there and talking at the same time. So Billy stood in the dining room between the two activities.

"Do you think we'll win this year?" Harold asked Barney and Jake.

"Why don't you ask them?" Barney replied.

"Better yet," Jake laughed, "why don't you ask Oklahoma?"

"How do you mean, buddy?" Harold asked.

"I mean that Nebraska always says we will win, but it seems as though that doesn't count. Oklahoma knows they will win and by exactly how many yards they will run for every touchdown and exactly in what quarter of play they will do it."

"That's blasphemy. That's a downright accusation of game fixing," Barney said with disbelief.

"No, no, no. That's not what I mean." An outsider could have seen that Jake was building up to get some grief off his chest. "I mean Oklahoma spooks us. We have just as good a team, we have a very good coach, we have the best uniforms, the loudest most loyal fans ... we have everything the best in the whole country. But we don't have the best luck."

Harold thought this was as good a time as any to goad his best friend, forgetting they were not in the saloon where most of their goading took place. "We won't win this weekend, if that's what you're concerned about."

Jake knew an egging-on when he heard one; he ignored it. "Remember one year when there was only two seconds left and Oklahoma ran ninety yards for the winning touchdown? Where were we? In the locker room? College players aren't suppose to get touchdowns in the last second of play. Oklahoma doesn't know this."

Harold drew in on his pipe. He knew the passion Jake felt for the Nebraska team; no one rooted or tooted louder than Jake over a game, no one was more hurt when they lost. Harold decided he had better draw an end to this train of thought before it ruined the festivities. "Maybe Oklahoma has a voodoo doll they call Nebraska and stick pins into."

Jake snorted. "I think the voodoo is in your head."

Barney grumbled, "Nebraska will win this one."

"Of course they will," Jake finally decided.

"Then why do you insult something you love so much, pal?" Harold inserted.

"Because I'm a buffoon, and you're a buffoon, and I am ashamed of every word I've uttered against my team. It's all poppycock."

Poppycock or not, Billy's head went from one man and then the other and the other. Such a conversation, and what in the heck is voodoo? He came to the living room, sat down on a very soft, deep cushioned sofa, and wondered at all that was going on: the women in the kitchen, the men in the living room, and he somewhere in-between.

Jake picked up the delicately designed dish of nuts and sweets and cheese balls and passed them to Billy. "Here, munch on some of this stuff, it will fill up your hungry stomach. I hope you will be as devoted to Nebraska as the rest of us are. We have a great team. Nobody wins all the time, you know."

Billy remembered what Jake had said about how he hoped Thanksgiving would be his favorite holiday, and now Jake said he wanted Nebraska to be his favorite team. The cheese balls and the nuts and the candy no longer looked like a big deal to the young, lonely boy because he wasn't seeing the tidbits of food— he was seeing a vision of Jake on that platter: his intended foster father was giving of himself, and there was no dish big enough to hold the neglected boy's joy as he took some of the token offerings into his hand and popped them into his mouth.

"Why don't you take the dish into the kitchen and see if your sister would like some too?" Jake coaxed.

Billy obeyed, but the moment he entered the kitchen he was hit with a wave of the emptiness he had felt some weeks before when he was told his father as well as his mother had left. At the moment it didn't matter that this kitchen was filled with women and George and chattering—it would take a while for any kitchen to feel full to him. He decided to not interrupt Angela with the dish; she seemed contented; he was hoping for his own contentment—Jake's concern helped a little.

Clara's dining room table with the extra boards was ample for the holiday feasters. Angela continued to hover next to Nell, and Billy sat snuggled up next to Jake who was snuggled up next to Nell. There they were, a foursome, like paper cut-outs strung together. Dolly smiled at the sight, Clara realized it also, where was Norman Rockwell?

Clara clapped her hands, offered another prayer—one that was sweeter than the one by the stove—and the eating and the swallowing and the talking began.

Afterwards Billy put himself elbow deep into scrubbing the pots and pans; the women, understanding the young boy's need for something familiar, took turns drying and parceling out leftovers. Jake stood by the kitchen door, much like Billy had done before the meal started; he watched; he waited; and he realized Thanksgiving would now mean more than gratitude for the land. Once he and Nell were married, Thanksgiving would also mean he belonged to someone; it might also mean he wouldn't have to go home after the eating because he would be at home— December twentieth was only three weeks away.

***

Jake woke up with a suddenness that caused his heart to boom in his chest. Somewhere in his subconscious he realized he had not discussed where he and Nell and the children would live after he married them.

He had assumed Nell would join him at his farm, but now with the children—maybe the law would say they couldn't leave the town area. Surely they couldn't all fit into Nell's small apartment.

His land. He couldn't leave his land. His heart pounded some more, and then the throbbing went to his head.

He ran outdoors into the morning's cold and pressed his palms against the hard, snowy ground. He couldn't give this up. All he ever had was this land, the ground, the earth with its dirt. Could a human being give him the security the farm had? Could Nell replace all that? Please God, I want Nell and I want the kids, but don't make me give up my soul for them.

It was a pathetic sight: Jake on the ground begging for his life. But he wasn't being unreasonable; he wanted to have everything he loved, and at the moment he was pleading to God to let him have everything. If Harold had been there, he would have told Jake to get his foolish body off the ground and into the house and onto the phone and call Nell about his concern. But Harold wasn't there, and all Jake had to accompany him was his link to the land, a link that could not verbally advise or comfort.

The guardian angels that helped him at the hardware store finally made an appearance, and Jake's body caught up with his panic. He shivered, stood up, and whimpered himself back to the kitchen with his pajama legs wet and bagging at the knees. I love my land, it has always been there for me, God for pity sakes, help me.

Prince and Mitzie, who had rushed out with him, came back in too. Animals know when something is wrong with their master, and this morning, something was wrong with theirs.

Jake sat at the kitchen table as though this would make everything all right. He thought about his mother who would talk about Alice once in awhile. She never got over the hurt. She had someone she loved very much at one time, and this someone was taken away. Just because you care for something doesn't mean it will stay.

Jake's thinking kept falling into pits. Nothing he thought was cheerful. How could he expect to keep his land forever when his mother couldn't keep her little Alice forever? Who did he think he was anyway? A mother's child is much more important than a man's land. His mother had accepted her grief, and so would he.

But not unless it was absolutely necessary. Oh God, help me to figure out how to get all those people I love onto my land and into my house.

Nell didn't answer the phone. She had left her apartment earlier than usual to help the orphanage with the special post-Thanksgiving breakfast the spinster sisters traditionally fixed. She took Billy and Angela with her because school was closed until the next week.

Jake waved for Prince to climb into the pickup and sit next to him; Mitzie was gone for the day into her world of mice exploration, concern for her master gone. Jake no sooner had the ignition turned on when he started to worry again. What about his pets? They can't live in town. An apartment probably wouldn't allow them.

As for the apartment, Nell had the only one available, and it wasn't anything to long for and cherish. Besides, the landlord had his own pets and lived directly below; surely he wouldn't allow Prince, the panter and barker, to interfere with his own panter and barker.

It wouldn't work out. Jake's mind narrowed for the umpteenth time in his life. It wouldn't work out. The angels came again but left without even trying. It just plain and simply would not work out. He should have realized that the minute he woke up in the morning. He should have called Nell, four o'clock or not, and told her she would have to live on the farm. No if's, and's, or but's. Oh how brave he was when away from her.

Okay now, what if Nell said he must choose between his land and his pets and her and the children? What if Nell said he must choose between being a farmer or being a refined city gentleman? How could he choose between two different worlds when he was born to live in just one? Could Nell possibly be that rough on him? In his hysterical mind, she had already taken him off his land, what more cruelty would she insist on next?

Jake's mental torment made up a few more things not yet established. How could such a wonderful woman be so unsympathetic? Besides all that, she wanted to learn to drive. She had already stripped him of his farm and his animals, and now she wanted to top that off with taking away his dignity of driving her places.

He certainly had to get to Nell fast before he thought of anything else she would ruin. The pickup hit every rut and every slick spot of packed snow with the determination that its driver needed to get somewhere in lightening-fast time. The man and the dog both arrived without incident except for the wheel alignment—it would have to be adjusted.

He stood at the front door of the orphanage with his knees locked in determination and his chest strutted out until his shoulder blades almost touched. He was on a mission, and he had to look like he was authority. He was scared. He rang the doorbell.

Nell swung the door open suddenly and wider than seemed possible for a heavy door to open. Jake immediately knew that a door opened in that manner of swiftness and strength meant Nell would fight him to the death over where they would live.

Nell smiled. "Good morning, Dear, come in. It's so good to see you. How about some coffee?"

Great, she was her wonderful sweet self again. She had probably forgotten how miserable she had made him in the few short hours he had been up.

"Nell." He looked at her and felt a great guilt for his evil thoughts. She had a way about her, and he had to be firm. "Nell. We need to talk."

Her smile disappeared, not because of what Jake said, but because of the way he said it. Gentle Jake wasn't very gentle right now. "What's wrong? Sweetheart?"

"Maybe everything."

"Oh?" ... tension had found a home.

"Maybe nothing" ... a glimmer of the guardian angels got through ... "that's why we need to talk."

Nell smiled a little. "I opt for the maybe nothing."

Jake forced a little smile of his own. "You can have the 'maybe nothing' if there is nothing. I'm worried, in case you haven't guessed by now."

Nell unclenched her hand and took Jake's and led him

into the small parlor laced with doilies on just about everything.

Jake ran his free hand through his curly hair and looked for a non-dainty place to sit. There weren't any. "Could we go to your place? There's too much fancy stuff in this room. I feel like a tea party is going to walk in any minute." If Jake had spilled out his concern to Nell as fast as he had rushed to get to her, he would have had everything settled before the lace doilies ever came on the scene. Fear made Jake run, and fear made him stop.

Nell put her fingertips on Jake's unshaved chin. Maybe she meant to slap it instead. "Is your new concern so bad, we have to be totally alone to discuss it?"

New concern? Jake started to worry deeper. What did Nell mean by that? What were the old concerns? Was she implying he was a fuss-budget? Was she going to make him quit that too, if indeed she really meant he was a fusser? First the land and then the pets and now the personality. He would have nothing left; he would be a shell of a man going to the altar. If Nell had heard all of Jake's thoughts from the time he left his farm in the morning until now, Jake would no longer have to worry about the altar or where they would live after the altar—she wouldn't want him anymore.

He had to calm down. He had to act like there wasn't anything too wrong. This was not easy for Jake to do at anytime, let alone after this morning of accelerated worry. He tried to smile again. "We really wouldn't have to be alone for this, but I don't like rooms filled with holey handkerchiefs."

Nell laughed. She decided Jake's new problem was way overrated. "Let me find one of the sisters and tell her I'll be gone for awhile. Wait here, Honey."

Honey? She had never called him that before. Jake's mind had gears in it that shifted back and forth from bad thoughts to good thoughts. He was now in the good-thought gear: what a nice person Nell is, calling me Honey, she must really want me. Now back to the bad thought gear: would she consent to live on his farm if the kids couldn't come? How liberated was she now? She called him Honey—how sweet; but honey was also sticky. That was it—Nell was sticky honey.

Jake opened the heavy orphanage door, and their shoes crunched on the crusty snow; and this crunching was the only sound either heard until Nell opened her apartment door and the phone rang.

It was the orphanage. Nell said 'oh my goodness' and a few other things and hung up. "Billy's sick. He has thrown up all over the kitchen floor. He got one of the sisters."

Jake felt like throwing up too; he could already smell it. Another delay in talking to Nell. He had been all set, primed to go a few more rounds with his future wife, and then Billy had to go and throw up. Throw up, throw up, throw up. Let the whole world throw up.

"I'll go get him," the recovered Jake offered. "You stay here and boil water or something."

Nell sighed. "Thank you."

Billy's mouth was turned down so far, Jake thought it might fall off. He put his arm around the boy's heaving shoulder and nudged him out the door in time for another episode to land in a snow drift, fortunately away from the sidewalk. "Come on, son, Nell will cure you." The snow crunched underneath again, but this time its sound was interrupted with an occasional gag from Billy. Jake took deep breaths to prevent his own gagging, and he wished Billy would take some deep breaths too—from his chest, not his stomach. "Breathe from your chest, son, your chest, easy though, not too deep." Billy gagged again, deep. Jake stopped by his pickup to let Prince out because it appeared the gagging would go on all day. With Prince panting and Billy gagging and Jake reminding to breathe again from the chest, the noisy trio arrived back at Nell's.

Billy threw up two more times before he calmed down enough for Nell to settle him into his narrow bed. Jake boiled the water he had suggested for Nell to do and looked for tea bags in the cupboard. He couldn't find any.

"Where are your tea bags?" he called to Nell.

"They're in my purse on the kitchen table."

265

"Your purse?" Jake put his hands on his hips. "Your purse?"

"Yes, open it up, they're right on top."

This was something else he didn't know about Nell, Jake worried. Another concern: was it normal to keep tea bags in a purse? He raised his voice. "Did you say 'your purse?'"

Nell came into the kitchen. She frowned. "I said my purse. Okay? I ran to the store right after you went for Billy. I was out of tea, and I merely stuffed the box into my purse. Okay?"

Jake didn't say anymore, but he was relieved.

"Now," Nell continued, "what did you want to talk to me about?"

Jake poured the boiling water over the tea bag. "I'm concerned about a few details."

Nell sat down at the table and squeezed the strength out of the bag with the back of a spoon. "Have some tea yourself if you like."

"I'm concerned." Jake started to leave with the steaming tea for Billy.

"So am I," Nell answered. "I hope Angela doesn't get this too. Or us. I hope we don't have to postpone the wedding."

Jake stopped short of Billy's room and returned with the tea cup, his mission aborted, choosing to ease his mind instead of easing Billy's stomach. "It's not the flu I'm concerned about. It's not the wedding either."

Billy gagged again, and Nell rushed past Jake and the hot cup and into the makeshift bedroom. Jake heard more throwing-up; he looked the other way although Billy was nowhere in sight; he started to drink the tea.

"He's too sick for anything in his stomach for awhile, even tea," Nell sighed as she returned to the kitchen. "Oh, I see you're drinking it anyway." She smiled a little.

"Nell, we really have to talk."

"We have all day, Jake. I won't go back to work with Billy the way he is."

Jake nodded. "That's good, because this might take all

day."

Billy gagged. Nell ran. Jake followed.

By early afternoon the crisis calmed. They had managed to get two cups of tea into Billy without it returning, and Nell was now free to spread homemade mayonnaise on four slices of bread and turkey. Their overdue appetites bit into the sandwiches with no respect for daintiness.

"So this is what it's like to have kids," Jake muffled through a stuffed mouth.

Unlike Jake, Nell waited to swallow. "I guess. Not much different than having brothers."

Okay, now was the time. No more delays, no more turkey, and no more gagging. One more gulp of tea, however, just one more gulp. Then a deep breath and: "Nell, we are going to live at my house and on my land. Aren't we?" There, it was blurted out with the finesse of a machine gun going off without warning.

Nell returned the bluntness with a startled look incapable of words.

Jake tensed. "Um-m. You look surprised." He became hot like a thousand prairies fires burning all at once and only on him.

"Well, I am." Nell stared into Jake's flushed face. "I assumed we would live there. The kids, too, if the County Board says it's all right." Nell wasn't through being puzzled. "Is that what brought you over here so early this morning? Was that your new concern?"

Jake relaxed until he slumped down so far in his chair that he almost slipped onto the floor.

Nell laughed. She was no longer puzzled; she had her Jake back again, the one she fell in love with, the one who worried too much, the one who wanted to get married but wouldn't admit he was already married. Married to his land.

She took his hand. "Jake, oh dear Jake, perhaps we should discuss the children." She hesitated. "You and I are the ones getting married. If you don't want Billy and Angela, then they will go back to the orphanage. This is all right with me, but I would want to continue to work there so I can be like a parent to them. They need that. We can give them a lot of attention outside of our home." She cupped Jake's face with her hands. "I said our home, your home, the one standing on your land. Okay?"

Prince barked. "Sh-h," Jake commanded with his eyes remaining on Nell and every word she had just said. "Sh-h. Don't disturb Billy. He won't want to come live with you if you're so noisy."

Prince accepted the reprimand and settled down to panting. But Billy, awakened by the sharp bark, called out.

"He wants Prince in with him," Nell said after she returned from the bedroom. She took the confused animal by the collar and led him to the patient.

Jake sat there and watched the entire procession. He made another sandwich and offered half to Nell. "You know what? I do want those kids. We're a family, all of us." He felt like sitting on the floor and crying, but this time from joy instead of grief. He felt so much joy that every nook and cranny of him was filled with it—filled and overflowing like rainwater spilling out of a full bucket during a heavy rain.

"Are we getting married in a church?" Jake asked thinking he would get rid of Harold's concern now that his was over.

"I haven't been to church in years," Nell said. She cleared her throat. "Are you disappointed?"

"Women usually go to church," Jake answered. "But no, I'm not disappointed. I don't go to church either. Too lonely. Dolly told me a person can't be lonely in church because God is there. But God is also outdoors and inside each kernel of corn and shock of wheat, and He is definitely packed inside every granule of earth.

Nell stared at Jake again, but this time in astonishment. "You really do love the land, don't you? But you'd better be careful who you tell your belief to—there probably aren't too many people who would appreciate hearing that God is packed inside a grain of dirt."

Jake laughed. "Oh, I don't know about that. Anybody who

knows that the Charmleys occasionally sent their children to Sunday School can believe anything."

"They sent them there to get them out of the house," Nell laughed also. "Let's continue that. Church is a good basic foundation. So let's wait with your version of life and God until they adjust to this one ... they are confused enough about the version they have now. Let's straighten that one out first."

"I'll fine-tune them later." Jake felt so good. God was evidently in his feelings also.

Nell nodded, she wasn't through with the subject. "Do you realize we are two old maids and two old-fashioned people who never asked the other what religion we believe in?"

"I'm a Christian, always have been," Jake said. "I assume you are the same?"

"Lutheran," Nell answered.

"You're a good woman, my Nell." He reached over to her. "And you are my woman, all mine. At last. Right?"

Nell smiled her enthusiastic smile that Jake loved so much. "Right. And you are my man."

Billy gagged through the sentimentality; he threw up, and Prince ran and slid out of the sick room, his ears pulled back taut. Jake boiled more water, and Nell scurried back and forth until the magic between their souls changed into the reality of loving and caring for someone else who at the moment was a gagging young boy.

"And furthermore," Jake said after Billy went to sleep again, "furthermore, those kids need land and open space to bounce around on. They need animals to pet and feed and play with. They need gardens to weed. They plain and simply need to learn about farming. Do you think we will be allowed to take them to the farm?"

Nell answered a probably. "I asked the sheriff a few days ago, and he said he'd check again to make sure it's legal, and as soon as that happens, we can move them out whenever you say okay."

"You mean we can adopt them?"

"Oh, I don't know. Possibly or maybe not. But we can raise them and love them and let them know somebody cares."

Prince whined and looked up at Jake. "He needs to go out. I'll walk him around town and be back before you miss me. Why don't you rest awhile, Nell? Put your feet right up there on the table and lean back."

"My feet on the table? You don't do that, do you?" Nell mocked surprise.

"Yes, and a few other undignified things."

"Like what?"

"Like nevermind. You'll find out soon enough."

Nell laughed and shoved her man and his dog out the door. She sat down and put her feet up on the kitchen table; they didn't look proper there, so she went into the sitting room and put them up on the coffee table—the kitchen table was meant for Jake's feet, not for hers.

***

The spinster sisters agreed to keep Angela until Billy's crisis was over. "No need for both to be sick," the one offered. So Jake stopped by the orphanage on his way back to the farm to look in on the little girl. She responded with head down in shyness and thumb nervously placed in mouth.

"Everything will be back to normal by tomorrow," Jake comforted, and finally Angela looked at him and nodded. He was certain if he stayed any longer, she would cry and he might too: she out of anxiety, and he out of happiness. Now was not the time to explain about her and Billy's future living arrangement; she was having a hard enough time trying to understand why she couldn't be with her brother. Children don't think in terms of catching germs from someone—they don't have to—adults, with all their fears about everything, do that worrying for them.

Jake ached to hold her and comfort her, but he felt as awkward as she. He thought of how his mother would not have felt awkward, of how she must have longed over the years to hold her daughter and say: there, there, everything will be all right. But his mother had lost that opportunity once Alice laid stretched out by her feet where she fell that ugly day. Jake hoped he could be to Billy and Angela what his mother wanted to be with Alice, and had been with him. He hoped he and Nell would have the children until they grew up. He hoped they wouldn't die like Alice or run away like Alvin. He hoped they would all live happily ever after. He hoped.

***

"Oh my golly gummy gosh." It was Clara again using her favorite words to relieve her disgust of Les and Lo. She had gone into the bathroom to clean the tub, sink, and toilet, and almost got mangled in the heap of clothes strewn on the floor as though this was the latest fashion in carpeting.

She would have given George her notice to leave this den of upheaval and sass, but she felt sorry for him, especially now since he was the sole heir of his twin brothers' woes. If it wasn't for George's soft nature, she would have had his brothers arrested just for the sake of it.

The sheriff eventually did what Clara had intensely hoped for: he put the twins in jail for not completely refinishing Barney's torn-up saloon. It had been a long drive to Omaha, and by the time the brothers arrived, they had worked themselves up to an even bigger sulk than they had left with, and consequently bought only a few tables and chairs from a worn-out outlet store on the edge of the city; they were the cheap, retractable kind that fitted into the back of their pickup so they wouldn't have to pay shipping costs.

George bailed them out so they could tend the farm while he drove to Omaha to properly buy Barney's replacements. "Are you sure you want these varmints back on your farm?" the sheriff said to George in front of the varmints as he turned the key in the jail cell. George nodded and early the next morning drove away.

He was lucky, the furniture market had a section of unmatched pieces of wood appropriate for Barney's casual decor. The legs of the tables and chairs were heavy and thick like maybe Henry the Eighth had used them. The new mirror was larger than the original, and the wall photos of Bogart, Monroe, and Gable were enhanced by the addition of Peter Falk's Columbo looking askance at his suspect along with a candid shot of Johnny Carson looking puzzled at one of his guests.

Five days later the furniture arrived, and one day later George and Clara were in Barney's helping him scrub down and clean up the grand new look.

"All this wood looks awfully good, it's so rich and warm," Barney smiled although he thought it out of place for what he was used to. He wouldn't say that though, he would certainly adjust, and probably in a few years there would be enough nicks, brought about by whatever causes nicks, to make the saloon look as good to him as the varied-colored plastic tables and chairs had.

Although all three were more than a little happy with the Beer Palace's new look, George and Clara didn't say one thing about how good things can come out of bad even after Barney thanked them over and over for the replaced furniture and their concern. Barney had suffered enough over the destruction—he didn't need to hear any words of wisdom.

***

"Well, it's about time I have some happiness, don't you think?" Jake said to Harold at the Hallgrens' breakfast early the next day. Jake had called Nell earlier about Billy's flu progress, and she suggested he have breakfast with Harold and Dolly and not come to her until the afternoon.

"I'm so happy for you both," Dolly said as she handed Jake a plate of steamy French toast. "And the children too. You and Nell will really appreciate each other after such a difficult courtship." She patted Jake on his elbow and added, "Even though you're doing your marriage backwards."

Harold stopped stuffing his mouth with huge bites of the sweet toast so he could feign surprise. "Just what do you mean by that, woman?"

"You know perfectly well what I mean. Jake and Nell are

marrying for the first time at past middle age when most people are ready for the rocking chair. On top of that, they are becoming parents. How many sixty-year-olds start a family?"

Jake cleared his throat. "Nell is only fifty-seven."

Harold shook his head in reprimand. "Those kids should be their grandchildren, not their children."

"Right," Dolly continued. "That's what I mean about doing things backwards. Jake's courtship was like that too. First he proposed and then he courted."

Jake syruped the toast and slashed his fork into its richness without the benefit of a knife.

"And another thing," Harold added, "do you realize he will have two delinquents for brothers-in-law? They're going to be his kin."

"Oh pooh," Dolly chided to her husband, "don't think of it that way. Jake's real kin have all passed on. Bless them. Except for that brother of his who ran away, and for all his lack of communication, he might as well be passed away too. Probably is, don't you think?"

Harold tapped his finger on the table, almost on Jake's syrupy plate. "Where are you two getting married? You haven't asked me to be your best man yet. When are you going to ask? After the wedding? Oops, you'll say, I forgot to ask. But then, that will be all right—it will be in keeping with everything else backwards with you and Nell."

Jake took a last swallow of his coffee. He tapped back. "Are you talking to me? I didn't realize you and Dolly knew I was here."

"It won't be much longer and you won't be. Dolly and I are practicing for that day. That's why we ignored you. Am I going to be your best man or not?"

"You're so romantic," Jake scolded. "I choke with happiness when I think of asking you after all these years of not being a groom. I've been trying to think of a real dramatic way of doing it, and what do you do? You preempt me. You might as well be a local TV station."

"You need preempting," Harold smugged back.

Jake continued. "Then you both—you too, Dolly—talk of my backward courtship and Nell's offensive brothers and our being too old for children. All I can say is that you two have turned into old maids. You think everything has to be done the way you did it and the way your parents did it and the way Adam and Eve did it, whether it works for everybody or not. Particularly you, Harold, my one and only best friend—well, best friend after Nell."

Dolly patted Jake on the shoulder in a 'there, there' fashion, and Harold started to stuff his pipe. They knew the nervousness of a new groom; they did not know the rustiness of their thinking.

Jake, though, didn't need their understanding. He wasn't nervous. He was different. He was beginning to feel a tinge of control over his life. The light had started to flicker. And it would probably get stronger.

Harold pushed away from the table and went over to pet Proudflesh lazily snoozing by his empty dish. "I'll be your best man anyway, buddy, you don't have to ask."

***

Jake left the Hallgrens that morning, half happy, half sad, because the French toast breakfast would probably be the last breakfast he would have with those precious friends of his. It was like leaving home—no more Hallgrens. Forevermore Nell.

As he drove away, he alternated between choking up with a sob and shouting out with a laugh. Choke, laugh, choke, laugh—like a car with engine trouble.

He drove slowly; he wanted to savor this event; he wanted to think about everything and look at everything and hear everything. He rolled down the window and heard birds flapping overhead; he saw a grouping of birches which was really one tree separated in four sections at the base. A clump of one tree, like a family. Nell and him and Billy and Angela. Then he noticed one lone birch a few yards away. Maybe that was Alvin, he mused. Or George. Hopefully—George.

***

274

While Jake was choking and laughing his way into town, Harold and Dolly were laughing about Jake's comment on their being old maids.

"I get such a kick out of Jake accusing us of being old maids. He's quite a character, isn't he?" Harold laughed some more as he knocked his pipe against the shed wall, tapped the warm ashes into his hand, and threw the black mess out the door.

"I'll never know why you clean your pipe that way," Dolly retorted when Harold came back into the kitchen. "Why don't you hit your pipe on the outside of the shed and let the ashes fall on the ground? That way you don't mess up your hand."

Harold eased himself onto a kitchen chair. "I do things the way my Dad did them."

"Everything?"

"Everything."

Dolly sighed. "Perhaps Jake is right—we are old maids. You still do things the way your father did, and I still chide you for it."

"Jake was only kidding about that old maid stuff, sweetie-pie. He's feeling his oats right now, and I can't deny that to him for the world. He and Nell will settle down pretty soon, kids or no kids, and we will all become four old and companionable friends. We'll each go to our rocking chairs and talk about the good old days."

Dolly shook her head no over her husband's pat idea of old age. She remembered the chair upholstery scene when he declared he and she were one person. Now, she supposed, he wanted to have Jake and Nell join them in becoming one person also. "It can't be done," she said. "My dear husband, you can't expect Jake to do what we do. He's had too many years of being alone to think the way you do. I don't even think the way you do about being one person together, and I'm one of your persons."

Harold got up from the table and started to walk to the living room as though changing the scenery would change

Dolly's thoughts.

It didn't. "Let's get out of our rocking chairs, let's be young again. Why don't you run for road commissioner?"

Harold almost ran back to the kitchen. "I would never run against Ralph. He's doing an okay job. I'm too old."

"You're younger than Ralph. What if something happens to me? You'll have a job to keep you busy, you can ask for more money to fill all the ruts instead of just a select few. We need more gravel roads, and the money is there for it, and you know it. It would make a good campaign promise."

Harold shook his finger at Dolly. "Nothing will happen to you. And there aren't that many ruts at any one time."

Dolly could only shake her head back and forth in resignation of her failure to make Harold admit he was the one in the rut, a rut that was no longer comfortable for her. She didn't welcome his remark that he was too old—she was older than he. She had to say something, anything, that would break into her husband's one-sided way of thinking. She tried to remember some of the wise things her mother had said. She tried to recall some things Jake had come up with over the years.

She smiled. Jake was wise, he wasn't an old maid, he had comforted her and Harold in their times of stress just as they had comforted him in his times. They had learned from each other although it had taken years to do it.

She smiled again at the memory of a comment Jake made sometime ago concerning a message they saw on a poster leaning up against a table at a flea market in Omaha which said: Things Take Time. 'What things,' Jake had laughed. 'You tell me what those things are, and I'll give them the time— everything else I want right away.'

Dolly looked over at Harold. "Wise and funny, that's what Jake is—wise and full of humor. We are the old maids, not him."

"No we're not."

"Yes we are."

"Nope."

"My dear husband of many years, why don't you open your mind to new ideas? I'll give you the key. Just as soon as

276

I find it myself."

Harold left to tend to Brie. Proudflesh loped after him. There they were, the three of them in the barn. Old maids. Old, period ... but, how wise they all were too.

In the kitchen, Dolly was realizing this also as she kneaded the bread dough; she kept flipping it over and over until it became supple and manageable and ready to be used for a higher purpose. Of course, that's what it was—nothing that hasn't been beaten up a few times is of much use. The dough wasn't meant to remain in a blob. Neither were they. Somehow she had to think of something, a right something, to say to Harold so he would quit thinking his life was over, to realize he was not a blob.

She finally remembered. It was something her aunt said many years ago when she heard her niece grump about turning forty. 'Dolly, look at me, look at how old I am. You're still young. Besides, we weren't put on this earth to be young. We were put on this earth to learn, and learning takes time— longer than what years you have already had. Wait until you're my age. Then you will know what I mean.'

Dolly was now her age, and that morning standing over the bread dough, she at last understood. Now the hard part came: convincing Harold.

***

As quick as the fairy tale of Jill running after Jack and his broken crown, things began to happen for Jake and Nell. The bride and groom started to talk, jabber, almost breathlessly over last minute details of their future life together as husband and wife, and as parents also.

"I asked Clara to be my matron of honor," Nell said before Jake even closed the door on his visit to her that morning of his last bachelor breakfast with the Hallgrens. "I thought about asking Dolly, but decided on Clara because she is not only my replacement, she is also very good for George to be around. I feel close to her for those reasons. Dolly said she understood. Dolly always seems to understand."

Jake had some news also. "It's official. I just came from

the sheriff. He said Country Welfare gave us the kids, we can be their foster parents. Now, where are we going to get married?"

Nell pointed to the orphanage. Those dear sisters offered the foyer without me asking. They didn't say anything about the reception though. Any ideas?"

"Barney's."

Nell grimaced. "Jake, Jake, Jake. My brothers desecrated it."

"And we will bring joy back to it, and maybe Barney too. We will make him feel how important his place is. I spent many hours there before and especially after I met you, sulking into his beer and condemning his pretzels. In memory of both that and your brothers' destruction, let us be the ones to bring some life into it again."

Nell didn't hesitate to agree. "The wedding is mine, the reception is yours. But I'd like to be the one to choose our honeymoon spot. Omaha, in amongst all those tall buildings and honking horns and Christmas lights that you have described to me. Just the two of us, our first Christmas together before we become parents. I told the children we would be home the day after Christmas, and we'd all be together and celebrate one day late. That way they will have two Christmases, one with Harold and Dolly, and one with us."

"Harold and Dolly?" Jake challenged. "I was just with them and they didn't say anything about taking Billy and Angela for us."

Nell poured Jake a cup of coffee, filling it extra full. "That is because Dolly called just before you came in. She said something about teaching Harold a thing or two and that maybe having the children stay with them during our honeymoon would do it, and wouldn't we love to have some time to ourselves before becoming a family?" Nell would have continued with more excitement, but she ran out of breath.

"Good idea," Jake said. "Whatever she wants to teach Harold is a good idea. He needs lots of teaching. The honeymoon sounds fine, any place will do. Just tell me where to be and when, and I'll cooperate fully." He chuckled then, thinking of what the Hallgrens would say about doing things backwards if they knew Nell was in charge of the honeymoon.

"I'm so looking forward to this, Jake. We will have a good life together. We have a lot of time to make up for." Her breathlessness kept her from thinking about something that had been nudging her since she set the wedding date; and for now, her conversation with Jake continued to block it out.

Jake went to Nell and kissed her. "I have an awful lot to be grateful for. A woman, our kids, and my land ... our land. How's that sound?"

Nell thought it sounded good. All they had to do now was wait for it to happen. As quickly as possible.

The Last Concern

Two days before the wedding all of Jake's anxieties seemed to have disappeared. Nell took them over. It was she who was nervous and doubtful, not about being married, but about being in bed with Jake for the first time and receiving his love and giving him love and all those things newlyweds do on their honeymoon and forever after. She was worried, quite bluntly, about the love-making.

She had never gone that far before—close, she had been close, but close was not the real thing. She figured Jake had gone beyond close in his past, don't all men? Maybe not, she thought, but probably for Jake, yes. Definitely he had. She was the novice. How would he feel if she didn't please him?

Jake had been so concerned about his concerns that Nell didn't realize she had concerns of her own; now was a fine time to worry about them; now was a fine time to say at the last minute that they shouldn't get married because she was concerned. Why hadn't Jake brought up the subject? Because he wasn't concerned or he certainly would have had another fussing bout. She, however, was concerned.

So she called. "I think perhaps we should talk over a few things before we get married."

There it was again—doing things backwards—Nell seemed to have caught the spirit from Jake. Although she wasn't as backward as Jake because she didn't wait until after the honeymoon to discuss those 'few things,' she came dangerously close.

At the same time Nell was concerned over her concern, Jake was in a state of entering the portals of heaven: he was finally getting married, and to Nell, of all people. Nell the wonderful lady, the strength, the absolute everything. Jake was a walking and breathing example of a man in a daze of euphoria that come to both men and women shortly before the 'I do' and 'I do too' part of the ceremony. He was absolutely not concerned about anything anymore. Walking through that tunnel that leads to the peace of heaven couldn't be any brighter to Jake than walking the few steps to be by Nell's side as the minister asked his intention.

Jake was in ecstasy, moving around as though his mind and his body were no longer together; if anyone had snapped their fingers and ordered Jake to bake a cake, he would have; if anyone had suggested he chug a gallon of whiskey for the fun of it even though it would kill him, he would have tried it anyway; and if he had come upon a tree without limbs and Harold told him to climb up, he would have done that too— done it and succeeded. Fortunately, no one knew about Jake's extreme condition, although they could have guessed it from his perpetual smile that made its first appearance the day Nell said December twentieth.

His state of amazement, nevertheless, started to end after Nell's phone call. She sounded a little, well, somewhat concerned. What did she mean: 'I want to talk?' Talk about what? Talk about life after the wedding, about life before the wedding, about life after death? What was there left to talk about for pity sakes?

"It's just an introduction to our marriage, Jake, but we definitely have to talk."

That introduction to marriage she mentioned sounded good to Jake. What a woman. Besides all her other admirable qualities, she wanted to treat him before the ceremony. What a woman.

"Let's get introduced," he laughed. "We'll take the kids to the orphanage, and then I'll take you to the farm." He laughed again. What a woman.

Nell let Jake's answer and laughter go by her as remarks made by a nervous groom. What a smart aleck. She got even more concerned. She again was concerned about her concern. What if he asked her to his bachelor party at Barney's the night before? Jake was the type who would do something like that. Her thinking continued to get ridiculously knotted until she asked Jake to come for her a few hours before supper time so she could fix him a meal in his own kitchen.

"We need to talk," Nell said for the fourth time as she put two potatoes into what would soon be her oven and cut up pieces of leftover chicken she had saved for a casserole. "Really talk. About how our marriage will be."

Jake started to back out of the portals to heaven. Nell's introduction wasn't going to be what he thought it would be. Her introduction was starting to sound like a lecture.

Nell inverted a can of peas into a sieve and waited until each drop of liquid ran down the drain. "We're not twenty years old anymore. We know better than to think there are any of those live-happily-ever-after possibilities for us. I know better, and you know better. Am I right?"

"Sure," Jake said. "Sure." He might as well be married to Dolly, the way this conversation was going. He said 'sure' a few more times and then the portal to heaven closed.

"First of all," Nell continued in a flurry of words to get them over with, "first of all, I don't want us to become so attached to each other that we move and think like one person. I still want to be independent."

Jake's perpetual smile stopped being perpetual on that last statement of his beloved, formerly dependent Nell. The last time she spoke of independence, she postponed the wedding.

Thank goodness for Nell's flurry of words because while Jake was still feeling stunned with his past fear of losing her and before he could panic with thoughts of another Waterloo of women and love, Nell quickly added: "I want to be independent with you, like letting some air come between us. You'll want to go to Barney's without me, and I'll want to have women friends and help at the orphanage, and maybe you'll want to take Billy fishing while Angela and I go shopping. Or something like that."

Jake brought back his smile. "As long as you live with me, you can call the shots." He wondered if that was what Harold had promised Dolly.

Nell frowned. "No, I mean we are equal. I want none of this stuff where one lords it over the other."

Jake's mind filled up with Harold and Dolly again. They seemed to be equal, even though Jake knew that if there was such a thing as a final word on anything, and Harold claimed he had it, it was Dolly who really did.

Jake didn't know what to say anymore on the independence thing, so he changed the subject. "I love you, Nell. I loved you after one look. It was one of those first-sighting types of love, one of those across-a-crowded-room kind of thing." He looked straight at her like he did when he first saw her at the barbecue. An amazement look. "And I still love you."

If Nell had been Dolly, she would have dismissed Jake's latest verbal outburst of love as something from a mushy movie scene. But Nell was not Dolly, and her reply of 'thank goodness for those crowded rooms' seemed appropriate for the occasion, although it didn't relieve her worry about the possible wedding night problem.

Nell put the pea and chicken casserole into the oven next to the potatoes, took a deep breath, and came over to Jake. She sat down and folded her hands on the table. "You don't want one of us to lord it over the other, do you?"

Jake said no and he meant it and he was tired of the subject. So he changed it again. "What was your real reason for going to Iowa? A piano can be shipped by a friend." Why did he say that? What was he, a private eye making devious remarks to a suspect?

Nell leaned back on that one. Way back. The abrupt remark and question pushed her there, and Jake couldn't help but notice the impact of his rudeness.

"I'm sorry. It's none of my business. After all, we agreed on being independent. You agreed, that is." Oh sure, another nasty remark. "I'm sorry again, dear woman, I guess I'm a nervous groom and am taking it out on you."

Nell recovered and shook her head. "I meant to tell you sometime, like next year maybe. You might not be ready for it now."

"What kind of a casserole did you fix for us? I can smell it coming out of the oven."

"I didn't come over here to fix you a casserole or to bake potatoes or to make us mad at each other. You asked about my reason for Iowa, and I will tell you, but please remember I warned that you might not be ready." Nell took another deep breath—like a judge might when sentencing a criminal to death—"I went to Iowa to see my boyfriend who dragged his heels so long on proposing that I decided to move to Nebraska with my brothers."

Jake wasn't ready.

Nell continued, and fortunately because it got better. "I went back to make sure he didn't want me. You see, I was really attracted to you. Did you know I walked around the hardware store twice so you would be sure to see me? I noticed from afar at the barbecue that you seemed so pleasant, and then Dolly told me later you would be quite a catch and you were definitely available."

Jake was still not ready.

Nell kept on going. "She told me so much about you and Harold and your farm that I got to know you before you even said hello."

Jake stirred a little. Who would have guessed? Certainly not he. Nell was there for the asking, almost, and he had thought he was climbing a pathless mountain in pursuit of a woman he worried would reject him. He stirred some more and reached for her hand.

"I'm not through yet, Jake. After our first date together, when I realized Dolly was right, I wanted to make sure it was all over between Bert and me before I let you into my heart."

Jake reached for her other hand. "And when did that happen?"

"All the time. It happened all the time until it finally became love. And it's still happening."

That should have been the end of a perfect evening, but it wasn't. Nell was frowning too much, and it was a distraction. Jake leaned back in his chair and cleared his throat. "Nell, you seem worried. Why are you worried? I can't wait to get married. Don't you feel the same? Things will be the same as now except we will live under the same roof and we'll have two kids in our laps. That's sort of what we're doing now."

Nell sat up suddenly straight. Jake had pulled the trigger on what was bothering her. She turned her eyes right into his and clipped out one word after another. "We're going to have more than the children in our laps—we're also going to have each other there."

Jake thought for a moment and then his smile returned with the response of a wilted flower given fresh water. "So that's what is bothering you ... the bed." Nell hadn't come to discuss equal rights or old boyfriends or how much they loved each other. She came to discuss their goings-on in bed. She was a fifty-seven year old nervous bride, and in one anxious statement, Nell had made Jake taller than she. Taller than Harold. Where was King Kong?

So it was then, right there smack on the kitchen table in Boone County, Nebraska, that a firecracker went off—a firecracker of realization that hit and exploded on the ceiling, spewing dust all over Jake.

The dust turned lights on all over the inside and outside of Jake's head and heart. He hadn't worried about their wedding night. He had thought about it, but he hadn't worried. Nell, after all, was perfect. And he hadn't picked up any concern on Nell's part because she had become so confident about everything once she got her apartment.

Jake quit smiling and closed his eyes as one does when met with a revelation that suddenly shatters years of whining, groaning, and complaining: he opened his eyes, got up from the chair, and put his hands on Nell's shoulders as though he was steering the wheel of a ship. This wonderful woman of his, this fair-haired package of loveliness who could have any man at any time in her life—with the exception of Bert in Iowa—had made Jake realize that height had nothing to do with manhood. And that is what exploded the firecracker, and that is what brought Jake down from his unrealistic seventh heaven and up from his self-made depths of Hell. The firecracker in his mind brought him to lean over Nell and hug her head with his, and in a very quiet and deliberate voice, explain that he loved and respected her too much to worry about her bedroom abilities, and he would appreciate it if she didn't criticize his either.

Nell took still another deep breath, but this time it was one of relief. Jake turned her around to him, cupped her face into his hands, and penetrated his eyes into hers. "Older people get married all the time, my dear precious Nell, and I've never heard of a national alert going out against it because of what may or may not happen in the bedroom. Have you?"

Nell's smile finally matched Jake's. "This is why I came tonight, so we could settle our thoughts about that, so we could really enjoy the wedding and reception and not worry about the honeymoon. I think our dinner just burned. How about some popcorn for supper?"

Jake went to the potato bin and pulled out a bag of corn. His eyes twinkled and so did his voice. "Let me pop this," he said. "I'll show you how to do it so there are no old maids."

Nell laughed at Jake's confidence, and then she cried with the joy that a calm brings after a severe storm. Jake had finally come to take the lead again, only this time it was nicer, not pushy like when they first met in the hardware.

She began to feel summer-warm, now that Jake had taken command of her wobbly boat; and when, in the middle of the television viewing with the popcorn only half gone and Jake caressing her here and patting her there, she felt at ease with the last thing she remembered him saying that evening:

"How much of you can I have tonight?"

***

The late afternoon following their talk of independence and bedrooms and old boyfriends and a few other things, Jake went to Barney's full of joy and camaraderie with 'the boys' at his bachelor party. He had forgotten about how he had verbally accosted Nell with her reason for going to Iowa; he had forgotten about how he had suffered so much when

Nell was gone; he had forgotten about how right he was to have worried. And of the other things he had not forgotten, he had somehow chose to not think about.

Harold would have told him that it was a spell Nell cast over him, a spell that all wives cast over their husbands, so they forget about things and become good husbands. Dolly would have told him that anyone who wants to make a successful marriage must forget some things, that there are no spells or one-upmanships or anything devious—that it's merely a case of decency and common sense. And Jake would have told both of them they were full of baloney.

But after he returned home from his last bachelor celebration and after he brushed his teeth, he sat on the edge of the bed and thought of how close he had come to losing Nell to that Bert person in Iowa. He was tempted to call Harold and jeer 'see, see, I had a right to fret and worry.'

But he didn't do that. He wept instead, and as his eyes dropped the tears and as his sinuses oozed congestion, Jake took a deep breath, blew his nose, and enjoyed a peace that a soldier feels only after a great battle—in Jake's case, a battle that began almost sixty years ago and only now ended.

***

Bad things happen, then good things.

The white cupola on top of the orphanage looked like the top of a wedding cake held up by three layers of floor. The outer portion of the gothic design was cheered with white trim on the red brick and decorated with long, wide windows and a generous, heavy door. The front bay windows, gracing either side of the front door, were like hands reaching out to embrace the incoming bride and groom and guests.

Although a number of people from a portion of Boone County were invited to the reception, such as the regular drinkers at Barney's and their wives, only a few were invited to the ceremony. These guests sat in the foyer on folding chairs put exactly in place by George as his contribution to the ceremony. The spinster sisters sat cross-legged at the ankles, their hands placed in their laps in an almost praying fashion; their postures showed more than propriety ... they were honored by the event.

Clara tried to straighten up her shoulders several times and finally gave up; she decided she could not undo years of habit just because she wanted to look dignified for one day. Harold did manage to stand up straight, so straight he was stiff. His eyes went to Dolly, then Jake, then Dolly, then Jake. He'd better concentrate on only Jake for now.

Dolly smiled with such a deepness, one would think she was the bride. This display of her smile was brought about by her thoughts that she had been the matchmaker. Yes, definitely, she had been the matchmaker.

George refused to sit down, and instead, leaned against the massive bannister's head with his arms straight down by his side and hands pressed against his legs as though he would be asked to carry out a coffin any minute. His serious face, which would have been better appreciated at a funeral, matched the formality of his pose.

Billy and Angela and the other children of the orphanage sat next to Dolly. They weren't beaming like she. They were too busy trying to not fidget and most of the time they succeeded, especially Billy and Angela who sat so still one might think they were hypnotized. Billy's stomach growled, and his face turned red, but no part of his body squirmed or moved. He was in a trance, and he had taken his sister with him.

Other than Billy's stomach, there was no noise: no throat clearing or jaw scratching or feet shuffling; if a mouse had been present, it would have been heard.

Then it finally came. After years of longing, whining, complaining, growling, worrying, talking—it finally came:

"Do you, Jake," Jake shifted his feet, "take this woman," Jake shifted his hands, "to be your lawfully wedded ..." Jake shifted his shoulders, "wife to have and to hold ..." Jake shifted his entire body toward and up to Nell.

"Yes, yes, yes."

"... from this day forward for as long as you both shall live?"

The minister waited; his hand motioned for Jake to answer.

"Yes. I said yes to everything. I really mean it. I promise, no problem."

Harold looked down at the floor, the place where most people look when they're embarrassed.

The minister smiled and turned to Nell. He winked at her. "How about you? Do you feel the same?"

Nell nodded and looked at her adoring groom. "Of course, Reverend. Yes to this man. We are definitely in this together."

They were married.

Nell bent her knees a little, and Jake stretched his legs a little. They kissed. It was as simple as that.

Dolly sighed at the backward order of the vows. Wasn't the woman suppose to declare hers first? Everybody she knew in Boone County had. Maybe this was the new way of doing things where any manner is acceptable. Oh well, everything about Jake's courtship had been backward. Might as well extend it to the ceremony.

Harold moaned and tried very hard to keep it inside; a little leaked out, though. What kind of a wedding was this? What kind of a deal is it when the bride and groom say anything they want anytime they want? Was the marriage valid? Jake and Nell had better get back to church: they needed to work on learning a little more formality with religious ceremony and propriety. Where did that minister come from? Surely not in Boone County where, Harold was fairly certain, winking at the bride during the ceremony was not done.

Harold looked at Dolly who gave him a facial expression whose message said to keep your remarks to yourself. That was hard for him to do, but he did it for Jake's sake. It was a good thing this was not the wedding of a stranger because he would have at least said something about the winking.

Protestant wedding ceremonies are relatively short, and as one guest was overheard remarking at one of them, 'to the point.' Jake's courtship of Nell had been short and to the point. Definitely, exactly, to the point: I see woman, woman sees me, I take over, she tells me not to, we finally agree, we pick up a few kids, we get married. No big deal, it happens all the time. Some of the time. Not too often. But it happened to Jake. It took him only four months to find a bride and marry her. Four months and forty years.

Regardless of the Hallgrens' doubts about the ceremony, Jake Blackburn and Nell Swensen were now married as much as the Hallgrens were, as much as the Tollivers, as much as the sheriff, and no less than all the kings and queens of England.

With the energy of their love for each other, and with the remembrance of their evening together two nights before, Jake and Nell had turned the antiquated setting of the orphanage into an expanse of newness for each other. They were now ready for their reception at the newly restored Barney's two blocks away. And after that was over, they would be ready for their future.

***

With time, anything can change; with time, everything can change. Jake's courtship and wedding showed both the anything and the everything. Probably no one was thinking such deep thoughts, however, because they were too busy sharing the joyful activity of the wedding reception when all the quietness, the seriousness, the nervous anticipation of the wedding is soon forgotten as the new husband and wife come together with guests to celebrate the beginning of marriage.

Whether the couple is twenty years old or fifty or five hundred and ninety-one, the wedding reception shows more of a new beginning to life than the ceremony itself because a ceremony is just that—a ceremony. Solemn and necessary. But a reception is an exchange of feelings that reflect how joyous one human being can feel for another. One does not have to be the new husband or the new wife to participate in this revelation. It is there for everyone, and it is usually very loud.

Jake and Harold were capable of being very loud. The din of their teenage years had not let up—it had only become less frequent as they grew older. And this day at Barney's was a day to be a teenager again. Not just Jake and Harold, but everyone invited between the portals of the saloon's narrow door. The noise that was restrained for the ceremony in the orphanage came out in the saloon as the wedding party burst in with the enthusiasm of young love.

Barney's was not the typical wedding reception place. There were plenty churches in Boone County to take care of such celebrations. For Jake, however, Barney's was his church.

Good old Barney's Beer Palace. It was the place where Harold determinedly drove Jake to comfort him after his mother's death many years ago ... not for the beer or the whiskey or the pretzels, or even the liverwurst sandwiches ... but for the camaraderie of men who will talk about things and extend a hand or offer a shoulder and ear to let the mourner know they are all in this life together whether they like it or not.

Good old Barney's. It was the place where Jake and Harold came together every Saturday to enjoy the closeness that beer drinking and pretzel eating can provide; it was the place where they had always talked and joked and poked fun; it was the place where Harold lamented about his daughter living so far away, and where Jake poured out his heartache over Nell; it was the place where feelings and comments and conversation flowed like beer flows from tap to mug. Barney's was the place where Jake felt closer to other people than any amount of church attending in his past had done. It was the place where he listened to some stern sermons from Harold and some wise remarks from the proprietor himself.

It was fitting, then, that Jake bring his happiness into the saloon in which he experienced both joy and sorrow and in which he exchanged fellowship about the land and farming. It was Jake's home away from home—and from Harold and Dolly's too.

Of course, everyone was at Barney's that day. The town had many walls, and somebody came out of every one of them: the Tollivers from the hardware, the widower Bennett from the drug store's pharmacy, the ladies from the quilting club and their husbands, Ralph the road commissioner and his wife and widowed daughter, Sam Sanger from everyone's favorite and only restaurant in town—everyone—every farmer, every shopkeeper, everyone, even the gossips. The Swensen twins were not there, but they were no longer considered an 'everyone' possibility.

On the walk over to the saloon, Jake squeezed Nell's hand an extra time in case she felt bad about how her brothers had mocked her and George. "Don't worry about Les and Lo, my dear bride, they're probably contently sitting in front of the television and grunting and shaking their heads about how short I am and how I don't deserve such a wonderful woman like you." Jake took a deep breath and put his arm around Nell's waist. "Ha ha to them—I have you now."

As Barney poured the champagne toast, Nell nuzzled her nose against Jake's ear. "Jealous, jealous. Everyone here or not here is jealous of me today. I've got the best man in town."

Jake's ego puffed up again at another of Nell's compliments. But this time he retained his real height, this time he didn't have to imagine himself taller, this time he knew he had all the stature necessary to win the heart of the lady in the green and brown checkered dress from that August afternoon barbecue. This time he felt at home with everybody, because for the first time, he felt at home with himself.

Billy and Angela drank orange soda pop for what would be the last time by order of Jake—the last time he would know about, that is. The children hovered close to the wedding cake, skillfully baked, iced, and donated by Mrs. Tolliver, as the orange liquid bit and slid over their sensitive tongues and down their waiting throats. They didn't know what else to do but to drink the soda and look at the cake because all of the toasting and back-slapping and hugging was something they hadn't been a part of before. They decided all that stuff must be something adults do, adults other than their parents, something maybe someday they would learn to do too.

Barney honored the occasion by removing his apron and not washing the glassware until after the reception. "Hold onto your glasses," he shouted at the start of the merriment. "This ain't the Ritz, they'll be no dishwasher working today."

Nobody held onto their glasses, and eventually the new owner of the town grocery recognized the problem and dashed to his store for stacks of paper cups. "Everybody hold on to your paper cup—this is all there is."

Once in awhile, when Clara wasn't gunner-golly-gushing to one guest or another, she noticed George standing over here and then over there, but never sitting down. Maybe he thought he didn't deserve to sit on the new chairs or to put his elbows on the polished tables. She went over to him just as Jake raised his third glass of champagne in a toast to George.

"Thank you, new brother, for not throwing me out of your house. But mostly, thank you for Nell. I need her more than you do."

George smiled and nodded. He looked at Clara, but he didn't say anything. So Clara did instead. Her leathery skin was softer now and her voice gentler than that first day in the Swensen kitchen. "I will toast you, Mr. Swensen, boss man. You are some terrific nice employer."

George's hulk looked down at Clara's small frame, and for a moment he forgot about how the saloon had looked after the destruction. "George," he answered her. "My name is George. Remember that from now on."

Barney was uncomfortable with all the remarks that closeness of spirits, both human and alcohol, can bring forth at such an occasion. He crossed his arms, leaned against the bar, and realized that everyone in the room, with the exception of the children, were happily overwhelmed with the alcohol content of the champagne. He brewed more coffee. No one had better leave drunk, not even a suggestion of drunk, even if he had to surrender all of his liverwurst supply. Besides, as long as he kept busy with such concerned chores, Jake and Clara might not come up to him with one of those embarrassing toasts.

"Barney, you're the greatest." Leave it to Harold to break into Barney's bashful silence with a salute from Jackie Gleason. "Here's a toast to you too." Barney looked the other way and wished Jackie Gleason really was here so he could tell Harold to go to the moon.

Finally the sandwiches that were cut into exact squares by the quilters and spread with mayonnaised chicken and ham and roast beef were gone. So was the wedding cake, with the exception of the top layer secretly stored in Barney's apartment freezer. Only a few hunks were left, scattered about on the largest rose-embossed platter in Boone County, only a few hunks to remind Jake and Nell of their choppy journey to the altar. If either Jake or Nell had been calm enough at the moment of the cake's demise, they probably would have considered the remaining large crumbs as a sacrilege of what their real love was. Fortunately, for the first time since they met, neither was in a philosophical mood. This event was not the time to be wise—it was a time to enjoy and experience and not worry about what either would think, or what Harold and Dolly would think, or what Aunt Sarah down the lane would think. Thank goodness for that.

As the warmth of the reception's drinking gradually left Jake's mind, his thoughts shifted to his parents. How so very long ago they were. They would have liked Nell because, Jake was certain from his mother's description of his sister, that Nell was Alice, alive and grown up. His mother would have been proud of his choice. His dear, dead, unknown-to-him sister would once again live in the Blackburn house.

That thought completely sobered Jake. He shook his head in one sharp, quick motion like it needed waking up.

Why did he have to think about his past family now? They were gone. They were dead. He and Nell were alive. Nell would not be a substitute for anyone. So it was there, at his wedding reception, just as it was in his kitchen two days before when he had been hit by the rocket of realization that his lack of height was so unimportant, when he was hit again by the same rocket. This time it told him that Alice's picture needed to move out of the living room and into the seldom-used sitting room. He would put it next to the wedding picture of his parents. Where it belonged.

***

Jake and Nell's ceremony was not the wedding of the century, although the town gossips might have considered it so with such a short man marrying a tall woman. It was, nevertheless, the wedding of all time for Jake—the one he thought he would never have—the union he had craved, the commitment he finally experienced.

Getting married, after all, is the thing for a man in love to do.

EPILOGUE

With Nell and the kids in his life, Jake felt tall now, he was at last content. So the following spring he said with great pride, "Let's have a family portrait taken."

The photographer arranged the foursome in the usual pattern except for one detail. Without any ado or explanation, the lensman placed a book on Jake's part of the bench. Jake stared at the book like one stares at an enemy. Then he laughed and sat down on it.